The Treaty

A new novel by David J Grant, the Treaty is the first in a collection of real people fiction stories. David J Grant is British and lives in England. For more information about this author visit the official website at:
www.davidjgrant.co.uk

DAVID J. GRANT

The Treaty

samosir
BOOKS

SAMOSIR BOOKS

Published by Samosir Books Ltd, United Kingdom

Copyright © David J Grant 2007

David J Grant has asserted his right under the copyright, Designs and Patents Act, 1988 to be identified as the author of this work

This book is sold subject to the condition that it shall not be by way of trade or otherwise, be lent, resold, hired out, or otherwise circulated without the publisher's prior consent in any form of binding or cover other than that in which it is published and without a similar condition including this condition being imposed on the subsequent purchaser

First published in Great Britain in 2007 by
Samosir Books Ltd
1-2 Universal House, 88-94 Wentworth Street,
London, E1 7SA

ISBN 978 0954 884222
Printed and bound in Thailand
Cover artwork by Clara Pages, Buenos Aires, Argentina

www.samosirbooks.com

To my family, and Susan

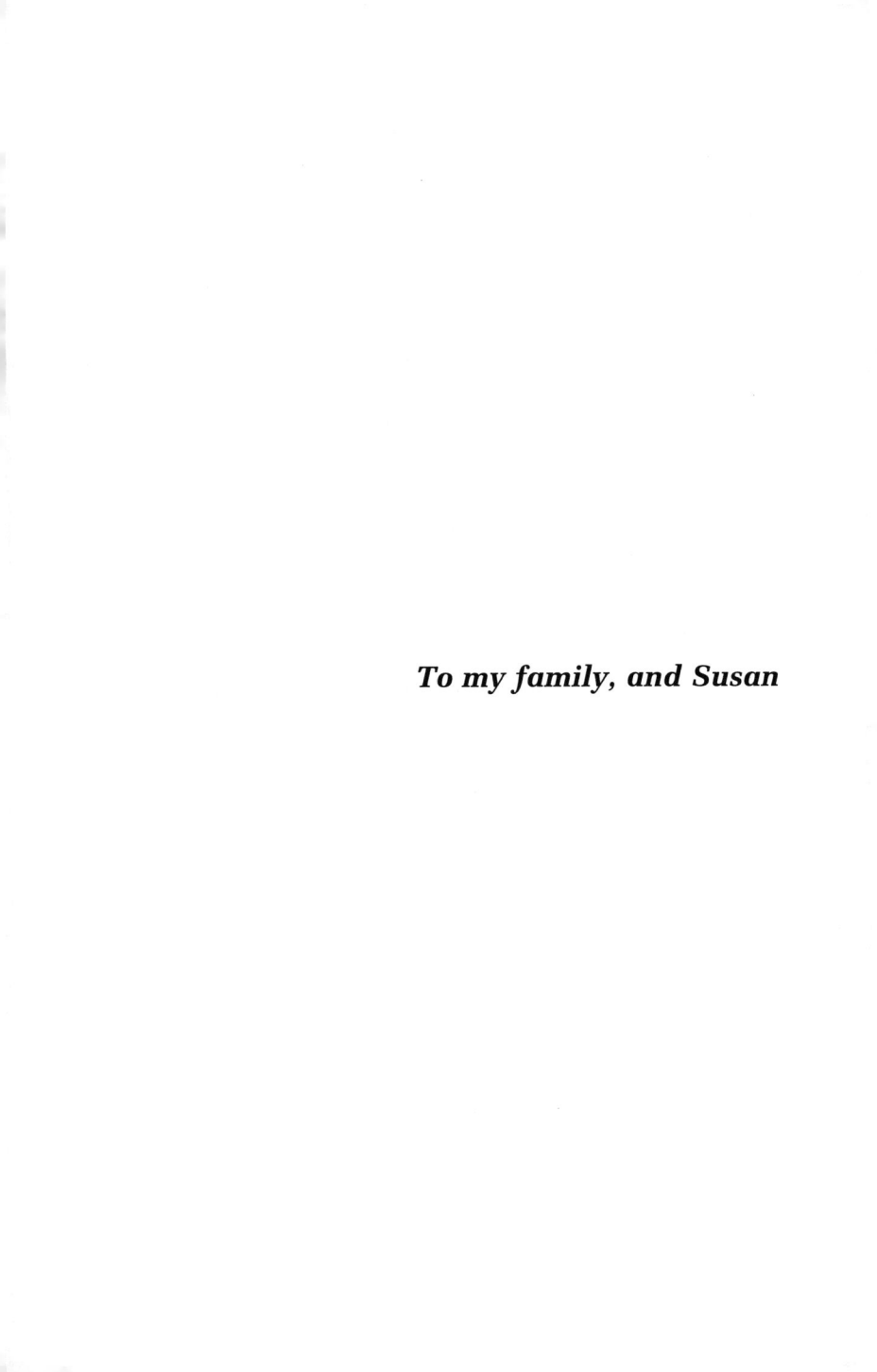

'No government can completely protect its citizens from all harm -- not by legislation, or by regulation, or by medicine, or by advice. Drugs cannot be forced out of existence; they will be with us for as long as people find in them the relief or satisfaction they desire. But the harm caused by drug abuse can be reduced. We cannot talk in absolutes - that drug abuse will cease, that no more illegal drugs will cross our borders -- because if we are honest with ourselves we know that is beyond our power'

President Jimmy Carter, August 2, 1977

The Treaty

1

Only seconds before the lift door closed an arm jammed between the sliding gates. Standing in the gap, a pallid-faced middle-aged man in a dark suit waited for a woman with distinctive henna dyed hair to catch-up. Dominic smiled at the man and then watched as the woman jumped inside the lift, panting and out of breath. The couple huddled together in front of a glass wall, whispering in a language Dominic didn't recognize. Stabbing at the control panel, he caused the doors to close and selected buttons to the fifteenth floor; he politely asked which level they needed.

'Same,' the man answered.

The view through the glass looked out across the London skyline, the lights from the moving traffic below flickering in the dark. Juddering to a halt, Dominic stepped to one side when the doors opened allowing the couple to exit first. They seemed to be in a hurry, but Dominic thought nothing of this and not feeling tired strolled over to a plate glass window giving way to an expanded view beyond the twinkling lights of the city boundary. He paused to look out, searching the horizon; identifying familiar landmarks. The book deal agreed that evening with a prominent distribution company would, he believed, cause a major political storm when it went on sale, fulfilling his ambitious dream to be rich and famous. Married to his beautiful wife, Emma, and blessed with a son he loved dearly - it could only get better from here on.

Out of sight, the same man who shared Dominic's lift had returned, this time alone. Advancing toward him with the stealth of a panther, the man in the dark suit made one final movement. For a split second Dominic would have seen his assailant's reflection in the glass, witnessed an arm lock around his throat, felt the pain of a Seberger silencer jammed into his temple. A muffled noise made by sub-sonic bullets travelling through the suppressor into his brain caused a now lifeless body to fold neatly onto the richly carpeted floor. The assassin's work was not finished. After searching through the dead man's pockets, he removed a key card to room 1504. Emma slept soundly under her silk sheets; she knew nothing of the pain. The assassin's powerful hands closed her throat in one firm grasp and suffocation quickly followed. Checking she was dead, he left the room heading out through a fire door at the end of the corridor and down a flight of back stairs. Rejoining his female partner waiting in a car opposite the hotel, in only few hours they would be in Calais, change their vehicle for the second time - ready to start the journey back home to the Czech Republic.

2

Water mixed with shards of glass showered panic-stricken shoppers when a gaping hole appeared in the supermarket roof. Andy stopped abruptly catching the full force of a loaded shopping cart on the back of his heel. Gasping, he dropped down on one knee and cursed at the young woman with black hair standing behind him holding the hand of a small boy. They watched as the chaos grew worse, and taking the woman's arm, he ushered them both toward beckoning staff at an emergency exit. Outside was pure bedlam, the mini-tornado had ripped branches from trees, and roof insulation and rubbish swirled across the car park.

'Where's your car?' Andy yelled.

The woman pointed to a black Mercedes SUV parked a short distance away and scooping up the child in his arms, they splashed through swirling pools of rainwater running together toward the vehicle. Not waiting for an invitation, Andy helped the little boy into the car before leaping into the front passenger seat. The woman, now behind the steering wheel, calmed the little lad cuddling him on her lap. With the doors firmly closed, it went eerily quiet; the next minutes were spent watching a silent movie of people rushing for safety.

Drenched by the rain and still in mild shock, he realized

his companion was quite young and foreign.

'How long do you think we wait here?' she asked, softly stroking the boy's hair.

'Not long I hope,' Andy replied, wiping the condensation off the window. 'If you don't mind I'll stay a few more minutes and then go look for my car.'

'It's okay you should stay until it is safe. Thank you for helping us, Toby could have been hurt.'

He responded by patting the little boy on the head. 'Hello Toby, I'm Andy. Let me guess your mummy's name, I bet its Mummy.'

This had the desired effect and made the woman laugh. 'I am Maria not your mummy isn't that right, *bonito*?' Toby shyly hunkered down and then suddenly Maria remembered the earlier accident. 'How's your foot, you were injured back in the store?'

Andy instinctively flexed his ankle and felt a twinge of pain. 'Oh God, I am sorry there's blood all over the mat.'

Maria leaned over and peered down between his feet.

'It's okay, it will cleanup. I think you must take your shoe and sock off.'

Reaching for the glove compartment, she rummaged around for the first aid kit; selecting antiseptic wipes while Andy continued struggling to remove his shoe and bloody sock.

'Can you manage to do that yourself?'

'Yes, thank you,' he winced, dabbing the wounded area with an antiseptic wipe.

Applying the dressing, he held it in place as Maria secured the bandage with a strip of surgical tape.

'Thanks that should stop the bleeding.'

Feeling self-conscious of his exposed foot, he struggled to pull his sock back on. Maria smiled at his frustration and, as she reached across his lap to place the first aid kit back in the glove compartment, there was a sudden tap at

The Treaty

the window. Struggling to sit upright, her head positioned directly above his crotch, Maria managed to reach the controls and opened the steamy window.

A rush of cold air filled the car as a policewoman peered inside. 'Is everything okay in here?'

'Yes, we are fine,' Maria smiled shyly. 'Apart from a small injury to this man's foot, we have our own first aid kit so it should be okay.'

'It's just a graze,' Andy quickly interrupted. 'How long do you think before we can leave?'

'We cannot let you go just yet, sir, the road has to be kept clear for the emergency services. Keep an eye on the patrol car parked in front of the store; I will guide you all out when it's clear.'

On that note, the policewoman smiled and moved onto the next vehicle parked up behind.

Toby was becoming restless, Maria scrambled between the seats into the back of the SUV. Searching through various plastic bags, she found several packets of assorted snacks. The little boy shrieked with excitement as she tore open a packet and placed them in his hands. Taking more notice, he watched as she squeezed back through the narrow gap between the seats, thinking how attractive Maria looked dressed in petite slimfitting Mango denim jeans and the same brand T-shirt. Flopping down behind the steering wheel, brushing her hair away from her face she offered Andy a packet of the snacks.

'Thanks, sorry to invade the car.'

'No problem, you must stay with us until it is safe to leave. Will you be able to drive?'

His foot was painful and he knew he could not get his shoe back on. Driving was out of the question. 'I'm not sure. The way things are turning out; I think I will have to find a taxi and then a hotel.

Maria looked concerned. 'Oh, are you not from this area?'

'No, I was on my way home from a business meeting.'

'I can drive you somewhere if you like? There is a small Courtyard Marriott close to here.'

He needed to get back to his apartment in Buckinghamshire as soon as possible, and then leave the following evening on a business trip to Madrid; he worked for an American telecommunications company, as a professional engineer. Still in his early thirties Andy's employers sent him around the world, usually at short notice, and today he was on his way home from an English assignment in Birmingham. Avoiding the heavily congested motorway, a storm had threatened and he had pulled into the relative safety of the supermarket car park.

'No, please, that would be asking too much.'

Maria shook her head. 'I insist. I hurt your foot. I would feel very bad to just leave you here.'

'Okay, if you insist. It would make things a lot easier.'

After an hour the storm eventually calmed down and seeing the policewoman standing by her patrol car and pointing to the supermarket exit, Maria struck the engine and drove over to Andy's car so he could retrieve his overnight bag and a laptop. Hopping on one foot over to his BMW, he comically returned and climbed back on board the SUV. They quickly joined the main road, and took in the scenes of devastation and damage caused by the freak storm. Roof tiles littered the highway, house windows smashed, huge trees uprooted and damaged cars and lampposts lay by the roadside. The journey was hazardous, and reaching the hotel Maria pulled onto the forecourt and struggled to park near to the main entrance.

Andy winced in pain and held his foot. 'I am never going to get a room here it's full to bursting point.'

'We can try another one further along the road; it's not too far out of my way.'

The Treaty

'I'm really sorry Maria you must be desperate to get home. I should not be causing you all this trouble. Perhaps they will let me stay here even if I sleep in the reception area. It is an emergency.'

'What about your foot, how will you get that treated so you can drive tomorrow?'

She had a point; it was turning into a costly nightmare. The local radio reported damage trees and blocked roads throughout the region and especially the route he needed to take. A taxi was probably out of the question and even then, there was recovering his car. He needed somewhere for the next 12 hours to get sorted out.

'Maybe you can stay at my employer's house?' Maria suggested. 'I work as the au pair for a family just a few miles from here, then in the morning I can take you back to your car.'

'Will your boss mind if you bring home a complete stranger?'

'No, he is very easygoing; anyway, they've gone away for the weekend. That is why I have Toby with me today.'

'I wouldn't want to impose on you anymore than I have to.'

'Please Andy this is no problem. You would not be in this situation if I had been more careful.'

'Well, if you are sure it would be okay.'

'English are so funny,' she giggled. 'This is normal in Argentina; we help people when there is a crisis.'

'Maybe you're right,' Andy agreed. 'We are very paranoid in England.'

'Yes, I hear this lot in your country. Nevertheless, please, you are very welcome. Jack our Gardner and his wife, Mrs Briggs, the housekeeper, will both be there. You can sleep in the guest bedroom.'

Andy thought about it, he was a free agent with no wife or girlfriend waiting back home. The decision was a no-brainer.

'I'm really grateful for the offer. If you're certain it will be okay, it sounds a whole lot better than the hotel idea.'

Pulling out onto the main highway, Maria carefully watched for her turning and was eager not to miss the narrow country lane. Powering through floodwater the Mercedes produced a backwash sending out waves of muddy water. He was impressed with her driving and soon began to notice the changing countryside with fewer houses and more hedgerows and grassy hillocks crowned with dense woodlands. At one stage in the journey, he read out the name on a road sign as it flashed by.

'Althorp House, is that where Princess Diana's family live?'

'Yes, that is where we are going. My boss lives on the edge of the estate in a house owned by Lord Spencer.'

'Wow, I didn't realize we were staying in a mansion.'

Maria laughed. 'I said on the edge. They live in an old farmhouse.'

'Where are you from Maria, no wait, let me guess? You spoke Spanish to Toby at the supermarket, so I presume you're from Spain?'

'Wrong answer,' she laughed, teasing him with her reply. 'Over three hundred million people around the world speak Spanish. Guess again?'

Studying her face, he tried to look for clues while Maria concentrated on her driving secretly enjoying the attention.

'You look very European, but could be from Central or South America. You're definitely not Brazilian, as you would speak Portuguese, perhaps; Mexico, Costa Rica, Colombia or Venezuela?'

'I will give you one clue, think of a place in South America where large numbers of Spanish and Italians emigrated in the eighteen hundreds.'

Andy thought about this then guessed at an answer. 'Argentina!' he cried waking Toby.

The Treaty

'Yes, you're right. My mother's family came from Spain and my father's family were from Italy. We are all Argentineans now.'

Rallying along ancient narrow lanes bordered by a stonewall, which snaked around the Althorp Estate, overhanging trees stole the fading light, casting a row of honey-stoned cottages in a hazy silhouette. Passing a thatched house, Maria negotiated a sharp bend and slowed the heavy vehicle to a halt in front of a red brick Georgian farmhouse. Manoeuvring the SUV along the gravel driveway, a short wiry little man swung open a heavy white painted five-bar gate and walked over to the car.

Maria opened her window. 'Jack, hello, sorry we are so late! I hope you have not been worried about us?'

'We heard the news about the storm. Mrs Briggs has been worried sick.'

Silencing the engine and unfastening the little boy's seat belt, Maria climbed down as Jack stepped forward to take Toby.

'Yes, it was very frightening - this is Andy. He was injured in the supermarket during the storm.'

'Hello, Andy,' Jack smiled.

'Is Mrs Briggs still here?'

'Yes, she's inside.'

Struggling to climb out of the car, Maria offered Andy her arm for support. 'Come on old man let me get you inside,' she smiled.

'Less of the old man,' Andy laughed.

She helped him into the farmhouse kitchen, guiding him to a wooden chair arranged around the traditional oak table in the centre of the room. None of the walls or floor bore any link with the past having been decorated in modern colours, and supporting essential household gadgets.

'Maria, you're back!' Mrs Briggs cried, carrying Toby in her arms. 'What on earth happened?'

Andy decided to stay silent while Maria gave her a short account.

'Well, you must both be very hungry after all that excitement. I will take Toby for his bath and put him to bed, while you and Andrew have something to eat. I have to leave soon Maria I hope that will be all right?'

Andy guessed the "all right" meant would she be all right on her own with him. Maria's reply seemed relaxed enough.

'Yes, that is fine Mrs Briggs; you go home at your normal time. Andy, would you like to try my Chicken Omelette Argentinean style?'

'Sounds great, what makes it particularly Argentinean?'

'Oh, chicken spiced and a few extra ingredients. I'm sure you will like it.'

Jack had disappeared outside and Mrs Briggs left the kitchen, leading Toby by the hand and listening to his version of events during the storm. Andy watched Maria expertly dice the chicken and prepare fresh spices, producing a delicious looking omelette in only a few minutes. They finished eating as Janet reappeared fastening her jacket ready to leave.

'I have settled Toby down and he went straight to sleep. The child is exhausted.' Moving up closer to Maria's chair, her voice dropped to a whisper. 'Now, are you sure you will be safe here on your own. I could ask my Jack if he would walk back to the house with me later this evening.'

'No, please, don't go to any more trouble, Mrs Briggs. You go off and enjoy your evening together. I will check Toby regularly as usual. We will be fine.'

'Very well dear, if you are certain. I'm just up the road if you need anything. At least you have Andrew here to keep you company, not that he is much use to you with that foot.'

Finding her own joke amusing, she went off chuckling to

herself all the way down the yard. Jack popped his head around the door and gave Andy a firm nod before heading off home too. With the house to themselves, Maria cracked open a bottle of Argentinean red wine.

'I'm going to take a shower and freshen-up,' she smiled, filling Andy's glass. 'Make yourself at home.'

He felt relieved to have a moment to himself and taking a few sips of the delicious tasting Malbec; he gradually began to stop worrying about getting home the next day and started to relax.

Maria returned to the kitchen dressed in a white bathrobe. This was the first opportunity she'd had to entertain a man since arriving in England from Buenos Aires, and she felt excited to be in his company.

'Can I use the bathroom?' Andy asked.

'Yes, it is just along the corridor. I will be in the lounge through there.'

Trying to remember the directions Andy struggled to his feet and negotiated a labyrinth of narrow passages to reach the small toilet. Maria meanwhile, flicked on the television in the lounge, catching the regional news, immediately seeing a report on the storm.

'Hurry Andy, our supermarket is on the television.'

Guessing he could not hear through the thick walls, she watched and listened how thirty people were in hospital after incurring injures during the storm. Thankfully, with no one killed she whispered a prayer in Spanish, thanking dear sweet Jesus for helping to bring Toby home safely. For the first time it dawned on her how very dangerous their experience had been. Meeting Andy had been a blessing, with the bonus that he seemed like a kind person. Most of her male friends in Buenos Aires were arrogant and conceited, and thought every pretty girl was chasing after them. He was mild mannered and had distinctive blue eyes, why would she not find him attractive. Talking about her family had made her feel homesick. In BA, she was always busy studying for exams, going with her friends to Tango classes; even learning sword fencing to help with fitness. Argentineans led a healthy lifestyle unlike most of the people she had met in England.

Following the noise of the TV, Andy made his way to the lounge and found Maria reclining on the settee.

'Hi, what's happening?'

'They showed the supermarket, thirty people have been taken to hospital.'

Standing in the centre of the room, unsure where to sit down, Maria tapped a cushion next to her. 'Sit here next to me. I won't bite.'

He clumsily sat down leaving one cushion space between them.

'Are you comfortable?' she smiled sweetly. 'Take your other shoe off and relax. Is your foot okay?'

Andy stretched his legs out. 'Yes it's fine. I should perhaps change the dressing soon - then I will be able to get the other shoe back on. By the way, does Mr Marsh have a computer connected to the Internet?'

Maria frowned. 'Yes, it is in his office. Why, do you need to use it?'

'I have to make changes to a customer's telecom system at about one o'clock in the morning. I can access it over the net, but I'm not sure my laptop will work from here and it will be quicker using an existing computer.'

Surprised by the request, Maria thought about it for a moment then decided it wouldn't be a problem, after all, he did say he worked in telecoms.

'Yes, it should be fine. I will show you where it is later, Dominic won't mind.'

'Thank you, I was concerned it may be a problem.'

Supporting new customers was Andy's main bugbear. He had to be available almost 24/7 and early morning was the

The Treaty

only time practicable to carryout modifications when the call traffic was low; he was committed to make the changes that night. Maria returned from the bathroom carrying a first aid kit and knelt down on the carpet. She started sifting through an assortment of bandages, plasters and antiseptic wipes.

'These should do,' she smiled.

'What does your boss do for a living?' Andy asked, looking around the elegantly decorated lounge room.

'Dominic is a publisher and the editor of a magazine, plus other specialist books on sport. You may have heard of him before.'

'How long have you known the family?'

'My father met Dominic in Buenos Aires earlier this year and Emma, his wife, was looking for an au pair. I was recommended for the job. I really wanted the opportunity to come to Europe.'

'Do you like it here?'

'Yes it's fun, but a little quiet. I will eventually visit London and other parts of the country.'

Sitting cross-legged on the floor, her mind was clearly somewhere else. Periodically she routinely flicked a loose strand of hair tumbling about her face and shoulders. Hours earlier driving along the highway during another mundane sort of day, Andy could never have imagined in his wildest dreams being here alone with such a beautiful girl. Catching him staring, she broke the silence by showing him a roll of bandage.

'This dressing is prefect. Would you like me to change it for you?'

'No, that's okay I can manage.'

He leaned over to take the items from her, but Maria refused to hand them over. 'I am down here now and will do a better job. I trained in first aid and I'm practically a nurse.'

Both laughing at this obvious lie, Andy reclined back allowing her to lift the injured foot and cradle it between her knees, she slowly began unwrapping the old dressing.

3

With only natural light illuminating the nape of her neck, Andy eased out of bed and searched for his car keys. Anxious not to wake Maria, he slipped on a white dressing gown, crept out onto the landing and made his way down creaking wooden stairs. Finding the office, he flicked on a desk lamp, powered up the machine and began logging onto the company website. Gaining access to his customers' telecoms switch, Andy swiftly made changes to international call rates and uploaded new software updates and began checking routes. Idly scanning the networks, he was able to reach the sequence of codes and numbers connecting Dominic Marsh's phone to his telecom provider's network. From the configuration and series of DNS numbers, Andy knew someone was intercepting the line. Mystified by who could be doing this, he began to wonder if Maria's boss was under some kind of investigation. Curious to find out more, he mischievously decided to search for clues on his computer. Cruising around the hard drive several recent files looked interesting, and opening one record in particular he found a web link. Clicking the hyperlink, this led him to another computer server and the forbidding response - Webyoo Lock encrypts this file. Seeing this as a personal challenge, he reached for his car keys off the desk detaching a small memory stick. Plugging it into a spare

USB port uploaded an illegal program used to generate passwords and to pirate software. Incredibly, Dominic Marsh had used a propriety encryption program that was not at all difficult to crack. In seconds, he opened the file and started examining the full content of the once secure data. The official looking documents appeared at first glance to be historic, and had been originated on a manual typewriter then more recently scanned into a computer. They related to a government treaty.

"DRUG CONTROL TREATY BETWEEN THE GOVERNMENT OF THE UNITED KINGDOM OF GREAT BRITAIN AND NORTHERN IRELAND AND THE GOVERNMENT OF THE UNITED STATES OF AMERICA.
The Government of the United Kingdom of Great Britain and Northern Ireland and the Government of the United States of America, Recalling the Senate decision of June 24 1947 it was ratified on that day a treaty transferring narcotic drug control from the League of Nations to the United Nations. This new Treaty between the Government of the United States of America and the Government of the United Kingdom of Great Britain and Northern Ireland signed at London, February 25, 1969, is an amendment by the Supplementary Treaty between the two States, and desiring to provide for more effective co-operation between the two States in the suppression of crime and, for that purpose, to end a new treaty for the implementation and management of narcotics in the two countries covered by the Treaty."

Reading each page, he saw reference to countries famous for their narcotics history: San Salvador, Panama, Colombia, Pakistan, Laos and Afghanistan. This was a comprehensive plan for the production, management and distribution of opium and cocaine throughout the world. The last page had the two signature panels ready for signing, and a third witness section:

> Either State may terminate this Treaty at any time by giving written notice to the other State through the diplomatic channel, and the termination shall be effective six months after the date of receipt of such notice.
>
> IN WITNESS WHEREOF, the undersigned, being duly authorized by their respective Governments, have signed this Treaty.
>
> DONE at London, in triplicate, this 25 day of February 1969
>
> FOR THE GOVERNMENT OF THE UNITED KINGDOM OF GREAT BRITAIN AND NORTHERN IRELAND:
>
> GEORGE BROWN
>
> FOR THE GOVERNMENT OF THE UNITED STATES OF AMERICA:
>
> WILLIAM P ROGERS

Not recognizing either signatory, Andy assumed they would have been leading political figures in their time. Intrigued and wanting to read more, he made the decision to copy all the documents together with three letters included in the same file onto his portable memory device. Next, he loaded another program and proceeded to remove any trace of his activities. He doubted Maria's boss would ever notice anything different - apart from the equipment operating more efficiently.

As the erasure program searched across the hard disk, wiping out temporary files and history tracks, the door opened startling him.

'So that is where my dressing gown has gone.' Maria giggled, stepping sleepily into the room. 'What are you doing?'

Andy clutched his chest, and sighed. 'You gave me a fright, I will be finished soon.'

'Baby, I want you back in my bed.'

'I'm sorry for waking you up.'

'No, it's okay.'

Not wanting her to see what he was doing, he moved from the computer in a single bound, held her in his arms and gave her a squeeze. 'Just a few more minutes, I'm almost finished.'

'Would you like a glass of water?'

'Yes, thank you. Take it with you to the bedroom I'll be there in a minute.'

As she left for the kitchen, he returned to the cleanup process only to find something had gone desperately wrong. His special software was erasing all the files he opened, including the documents. Hitting keys in a mad panic, he tried to stop the program but it was too late. All the files he copied had disappeared off Dominic's computer. It would have been possible to return the data saved on his memory stick, however some of the dates would all be different - a give-away to Maria's boss. Deciding there wasn't enough time to make the necessary changes he did nothing instead, in the hope Dominic had backups saved elsewhere. Turning off the computer he removed his equipment and returned to Maria in bed.

4

A group of girls dressed in uniform jostled for attention at the hotel's check-in desk. Competing with the airline crew at the Holiday Inn, Madrid, Andy exchanged banter with a pretty flight attendant while waiting to register. He had arrived in Spain to help colleagues present a one-day telecoms seminar, and after eventually retrieving the key to his executive room, he headed to the fifth floor. Kicking his shoes off, he lay down on the queen-sized bed and replayed the past 24 hours over in his mind. Mrs Briggs had arrived unexpectedly first thing in the morning and banged on the bedroom door. Maria made him stay quiet, and then asked him to creep into a spare room when the housekeeper was not looking. With his injured foot magically better, Maria gave him a lift back to the supermarket car park and after saying their goodbyes, he made a promise to stay in contact. He had already decided this would happen and planned to arrange another visit as soon as he returned from Madrid. The phone rang, making him jump and disturbing him from his thoughts. He reached over and picked up the receiver. It was Tony Celentano, Andy's UK boss, who was staying in the same hotel.

'Hi Tony, I'm in 504. Did you have a good trip over here?'
'You are joking. If I ran that Easy-Fly/Jet bullshit, I wouldn't pay their staff in pennies. What happened to you on Friday,

you vanished off the face of the earth? My room was crap when I got here, and I insisted they move me to the tenth floor at no extra cost. What's your room like?'

'Oh, fine, no problems. Sorry about Friday, motorway was a nightmare during that freak storm.'

'I thought perhaps you had been blown away. I'm getting changed and meeting the other guys at seven in the bar, see you down there.'

Andy was pleased he didn't have to rush and returned to flashbacks of Maria sitting by his feet. He recalled accidentally deleting files from Dominic's computer, and began to worry what Maria would think if she found out. Feeling suddenly anxious, he decided to take a shower and get ready to meet with his colleagues in the bar. Expecting to be first, Andy was surprised to see Larry and Joel sitting in reception.

Joel grinned broadly and stood up to shake his hand. 'Hey Andy, how u you doing? Have you met Larry before?'

Larry stood up and extended a beefy fist. He was a big man weighing around 250 pounds. Andy recalled seeing him once before on an earlier visit to his head office in Utah.

'Yes, I think we met when I came over last year.'

'When did you get in?'

'A couple of hours ago, I've spoken with Tony and he is on his way down. Well, that's if he hasn't fallen asleep.'

They all laughed and sat down at the table. Joel and Larry ordered iced water for themselves and a beer for Andy. Continuing with small talk about their respective journeys it was not long before Tony arrived. He was a larger than life character, usually the centre of attention and came with none of the formal handshakes and polite conversation about the weather - it was just a round of raucous bear hugs and backslapping. He made his entrance, smiling from ear to ear with a cigarette between his fingers

The Treaty

ready to light up as soon as he was in the smoking area. Joel delivered the first hug and then Larry gave him the same enthusiastic welcome. When glances from other guests signalled they were making a lot of noise, Andy called the waiter over and ordered more drinks. Over dinner, they talked business and finished off with a plan to meet first thing for a pre-seminar breakfast.

With delegates due to start arriving at 10am, Andy's job was to greet visitors and check they had registered before issuing a welcome pack. Earlier that morning Tony hired a translator, offered by someone at the hotel, thinking this could be useful during any negotiations later in the day. With preparations well underway, Andy caught sight of an attractive woman approaching. Smartly dressed in a white top and fire red trousers, she was tall and slim with piercing green eyes.

'*Hola*,' she smiled confidently. 'I'm looking for Tony Celentano.'

Andy explained he worked with Tony and asked if he could help. She said her name was Fatima and was there to act as a translator.

'I received a phone call from the hotel one hour ago, so I've no idea what I am supposed to do.'

Andy impulsively touched her arm, and feeling her tense, he quickly withdrew his hand. 'I'm not sure, either,' he smiled, feeling slightly embarrassed. 'You can help me out here if you like; I've been having terrible problems understanding the delegates.'

'Sure,' she replied.

After the seminar, Fatima circulated among their guests helping with translation. Andy was busy too offering technical advice, and it was not until the last delegate drifted off that they were able to congratulate everyone on staging a great event. Fatima had been a huge help, impressing everyone with her grasp of electronic engineering and telecom terminology. At some point in their conversation, she asked if they knew Madrid and offered to show them the nightlife. Andy responded positively. He could not face another long boring evening staying in the hotel, while Joel and Larry preferred to check out a Mormon Temple and Tony announced he was too tired and would settle for an early night.

Meeting later that evening in the hotel lounge, Fatima turned heads coming through the foyer dressed to kill. Andy felt positively proud leaving his colleagues behind accompanied by this beautiful woman. Taking a cab to downtown Madrid, they took a short walk through the tourist parts of the Royal Palace gardens before deciding to eat. Spaniards dine late in the evenings, and Fatima suggested a specialist restaurant where they could watch a cabaret then have food.

'I don't think Joel and Larry would have been comfortable in this place,' she told him. 'It's different and very popular with young people.'

It was exactly that, and Andy had immediately suspected something was not quite right about the people working there on entering the joint. The girl on the door seemed ordinary enough, but once inside all the men waiting tables were muscle boys in black leather waistcoats, which showed their pecks and wore dangling chains decorating their biceps. Serving behind the bar the attractive girls were, according to Fatima, all men in drag, although, he could not possibly tell. Seated among tables of students, hen parties and couples having a fun night out, they settled down to watch the raucous and at times very funny performance. Fatima did not drink any alcohol back at the hotel but was now happy to share a bottle of red wine with Andy, and after the first two glasses, there was a noticeable change in her personality. Gone was the professional businessperson and now, sitting up close with her arm wrapped around his, she pushed her head back and burned a gaze directly into his eyes.

'What have I said?' Andy smiled.

'Nothing, you have not said anything. I just want to look at you.'

He laughed nervously, taking a sip of his drink.

Moving closer, her lips to his ear, she whispered, 'What would you like to do after the show?'

He felt suddenly hot. '...I don't know, what would you like to do?'

Without warning, Fatima jumped and grabbed his hand. 'Come, I will show you.'

There was no room for debate and weaving among a maze of tables, they ran down the stairs and back out onto the busy street. On reaching the outside, she immediately began kissing him like a demented vampire. Pausing for a second, she began leading him by the hand to a waiting taxi and whisked him off into the night. There was no conversation and he did not have clue where they were going, as if it mattered. The driver's eye reflected in the mirror told him he had seen all this a thousand times before. Leaving the commercial district the journey lasted no more than ten minutes before drawing to a halt alongside a nondescript apartment block. Andy was not naïve and hoped he knew where this was leading. Confirmation came only minutes later while enjoying some of the noisiest sex he had ever experienced.

Calmer, as if sated by her latest victim, Fatima casually asked him. 'Have you ever made love to a black girl before?'

Surprised by her question Andy struggled to think of a quick response. 'Uh, all I can see is a very pretty girl with dark olive skin, gorgeous eyes and a smile to die for.'

This sent her into a fit of giggles. 'At the hotel when you

touched my arm it was like an electric shock wave, I knew from that moment I wanted to make love to you.'

'Now I feel stupid. I thought I had offended you by being over familiar.'

'You English are so stupid. Why are you always so afraid to speak your feelings?'

Fatima climbed out of bed and walked naked into the lounge. She disappeared for a few seconds only to return with the beautiful sounds of Madame Butterfly drifting into the room behind her.

Andy sat up in bed. 'I love this piece of music. How did you know it was my favourite?'

'I didn't,' Fatima smiled, lifting the silk sheets and sliding under them. They snuggled up close, and kissed.

It was a hot sultry night in the Madrid suburb making breathing difficult, even with the bedroom window wide open. Trying not to make any noise Andy slipped out of bed and went in search of a drink. Finding the kitchen, he filled a glass with water from a plastic bottle in the fridge and carried it through to the lounge. Scanning the neatly furnished room illuminated by soft orange shadows from the streetlights below, he sat on the sofa. The room did not have a lot of furniture, a small coffee table in the centre with an Ikea style unit at the side displaying a variety of books and papers. Fatima's handbag was lying on the edge of the sofa, where she casually dropped it down at the height of their passionate entrance into the apartment. From where he was sitting, he could just make out some writing at the top of a piece of paper jammed in the zip, a row of numbers curiously matching those from his own local phone code. Tempted by the coincidence, he worked the fastener and eased out the paper far enough to see it was a fax letter. Scanning the message, he quickly realized this was the same fax he sent to the hotel confirming his arrival time. Carefully returning the page, he closed the zip, finished his drink and tried to figure out why she would have this document. Maybe, he thought, the hotel gave it to her so she could remember the name of her client. With this odd event on his mind, he returned to bed and, unable to sleep, he felt anxious to find out more about the fax. At one stage, he was even tempted to wake Fatima, but as dawn approached, she began to stir herself moving closer to him and clearly intent on more sex. With the letter still on his mind, he stopped her by asking if he could take a shower to cool himself down. Watching him leave the room, she reached for a mobile phone left down on the floor by the bed and made a call. Hissing instructions into the phone in fluent Arabic, she ended the conversation by throwing the device back on the floor. With Andy still in the shower, she left the bedroom, and then soon after someone from outside the apartment knocked on the front door. Wrapped in a bath towel Fatima sprinted to her spare room, picked up a small plain envelope and went to greet the visitor. Speaking quickly to a bearded man, she handed him the package and abruptly closed the door in his face.

Unaware what was happening Andy came out of the bathroom, and finding Fatima gone, pulled on his boxers and went in search. With the smell of fresh coffee wafting through the apartment, he discovered her lying full length on the sofa wrapped in the same white bath towel. Moving her legs, she cleared a space by her feet and beckoned for him to sit down. Meekly obeying, he plucked up the courage to speak about the fax number and began to massage her ankle. Gradually squeezing the calf muscle, he moved higher up the thigh. Fatima's pulsating breath increased in frequency, encouraging him to work harder. Pushing his fists into her abdomen and resisting her feet pressing against his groin, he continued the massage deeper and deeper, making her excitement rise to a fever pitch. Gently continuing as she began to calm down, all he could hear was an almost indiscernible whimper. Turning onto her stomach, he continued kneading with long strokes and all the time trying to gauge the best time to speak. Sliding his hands to her shoulders, he gently squeezed the knotty muscles, massaging the arm and side of the neck. He held her shoulder with both hands and moving up and down, forward then backward he watched her squirm with pleasure. Fatima could feel a growing sensation of heaviness as the shoulder and arm relaxed. Finally making circular movements with his fingertips under the shoulder blade, he began to speak softly.

'Fatima, last night when you were a sleep I came in here and saw a piece of paper sticking out of your bag. It is a copy of my fax to the hotel. Why do you have it?'

She stopped moving and lay silent. Turning her head to one side, she rested it on her forearm, the page still protruding from the bag on the floor by her head.

'Baby, it's nothing I was asked to translate it at the hotel by the girl in the business centre.'

Relieved she was not angry; Andy resumed the massage and accepted her explanation.

She turned back over to face him. 'There is something I should have shown you last night.' Reaching for her handbag, she produced another sheet of paper, and handed it to him. 'Did you know this?'

Scanning the page, Andy could see it was a copy of a newspaper article printed from a website with the headline; "Couple Gunned Down in Hotel Shooting". He quickly read the first line; "*A husband and wife staying in a North London hotel were brutally murdered in two separate incidences. The motive was thought to be robbery…*"

Andy frowned. 'Why are you showing me this?'

'Carry on reading.'

"*…Police visited the victims' home in Northamptonshire to search for further clues. The man has been named as Mr*

Dominic Marsh, publisher of a popular magazine and his wife Emma Marsh..." Andy's mind raced. "*...Police would like to contact anyone who had dealings with the couple recently. They were also anxious to speak with any visitors to their home, and in particular, they urgently need to talk to a Mr Andrew Davies, described as the friend of Ms. Maria Farnese, the couple's au pair. Mr Davies is reported to have stayed at the family's home on Friday evening. Inspector Colin Sharp, in charge of the incident said," It is understood Mr Davies is on business somewhere in Spain, and we need to make contact with him and eliminate him from our enquiries...*"

Andy was speechless and read the news story over again to make sure it was referring to him.

'When did you say you got this?'

'Just before we left the hotel to go out last night,' Fatima replied. She reached and grasped his hand, speaking very gently. 'You obviously knew nothing of this. It must be a shock.'

'Yes, it is a very big shock. I cannot believe you kept this from me all night, I would have gone back to London.'

'Baby, I'm sorry, I didn't get chance to read it when the girl gave it to me to translate. I slipped it into my bag together with the fax planning to look at it later. They ask me to do these things all the time, I never realized it was so important and directly affected you. It was only last night when I came in here to read these papers while you were sleeping that I understood the significance. Did you know this girl and these people very well?'

'I met Maria last Friday for the first time; I didn't know the couple who have been killed. Poor Maria and their little boy Toby, I feel so sorry for them.'

Andy explained about the storm and meeting Maria. He told how they stayed together just that one night and how he had arranged to meet her again when he returned to

England. He went in search of his mobile and began calling the number she personally stored in his phone seconds before they parted.

'It's still very early in the morning, she's on voice mail.'

'Andy, why do you think the police are so keen to see you?'

'I don't know. I will call them from the hotel room.'

'If this man Dominic was a journalist and wrote about people, perhaps they suspect you had a reason to be there, other than meeting Maria?'

He calmly digested what Fatima was saying and tried to understand her logic. 'I don't get it, why would they suspect me of anything? I never even met them.'

'Did anything unusual happen while you were staying there?'

Andy blushed and avoided telling her about Maria. 'No, I don't think so. Ah, I did borrow Dominic's computer to do some work.'

'Yes, Andy, maybe they think you were looking for something. Did you find anything strange?'

Even though he was in shock, Andy suspected Fatima may have another agenda, but could not figure out what it was and decided to play along.

'No, not really,' he lied. 'I searched around on the hard drive just being curious; it wasn't for any particular reason, but I may have accidentally deleted some of his computer files.'

All the time he had been speaking, he watched Fatima's body language and there had been a noticeable change. She was more intense, even excited by what he was telling her.

'What were you looking at?' she asked.

'There wasn't anything. All I could see were files from past editorial used in the magazines.'

'Did you open any of them? The police may be able to

The Treaty

tell if you did.'

'I doubt that. There was one file I saw but it was encrypted, something about a treaty.'

Fatima's jaw dropped and her mouth gaped open. She visibly flinched as he said those words.

'Andy, did you make a copy? The police will know.'

'Look, you're being ridiculous. Why would I copy the damn thing? I must try to call Maria again. Is there anything else you've forgotten to tell me?'

The sympathy and warmth displayed by Fatima just seconds before was suddenly gone - she was aloof and composed. 'I've told you everything, and I'm sorry about your friend and her family. I just wish you had mentioned the au pair before you had sex with me!'

Andy immediately felt pangs of guilt, not for Fatima but for Maria.

'I'm sorry. I didn't...I really must get back to my hotel.'

'I'll call a taxi.' She picked up her landline phone, punched in a number and began speaking in Spanish. She replaced the receiver. 'The taxi will be outside in ten minutes.'

'I'm sorry if I was angry, I'm really shocked by what happened in England.'

'Don't worry about it, I've enjoyed meeting you.'

Ignoring her sarcasm, he left the room to finish dressing. When he came back, she was waiting by the door.

'Take care, and thanks again for your help at the seminar.'

They kissed formally, with none of the passion from the previous night, and he left her apartment and headed outside to a waiting taxi. Arriving back at the hotel, he brushed passed a tired looking concierge and headed up to his room. Standing outside the door he searched through his pockets for the keycard, and realizing it was missing guessed it must be on the other side of the door. Making a quick sprint back to reception the sympathetic receptionist produced a duplicate, showing she was used to dumb-ass customers losing their room card. Once inside he immediately began trying to phone Maria, and waited for an answer.

'Hello, Maria's phone, who is this?'

'I was expecting Maria. Is she there?'

'Is that Mr Davies?'

'Yes.'

'We've been trying to contact you, sir. I could not find your number in Maria's phone. I'm Inspector Colin Sharp. Maria is in hospital recovering from shock. She collapsed shortly after we went to see her. Have you heard what's happened to Mr and Mrs Marsh, her employers?'

'Yes, I've just been told. Is Maria going to be all right? I will be back in the UK as soon as possible, at the moment I am in Madrid.'

'Ah Madrid, we knew you were in Spain somewhere. Maria is ill, but I understand she is conscious now. You will have to call the hospital to find out more. We are still trying to piece everything together and you may be able to fill in a few gaps, especially about the weekend. When can you come in to see me?'

'I'm flying back today, late this afternoon. Is that soon enough, I have to drive from Heathrow?'

'That'll be fine. We just need to chat about the hours prior to the incident and your visit to Mr Marsh's home. I'll look forward to seeing you then Andrew, take care and have a good flight.'

Andy snapped his phone shut and immediately started to pack. He was still in shock over what had happened, and discovering now Maria was in hospital, he felt overwhelmed and a little shaken. Checking his few belongings, he suddenly noticed something was missing; his laptop bag had been on the floor by the desk. After searching the room from top to bottom - in the wardrobe, underneath the bed, he called reception to make sure they had not taken it for security purposes. Finally, it began to dawn on him the computer had been taken. Remembering his car keys and computer memory stick, which were together in his overnight bag, he furiously sorted through a jumble of underwear and socks. Out of growing frustration, he tipped the contents of his bag onto the bed, and watched his car keys bounce out with the laundry. Relieved to have found them, he immediately noticed the memory stick was missing. This was the last straw, and he thanked God he had removed the files he copied off Dominic Marsh's computer before he left for Spain. Feeling a wave of depression and despair, he crashed down on the bed and lay amongst the dirty laundry. He grabbed hold of his bag and threw it across the room. With his eyes closed he began to recount the past few hours and the chain of events that had taken place. Two people were dead, he had been robbed, and there was Fatima - what part did she play in all this? Why did she have his fax and the newspaper article, and why did she act so strangely when he mentioned the treaty?

5

Tim walked into a bright office and was shown to a chair placed in front of a plain wooden table. He sat down opposite the smartly dressed middle-aged woman who was conducting the interview inside Paddington Green Police Station, home to the UK anti-terrorist squad.

'Thank you for coming,' she smiled.

'That's not a problem; my office is close by in Charlotte Street.'

'So Tim, how long have you lived in London?'

'I came to Europe back in the Eighties. I'm still an American citizen, but classed as a local in my neighbourhood.'

Reaching to switch off the tape machine used to make an obligatory recording of their conversation the woman then stopped him mid-sentence.

'Sorry Tim, I will have to start this again I should have began by introducing myself - okay here we go.'

Snapping down the switch this caused the ancient recorder to start-up once again.

'My name is Caroline Lovelace-Jones and I work for a branch of the Home Office. I am looking into one or two security issues indirectly related to the murder of Mr and Mrs Dominic Marsh. Tim I understand you knew Dominic and Emma and were close friends.'

The Treaty

Tim Franklin was the American born literary agent employed by Dominic Marsh, and had met with his client only hours before the fatal shooting. After the interview by local police, his file came over to Special Branch at their request and forwarded to Caroline.

'I've known Dominic for years, right from when I first arrived in the UK. He was always a bit of a rebel and made enemies, but I never dreamt anyone would want to kill him.'

'Well, the police are not sure what the motive was; it could have been robbery. His credit cards and money were stolen.'

'When I lived in the US I had another client called Danny Williams, he was working on a book and claimed it would confirm rumours linking George Bush Senior with a drugs and sleaze scandal. They found Danny's body in a hotel room in Martinsburg, West Virginia, apparent suicide and hence my skepticism.'

'I'm sorry about your friend. The reason we have asked for your help is because I am working on a special project and one or two things in your witness statement interested me.'

'Like what for example?'

Caroline ignored his question. She was more interested finding out what he knew of his client's recent past. Her real job title was Bureau Chief of MI-21's Madrid office, with the special responsibility of tracking suspected and known terrorists.

'Tell me about the book Dominic was writing - was he planning some kind of exposé?'

'This will sound crazy, but I'm honestly not one hundred percent sure. It was a nightmare trying to promote the damn thing to foreign publishers. All he would give me was a very brief synopsis that practically gave nothing away; apart from saying the story was political dynamite.'

'Was he being so secretive because he expected trouble? Someone may try to stop him from publishing perhaps.'

'The answer is, I really don't know. Dominic kept information a secret and he believed it was a currency in its own right. When I told him how difficult it was to be taken seriously, he would laugh saying they will miss out and should go on his reputation and history of exposing corruption and dodgy politicians.'

'Yes, I see from his file he owned and published a satirical magazine and, by the looks of things, always seemed to be getting into trouble and sued in the courts. What did his project actually comprise of?'

'Film, newspapers, books...first he planned to write a series of articles followed by the book and hoping for a movie deal later.'

'So how did he come by this information, any clues?'

'I knew absolutely nothing about it until we met at his hotel on Saturday afternoon, the hotel where he died. We had a meeting with a prospective major distributor for the book who amazingly agreed with a deal. Dominic confided he had paid a corrupt bank official in Argentina for a whole bunch of supposedly secret documents stored in a private safe-deposit box. They had been lying there for almost a decade. The owner had apparently died. He met this guy at the Latin American Book Fair in Buenos Aires, and claimed there was enough evidence in the files to prove the US and Britain had signed an illegal narcotics treaty in the 1960's.'

Caroline smiled and quickly wrote something down in her notebook. 'Did you believe the story? Perhaps more importantly, what relevance would it have today?'

'Dominic was the sort of guy you took seriously, as sooner or later he would come up with the 'real deal' and I'm on ten percent for life. I asked him the same question - why would anyone be bothered about this now. It was ancient

The Treaty

history to most people. His reply was he believed this agreement was still in force and operational to this very day.'

'Did he mention any names, Westerners we might know, business people? Who were these mystery figures?'

'You will think this is absolutely comical, but he let slip the names of a couple of senior royals.'

'Go on Tim, make me laugh?'

'Prince Philip and Diana amongst others - you do know he lived close to Di's old home at Althorp?'

Now Caroline was uncertain how seriously she should take Tim's evidence. She did not want to be made a fool of and was growing impatient, which was made worse by the fact it was several hours since her last cigarette.

'Is this a joke Tim, because if it's not, your client was probably sold some barmy conspiracy theory not worth the paper it's written on? I thought Dominic was an intelligent man. Are you sure he was not winding you up, did he have a sense of humour?'

'Yes, he was well known for making practical jokes, but honestly Caroline, I've never known him to be more serious. This story was going to make him famous; he really believed that it was true. After he married Emma, and their son Toby was born, they rented a house on the edge of the Spencer Estate in Northamptonshire, to be closer to Emma's folks. From what I gather it was probably there he somehow made the Diana connection.'

'I thought Mr Marsh was based in London, his office was definitely here.'

'He commuted, staying in London three nights a week. Don't forget he was nearly twenty years older than his wife and probably needed some space. To help Emma they had an au pair, a young girl from Argentina as it happened. The last time I visited she was teaching them all Spanish, one big happy family. The police told me about her collapsing when she heard the news.'

'Yes, it must have been devastating. I believe she is recovering in hospital. Tim - before we finish is there anymore you can tell me; did he specifically link Althorp in anyway with those papers? In what context were the royals supposedly involved?'

Tim leant his elbows on the table, and sighed. 'When Dominic received the documents, the guy from the bank was certain they originated out of Northamptonshire. I suspect this bank dude was hawking them around to anyone he thought could pay the price. Dominic must have made the connection with Althorp and the royals.'

'Well, Tim, thank you for taking time out of your busy schedule. Have my card, and if you hear or remember any additional information give me a call or email.' Tim accepted the card and shook Caroline by the hand saying,

'Thank you, I will. It is so sad that it had to end like this. Dominic took risks but he could never have imagined anything like this happening.'

'Well, as I said at the start, we don't yet know what happened.'

Caroline stood to show the interview was over. The female officer who welcomed Tim in reception returned to escort him from the building. Caroline sat back idly making small ticks with a pen on a sheet of notes, matching words gleaned from other covert conversations, Althorp, Buenos Aires, Prince Philip, the treaty.

6

Inspector Colin Sharp led Andy into a small newly decorated interview room; he was a slim, gangly man, at least six-foot five inches with little or no hair on his head. Observing through a two-way mirror Caroline Lovelace-Jones sat in an adjacent room, waiting patiently for this second interview to take place.

'Thank you for making it over here so quickly Andy, as you can imagine time is of the up-most importance in a case of this nature.'

'I can imagine,' Andy replied, looking nervous. 'Do you know exactly what happened to Maria?'

'Please take a seat and we can go over everything.'

Andy did as asked and the two men sat opposite each other at an interview table.

'I plan to visit Maria in hospital after we're finished here. Is she going to be all right?'

'Yes, Andy, she's fine. I have personally been to see her and she was sitting up in bed answering questions. Apparently when our people arrived at the house to break the news she suffered an anaphylactic shock, which caused a restriction to her breathing and her heart to stop for a few milliseconds - long enough to send her into unconsciousness.

'Poor girl,' Andy sighed, 'she seemed like a very sensitive

person. I can only imagine how shocking the news would have been for her.'

'You must be keen to visit her, so I will try to get through these questions as quickly as possible.'

'I'd appreciate that.'

'Did Maria tell you anything of interest about Dominic Marsh?'

'Not that I recall, she appeared to like him. He sounded like a very kind man. She mentioned they had spoken about taking her with them when they all went on holiday. I didn't get the impression he talked about his business.'

'According to Janet Briggs, the housekeeper, you arrived with Maria after a storm with an injured foot. How did that all happen?'

Andy explained about the mini-tornado. This had been in all the national newspapers and on TV, especially the damage to the supermarket. He told how Maria caused the injury to his foot with her supermarket cart, causing the Inspector to chuckle; he clearly had no problem believing Andy's description of the events.

'What I am not too clear about is what happened later, during the night. I don't mean in the bedroom, but when you got up to use the computer.'

Andy blushed, and the Inspector peered down at his notes.

'According to Maria about twelve thirty in the morning you left her bedroom and went downstairs. Can you explain to me what you were doing on Dominic Marsh's computer?'

Having anticipated this would be a material question; Andy took a deep breath and launched into his well-rehearsed explanation. After what had happened to both the Marsh's and after his strange encounter with Fatima, he felt so concerned for his safety he decided to say nothing at this stage about opening the encrypted files.

The Treaty

'I work in telecoms, and I had to make rate-changes and install an upgrade onto a client's telephony switching platform. This piece of equipment manages all the calls and billing, which I gained access via the Internet.'

'Why at that particular time in the morning?'

'We can only play around with a customer's equipment when call traffic is at its lowest volume, otherwise they would lose a lot of revenue through calls not being completed.'

'So you have to switch the machine off?'

'No, but during the rate-change and software upgrade some calls may not complete, so if we choose a time when few calls are being made then the disruption is kept to a minimum.'

Pausing again to read his notes, the Inspector twirled a pencil around with his fingers before glancing up, making full eye contact with Andy.

'After you had finished making the upgrades did you close the computer down and go back to bed,' the Inspector asked, 'or did you play around for a while and perhaps have a little look on Dominic Marsh's hard-drive?'

Battling to stay calm, and desperate not to show how nervous he felt, Andy launched into his prepared piece.

'I more or less closed down immediately after finishing the work. Maria came into the room to find out if I was going to be very long and I began to shut down.'

The inspector leaned a little closer and stared hard into Andy's eye. 'You shut down the computer?'

Andy nodded. 'Yes.'

'Okay, well, my boss requested this next question; I am literally ticking the boxes you understand. Did you copy any data or other information from Dominic Marsh's hard drive, or email anything to yourself from his computer?'

'No, as I've already explained it was a simple upgrade and rate change, I do these everyday of my working life.'

'Maria said in her statement she thought she saw you use a memory stick.'

'Yes, that is possible I have one, or did until it was stolen. I used it to store passwords for access to customers' equipment over the internet.'

'Just one last item and we're practically finished,' the Inspector grinned. 'Our technical gurus say there were no traces of any activity on the machine, no history or log files, no internet trail, which they thought was a little unusual. Do you have an explanation, not too technical of course?'

'When I finished working I used a piece of software called a Scrubber. This removes all the old rubbish and history files, including any trace of the passwords and login details I used to gain access to my customers' telephony switches. I didn't know how safe the machine was, it could have been infected with Spy ware or a keystroke logger used to record passwords and other secure information.'

'You mean the sort of stuff used by fraudsters for phishing, to get peoples' bank details and account passwords. I can see the logic, but surely Dominic Marsh would have been pissed-off, discovering you made all these changes to his equipment without him knowing?'

'The only thing he would have noticed was increased speed reaching the Internet and improvement in functionality.'

'Andy, thank you once again for coming in to see me and please let me know if you have any new travel plans in the next few weeks. We may need to talk again.'

'Yes, I often have to go abroad at short notice as part of my work, but I will let you know when this happens.'

Caroline watched Andy leave, chiding her self for admiring his looks and wondered if he could be more involved. Based on his evidence she had doubts. Maria showed no loyalty toward him, making it clear they had only met that

The Treaty

once. It was probably just a coincidence. Andy had stayed at the house and Maria fancied him so she let him share her bed, it was a common affair - but that still did not explain everything. If he did not already know her, how had Fatima managed to identify him so quickly?

7

Paul approached and peered down at his employer who was fast asleep in an armchair. His breathing was so shallow it appeared to have stopped altogether.

'Excuse me sir, I will be leaving shortly. Is there anything further you need, can I help you into bed?'

Waking abruptly and looking around, Philip cleared his throat. 'Michael, what bloody time is it?

'I'm Paul, sir, and it's ten o'clock.'

'Paul, yes, put that damn table light on, there's a good chap, see what we're doing, and brandy, top me up then off you go?'

'Do you need assistance getting into bed, sir?'

'No, I'm fine, not ready yet, no need to shout - it's too early.'

Paul finished pouring out the brandy, desperate to finish his duties for that day and hand over to Michael.

'Would you like the television on, sir?'

'No, leave the bloody thing off, it's full of depressing news.'

'Goodnight sir, Michael will be here if you require anything further. May I remind you of your appointment at eleven o'clock in the morning with the Duchess of Cornwall?'

'Yes, I know, I'm not a gibbering idiot just yet.'

Settling back in the armchair, Prince Philip took a sip of

The Treaty

his drink and began to feel less agitated as the brandy did its work. It had been a busy day for an eighty-four year-old man - visiting a bunch of geriatrics in a new hospital opened by the Queen. Now it was time for serious business. Charles's marriage to Camilla had brought them one-step closer to appointing his successor. She was perfect for the role and he was confident she would not let them down. It was time to start handing over the huge burden to a younger person, and thank God, the right one had finally come along.

Camilla had been on his radar for years, and he was angry when Charles let her go off to marry that other fellow the first time around, so ridiculous, so many problems could have been avoided. Although, he was partially to blame in letting Ted Spencer talk him into using his girl Diana. There was never a chance in hell it could have worked. His next mission was to hand the responsibility of Consort over to Camilla. Of all the people to succeed him, she was undoubtedly the only one he knew with the mental capability to handle this onerous and difficult job.

Nights seemed long and drawn out when you got to Philip's age. He did not sleep well, perhaps made worse by frequent catnaps during the day. This gave him a lot of time to think about the past, sometimes too much time. With all the outward signs of a man of great privilege and wealth, it was not public knowledge how hard and very insecure his early life had been. He was the youngest of five and his parents were members of the European aristocracy that ruled in the early part of the 20th century. His mother came from wealthy German parents, born in England and related to Queen Victoria. Named Victoria Alice Elisabeth Julia Marie, she was profoundly deaf, and could lip-read in four languages. Her official title was Princess Alice of Battenberg taken from her father Louis of Battenberg and her German mother Victoria of Hesse.

Philip's father was Prince Andrew of Greece and, shortly after Philip was born, Andrew faced a close encounter with death. Greece had been taken over by a new military junta and Andrew's brother, King of Greece, was deposed and fled the country leaving Andrew to face trial and a sentence of death by firing squad. Working behind the scenes, Andrews's brother-in-law, Lord Mountbatten, arranged a rescue by the British Royal Navy, who snatched him from his captors. Growing up in Paris in a household of girls made Philip appreciate the importance of wealth in maintaining any kind of independence, and it was probably then he vowed to one-day recover his families lost fortunes and make sure his life would be very different from that of his parents. Recalling how hard it was for his mother and father, who had been brought up with great privilege and who were effectively reduced to living in poverty, at least by their standards, he wondered how his own family would have coped if the same disruption happened to them.

Self-analysis was not new to Philip; he was a loner and used to deep thought, probably helping to bury the more painful of his life experiences. One particular recurring nightmare was the terrible tragedy of his youngest sister Cecile. Determined to attend a wedding in England while heavily pregnant with her fifth child, the whole family set off from Frankfurt airport. In heavy fog, just outside Ostend, the plane's wing clipped a tall chimney causing it to crash - only their youngest child Johanna survived. Despite this, the wedding took place in full mourning dress and five coffins accompanied the newlywed's back to Darmstadt for burial. In shock after the loss of his sister, he rarely talked to anyone about her death. Later his guardian and mentor Uncle George, also died leaving the young Philip living alone in England. Taken in by another uncle, his mother's brother Lord Louis Mountbatten, he helped arrange for entry into Dartmouth Naval College.

The Treaty

Here Philip first met the thirteen-year-old Princess Elizabeth, who he later married. Philips own father's life practically ended with the demise of Greece's monarchy. Cast out a penniless iterant without even a surname, he never properly recovered, eventually abandoning his family in Paris and moving to Southern France, where for years he lived with Countess Andrée de La Bigne.

After Philip's own marriage to the future Queen of England, he thought his life was now perfect. With his naval career going well and the birth of a son and heir, everything suddenly changed with the unexpected death of Elizabeth's father, King George VII. Philip soon discovered he could no longer continue with his own career and was to become the Queen's fulltime Consort, performing countless royal duties, travelling the commonwealth and meeting with world leaders.

In 1964 Britain elected, for only the second time in its history, a socialist government, under the leadership of Harold Wilson. Philip feared they were under threat; he suspected constitutional changes that some MP's may try to get rid of the royal family. Thousands of people in Britain supported Communism. During one visit to London, Russian President Khrushchev was reported saying he had not met with so many committed socialists since the days of Stalin. Moves to turn Britain into a republic with an elected head of state were the goal for several key members of the Labour Government, who despised the royal family and all it stood for. With his own experience of living in exile and a real fear that history could be repeating itself - he knew he must take action. Everything they owned, their lifestyle in Britain was up for grabs and could never be taken for granted. The monarchy was as expendable in Britain as in most other European countries. Both Philip and the rest of the family faced the choice of either losing their rank and privileges living in Britain, or moving to another country to start over again. He believed his personal duty was to protect his family in the same way his father had tried so hard to do, almost losing his life in the process. The ultimate weapon for success was personal wealth, something his own father lacked plus a powerful ally. At that time, Philip had neither.

The Treaty

8

A black Jaguar motorcar swept smoothly off the slipway, joining the M4 into Central London. Camilla hunkered down in the back seat still feeling self-conscious of her new celebrity status and nervous about meeting her father-in-law, Prince Philip. When she left Highgrove that morning, husband Charles was cynical about the reason why his father had called this meeting saying he probably wanted her to take over some awful charity that he can't be bothered with anymore. Suspecting he was right, she decided to listen to what he had to say and not be pressured into accepting any old job. Since their wedding, her life had started to improve dramatically, and even the media were more respectful toward her. Slowly but surely she was building bridges with the family and with the British public. Who knows she thought, one day they may even like her as much as they did Diana.

* * * * *

Speaking while opening the thick velvet drapes, Michael moved to start laying out his employer's clothing for that day. 'Good morning, sir, it's nine o'clock.'
  'What's that? What bloody time is it Paul?'
  'It's nine o'clock, sir, and you have an appointment at

eleven with the Duchess of Cornwall. It's Michael sir.'

His head ached from drinking brandy the night before and he knew it would take awhile for this to clear.

'She will just have to bloody wait until I'm ready.'

With Michael's assistance, he dressed, and despite insisting on his usual full English breakfast, he still managed to be in his chair by the time she arrived. Inline with time-honoured protocol Michael announced the arrival of his guest.

'Show her in - and Paul, I don't want any further disturbances, at all.'

'Yes sir.' He left the room muttering under his breath, 'Its Michael you old fool.'

Camilla was shown into the room and went over to greet Philip, stooping to kiss him on the cheek telling him not to leave his chair. She had not been to the Palace since returning from their honeymoon and noticed how frail he looked; unaware this was more to do with alcohol than his age.

'Sit down old gel, how are you? Charles must be wondering what the bloody hell this is all about.'

Smiling, she confirmed her own curiosity and continued making small talk. 'Are you looking forward to your America trip? Charles told me this will be one of only a few occasions you have actually been abroad for a proper holiday.'

'Not so keen on flying at my age, and it would be even better without all those blessed Americans everywhere. Still the Queen enjoys it and likes to see her horses every now and then.'

Philip had a famously short attention span and moved on with the main purpose of their meeting.

'Well, Camilla, I'm not going to beat about the bush, I asked to see you for a serious and important conversation.'

Sitting up straight and edging closer, he now wore a fearsome expression and looked her in the eye. Gone was the frailness of old age, the demeanor had dramatically changed to one of aggression, a manner designed to dispel any sign of weakness on his part. Camilla had previously listened to Charles describe this posture, used to intimidate and strike terror into him when he was a child.

'Now that you are married to Charles,' he began, 'what I am going to divulge has to remain a secret between just the two of us, and when I explain you will understand why. Do I have your word that nothing you hear from me during this meeting will be discussed outside this room?'

Meekly nodding her agreement, surprised by the speed he had changed his tone; she answered back, 'Yes, of course.'

Relaxing again, happy the importance level of their meeting had been established; he cleared his throat, took a sip of tea and began speaking in a slow measured tone. 'I'm eighty-four years old and living on borrowed time, its essential our family remains at the centre of power in Britain. You have to understand this has been a damn hard show for me to run on my own.'

Unsure where the conversation was leading, Camilla listened patiently as he rambled on.

'You won't remember, but in the sixties our situation was very different to how it is now. You see my dear I had to take action. It was not good enough to sit back and let events take their course. There were only a few of us who could see the bigger picture, and together with my cousin Bernard, did you know him? Prince Bernard married to Queen Juliana over in Holland, well, with Bernard; we came up with a plan.'

Camilla managed to stifle a yawn, not having counted on this history lesson or tour through the family archives. Oblivious to her boredom, Philip rambled on becoming lost in his own consciousness as he pulled the story together.

'...There was only Bernard and Uncle Dickie I could rely on. We shared the same sort of ideas about what was decent and how things should be run. Bernard invited me to join his club, a bit of a strange set up. Everyone was jumpy in those days, what with the cold war. Those Russians were a scary bunch, they killed half my family, you know. Anyway, Bernard had been involved with this group for sometime, made up of prominent people mainly European and Americans. We had all the top names at the meetings, Kissinger, Nixon and Macmillan; even old De Gaulle paid a visit. It was so bad over here in Britain they would not invite our own Prime Minister, that little fat chap Wilson, he was suspected of being too close with the Russians. We always met at the same place, the Hotel de Bilderberg in Holland, have you heard of it?'

Only half listening, her mind had wandered ahead and Camilla mouthed either a yes or no when she thought it appropriate. Trying to work out where this convoluted discussion was leading and why he had made such a fuss about it being secret. What had she gotten into? It all seemed so simple before the wedding. Back then, her only objective was to marry Charles, a mission she had pursued for almost two decades. Now that had been achieved she had hoped to settle down into some kind of normality, well, as normal as possible being married to the heir of the throne.

Philip raised his eyebrows. 'Pay attention, dear?'

'Yes, I am sorry,' she replied, straightening her posture. 'I was listening; it's hard for me to take everything in. I am not sure where this discussion is leading, or what you want me to do for you.'

'I haven't got to that yet. I am sorry old-gel, but it is complicated. You must try to keep up.'

Embarrassed by his chastisement, she recalled Charles

warning not to take any nonsense and made an effort to concentrate on his ancient history.

'As I was saying,' Philip sighed, 'there was only us three against the world at that time, the people who I could trust. We had all witnessed how politicians treated Royalty once they turned to republicanism. My wife's wealth, possessions, and that of the children's would be up for grabs by thieving politicians. Bernard's income came from his wife and so did mine. Uncle Dickie wasn't rich; we needed independent incomes, not handouts from governments to be really secure.'

Feeling impatient, Camilla could not see the point of what it was he was trying to say and even began to suspect he was going senile. She debated whether to make an excuse to leave the room and call Charles, but instead she interrupted Philip in mid-sentence.

'I can see how you must have been very worried about the future,' Camilla said. 'I'm just a little confused about how I could be involved in your family's private arrangements made all those years ago.'

'It's important, and you have to hear the full story. Put up with me for a few more minutes, I'm leading up to a new role for you in the Royal Family.'

Shocked by this revelation, he now had her full attention. Camilla felt anxious to hear what he had in mind. She knew Philip could not be dismissed; he was after all still the head of the family.

'Uncle Dickie, when he was Lord Mountbatten was the last Viceroy of India, before they were granted independence. Did you know that Great Britain in the nineteenth century was the largest supplier of opium in the world?'

Unimpressed by this piece of trivia, Camilla renewed her concerns about the state of Philip's mind and, ignoring the question, allowed him to ramble on.

'We supposedly ended the trade at the beginning of the

1900's, but still played a major role producing all sorts of chemicals and drugs in India and Hong Kong. This was before WWII, and afterwards the communists led by Mao Tse Tung changed it all.'

His expression suddenly went smug, trawling back through his memory closing his eyes to savour this particular part of the story.

'I had a plan of my own, a simple one really. My idea was to copy the same techniques used by the British in India, to show how we could produce and distribute opium on an international scale, in exactly the same way as before - selling it to the Chinese and anyone else that wanted the bloody stuff. The British had perfected methods for over a hundred years manufacturing and distributing narcotics, and Uncle Dickie knew how it was done from his stint running India. In fact, we copied a lot of the information from notes and treaties and used this information to produce our own documents. Next, I submitted my idea to the Bilderberg committee, who initially did not grasp the significance until President Nixon heard about the plan. It was not lost on that old crook - he loved the scheme, which apparently tied in with some of his own ideas to control production and the markets for narcotics on a global scale. Later in the same year, nineteen sixty-eight I think it was, we all got together and thrashed out an agreement. I had help from some lawyer chap Bernard introduced me to, an expert on international law, Mardjono Deradjat, little Asian feller from Indonesia. They had a lot of them in Holland, it used be to be a Dutch colony you know. He turned up again fairly recently, I'm still trying to contact him.

Not waiting to hear why he wanted to speak with Mardjono, Camilla prompted anxiously for him to keep talking. 'What happened next? How did you get the document officially sanctioned? Surely Parliament could never

The Treaty

have been involved.'

Philip cleared his throat, and reached for a tissue from the box on the table by his side. He coughed a disgusting amount of phlegm into the flimsy paper. Camilla had no choice but to wait until he resumed, trying hard not to watch.

'After the agreement was completed,' he continued, wiping his mouth, 'we arranged a meeting to coincide with Nixon's state visit to London. It went incredibly smoothly, everyone was so taken up by the visit to Buckingham Palace and the meeting with the Queen. We even managed to slip the signing ceremony in between two banquets.'

Unable to hide her disbelief any longer, Camilla challenged him openly at the first sign of a pause. 'I'm really sorry, Philip, but I just find this hard to accept. I mean, how could the Royal Family become involved to this extent? Surely someone would have leaked information to the press, or politicians. It would have been political suicide for anyone to sign an illegal treaty without the approval of Parliament and the US Senate. Who decided do this?'

Philip smiled. 'You have to believe me my dear, because it's true. Nixon did not waste anytime handing a pen to old Bill Rodgers, his Secretary of State. At the same time, I tricked our Foreign Secretary, George Brown into adding his signature. Brown loved a drink; eventually it killed the poor old sod. We had the whole thing wrapped up during the visit. You can check the dates. I think it was in February 1969. You see my dear it had to happen - I did not have a choice. The financial benefits, which have accrued over the years for this family, ensure you will never face the threat my mother endured. Camilla, I want you to succeed me and eventually takeover my role managing the treaty here in Britain.'

Philip was filled with self-belief, knowing that regardless of what she thought he had acted properly and done the right thing - at that time. As the years rolled by and the threat of republicanism drifted away with the end of the cold war, he had doubted the necessity for the scheme. However, it was too late to end the treaty now. He was deeply involved, and too many people depended on it, especially on the opposite side of the Atlantic. There was no alternative but to carry on managing his part of the contract. He had to see it through into another generation, for their sake.

Camilla looked stressed; she was being asked to do something she vehemently disagreed with and to play a leading role.

'I simply do not understand why this all rests with me, why not Charles or his two brothers and sister - why me?'

'Don't think for one minute I haven't considered them all in turn, but not one of them has the inner strength to carry this forward. I've watched you grow for nearly thirty years and I know you are the right person to succeed me.'

Nothing more was said as she began to gradually come to terms with the reality of what he was asking her to do. Here was Prince Philip, the head of the Royal Family, outlining the terms and conditions for full membership.

'Have you approached anyone else to succeed you in the recent past? What about Diana?'

'Of course, at one time I was impressed. She had a very strong character, an anger that I liked, despite her angelic public image. I even discussed the treaty with her.'

'You actually told her the same things you are now telling me - how did she react?'

'Quite surprising really, she was very easily convinced, unlike you.'

Philip smiled, meaning this to sound like a compliment. Camilla continued with questions following the same delicate route.

The Treaty

'So, how did you leave things with Diana,' she asked, 'was an agreement made to succeed you?'

'Yes, more or less. We had several meetings when I gave her all the background information.'

'I'm surprised you trusted her given your past relationship'.

He nodded in agreement. 'It was complex. I installed her as the head of some appropriate charities that we used to deliver funds. She became attached to fundraising for Land Mine victims for some bizarre reason, which did not particularly bother me. We could only ever use a fraction of the money donated and the balance had to be re-distributed under the terms of the treaty to different parties.

'You mean kick-backs?'

'That's too simplistic. The payments for expenses had to be channeled through legitimate sources, and here, money was received as grants for mine clearance from other charities our organization controls. Diana believed her charity should be retaining more of the revenue and started to interfere directly in operational matters.'

'Was she right to do that, if the money was not going where the donors intended?'

Philip chuckled. 'Now you're being naïve. This money was not donated - it came from the sale of narcotics and was being laundered. It had all been working fine for years, and she could have jeopardized the whole institution.'

'You should have seen this coming, bearing in mind Diana's personality and infatuation with a 'Mother Teresa' lifestyle?'

'Perhaps I was being ridiculous, thinking that she could take over managing the treaty. I was never that convinced by the fuzzy logic she used to justify her good causes. Bearing in mind there are too many people on the planet already, without helping more in third world countries, who will eventually die anyway - if not from starvation then from Aids.'

Dismissing his uncharitable view having heard it expressed in public before she asked, 'When did you eventually fall out with Diana?'

'I wouldn't say we ever fell out; it came to a head a year or two before she died. What particularly upset me was when I saw pictures of her swanking around on luxury yachts one minute and pleading poverty the next. The final bust-up came when she threatened to tell people about the treaty. According to Diana, her brother's pals in Cape Town had heard rumours of an illegal narcotics distribution scheme implicating me in particular.'

'So who started these rumours? Did you ever find out?'

'Diana thought they came from Thatcher's boy Mark, he was living in South Africa. It was nothing really new, these tales had been in circulation implicating various political figures, and most of it was complete nonsense.'

'Not this story, though?'

'Let's say they may have been on the scent. What I did not know at the time was that Diana had been in contact with that lawyer I mentioned earlier, Mardjono. He arrived unexpectedly at her hotel when she was visiting this place in Asia somewhere, during one of her visits. He had one of the only signed copies of the treaty, which was a mistake. We never intended he should go off with this. Apparently, in return for her help in increasing the aid for the charity Mardjono was involved with, he gave her a complete set of the documents that made up the treaty.

'So where are they now? Did she pass these back to you for safe keeping, or to be destroyed sounds like a better idea.'

'My dear, you must be joking. She told me nothing at all about this, in fact, we only recently discovered they were still in existence.'

The Treaty

Camilla looked relieved. 'Oh well, at least you have them back now. It would be disastrous if they went missing again.'

Now was Philip's turn to redden with embarrassment, a site she had not witnessed before. Using another tissue from the box, he cleared his throat before answering, 'Unfortunately, we do not have them yet, but my people are working on this. Diana hid them very effectively.'

Following a stunned silence, a different Camilla responded, speaking icily and condemning such ineptitude. 'Bearing in mind what you are asking me to do, I am not feeling very reassured knowing a complete set of these documents are out there ticking away like some political time bomb. What do you think would happen to Charles, in fact, the entire family, if our involvement in this treaty became public knowledge?'

Philip warmed to Camilla's feisty nature, feeling even more confident she was the right person for this job.

'My dear, please don't worry,' he said softly, 'we have it under control and all the documents are being secured as we speak. I would prefer not to go into any more detail.'

Sitting upright, Camilla steeled herself to ask the next provocative question that was engraved on her mind. 'Considering everything you have just told me - was Diana killed by your people?'

'No Camilla, she died in a car accident as you already know.'

'Thank you, I hope you will understand why I had to ask that question.'

'No, but I do respect your right to ask it.'

With that said the conversation started to dry up, as both of them were occupied by their own separate thoughts. Philip began to look tired and Camilla was keen to leave and take some time to think what she should do. There was a lot more questions she needed to ask and she still had her reservations however, Philip had been open, showing he trusted her. Maybe this was her one chance to win a major role in wider affairs of the family.

'I think I should leave now and have time to think, but I will agree with a new role and to help you since I am married to Charles and a part of his family.'

Philip beamed back; Camilla was a strong person who would come through for him. He was even more certain of his decision that she was perfect to become the new leader of the treaty in Great Britain.

'Thank you my dear, and I am very grateful you've agreed to help me. Perhaps in the next few weeks we can meet regularly to discuss various projects and charities that are important to the organization.'

'One immediate problem I have is that I hate the thought of secrets from Charles. What shall I tell my husband?'

With a raised eyebrow and a big grin Philip answered, 'Why, the truth of course! You have been invited to take over some of my official charity work.'

The Treaty

9

Echoes of applause bounced around the huge glass and steel auditorium, welcoming the entourage of important looking dignitaries onto the stage. In a lounge, overlooking the event an octogenarian man walked slowly across a richly carpeted floor flanked either side by aides, who guided him toward a small group of men in suits. George Bush Senior advanced first to greet his old friend and they shook hands.

'Phil, it's good to see you again. How was your trip down here?'

'Wonderful to see you George, the flight was fine, slept through most of it.'

The convention centre in Monterrey, Mexico, was a two-hour flight by private jet from the Kentucky bloodstock farm, where Prince Philip was taking a rare and private holiday outside the UK, together with The Queen. Their host in Kentucky was a former American Ambassador to Britain and horse breeder, like the Queen. He also happened to be close friends with the ex-president and invited Philip to visit the conference during his stay to meet with executives at a special two-day event hosted by Healthy Verve International.

'We appreciate you were able to drop in Phil. You've met my son before, I think?'

'Yes we speak regularly. How are you, John?'

'Doing fine sir, it's a real pleasure meeting you again. Are you enjoying your holiday in the US?'

'Indeed, my wife breeds horses, you know. She has a couple permanently looked after at the farm where we stay. It's good for us to be able to come over and visit occasionally.'

'Excellent, do you ride yourself, sir, or have you given that up now?'

'Used to play blithering Polo and let the horse do most of the work, tell me John, who are all the other bods here?'

'Mainly executives from Healthy Verve, they host the conference every year.'

Philip turned back to address George Bush Senior. 'Splendid place this George, I had a quick look in the main hall as we passed just now and it's full. I was surprised to hear so many American accents, thought they were all trooping around my homes in England.'

More polite laughter from the group caused the heads to turn of other important officials, who were standing around hoping to be introduced.

'How many people do you think are here? Looked like thousands.'

George beckoned toward one group of men standing close by and to Jim Turner, who bounded across the room.

'Jim, I want you to meet with Prince Philip. Jim is the CEO of Healthy Verve and responsible for global operations.'

'Good to meet you sir, and thank you for taking the time out to visit.'

'Least I could do since I was in the area so to speak. Tell me Jim, how many bums have you got on those seats in the hall?'

Jim smiled. 'Well, sir, we expect around ten thousand in total, arriving from all over the globe. This is our major jamboree and a massive morale boost for the distributors and network organizers.' Jim directed Philip over towards a large plate glass window looking out over the auditorium. 'Let me just show you out here, those people seated nearest the stage are our top five hundred in-country executives. Behind them are about two thousand of our best dealer managers who each account for at least twenty million dollars worth of annual revenue. The rest of the audience is made up of managers and team leaders from all around the world, who have achieved targets and earned substantial commission.'

When Philip first arrived, he witnessed a mass of people streaming into the conference centre carrying rucksacks and shoulder bags with their country or city name emblazoned - Seoul, Boston, Singapore, Sydney. It truly was an international event.

'That's amazing. How the hell was you able to persuade them all to come?' Philip asked, in awe at the size of the event.

'I can tell you they didn't need persuading - these are some of the most committed people you are likely to meet. The past twelve months has been a terrific year, especially now supplies are more stable from Asia, helped by our troops back in Afghanistan.'

Philip turned back to address his friend. 'Not like in the old days hey, George? In the Seventies we had the one CIA controller in Kabul, now there are bloody hundreds of them.' Laughing George countered, 'Back then all the goods came from Turkey, until your socialist chums at the UN put the lid on it.'

The men laughed at their ludicrous operations in the early days, and then Philip returned his attention back to Jim. Indirectly, Philip was a major shareholder of Healthy Verve through numerous charities and trust funds and had a keen interest in the operations.

'What puzzles me Jim is how the devil you run a global

operation of this size?'

'It's a complex structure sir, and we have the regular management meetings with all our partners. For example, you just saw through that window, the executives who we invite to meet and share success stories on a regular basis.'

Philip shook his head. 'It's unbelievable and all with no outward sign of infrastructure or national promotion. This is truly the most amazing success story, chaps.'

'It does not end there, sir, we bring rewards to some of the world's poorer countries and employ the rich world's minorities and unskilled. Some of these people would still be breaking into homes in Great Britain, if it were not for Healthy Verve.'

George Senior could see Philip's eye glazing over as Jim rambled on. Sensing he had endured enough, he came to his rescue.

'Jim, is the meeting room set up for us to use?'

'Yes sir, whenever you need it.'

'Thanks for filling Prince Philip in on the logistics. There will be more time to go over things with him later.'

'No problem, sir.'

Jim and Prince Philip shook hands, and as Jim strode away, George moved closer to his friend and whispered in his ear. 'Jim has organized a session between Richard Diago, Chairman of the New York Stock Exchange and Raul Reyes of the Revolutionary Armed Forces of Colombia (FARC). It should be very interesting. I would like to introduce you to them both before we leave here today.'

Philip's expression and raised eyebrow showed he was clearly unsure if this was a good idea.

'Of course, I will leave it up to you, Phil. These people may not be your bag so to speak. They are meeting here to send a positive signal from the US financial services to Latin American investors, and to discuss ways for foreign

The Treaty

investment and the future role of US businesses in Colombia. Reading between the lines, Phil, we need the Colombians to invest some of their cash back into the US financial system. It's estimated there is about five hundred billion to one trillion dollars being laundered every year. If we can circulate this money through US and European blue-chip stocks it will strengthen the dollar and bring down interest rates, helping you at the same time.'

'Don't pretend to understand all that George, but if you think it's important, wheel me in. I am all for helping to keep up the price of my shares.'

Jim Turner interrupted saying the meeting room was ready to use. Taking hold of the prince's arm, they walked the few metres to a small room reserved for the Chief Executive and his guests.

'Are these chairs okay for you Phil, can I get you one with a straighter back?'

'No, this is fine, just let me settle down here - could do with another drink. Is there any gin to go with that iced water?'

George quickly summoned an aide and sent them off in search of alcohol for his friend. Philip seemed a little distant and was clearly tired from the travel and activity surrounding him. George was the youngest by four years and realized he would soon be entering this important and final stage in his life. He recalled those early days in the sixties and seventies when meeting Philip in Holland. George, like his father, had been tapped by the Skull and Bones secret society when he was a student at Yale. Later he was granted automatic membership to an equally secretive European based organization called The Bilderberg Group. In the same way that Skull and Bones members provided support during his presidential campaign by rallying huge sums of money, the Bilderberg Group helped members from around the world to achieve their goals. It was here that Prince Philip and his uncle Lord Mountbatten first floated their big idea for the treaty.

'Well Phil, what do you think of our efforts? Did we do the treaty justice?'

'George, I've said this many times over the years on numerous occasions and will say it again, it is all very impressive.'

'Quite ironic Phil, don't you think, both of us have spent a large part of our adult lives sharing a secret that's been of huge importance to global peace and prosperity.'

'You're right; there would have been a lot more seventies and eighties style recessions if we had not got together all those years ago.'

The two great men paused while Philip's gin was set down on the table and the waiter left the room. Taking a sip, he gave a sigh feeling the rush as the alcohol entered his bloodstream.

'My word that's better George,' he chuckled loudly, keeping his fingers wrapped tightly around the glass. 'I'm ready for anything now - fire away!'

'Well, it's still looking good from over here; the only major concern from our side is the uncertainty of your eventual successor. What is the take on that now - neither of us are getting any younger?'

'I'm pleased you've mentioned this, I am working on a replacement but it will take a few weeks to implement. My eldest son is now settled and I hope to make some important changes.'

'That's good to hear, we will keep it to ourselves for now, and I'm not meeting with the Bilderberg committee for several weeks so there is no urgent panic, unless you suddenly drop dead.'

Both men roared with laughter at this very real prospect.

'How you getting along with young Bill, George Senior asked. 'The Queen must really like it over there on his

The Treaty

farm?'

'It's very relaxing,' Philip nodded, sipping his gin. 'He is the perfect host and makes us both feel very welcome.'

'You've stayed there a few times I believe?'

'Yes, that ranch in Kentucky is the only place we have been on holiday outside the UK during our married lives. When you travel as much as we have, Scotland takes some beating.'

'Sure you are right, and it's good to hear he is taking good care of you and The Queen, he has been a solid friend to me to over the years.'

'Did you ever get to meet his grandfather? He was a real character. My Uncle Dickie, Lord Mountbatten, knew him well. They both had strong business connections in Germany.'

'Yes my family was also connected through business when we were in oil. His grandfather ran into problems selling petroleum to the Germans during WWII. Poor guy, he died not too long after being fined by a Senate Committee. Bit of a disgrace for the family, but these things happens.'

'Too true, George, been there myself more than once.'

Leaving the conversation at that point George Bush returned to more immediate matters that concerned him.

'Okay Phil, down to some business I need to discuss with you before the next Bilderberg committee meeting, any more news on the missing documents?'

Philip cleared his throat, and took a sip of Gin. 'As I understand it a plain photocopy of all the documents turned up in a bank vault in Argentina, of all bloody places. Some chap in London has been boasting he has a copy and plans to publish a book or some such thing, but as far as we are concerned it's not going to happen.'

'That's good to hear. The thought of information falling into the wrong hands really worried the Bilderberg

Committee. Where the hell did they come from?'

'It has to be the lawyer chap Mardjono. We were very foolish, George. We should never have let the lawyer's copy of the treaty out of our sights.'

'How certain are we Diana had the original signed version of the treaty?'

Philip shrugged before picking up his glass. 'We're not one hundred percent; she may have only had this copy that has turned up. The return address on the envelope found in Buenos Aires was close to Althorp, near Diana's family estate. That's all we know.'

'So, Mardjono may still have them? Assuming he is alive.'

'You have to remember George that until Diana came out with her ridiculous demands for us to give more money from the landmines charity to farmers in Laos, we didn't even know Mardjono still existed. There was a lot of ignorance at that time. The problem was she didn't know most of the 'donations' came via the World Wildlife Fund on behalf of the treaty and our organization - the profits had already been ear marked. Possibly jaded that we would not agree to help, for some unknown reason she foolishly warned Mardjono he was in danger. We came close to catching up with him somewhere in the north of Laos, and he was badly wounded by a terrorist group, lost the use of both legs, but he still managed to disappear off the face of the earth. Could be dead for all we know. The fact remains; he certainly met with Diana and may still have kept the originals as future collateral.'

George Bush Senior shuffled and scratched his temple. 'It must be possible to qualify Mardjono in or out of the jigsaw. Any idea what the current game plan is?'

'I have insisted we stick to the original plan approved by the Bilderberg Committee and stop any third-party from leaking copies of the treaty. We must then find Mardjono

The Treaty

and the original papers. To complicate the situation, a division of the British security network called MI-21 has got involved. I have been told by my security advisor they are predominantly a terrorist monitoring group, their bureau chief inadvertently stumbled on evidence of the treaty's existence. They are not sure what to make of it at present, and have support from Downing Street to dig deeper. It's uncanny George, after all these years the Treasury gaily spend most of the cash we generate in the UK, yet cannot figure out where it really comes from.'

'We have the same problem in the US, what a bunch of morons. Imagine if we had not stepped in during that last Wall Street bubble in nineteen ninety-nine, buying huge numbers of shares in blue-chip stocks. The whole shebang would have collapsed like a pack of cards. Instead we let our old pal Alan Greenspan, take the credit.'

'Amazing,' Philip smirked, his face now glowing red from the affects of gin. 'Yet what thanks did we get, not a word?'

Hearing the two men roaring with laughter, a senior aide waiting outside knocked and entered the room moving to replenish Philip's empty glass.

'What I propose George is we do nothing for a while and let these government security bods take us to our man. That will at least confirm if he is still alive. If he's dead and the original documents have disappeared with him, then fine.'

'Sounds like a good plan,' George nodded. 'On the other hand what if Diana did have the original papers and hid them before she died - any ideas?'

Prince Philip stared blankly through watery eyes, and did not reply. This was his worse nightmare scenario and seeing his friends discomfort George changed the subject.

10

'Oh, this is quaint. Whose apartment is it?'

'I use it occasionally when I stay in town it belongs to the department. Where did you say you were going?'

Kicking off her shoes Camilla sat down on the oatmeal coloured settee. 'I'm supposed to be having tea with an old school friend; Charles is too preoccupied to notice what I do in the week. Richard, sit down on the sofa and tell me what I should do next.'

Sir Richard Parsons had known Camilla since they were both in their teens. She was a regular spectator when he played polo and they dated a couple of times. He lost contact after joining the army, meeting on the odd occasion at family and friend's weddings, more recently funerals. Unexpectedly, a few weeks before, she had phoned his office in Mill Bank and asked for a meeting. At first, he could not understand what it was she wanted him to do. Her marriage to Prince Charles placed their friendship in an entirely different league and he had to be very careful, especially in his role as the security advisor to the government, however, it soon became obvious that Prince Philip had engaged her in some clandestine activity and she needed help; he found it hard to refuse.

'You just would not believe how hard it's been trying to deal with the problems I now have, and at the same time

The Treaty

being unable to talk to anyone else about them. I have George Bush senior and his son phoning me at all hours if they're unable to speak with Philip, Charles gets so angry.'

'Explain to me again Camilla, what do you have to do?' Sir Richard asked, sitting down on the sofa beside her.

'It's this bloody treaty I told you about. I still cannot believe Philip became so involved with the Americans. It would destroy the Royal Family forever if this went public, and it's probably the worst betrayal by a monarch since Charles II made his secret deal with the French.'

Sir Richard frowned. 'What secret deal was that? My history's shocking.'

'If you don't know you will have to read about it some other time, I forgot you went to Eton.' They both laughed as he cracked a joke about her Swiss finishing school.

'I don't understand what this treaty is about, Camilla. I mean, Philip didn't sign the document did he, why is he involved? He would not care about scandal anyway; nothing has seriously damaged him or the Royal Family to the extent you're suggesting. You have to remember if a treaty were approved between the British and Americans in secret; it would have taken place in a different world to the one we know now. Only a few years earlier we had an Empire, with Winston Churchill, Stalin and Roosevelt carving up Europe, Africa and the Middle East over a bottle of Vodka. I can understand how Philip and Lord Mountbatten may have felt vulnerable and concerned for this country in the late Sixties.'

'Richard there is concern and there is gratuitous greed. This treaty may be responsible for wars and much of the terrorism we have in the world today. Narcotics were not such a big issue in the sixties, since then the market for illegal drugs, heroin and cocaine in particular, has grown dramatically. This could not have happened without the control and organization established by the treaty. Philips involvement was to conceive the plan and make it happen; in return, he gained financial independence from both the Crown and the State. You have to admit one thing; it's been a huge success.'

'Successful in what way,' Sir Richard asked. 'Do you mean in personal financial terms?'

'I've met with his financial advisor, the same man who's advised the family for over thirty years and helped raise the money for George Bush's first Presidential campaign. He explained to me how, through a series of hedge funds and other financial instruments, they have accumulated billions in offshore trusts. Quite simply, if there was a revolution in Britain tomorrow, and the family was kicked out, the Royals would want for nothing.

'You are saying Philip actually receives money from the sale of illegal narcotics. It's incredulous! Surely it can't arrive in greasy brown envelopes?'

'Of course not,' Camilla snapped. 'Actually, I am out of my depth here. As I understand it the trusts are based in the Caribbean. Money is invested in both the finished product and raw materials for narcotics - fields of poppies and coca leaves I assume, and legal commodities, corn, rubber, orange juice, pork bellies that kind of thing. As the price of these rise and fall, huge profits are earned based on the trends without ever seeing the product. Arpad Takacs, his advisor, is an expert and rarely gets his sums wrong. The importance the treaty has made is in controlling the markets in the area where the narcotics are produced, of course, you already know that.'

'Since we first spoke about this Camilla, I've checked our files and there is practically nothing that would stand up in court implicating Philip. As for the signed version of the treaty, we are no further on finding it and in all probability Princess Diana did hide it somewhere.'

'But where, Philip mentioned she sent a draft copy to

The Treaty

Susan Barrantes in Argentina, perhaps she sent the original as well - oh my God, maybe Sarah Ferguson has it now?'

'Sarah Ferguson? Listen Camilla; I'm telling you some classified stuff here, I would get my balls chopped off if this leaks out. MI-5 trawled through Diana's personal effects looking for documents. We received instructions from high up at Buckingham Palace and at the time, it didn't make a lot of sense, but now I realize what they were looking for. Even the court case against Diana's butler, Paul Burrell, was an excuse to pull in anything she may have given to him for safe keeping, we went through his belongings with a fine tooth comb, and nothing.'

'What about her brother Charles Spencer? Philip told me Diana threatened to tell him about the treaty. Maybe he has it now.'

Sir Richard shook his head. 'No, if he had it he would have used it by now. There is no love lost among the families.'

'This is unbelievable Richard, the ghost of Little Miss Goodie Two Shoes hanging over me like the sword of Damocles?'

'I don't like the way this is affecting you. Why don't you give it all up and return to being a normal person again?'

'Sod that, I've waited too long for this to happen only to fall at the first hurdle. C'mon Richard, What do you think I should do?'

'Damage limitation seems to be the right approach, and in fairness to Philip this has worked well. The press speculation will not harm his reputation and may even enhance it! The method he has employed damping down speculation and making sure no real evidence exists has been spot-on.

Relaxed in the domestic surroundings, Camilla sat with her feet tucked underneath her, confident she had at last found a safe pair of hands in Richard.

'So who did you say lives in this apartment?'

'It's normally used by a colleague, Caroline Lovelace-Jones; she stays here when visiting our office in London. She's based in Madrid.'

Camilla threw back her head in mock surprise. 'So you two are friends. Is there anything you are keeping from me, Richard?'

'No, of course not, she's a senior employee.'

'Well, technically you're my employee now.'

He jumped from the settee and went into the small adjacent kitchen. 'Fancy a glass of Champagne while you are here, how long do you have?'

'Yes, why not, I can stay another hour. I'm really enjoying my little outing.'

11

The overpowering smell of disinfectant permeated through a maze of hospital corridors. Maria had been moved from A&E into a special coronary care unit under consultant cardiologist, Dr Richard Griffin. Following the confusing array of signs, Andy found the entrance to her ward and waited for a nurse to punch in the entry code allowing him access. Maria sat uncomfortably upright in bed. Andy was surprised how well she looked; with just a touch of makeup she appeared every bit as stunning as in his frequent and graphic daydreams. Looking equally pleased, Maria was secretly relieved he was as good looking as she remembered and was not a figment of her unconscious mind. Andy moved closer and they kissed shyly in front of the nurse who discreetly left the room.

'I was really worried when I heard what happened. How are you feeling now? You look really well.'

'I'm sorry, it was impossible to contact you. I was unconscious and no one else knew where you were.'

'What are your plans when you leave the hospital?'

'I don't know yet. I suppose I will have to return to Buenos Aires. There is nowhere else.'

He had already given this question some thought during his drive to the hospital and was not ready to let her just go off never to be seen again.

'Listen, I've been thinking. You could always stay at my apartment for a while. I live close to London; it could be ideal while you decide what to do. I have a spare room, you can just kickback and relax.'

Desperately hoping he would suggest this, she wrapped her arms around his neck and kissed him on the cheek.

'Andy, thank you, the thought of staying in the village with Mrs Briggs and Jack would have driven me back to Argentina very quickly. They are very kind people, but I need a fresh start. I promise I will be no trouble.'

Throughout Andy's visit, they avoided any discussion about Dominic and Emma Marsh. Maria was still convalescing and he knew the police had been frequent visitors, so too had Mrs Briggs. Toby was staying with his grandparents in Oxford, and Andy assumed he was too young to understand what had happened to his parents. It was a terrible tragedy. They made enquiries about how long Maria would have to stay at the hospital, and were told he could return to collect her in the next three days if the doctor gave her the all clear.

Andy was working from home when he received the call from Maria, asking if he could pick her up. This was good news; it had only been two days since his visit. Immediately preparing to leave he zoomed off down the motorway to Northampton to fetch his new flat-mate. Reaching the hospital around midday, he sprinted up the stairs retracing his steps from the previous visit to her room and found her dressed and happy to see him. On the way back to Little Chalfont they took a detour and dropped by Althorp, so Maria could say goodbye to Jack and Mrs Briggs, also to collect the rest of her possessions. Mrs Briggs seemed genuinely sad Maria was leaving, and made her promise to visit them before returning to Argentina.

Arriving home in the early evening, Andy helped her out

The Treaty

of the car and up the stairs to his apartment situated above a dentist's surgery. They had the two large bedrooms with a separate lounge, kitchen and bathroom. Maria looked ecstatic with her new home, and Andy explained how they were less than a five-minute walk from Chalfont and Latimer Railway station, with regular trains into central London. Quickly establishing a daily routine where he went off in the morning to meet clients most days and spent the occasional day at home. Maria soon returned to full health and began contacting the few people she knew from Argentina who were living in England.

On one particular Saturday, two weeks after she had moved in, Maria arranged with a girlfriend from Buenos Aires for a shopping trip in the West End. She seemed excited about the outing and promised Andy a present when she came back. Watching her leave he found her excitement endearing, and felt pleased she was enjoying being with him. Sitting down at his desk planning to catch-up on some work, he noticed Maria's small black pocketbook had been left at the side of the desk. It was normally kept in her bag, but he had seen her use it earlier and she obviously forgot to pick it up when she had finished. Flicking through, he could easily translate the dates for hospital appointments written in Spanish and read her reminders of family birthdays - discovering for the first time she had a sister called Mercedes who she had not mentioned before. Turning each page back to when she lived in Buenos Aires, he suddenly focused down on four words, "12:00 Fatima Café Tortoni."

Intrigued by the name he placed the book down then picking it up again continued leafing through, finding another entry on April 24 saying simply, "phone Fatima". Turning to the alphabetically coded address section, he stopped on the letter F. There in neat handwriting was Fatima's name together with her phone number. Pulling his wallet from his trouser pocket, he removed the business card she had given him during the seminar in Madrid; the mobile phone number was the same. Feeling an immediate sense of panic, he wanted to phone Maria and demand an explanation, but calming down realized this could be counterproductive. Maybe, he thought, there would be a simple explanation, coincidence perhaps. Argentina had strong links with Spain, their paths may have crossed - he could not rule it out. Unfortunately, by nature Andy was not an optimist and paranoia began to kick-in. What, he thought, if they were planning to rob him or frame him in some way? He had to think fast to avoid disaster. His attraction to Maria could be blinding him from the obvious. Perhaps Fatima and Maria were working together, a couple of con merchants looking for a single, love hungry sucker whom they could take for every penny. She may eventually even agree to marry him, then get his cash and disappear back home. Perhaps the whole storm thing at the supermarket was not just fate or destiny, but a rich opportunity seized on as part of their plan. The fact was he had no choice other than to wait until she came back home to find out what was going on. Continuing to churn over these irrational thoughts it was suddenly a relief to hear a key in the front door. He could hear Maria running excitedly up the stairs.

'Andy, are you there?' she shouted. 'I've had a great day. I've bought you a present - I hope it fits.'

Skipping into the lounge with eyes wide with excitement, she handed him a bag then reached up giving a hug.

Trying to act normally he opened the bag. 'Great, a sweatshirt thank you I'm sure it'll be fine. I'll try it on.'

'I have spent lots of money,' she puffed, falling onto the sofa. 'We went to Camden Market. Do you know that place? It's really cool.'

Following him through to the kitchen, it was almost

The Treaty

impossible not to register the tense atmosphere.

'Andy, are you okay? Is something the matter, please tell me?'

Andy finished making coffee and turned to face her. 'I need to discuss something with you.'

Maria dropped her smile. The excitement was gone. Instead, she looked out through wide frightened eyes fearing what he had to say. 'Discuss what, Andy?'

'I found something while you were out shopping. It's in the lounge.'

She raised her arms and blocked the doorway as Andy tried to leave the small kitchen.

'What are you doing?' he frowned.

'Tell me what it is?' she said in a trembling voice.

Andy wondered if she had already guessed he had discovered her secret.

Gently moving her to one side, he walked passed leading the way along the corridor into the lounge. Pausing by the desk, he picked up the notebook and turned to the page he had marked with Fatima's business card.

'How do you know this woman?' Andy asked, fighting to remain calm.

Examining the card, Maria turned it over and stared at the blank side, using the time to find something acceptable to say to him, but knowing it was impossible. Taking her by the arm Andy prompted her again.

'Look at me please, this is really important. How do you know Fatima?'

She began to splutter. 'We met in Buenos Aires and I don't know her that well, not properly.'

'Listen, you either know this woman or you don't! Which is it? I have to know.'

Andy's face was now red with rage. She had never seen him like this before. Pulling her arm away, she pleaded. 'Please don't shout you're frightening me. Why is this so important?'

Calming down, he realized this was getting him nowhere and he decided to take a softer approach.

'Maria, I'm sorry, I just don't know what to think, but you're making me feel worse by not being honest. I asked a very simple and direct question. How well do you know Fatima?'

Maria sat down on the sofa and began to sob into her hands. Stooping down Andy prised her fingers open to reveal swollen red eyes. He tried to comfort her.

'Please speak to me,' he whispered, 'and tell me how you know this woman. I am not cross with you I just need to know. I have a feeling she may be very dangerous.'

'Why do you think that?' Maria sniffed, tears streaming down her face.

He began telling her how they met in Madrid, about the newspaper cutting and how she had cross-questioned him, particularly about Dominic's computer.

'Was it all a set up? Did you tell her I would be in Madrid?'

She started crying again, and growing impatient this time he stopped her burying her face in her hands and raised his voice unable to quell his anger.

'Maria, please! You must tell me what happened. Are you still in contact with Fatima? How long have you known her?'

Stiffening, she sat back in her seat and took a deep breath. She knew she had to tell him everything.

'I am so sorry, Andy, this all happened before we met. I did not mean to get you involved, or to tell you a lie. I met Fatima at a conference in BA about one year ago. I was with my mother and older sister; they are both members of the Eva Peron Organization, a political group for women.'

'Why didn't you tell me you had a sister? I assumed you were an only child.'

The Treaty

'We had a big argument just before I left Argentina. It is a long story and has got nothing really to do with this, well, maybe a little, although, I would prefer not to talk about it right now. Fatima had been living in Brazil; she has family there and came with a woman who was also an activist for Muslim women's right. We stayed together for a few days and became good friends. One evening I invited her to my Tango class at the University. The Professor of Tango, Luis Boccia, really liked her and danced with her all night. He is very famous for teaching tango and taught Madonna for her role in the movie *Evita*. We had a great time and later went back to her hotel for some food and wine. When it became too late for me to travel home, she asked me to stay with her in her room for the night and this was when she told me about her husband, and how British narcotics agents had murdered him. They could have been army or secret service, I don't know. He was accused of involvement in narcotics and her baby daughter died in a separate incident. The next day I was introduced to her Brazilian friend who invited me to join her women's group.'

All the time Maria was talking Andy listened intently, trying to understand how this could be connected with the treaty and what it all meant to him personally.

'Maria, are you sure she was telling you the truth? There were no photographs of a baby or a husband in Fatima's apartment.'

She shrugged her shoulders. 'I don't know, I am just telling you what happened. Fatima did say she had a contact in London, who own property and businesses in the UK, they have a big store somewhere in the city.

'Was it called Harrods?'

'Yes maybe, I don't know. This person told her about a treaty and that it was still in operation. Another man, high up in US politics told her about a drug's treaty controlled by the USA and Britain. Fatima then started to believe it was because of this agreement her husband had been murdered. Her Muslim friends in London told her that before Princess Diana died in Paris, she mentioned sending documents concerning the treaty to a English woman living in Buenos Aires called Susan Barrantes.'

'I've never heard that name. Who was she, did you find out?'

'Susan Barrantes is famous in BA. She was the mother of Sarah Ferguson, wife of Prince Andrew. Susan was a well-known society figure and I can remember when Princess Diana came to Argentina not that long before she died. It was over ten years ago, and my mother took us to hear her speak at a rally for women held in the city. I remember her so well. She looked beautiful and talked with passion, demanding respect and political power for women. There were even shouts from the audience, people from poor backgrounds, calling her the new Evita.'

'So, in what way were you involved with Fatima and what about your family and friends? Didn't they mind what you were doing?'

This question touched a raw nerve and Maria began to cry again, all the while clutching a small silver locket around her neck, and then through streaming tears, she pleaded for his forgiveness saying how sorry she was.

'Andy, I deserted my family who I love so much. I hated myself and thought that I was betraying everyone, and now you will hate me too.'

'Why?'

'Because I was in love with Fatima, that's why!'

Seeing his face drop and with a look of utter despair, she grasped his hand.

'Andy, please forgive me, she cast a spell on me. I could not refuse her. Perhaps in time I will be able to make amends to my family and they will be proud of me.'

The Treaty

Unsure what it was she meant and without explaining any further, Maria suddenly stopped crying and began speaking animatedly and going over events leading up to the present.

'Fatima told me she believed Susan Barrantes had stored the documents in a safe deposit box at the Banco de la Nación Argentina, where my father worked, and that my father had sold them to an Englishman. The Englishman's name was Dominic Marsh.'

Andy frowned, 'Your father?'

Maria nodded.

It was all starting to make sense. The stuff on Dominic's computer, Fatima, and the probing questions asked during the police interview - they were all searching for the same thing, copies of the treaty.

'What exactly did your father supply to Dominic Marsh?' Andy asked. 'Was it a computer file or hard copies?'

'I'm not too sure. Flimsy paper copies, not the original signed documents.'

'So what happens when Mrs Barrantes turns up at the bank to open her safe deposit box and discovers it's empty?'

'She will not care.'

'Why not I don't understand?'

'She was killed in a car accident.'

'My God that's really sad - I didn't even know she had died.'

'It happened a year, or so, after Princess Diana died in Paris. My father thought that perhaps no one else knew the deposit box existed apart from the bank employees. He robbed them for their historic value unaware of any political significance.'

Andy rubbed his eyes and sat down on the sofa beside Maria. 'If he had known, he probably could have charged ten times as much for them.'

'Maybe, but there was a limited number of people he knew who would have any interest in them; it was luck meeting Dominic.'

'OK, so how did you manage to arrive here, you know, to England, working in Dominic's house. Come on, you have to tell me everything if we are to stay friends?'

Maria drew a deep breath and reached out touching his arm. 'Fatima brainwashed me. She told me she needed a copy of those documents and that nobody would ever know. I wanted to help her so much. She had experienced so much pain. I persuaded my father to ask Dominic if I could work for them as an au pair looking after little Toby. I think Dominic felt sorry for my father. Argentina was coming out of the worst financial crisis in its history. It was the least he could do. He was kind and let me into his home, and now he is dead.'

Tears filled Maria's eye. She had betrayed her father's trust and Dominic's generosity.

Andy's heart ached. He found it incredibly hard watching Maria suffer like this. 'I'm sorry Maria, but I have to ask - I have to be sure! Are you still helping Fatima?'

'No!' She yelled. 'I haven't spoken to her since Dominic and Emma were killed.'

'Why did you need to give her all that information about me? Did you not realize it could have placed me in real danger?'

'I was afraid Fatima would find out. She phoned daily and I would tell her what had been happening and answer her questions. You and I had just met; I was not even sure we would ever see one another again after that one night; you could have been married with children. I would never do anything to hurt you now, I love you.'

He had not been expecting her to say this and it was the first time either of them had admitted they were in love. Tears started to flow again, as she realized there was a high

The Treaty

risk he would ask her to leave and end their friendship. Lifting her head and taking a tissue from a box nearby, he wiped her face.

'You've got panda eyes,' he smiled.

She stopped crying and began to laugh - the tension between them melting away. He gave her a gentle peck on the nose.

'Maria, have you told me everything, I must know the truth.'

'Yes, that is everything I can tell you. I've been very worried; do you think Fatima had anything to do with Dominic and Emma being killed?'

He thought about this then reassured her. 'No, I don't think she did. She wanted Dominic alive so that he could lead you to those documents in his house. It would have been stupid for her to have him killed.'

'I've prayed every night to dear sweet Jesus, every night, in the hope I didn't cause their death.'

'Promise me no more secrets. If Fatima makes contact, you must tell me. We both could be in danger.'

She nodded her head, acknowledging this possibility.

'I will, I promise, definitely no more secrets.' She hugged him back and they kissed warmly. Andy, while having nagging doubts, knew he was going to have to learn to trust Maria all over again. He had to believe her sincerity and thought that perhaps she had been naïve; her affair with Fatima was something he could only blank out from his mind.

Deciding to change the subject, he told her about his next trip abroad to Asia. 'I will be away for almost the whole week. I'm going to Laos, a small country next to Thailand.'

Maria tried not to look disappointed. 'Oh okay, I will be fine. You did say you would have to go away some of the time.'

Feeling guilty after having shouted so much earlier he

wanted to say something positive, and then on an impulse he had a flash of inspiration.

'Why don't you come with me - the company doesn't mind if I share my room in the hotel. It costs just the same, anyway.'

Her face broke into a wide grin and clapping her hands together, she flung her arms around his neck. 'Fantastic, I've never been to Asia before!'

'We can stop over in Bangkok, but you will need to sort out a Visa and make sure you can return to the UK without any problems.'

Pleased with this decision, despite what had happened, he really wanted their relationship to have another chance.

12

'Excuse me, can you tell me where the Mill Bank conference is being held?'

Caroline Lovelace-Jones was at the entrance to the Houses of Parliament; she was running late and tapped her fingers agitatedly on the side of a little wooden security booth. The white haired man in uniform pointed in the direction of St Stephens Hall.

'Go through the reception and central hall,' the man smiled. 'Passed old Lord Falkland, the statue with the broken sword, those Suffragettes chained themselves to it. Carry on along the corridor and you will see more directions on the left.'

Thanking him, she cursed for not staying in London the night before and avoiding delays at Madrid airport. Trying to remember the door attendant's instructions, she blamed Emmeline Pankhurst for her being at the conference in the first place. Without women's liberation, she would have a husband and be home raising children instead of having this nightmare day. Her boss, Sir Richard Parsons, requested she address an audience from the Home Office made up of security specialists from MI-5 and police chiefs. Following the signs, she eventually found the correct venue, and pushed hard against a door and entered at full speed into a room full of delegates all quietly seated around a large rectangular table. One man thoughtfully pulled out an empty chair allowing her to squeeze in beside him. Immediately sensing it was hot, she had to get up again and struggle in the confined space to remove her suit jacket. Meanwhile, Sir Richard was standing at the head of the table and tapping his pen on a sheaf of papers, waiting for Caroline to be seated.

'Good morning Ladies and Gentlemen, thank you for coming to Westminster at such short notice. My name is Richard Parsons and I am the government chief Security Coordinator. I will get to the point. I've been tasked with investigating the growing speculation about senior establishment figures here in the UK, being involved with an illegal narcotics treaty, which was apparently cobbled together more than thirty years ago. You may think this type of conspiracy theory, call it what you will, would not normally warrant such an exercise, however, the Prime Minister is of the opinion these rumours in the media is damaging to our international reputation and relationship with the USA in particular. He is also mindful of links to senior members of the Royal Family causing unwarranted distress, when they can ill afford more damaging publicity. What I propose is to bring you up-to-date with the story that is doing the rounds. Following the murder of two people at a London hotel, it has been discovered one victim; a man called Dominic Marsh, planned to publish details of this supposed secret narcotics treaty. I can also tell you currently there is a parallel event concerning ongoing investigations, which may be connected and which you will hear more about in the next few minutes.

I have invited Caroline Lovelace-Jones, Bureau Chief of MI-21 Madrid office, to explain her role and Professor Colin Trenched who is an authority on illegal narcotics, and who more importantly was around at the time this supposed treaty was planned. To open our discussion, I will be asking why Dominic Marsh, a modestly successful publisher, who produced an outrageous publication was murdered. Motives for the double murder of himself and his wife, Emma Marsh, range from robbery to a planned contract killing. He lived with his wife in a rented farmhouse in rural Northamptonshire, located on the edge of the Althorp Estate owned by Princess Diana's Brother Lord Spencer. The couple left behind one small child, a boy, and the au pair. I mention the au pair because on the same weekend the crime was committed she had a visitor, a man named Andrew Davies, who she met during a freak storm only hours before Marsh was killed. Andrew Davies may or may not be material to this investigation, although, you will hear more about this from Caroline in a few moments. Davies is English and had no apparent connection with Dominic Marsh and his wife Emma, and had not known the au pair, Maria Farnese, before their meeting. Dominic Marsh's literary agent has since said in a statement, "My client claimed to have a copy of a secret document and planned to write a book." He believed it was dynamite, and would sell millions of copies. Right, that is as far as I will take it, now and next I will hand you over to Caroline.'

Straightening her skirt, Caroline walked to the head of the table. She was a tall blonde, with the kind of good looks and figure a woman in her early forties has to work hard to keep. Standing next to Sir Richard, she began to speak slowly with a pronounced Oxford accent.   'Thank you, Sir Richard and good morning everyone. Fast-forward to last Monday evening, the weekend of the murder and to a hotel in Madrid. Andrew Davies flew there from Heathrow Airport, soon after leaving Althorp, where he just spent the night with Maria Farnese. He was in Madrid on business with three other colleagues who earlier that day hosted a telecoms seminar for their employers - *start the video and dim the lights, please.* You see the reception area of the hotel; Andrew Davies is sitting at a table next to the pillar on the right together with his colleagues. Watch the girl in the red trousers entering from the right, she walks through reception and makes her way toward the group and greets her team. Tony Celentano first, he is Andy's line manager in the UK, next the American's Larry and Joel and leaving Andrew Davies until last - *stop there please.* I cannot read your minds, but you are probably thinking beautiful figure, stunning looks. She is in fact Moroccan by birth with a French/Brazilian heritage, and goes by the name of Fatima Habiba Labaua. Fatima is a senior member of a Madrid terrorist cell, and considered to be dangerous.'

A low whistle from the audience summarized the moment. Fatima was a name they only ever saw in security briefings and seeing her image came as a surprise.

'For those of you who have not heard about this woman's reputation, I have to say it is difficult to rate her seniority. Respected by those who work for her, she commands a lot of influence in her organization. Academically bright, speaks eight languages and runs a translation bureau as a cover. Her father was a senior Diplomat and her mother is Brazilian. Fatima was educated in New York and Washington and travelled around the world on diplomatic missions with her late father. She has a reputation for getting exactly what she wants, and who she wants. *Lights back on please.* You may have noticed from her body language that while she was talking to Tony Celentano, Andrew Davies is the real focus of her attention. Are there any questions at this point?'

A man sat on the far side of the table waved a hand in the air. 'Excuse me Caroline, Mark Chapman, Internal MI-5. Why haven't the Spanish lifted Fatima on suspected terrorist charges?' 'Thank you Mark, the simple answer is she has political friends in high places here in Europe and the USA.

The Treaty

When there is any trouble, she is a zillion miles away from where it happens. I am still puzzled why she singled Davies out and how she knew he was in Madrid. We suspect she had inside information and a strong ulterior motive, or Davies is in someway connected with her - not impossible. We are increasingly finding terrorists turn out to be the most unlikely suspects, and not the stereotypes we first thought of.'

Sir Richard Parsons stood up and approached Caroline. 'Okay, thank you Caroline, we will return to the terrorist aspects of this mystery later on. Before then I would like to introduce my next speaker Professor Trenched.' Caroline was still squeezing back into her cramped seat when a white haired man entered the room and strode up to the front and stood alongside Sir Richard. Dressed casually in a checked jacket and cotton Chinos, he looked a stereotypical academic in a room full of *suits*.

'Thank you Colin for your presence here today. Professor Trenched is from the London School of Economics, he is a global authority on the illegal narcotics industry and a Consultant to the United Nations.'

'Thank you, Sir Richard and good morning everyone. I will be as brief as possible with such a huge topic. For those interested further, I will leave behind copies of my notes and a recent white paper.' Clearing his throat, he turned to face a screen displaying a table of statistics. 'It's important to get a handle on the size of this industry, to understand why people in high places, even leaders of entire nations, are prepared to put their lives on the line for a slice of the action. The narcotics industry is said to be worth anywhere between $50 billion and $300 billion at retail, and according UN estimates could be almost as valuable as the oil and gas industry in 2004. It operates outside the law, none of the businesses involved are listed on any stock exchange and there are no accounting firms or interfering analysts researching the dynamics of this industry. Some 200 million people or 5% of the world's population aged 15 to 64 used drugs at least once in 2004. This is 15 million people higher than the previous year's estimate, but remains significantly lower than the number using psychoactive substances (tobacco: around 30%; alcohol: around half of the general adult population).'

'Excuse me Professor, Richard Kent, Home Office; do these figures take into account seizures and other losses to the drug dealers?'

'Yes, these numbers take into account the amounts of drugs seized by governments and lost for one reason or another. We can see from this next slide, how the value of drugs increases substantially as they move from producer to consumer. The relative importance of the size of the market is more pronounced if compared to the exports of individual products. Global exports of wine, beer, and cigarettes in 2004 were just a quarter of the wholesale value of illicit drugs. Dealers require a robust international currency and the ability to move large sums of money - the US dollar being their preferred choice. A UN study has shown that out of $400 billion in United States currency notes in circulation, $300 billion circulates outside the US. This global circulation of currency is supported by the Federal Reserve Bank, which annually prints $16 billion for shipment abroad - at a near 100% profit. From the Americans point of view, they do not have a problem while the dollar bills are not returned to the USA. They constitute an interest free loan with no terms of repayment as long as they remain outside the country. That ladies and gentleman is about as much as I can tell you in such a short period any questions?'

Sir Richard stepped forward. 'Is there any indication of central governments being involved in trying to control the production and distribution of narcotics?'

The Treaty

Colin Trenched paused before replying, raising his eyebrow at the naivety of the question. 'I think we can safely say that over the past two centuries it has been mainly governments that have ensured the successful expansion of this industry. Imagine the benefit of owning the market for heroin and cocaine.'

'In reality Professor, surely it's ludicrous to suggest any modern western government can orchestrate the cancerous growth in the use of narcotics. I mean, what possible justification would they have?'

'As you can see from these statistics, the value of this global industry is staggering and if we have national designs on controlling areas of the oil and gas industry in various parts of the world, we simply must control the production and distribution of heroin and cocaine. Afghanistan, right now in 2005, accounts for over 80% of the world's opiates and business is booming! With increasing numbers of UN forces coming into this country and regulating the market. I am confident we shall see production rise to meet over 90% of the world demand for opiates in the next couple of years. '

'Well we shall have to wait and see if the Professor is right. There will be further discussion on this topic after we have our break. Grateful thanks to you Professor Trenched and we really do appreciate your introduction to this very complex industry. Meanwhile time to stretch your legs - coffee and tea is ready and smoking is allowed on the balcony at the end of the corridor, back here please in fifteen minutes.'

The small assembly began filing out of the tightly packed room. Sir Richard caught up with Caroline, who was heading for the balcony with a cigarette between her fingers all ready to light up.

'Caroline, have you got a second. How close do you think Fatima got to Andrew Davies, is he a security threat do you think?'

'We had twenty-four hour surveillance on her apartment and he stayed over after a night out, leaving about six-thirty in the morning. Is he a threat? More like a possible victim if he's not careful. We are still not sure how she made a connection with him, but in her case, you have to rule out co-incidence. I was surprised to hear the police have let him go off on a trip abroad; both he and the Farnese girl are booked on a flight to the Far East. Laos I believe.'

'Why wasn't I told about this? I really do believe someone should have informed me earlier; I want the girl and Davies kept under surveillance, this is short notice for you Caroline but could you go out there? I think you know what the two of them are like and understand the sensitive nature to the background of this case. We don't want to bring in new people at this late stage.'

Caroline paused for thought finding it hard to think of an excuse. She did not really want to leave her post in Madrid at this time but at the end of the day he was her ultimate boss.

'Well I suppose I can reorganize, yes, of course, I will call my PA after the conference to make the necessary arrangements.'

'Excellent and thank you so much for coming over, I thought your talk went down well. Oh, and I understand congratulations are in order. I'm pleased you got the promotion to Bureau Chief, well done.'

'Thank you; I'm really enjoying the new location. Madrid is such a beautiful city.'

'I strongly believed you were the right person, despite the high caliber competition and made my views known to the selection board. When are you going back to Madrid?' 'I'm staying at the apartment just for one night, and then return in the morning.' 'Have you any plans this evening? Perhaps you would like to have dinner. I know a splendid

The Treaty

little place and very discreet. What do you think, perhaps for old time sake?' Caroline raised a smile, she knew it was payback time; her great job was down to him.

'Yes, I would love that Richard, what time?'

'I'll have my car pick you up about eight o'clock.'

13

Flickering candles cast dancing shadows across her motionless body. Fatima lay outstretched listening to the final aria from Madame Butterfly; sharing the woman's pain and anguish in a forlorn hope her husband will return, knowing the truth he is gone forever. When Philippe was shot dead and her baby daughter suffocated in her sleep, the future for her died too. From the bottom of despair, she had gradually found the strength to survive on hearing the voice of God. She had crawled back to a new kind of existence, in a world tainted with hatred and bitterness - a world in which she would devote the rest of her life to seeking revenge. This was the will of God, to win back power for the faithful. Punishment, when it came, would be swift with their denouncement and banishment. Immortal words from the Holy Koran were a source of peace, where death would have been a happy substitute. She chose to live and fight, to win the truth for God and her people. This was her life now and the right thing to do.

"O you who believe!
Equality is prescribed for you in the matter of murder:
the freeman for the freeman, the slave for the slave, the
woman for the woman, but if any remission is made (to

anyone) by his (aggrieved) brother, then the recognized course must be adopted and payment made to him in a handsome manner. This is an ease and a mercy from your Lord, and whosoever transgresses the limit after this, for him there shall be painful chastisement."

Each day a new page from the holy book filled her heart with inspiration; along with the certain knowledge that only through death would she see Philippe and their baby daughter again. At times when the pain and torture of her grief seemed so great, a happy and kinder substitute would be death instead of this lonely existence. Her duty now was to seek out the truth, to fight and win for her love of God and her people - this was the right thing to do.

Shattering her stillness, she silenced the shrill tone from a mobile phone. Deadening the music and in some confusion she forgot to check the identity of the caller, something that had never happened before.

'Fatima, its Andy, remember me?'

Aware her calls were always monitored she gave a cautious response, ever ready to cut the connection.

'Where are you? I thought you said you were coming back to Madrid. Tell me what has been happening with your girlfriend. Is she okay now?'

'I'm sorry I should have called, things have been hectic.'

'You were so angry when you left; I thought I would never hear from you again.'

Andy ignored this last comment determined to keep their conversation upbeat.

'My computer was stolen from the hotel when I got back after seeing you. I'm still trying to replace all the files and software.'

Her gaze drifted over to a black laptop case at the foot of a desk. 'At least you were not injured and got home safely.'

Andy guessed this was a good time to hit her with the real purpose for his phone call. 'Fatima, I know about you and Maria, I know she gave you information about my trip to Spain.'

Each syllable struck her skull like pieces of shrapnel, and while still in shock realized she had committed a grave an unforgivable error. This gaping hole in her security over the public network was potentially terminal and she had minutes to escape. Never having anticipated Maria would betray her she began to babble her response.

'I'm not sure what you are talking about. I'm sorry, but I have to go. I will contact you very soon and you can tell me all about this, ciao.'

Smashing the tiny phone into the wall and screaming with rage, debris flew in all directions as she scrambled to her feet. Using an encrypted device, she immediately contacted her driver, barking instructions at him in Arabic while grabbing at clothing and important equipment. An elderly housekeeper arrived, who would take her place after she left and would deny all knowledge of Fatima's existence. She had just made a catastrophic and usually terminal error.

* * *

'Miss Lovelace-Jones is on the line, sir.'
'Thank you put her through.'
'Caroline, good flight back to Madrid?'
'Richard, we have made a positive link between Fatima and Dominic Marsh's au pair, they are definitely working together.'

Richard leaned closer. 'You mean Maria...what's-her-name...Farnese?'

'Yes, we intercepted a call initiated by Andrew Davies,

The Treaty

he blurted out that Maria told Fatima he was travelling to Spain. That is why she was waiting for him to arrive and made sure she was offered the translator job by her friends at the hotel.'

'So that puts Davies in the clear. He does look like a possible victim as you said.'

'Sort of, I am still convinced he is hiding something and possibly did see or even copy the documents off Dominic Marsh's computer.'

'Why do you suspect that? Is there any evidence?'

'Well, Maria disclosed in her own witness statement that he used a memory stick, and why else would he remove all the history files off the computer when he had finished.'

'I think the jobs getting to you, Caroline. He explained all that in his own statement, it sounded credible to me.'

'Call it female intuition, then. I can tell when a man is lying.'

Richard smiled. 'I'll remember that. Okay so if he did make a copy what was his motive?'

'I don't know Richard, any number of reasons - curiosity being one.'

'Well, we will have to go with your intuition theory for now. This makes me even more convinced you have to follow them to Laos. Is that all booked and cooked?'

'Yes, I leave on Friday ahead of them. Giving me a day to organize things and get over any jetlag. I understand Davies has meetings starting on the Monday in Vientiane, that's where I'll be staying.'

'It was unbelievably careless of Fatima taking that call, have they picked her up?'

'We informed the Spanish and they sent in people from TEDAX and Unidad, just incase there were any explosives in the apartment, by the time they arrived she had packed up and gone.'

'Has she left Spain?'

'Almost certainly, she has homes in Paris and Marrakech.'
'Well thanks for the update Caroline, be careful and stay in touch.'
'Ciao'

14

James waved enthusiastically, weaving through a crowd of excited men chattering in small groups outside the bar. Andy signaled back to show he had seen him, and beckoned him over to his table near to the entrance. The Black Eye was a gay bar located behind St Martin-in-the-Fields Church, close to London's Leicester Square.

'Stand up and let me see you!' James laughed. 'You look really well; you must be in love again?'

Andy gave James a warm smile and stood to receive an embrace from his favourite cousin.

'You look well yourself, obviously still enjoying life in London.'

'I would prefer the South of France, but as I have to work then, yes, London's fine.'

They laughed again as they sat down.

'Where have you been hiding?' James asked darting glances around the bar. 'All I ever seem to get from you these days is the odd email and a card at Christmas.'

When Andy first moved close to London, he used to meet with James regularly. He loved his cousin's dry sense of humour and laissez faire attitude. In recent years his work had made a normal social life almost impossible, and pleased finally to find the time to meet up, he felt a tiny bit guilty as he had an ulterior motive. James was a civil servant and senior business analyst, an Oxford graduate with a Masters degree from the LSE (London School of Economics) in Philosophy, Policy and Social Value. He never doubted James would be a high flyer and was destined to reach dizzy heights in government or business.

'So what is the crisis, Andy? I am dying to know. Does it involve another man's wife and possibly sex?'

More laughter followed as Andy shook his head. 'I came by some information that could be something, or nothing, and it's made me curious enough to want to dig a little deeper. The only reason not to say what it is at the moment is because I'm not sure if it's legal, and could implicate you if there was a problem later.'

'Now you have my full attention, and you're right, I don't need anymore scandal, my lifestyle is dangerous enough.'

Andy tested the water and asked. 'Have you ever heard about a secret drugs treaty supposedly made between the US and UK government in the late sixties?'

'It has a familiar ring to it. Something like that was doing the rounds when I was at Uni. The problem is there have been so many conspiracies, which do you believe? Why, do you know something?'

'OK, James, I have to tell you more about a recent event so that it makes any sense. Did you read about the murder of a couple in a North London hotel a few weeks ago?'

'Yes it was front page news.'

'Well, I have it on good authority that the police suspect this was a contract killing, not a robbery as reported.'

'I would not be surprised at all, similar shootings happen practically every week in London these days. But what has it got to do with you?'

Andy decided to ignore the question.

'This might sound weak, but these two murders may be connected to this drugs agreement I just mentioned. One victim may have been planning to write a book and dish the dirt on some very senior establishment people.'

Listening carefully, James sipped his pint of Kronenbourg. 'Andy, there is one problem here, the biological clock is ticking. Many of the originators, if it turned out to be true, could all be dead and once that happens nobody really cares anymore what happened thirty or forty years ago - especially in regard to some silly treaty.'

'But what if this guy who was murdered stumbled on new evidence that could prove this drugs treaty is still operational, who knows what affect this is having around the world?'

Andy caught the eye of a waiter, or the waiter caught his eye - unsure who got there first. Decked out in a tight T-shirt and beaded necklace, he sashayed over and collected their glasses.

'Look, Andy, I'm an economist trying to predict the future outcome of government policy and the affects it is having on peoples' lives. Governments and businesses make whimsical decisions all the time, sign treaties and contracts that, with hindsight, sometimes turn out to be poor value.'

'Yes you are right. I would just like to find out if this agreement or treaty ever actually existed and if it is dead and buried.'

James was a high-flyer and was used to making decisive executive decisions.

'Okay, here's what I propose we do. I will call my old tutor, Professor Trenched, at the LSE; he is an expert in this field and wrote a book on the illegal drugs industry not that long ago. I recently recommended him to colleagues working in the Home Office only last week when they wanted someone very discreet and respectable to address a conference on this same subject. He went along, spoke for less than one hour, and told to invoice them for a grand. He is good man, one of my people. The thing is

Professor Trenched used to be a real left-winger, and always out front on 'ban the bomb' marches - ironically, together with Jack Straw our present Foreign Secretary. Colin will tell you everything he knows any drugs agreements going right back to the sixties.'

'James, that's fantastic! More than I hoped for, you really are a star. Listen, you and Rupert should come to stay at my place for the weekend and meet Maria, you can experience an Argentinean Asado and have a few beers.'

James immediately switched into a camp parody. 'Maria? Now there's a new name! You didn't tell me you had a new girlfriend.'

'Oh, didn't I? She is from Buenos Aires and has been staying with me for a few weeks. It's a long story.'

'I'm there already! Which weekend can we come over? I want to know more!'

Andy chuckled promising to phone and arrange a time.

15

'Mr Davies has arrived Professor, would you like me to bring him up to your office?'

'Yes, thank you, Barbara. He will get lost wandering through the corridors.'

Replacing the receiver, Colin Trenched left his desk to clear a seat for his visitor, moving a pile of papers and stacking them onto another chair. He had occupied this same office for over 20 years; it was like a second home. The room had enough space for a desk, two chairs and an extendable table. A large bookcase along the left wall rammed from floor to ceiling with boxes of academic papers and books left an area for a few photographs. One picture was of an African King who attended his lectures at the LSE, and another dusty image of former student and comrade, John Whitaker Straw (Jack Straw) the reigning British Foreign Secretary. Colin had been graying since a student, and his hair was now completely white. Despite that, he looked younger than his 68 years and was proud of his fitness. Having graduated with a first class honours degree in Philosophy and Mathematical Logic from Lincoln College, Oxford in 1959, he had travelled around post war Europe for two years becoming a devout socialist. Unable to decide on a career, he enrolled on a postgraduate course at the LSE to complete a Masters Degree in

Economics, and later became a senior lecturer before accepting a Chair. He remained at the University to the present time. Besides his teaching role, he managed a research contract and published numerous academic papers on the Illegal Narcotics Industry. He was Chairman of an official government committee on drugs and an adviser to a similar UN committee.

Hearing a knock at the door Colin looked up to see Barbara, one of the admin secretaries from the office on the ground floor, pop her head inside the room.

'Mr Davies is here Professor.'

'Thank you Barbara, wheel him in.'

Andy moved among the boxes of papers stacked on the floor as Colin Trenched stood up from behind his desk stretching out a hand in welcome.

'Delighted to meet with you dear boy.'

'Likewise, Professor Trenched.'

'Would you like a cup of tea or coffee?'

'Yes tea, please.'

'Barbara, can we find a clean cup and saucer for our guest, he would like some tea.'

Smiling she nodded bustling away.

'So, how's James?' Colin smiled. 'His call was such a lovely surprise.'

'He seems fine. Working hard and playing hard as usual.'

'He was a bright student.'

'Yes, he told me you taught him here at LSE. He spoke very highly of you.'

'Did he now, well I hope I will not disappoint you,' Colin laughs. 'James did not tell me an awful lot, apart from the fact you met with him recently and wanted to know if I knew anything about some historic narcotics agreement.'

'That's correct. I just hope I'm not wasting your time.'

'Well, I am sure you're not, fire away.'

Andy began with an edited version of his bizarre meeting

The Treaty

with Maria and the chance discovery of information regarding the treaty - admitting for the first time he had actually seen the documents, although, neglecting to mention he had made a copy. Voicing his concerns about the shootings in the London hotel and fearing links to someone preventing publication of the documents, he asked if it was conceivable, the treaty was still be in operation.

The Professor had appeared to be listening intently. After Andy stopped speaking, he waited seconds for his delayed response and began to fear he had drifted off uninterested in the subject.

'Andrew, what you have just told me fills some important gaps in my knowledge.'

There was a knock at the door interrupting his flow as Barbara returned to the office with two steaming mugs and placed them on the desk in front of them.

'Thank you, Barbara,' the Professor smiled. 'We are obviously all out of cups I hope the mug will do?'

Reaching over he picked up his drink. 'Thank you it's just fine.'

The professor waited until Barbara had left the room before continuing. '...Just recently I gave a talk about the illegal narcotics industry to government and security officials inside The Palace of Westminster. I think there is a strong possibility the conference I attended related to what you have just told me. I have indeed heard about the treaty conspiracy theory, and followed these stories for many years. James may have told you my political views. I believe inherited titles and inherited wealth has damaged the development of our great country. These are personal opinions you understand. However, I would dearly love to find a link among any senior establishment figures with this treaty and the Royals in particular.'

'The Royals - I don't understand?'

'Yes, Andrew. I have suspected their involvement with

the existence of a narcotics treaty for a long time, but until now, I do not believe there has been anything more than anecdotal bits and pieces to link the rumours - some of which implicate the Queen's husband Prince Philip. The missing proof is signed documentary evidence with an indication to how it all operates - money changing hands through offshore trusts, that sort of thing, and evidence which I suspect does not exist. What you have discovered however, is significant even though it will always be claimed the documents you saw are clever forgeries.'

Andy feigned incredulity, as he already knew from correspondence Prince Philip was in someway linked, but was eager to discover any new evidence.

'Why would the Royal Family become involved with something so scandalous? It would destroy them forever if this were exposed.'

'Quite,' Professor Trenched replied, raising his eyebrows. 'This is not a brush-off Andrew, but it would take time for me to expand on my theory. A couple of things you may want to research yourself is an organization called the Bilderberg Group, and do some reading on Prince Philip's life, particularly living in Europe before WW11. It may answer some of your questions about what could lead an outwardly privileged man to harbour seemingly irrational and insecure thoughts, particularly when viewed in a modern day context.'

This was a sensitive subject and extremely controversial. Colin Trenched was not isolated from the politics they were discussing and despite James being a close friend and Andy's cousin they had only just met.

'Is there anything else I can help you with, Andrew? I am fascinated by the subject and happy to talk about it anytime, please feel free to come and visit.'

'I'm really grateful for your time Professor, and will let you know if I stumble across anything new.'

The Treaty

'It was a pleasure, dear boy, and pass-on my regards to James when you next see him.'

Standing to leave, Colin reached out across the desk again and shook Andy firmly by the hand

'I think you may have stumbled across something here and you must take care how you unravel this story. The treaty seems to have a life of its own and may be a dangerous area of research, especially if you get too close to the truth!'

On that final note of caution, Andy made his way back through the labyrinth of corridors and stairs and out onto the London streets. His mind buzzing, he now had a real thirst to find out as much information as he could, and with no more work scheduled that day, he decided to take a trip to the British Library and conduct some research of his own.

16

'Good afternoon ladies and gentlemen welcome aboard TG911 Thai Airways flight to Bangkok. My name is Captain James Pickard I would like to apologize for the delay. We will be pushing back in precisely twenty-four minutes, so meanwhile please make yourselves comfortable and enjoy the flight.'

Andy fidgeted in his economy seat.

'Are you okay,' Maria whispered, massaging the back of his hand. 'Do you have enough room? Thank you for taking me with you, I'm really looking forward to seeing Bangkok.'

Andy clipped his belt over his stomach and stretched out his legs. 'I'm hoping we have time to do some sightseeing. Perhaps we should take a tour; it's the best way to see a lot in a short time.'

Since the incident with the address book, they had not spoken about Fatima. Occasionally, Andy dwelt on Fatima's reaction when he challenged her on the phone about her friendship with Maria. Unsurprised by her subsequent lack of communication he was equally unaware she had left Spain, now hunted by Interpol. People at MI-21 believed Fatima had links to the same organization planning a series of outrages in various European capitals following the Madrid train bombing. Eavesdropping on that conversation with Andy, connecting Fatima to Maria

The Treaty

had been a major coup and now they feared she would seek revenge targeting both Andy and Maria as a potential threat to her game plan.

Andy normally travelled business class on international flights, and exchanged his ticket for two economy seats half-hoping for a free upgrade back to business class. The flight however was almost full and seated toward the rear of the Airbus; they could not know the true reason for the aircraft's delayed departure. Only minutes before takeoff their flight was abruptly cancelled. A message had been received by the cabin crew ordering them to take on board another passenger. Expecting someone very famous the crew obeyed instructions and unlocked the doors. Only to their disappointment it turned out to be a very nondescript looking businessman. Taking his seat Barris Vaughan was a powerfully built, six feet two inches tall, ex-SAS paratrooper in his early forties. Grey hair and a Seventies style moustache, gave this Welshman an inconspicuous appearance, masking the true purpose of his journey. Barris had served for 20 years in the British Army and had fully expected to complete a twenty-five year stint before taking a generous pension into retirement, when his career abruptly ended after a series of misunderstandings involving very young girls. Forced to resign, now working for a secretive security organization, he was trained to carry-out instructions without question. Earlier on that same day after receiving a text message, he immediately reported to the Thai Airlines information desk at Heathrow Airport, where staff handed over a plain manila envelope containing details of his next assignment. Inside the envelope, he found a set of documents confirming his flights to Vientiane in Laos via Bangkok, together with photographs of a man and an attractive young woman - both onboard this plane.

17

'Please leave the small rucksack.'

Struggling to keep charge of her luggage, Caroline ordered the over-enthusiastic porter to carry her suitcase into the hotel. Having been in the air for over thirteen hours with just a short stop in Bangkok, she desperately needed a shower followed by sleep. The Lao Plaza, Vientiane's smartest hotel, used mainly by rich Asians and western business visitors, seemed out of place in one of South East Asia's poorest countries. Passing the armed guard, two smartly uniformed door attendants welcomed her into the spacious glass and brick foyer, decked out with fully-grown trees and a variety of tropical plants. She joined a short queue and waited to register.

Despite the long journey, Caroline liked Asia, seeing this as an excellent opportunity to travel somewhere different and to catch-up on CIA gossip with her friends from the US embassy. Searching the Gucci rucksack to find her passport, she fingered the photographic images of Andrew Davies and Maria. The brief given to her shortly before leaving Madrid was sketchy, and all she knew was Andy had business here for about one week and the couple planned to stopover in Bangkok on their way back to Britain. He would be meeting with people at the Lao Telecommunications office in the capital and supervising

The Treaty

new equipment installation. They were staying at this same hotel. Checking in, she headed to her room, and still fully clothed lay on the queen-sized bed and in a matter of minutes was fast asleep.

18

Scanning the unfamiliar dishes on the menu Maria struggled to choose something to eat.

'I don't understand what these are, Andy. What are you having?'

'I fancy the prawns. The fish sounds tasty, too. It's cooked in a Chinese style, but it's spicy.'

'Do you think it's fresh?'

'Definitely, it was probably caught in the Mekong this morning.'

This was their first meal out together in Vientiane, the capital city of Laos, situated on the banks of the Mekong River. Still relatively unexploited by tourism, most of the visitors were either on business or adventure travellers and backpackers. Their restaurant featured prominently in the Lonely Planet guidebook, and seemed popular with other westerners.

'That man at the bar looks drunk,' Maria whispered, indicating with a nod toward the circular bar in the centre of the restaurant.

Andy had noticed the man at their hotel earlier, as he had a distinctive grey moustache. Balancing precariously on his seat he slouched over the bar. Each time he raised his glass drips of liquid splashed onto his Chinos forming damp patches. Once or twice, turning sideways he looked

The Treaty

directly at them. Andy suspected he was attracted to Maria, who looked stunning in a white skirt and skimpy top. In fact, she had caused quite a stir in the restaurant, and he self-consciously felt eyes on them from people at various tables around the room. The man with the moustache turned away and continued a heated conversation with two young Australian guys seated close by. Odd words floated across above the background noise, Nam, Laos, bombing, Americans - the talk was all about a war that ravaged these parts in the 1960's and 70's.

'Why do they have to drink so much?' Maria commented. 'Are you like this when you travel on business alone? Do you get drunk?'

'I would more than likely be in my room, preparing for the meeting tomorrow.'

With a teasing smile, she reached over and taking his hand gave it a gentle squeeze. 'Are you certain? I mean, what about that woman sat by her self. She looks European and is very attractive. Wouldn't you be tempted to chat - her up?'

Andy discreetly glimpsed at the lone woman eating with chopsticks and reading a book. Her dress sense screamed English with big-hair in an old-fashioned style. She could easily have been a governess left behind by the Europeans when they ruled this part of Asia.

'You agree she is attractive, maybe looking for the right man. It could have been you!'

Andy smiled. 'Now you are being silly, why would I possibly want an older woman when I have you sitting here? I'm really pleased you came.'

'Yes, me too, it's fun to come on one of your trips. We can spend more time together, what time is the meeting tomorrow?'

'Early, eight thirty. Asang is picking me up at the hotel and the rest of the day, you will be on your own. Are you going to be okay?'

'Yes Andy, don't worry. I plan to have a long sleep then swim in the hotel pool and generally relax.'

'Great, I know he will want to take me to lunch somewhere and perhaps show me his city. It's the usual custom.'

Finishing off their meal, Andy suggested they take a slow walk back to the hotel as he still had calls he needed to make. The woman folded her book and asked for the bill, while the drunk at the bar and his new friends fell over tables and flagged down a passing Tuk-Tuk.

'Come on, Barris!' the taller of the two Australian men shouted. 'Let's go find some girls!'

19

Asang waited patiently in the foyer of the Lao Plaza for Andy to arrive. He was early, but this did not matter as he enjoyed the opulence of the hotel, an experience few of his fellow citizens would ever enjoy. Asang was mindful of the money foreigners brought to his country, accepting Laos must modernize. He was 32 years old and studied electronic engineering at a Russian University. Fluent in French, Russian and English he mixed easily with the newcomers unlike the rest of his family. Uncles, aunts and even his father all suffered terribly during the 1960's when the country was divided by a secret war in support of the Americans.

Laos is land-locked and sits with Thailand to the west, Vietnam on the east, Cambodia south with Burma and China in the north. The Royal Lao Government fought a bloody civil war supported secretly by the Americans, who then used them unofficially to transport supplies and equipment to Vietnam; preventing thousands of fighters from North Vietnam reaching the south of the country. During the Vietnam War, Laos became a major supplier of gold on the black market, which they sold to American soldiers serving in Vietnam. By the late 60's, this had changed and the only worthwhile product they had to sell came from the mountains in the North, along the border with Burma, where they grew poppies to make into opiates.

Asang kept his eye firmly on the lift doors in the hope he would recognize Andy when he did arrive. There were not that many guests staying in the hotel, and finally he caught sight of him as the lift doors flung open. Leaping to his feet, Asang nervously approached Andy and extended his hand ready to greet him.

'It's good to meet you finally,' Andy smiled. 'We've spoken so often on the phone.'

Returning to where he had been sitting, and the waiter summoned, they made small talk about Andy's journey and his first impressions of Vientiane. The conversation quickly moved to technical issues. After finishing their drinks Asang suggested it was time to make a move. His plan was to go to the telecoms site where the equipment was located and later, if Andy had the time, he would take him to his favourite restaurant.

On the way to the office, he told Andy all about his family and four young children, as he powered the dust covered Isuzu Japanese SUV through the back streets of the city. Bouncing over potholes and weaving in and out of Tuk-Tuks, they reached a white two-story building displaying the telecoms company logo. Leaving the vehicle, Asang took the lead, bounding up a flight of wooden steps fixed to the outside of the building that led to a first floor office. Andy followed, and before entering, removed his shoes choosing a pair of flip-flops from a random selection by the door.

Once inside, he followed Asang to the area where his equipment was stored. It had arrived direct from the USA, all carefully packaged and ready for assembly. His colleagues had done a great job, wrapping every nut and bolt and making sure all the cables had the right connectors. He estimated that it would take about two days to complete the install and one more for final testing; this would

The Treaty

allow them enough time to stop over again in Bangkok.

The first mornings work went well, and Asang had not forgotten his promise to take Andy out to lunch. The restaurant was only a short drive from the office, and turning right down a bumpy dirt track they headed toward the banks of the Mekong. At first sight it all looked rundown, a plain wooden structure stood on a platform supported by stilts built over the grassy river bank. Thailand was clearly visible in the distance and Asang chose a table overlooking the immense stretch of water - the tenth largest river in the world and lifeblood for millions of people along its route.

Glancing down at the menu, it looked incomprehensible to Andy.

'I think you'd better choose Asang, I haven't got a clue what to order.'

'No problem let's have a variety. Do you like fish? It is their specialty here, fresh from the Mekong, of course.'

Drinks arrived and they continued chatting about the possibilities for new business in this expanding country. The plan was to install several new systems in the north and the southern regions. Much of the east was unoccupied and dangerous, especially the border area between Vietnam and Laos along the iconic "Ho Chi Minh trail."

Changing the subject Andy asked rather naively. 'Has the war been completely forgotten by the younger generation in Laos, or does it still impact on your lives?'

Asang turned his gaze away for a second and looked out across the brackish water coloured by soil washed down from the mountains.

'It's difficult to summarize how I feel or how people my age are feeling,' he replied, turning to Andy. 'We all live such different lives. During the Vietnam War Laos was a sideshow - a secret war. We had over two million tons of bombs dropped on our country, the Americans admitted that many of those bombs were experimental devices, and a third failed to explode. Our countryside is still littered with them, and thousands of my people have been killed since the war ended. So, the best answer I can offer is, yes, we do still live with the war everyday of our lives.'

Andy squirmed in his seat, and then had a sip of beer before mumbling an apology for asking such an inane question. Seeing his discomfort, Asang smiled back and waved his hand, summoning the waiter over to their table.

'What are we, two old men talking about the war? Let's have some great food.'

Relieved his friend was not offended Andy raised his glass. 'Great idea, I will drink to that.'

When the food arrived, it was everything Asang had promised with a whole fish beautifully dressed, complimenting a range of spiced dishes. The two began to eat in silence; Andy tried a dish called Lop-stir-fry made from ground pork with sausage and many herbs served in cabbage leaves. He could see the French influence in the grilled steak, and used the sticky rice to mop up the sauces.

Speaking unexpectedly between mouthfuls of rice, his thoughts leaping back to their earlier more serious discussion, Asang announced, 'We were very sad in Laos about the death of Princess Diana. She helped our country with the charity for clearing mines.'

Thrown by this sudden introduction into their conversation he could only agree saying, 'Yes, it was a great shock in Britain and practically the whole world, she was killed in a terrible car accident.'

'Her work continues here in Laos.'

'That's good to hear, it would have been a shame if the money stopped just because she was no longer here to make people aware of the problems.'

Asang nodded in agreement. 'A short time before she died, someone from our company met the Princess in her hotel when she visited Vientiane. He spoke very passionately about her.'

'Really, who was that?'

'His name is Mardjono Deradjat, he used to be Lao Telecoms contracts manager, but he is retired now. He was a lawyer and helped to manage a charity when he lived here in the city. He met her to talk about the charity.'

'Are you sure he was telling the truth?'

Asang laughed at Andy's disbelief, thinking he was making a joke. 'Yes, it's true; apparently he had many stories about the Americans and the British when he worked in Holland. He claimed to have talked with Henry Kissinger on how to meet with the Chinese and help to end the war in Vietnam. According to Mardjono, even the US Secretary of State didn't know about these talks.'

'Is that why Princess Diana met him, because he knew all these westerners?'

'Yes probably but not only for this reason. When he worked in Holland he was involved in the agreement between America and Britain to sell our opium and distribute it in the west.'

Stunned into silence, Andy was suddenly aware he could be talking about the same documents he found on Dominic Marsh's computer.

'What are you saying, there was some kind of formal arrangement between the US and Britain to distribute narcotics.'

'Yes, of course,' Asang laughed. 'You sound surprised, Andy. I lived in Russia remember, it was known about. The Mafia worked closely with the treaty cartel, they had to do this.'

'So what has happened to Mardjono?'

'It was sad. He was travelling in the North of Laos when his car was shot at by terrorists and he was badly injured, losing the use of both his legs.'

'My God, when did that happen?'

'Oh, before I joined the company, perhaps maybe seven or eight years ago, Nhia Tou Yang had already taken over his job when I came. If you would like to learn more about all this, I will introduce you to Nhia when we get back. He may still be in contact with Mardjono.'

Andy could not believe what he heard, and began to wonder if perhaps he was just unbelievably naïve. According to Asang, the treaty story was true, and like the Vietnam War was just another piece of history.

20

As Caroline finished her coffee, she watched Maria enter the breakfast room dressed in figure hugging almost transparent white pants and a matching cropped top; she had seen Andy leave the hotel earlier that morning. Musing over how slim she looked and comparing the size of her tiny bum to her own mature deriere she summoned the waitress ordering more coffee. Spreading out a map of Vientiane on the table in front of her and planning a route to the US Embassy later in the day, she looked up in surprise when Maria appeared at her side.

'Excuse me, please. I am sorry to disturb you, but do you speak English?'

Caroline nodded answering. 'Yes, I do.'

Maria smiled. 'Could you tell me if your map shows how far the shops and market are from the hotel?'

Caroline peered down at the map. 'Yes, I'm sure it does. Why don't you sit here and we can both take a look, I want to go shopping myself sometime today.'

'Only if you are sure I am not disturbing you. It's very difficult for me here, my English is okay but I sometimes find it hard to understand directions in the Lao accent.'

Caroline laughed, saying she had experienced the same problem. Maria went to her table and returned clutching a shoulder bag, and leaving the puzzled waitress to find her with her breakfast.

'Where are you from?' Caroline asked, sipping her coffee.

'Argentina. Are you from England?'

'Yes, how can you tell?'

They laughed again at Caroline's joke, her English accent being so pronounced.

'I thought you looked English, but then, you may have been Australian or American.'

'I speak Spanish if you prefer?' prompted Caroline.

Maria's face lit up, immediately switching to her native language. She said it was so tiring speaking English all of the time. Caroline's Spanish was excellent and the two women enjoyed talking about their first impressions of Laos. Maria mentioned she was travelling with her boyfriend and Caroline explained she was there on business as a buyer of new age art and crafts for a large retail chain. Eventually, they looked at the map and planned a route to the market and shopping area.

'Why don't I meet you down here later this afternoon?' Caroline smiled. 'Perhaps about three o'clock when it's cooler and we can go together?'

Maria liked the idea. 'Yes, let's do that, I will phone Andy and let him know in case he returns to the hotel early, although, I am not expecting him back before eight o'clock this evening, or even later.'

Exchanging room numbers, they agreed to meet in the foyer. Maria finished her lite snack before heading back to her room. Caroline stayed behind searching in her bag for a mobile. Pleased to have contacted Maria so easily, it was now possible to go out for a few hours by herself and exchange gossip with her friends at the American Embassy.

The hotel staff began clearing tables and preparing for lunchtime, but annoyingly one guest remained, it was Barris Vaughan. He was fighting a hangover after his night

The Treaty

out with the two Australians. They ended up in a club of some kind, and all he could recall was a dirty room and a small girl who would not do as she was told. Smirking he sipped the last of his coffee, finished a duty free cigarette and made plans for the rest of that day.

21

Lying next to the pool on a plastic sun lounger, Maria recalled Christmas holidays as a child. It was their summertime and every year the family would drive to the ferry crossing the Rio de la Plata to Montevideo in Uruguay and stay in a rented villa for a huge family party. This hotel pool area was quiet apart from a woman with two small children splashing about in the shallow end. The same man they had seen the night before, who was drunk in the restaurant, sat at a table on the opposite side of the pool. He appeared to be reading a newspaper and sipped a bottle of beer, while making the occasional furtive glance in her direction. Wearing a modest two-piece swimming costume, Maria covered herself with a towel to shield her body from the sun and the man's preying eyes. Glancing at her watch on the white plastic table next to her, she eventually decided to return to the room. Her plan was to take a shower, have a little siesta and then have something to eat, by which time she would be ready to meet with Caroline and go shopping. Andy had already phoned to make sure she was okay. He was sweet she thought, worrying about her, and he sounded pleased she had made a friend so quickly and was not getting bored.

Gathering up the items she brought with her to the pool, Maria swung her legs off the lounger and straightened the

The Treaty

towel she was using as a wrap. Walking away from the poolside, conscious of Barris Vaughan's greedy eyes tracking her every move; she disappeared inside the hotel and hurried to the room. It was still in the same state she had left it in, and felt disappointed the room maid had not been to tidy things up. Removing her towel and swimming costume, she jumped in the shower, and in less than ten minutes was padding around the room in her underwear. The noise of the TV and the air-con unit above Maria's head masked the sound of heavy footsteps approaching the door. After a few initial taps, the visitor knocked louder finally attracting her attention. Guessing this was the room maid, she quickly searched for a bathrobe and grabbed the one Andy had used earlier. Expecting the door to fly open at any minute, she was surprised when it went quiet. Moving closer and unlocking the catch she was just about to turn the handle when the heavy wooden door suddenly swung inward knocking her off balance. A powerful blow from a fist followed through smashing into her face and throwing her down to the floor. With the escape route now firmly closed and tasting blood in her mouth she was unable to speak, only semi-aware of what was taking place. Lifted bodily from the floor, more blows landed on the head and chest sending her reeling back against the bed. Barely conscious - hardly able to breathe with her ribs crushed under the weight on top of her, the air expelled from her lungs leaving her gasping for breath. Her mouth filled with blood and saliva and between lapses of consciousness, there was a familiar smell of tobacco and beer close to her face. She could see her grandfather, he was picking her up in his arms - they were laughing as they waltzed by the kitchen table, knocking into a wobbly chair. He was taking her upstairs to bed while her mother looked on feigning anger, then she smiled blowing her a kiss - goodnight.

22

'Asang thank you for such wonderful food.'

'I'm happy you liked our cuisine it's different from Thai in so many subtle ways.' He glanced at his watch. 'Excuse me, please. I have a meeting at my office in town we have to leave.'

'No problem. Don't let me interrupt your day.'

'If you wish I can introduce you to Nhia, Mardjono's friend?'

'Yes, excellent. I'm interested to speak with him.'

Arriving outside a four-storey building close to the city centre, Andy waited in the executive suite on the top floor where Nhia had his office. He arrived from another part of the building, cutting short an internal meeting to greet Andy. Smartly dressed in an Armani style suit, Nhia was older than he expected - probably in his late sixties. After a firm handshake, he invited him to sit down on a small sofa. They waited while a girl poured a watery brew into two cups.

'Well, Andy,' Nhia smiled, stirring his tea, 'it's good to meet you. Asang has told me you have been talking about my predecessor Mardjono Deradjat. How can I help you?'

Andy had already prepared questions in his mind and was determined to discover something new about the treaty.

The Treaty

'I'm fascinated by Mardjono's life in Europe and some of the people he apparently knew. Are you still in contact with him?'

Nhia responded positively. 'Mardjono is a great man, he taught me this job here and I owe him a lot. He does not walk you know, he spends most of his time lying on his bed at home. I have spoken to him perhaps once in the past twelve months and we occasionally write to each other. I think he is very happy where he lives, overlooking a beautiful lake in Northern Sumatra. Do you know Sumatra?'

Andy lied, saying that he did, but his own geography was sketchy about that part of the world.

'I can give you his address if you want,' Nhia continued, 'he loves to speak about the past and would be pleased to talk to an Englishman. He has so many wonderful stories, even about your own Royals. You will know from your history lessons at school about the narcotics treaty between the US and the British. Mardjono wrote the entire legal document, did you know that? You must agree he is a famous man in your country, too, yes?'

For the second time Andy lied, saying the treaty would be familiar to the older generation, however, people his age did not know very much about this agreement. Nhia was not at all surprised saying it was the same in his country.

Placing his cup on the table and leaning back in his chair he said, 'Some young people know nothing of the war and are more interested in going to disco dances, they do not respect their elders in the way we did.'

'Did Mardjono ever show you a copy of the treaty?'

'Yes, he had his own copies. I saw those papers.'

'The people he worked for in Holland must have really trusted him.'

'Of course, Mr Kissinger kept in contact for many years.'

'Do you think Mardjono still has the documents at his home in Indonesia?'

Nhia thought for a minute. 'I don't know for certain, however, I do know what happened to one of his copies. He gave it to your Princess when she came to Vientiane.'

'Why would he do that?' Andy asked, sounding surprised. 'Surely he considered the papers of historic value?'

'Princess Diana's charity helps pay for clearing mines and unexploded bombs from our countries agricultural land. Mardjono asked for her help in having the donations increased, inline with the treaty requirements. He told her too much money was being paid to the poppy growers and other officials, also money was paid to organizations, in particular Healthy Verve.'

'Healthy Verve,' Andy echoed. 'Sorry you have lost me, who or what is healthy verve?'

'Nearly all narcotics are distributed by Healthy Verve in Asia; this is the same company in Europe, no?'

Andy admitted he did not know this name; drugs were not something he had experienced apart from smoking a little cannabis at University. He began to wonder if this could be another of those parallel worlds he discovered from time to time. When James had told him he was gay, he had no idea what a comprehensive and different lifestyle his cousin had been living. Gay bars and café's, shops and cruises, holidays and even gay mortgage brokers. It was a synchronized world, operating alongside his - maybe the world of narcotics was the same.

Nhia began to explain further. 'Healthy Verve is everywhere like McDonald's.' He laughed at his joke and walked over to a computer at the side of the room. Flicking a switch, he began searching for a document. 'I'm the secretary for the same charity and this is the last summary showing the donations, you can see for yourself where the money comes from.'

The Treaty

Andy stood by his side and scanned down the list of organizations, his eyes fixed on the United States mine action programs in Laos, contributing more than 23 million dollars. The bulk of this funding came from the UNDP Trust Fund, with commissions going out again to Healthy Verve.

Nhia pointed at the monitor. 'You see on the screen? The American funds together with the British come in and out to pay our farmers and feed their families for growing the crops.'

'And the crops are?' asked Andy.

Nhia looked at Andy as if he was stupid. 'Poppy of course, we make it for export. It is our only crop that is worth anything.'

'Sorry, yes, but I still do not understand why Mardjono involved Princess Diana in this?'

Once again, Nhia looked perplexed at Andy's ignorance. 'Your Princess Diana was controlling the payments.'

'I see!' Andy smiled, trying to hide his shock and surprise. 'So he asked Diana if she could help change the payments system.'

'Yes, that's right. Too much money was leaving Laos, and he told your Princess that the treaty had approved more for our people. She did not have her own documents and Mardjono offered to lend her one of his copies and to show her the authentically signed version, delivering them in person to her hotel. Diana was fascinated and pleaded that he leaves some of the papers with her overnight so she could read the full version of the treaty, especially the part that applied to Laos.'

Andy jumped in with a question. 'Do you know if he gave her the signed version to keep?'

'Andy, I'm not sure, you will have to ask him that question yourself. All I recall is when Mardjono phoned the next day to arrange collection he discovered she had left for Bangkok without leaving any of the documents she borrowed. At first, he said he was angry and disappointed she should do this to him, since he had trusted her. Then later, when things seemed to get better, he believed she had made a big difference. He was getting old and had not been in contact with Kissinger or anyone else in Holland for several years. The Princess, he thought, would perhaps use the treaty astutely, especially as she seemed to be helping him to make life better in Laos.'

'Would you mind giving me Mardjono's address?'

'Yes, I have it here.'

Within seconds, Nhia had printed out Mardjono's full contact details. Andy thanked him and prepared to leave, saying he had enjoyed their meeting and had learned a great deal.

Waiting for Asang to return, he thought about the ramifications of what he had just discovered. According to Nhia, Princess Diana had visited Vientiane in the early 1990's. He had just seen for himself payments passing to Healthy Verve quite recently and Diana knew about the treaty. Apart from her death, nothing else had changed; logically it could still all be in operation.

Rallying through side streets on their way back to the Telecom site, Asang made short cuts passing by ornately decorated colonial buildings and a traditional temple site.

'How was your meeting, was it helpful?'

'Yes thank you,' Andy smiled. 'He's plugged gaps in my general knowledge. I have to say I am so ignorant of my country's history.'

'Do not worry about it, when you have only ever lived under a communist system as I have, you learn to accept that not everything is as it appears to be. The simple fact is for the past thirty years, or more, Britain and the USA continuously expanded their economies, and narcotics have financed a lot of that growth and prosperity. Your economists and big banks call these billions of profits "*invisible earnings.*" That's why you don't know about them.'

Andy responded by laughing loudly in a disparaging way. 'The UK and America are democracies and we have a free press. We are experts in financial services - that's where we earn a lot of money from invisible exports. How could the treaty be kept a secret for so long?'

'By confusion, my friend, you should have lived in Russia; they are the masters of this art. For over seventy years, even some of your top economists believed the lies and statistics produced after the October revolution. It was all smoke and mirrors. The roots of communism were not working. Eventually the system crashed and this will probably be the outcome for the West.'

'Asang, I am a telecoms engineer not a merchant banker or politician. I have no idea if what you say is true. I am suspicious of this kind of conspiracy theory, and find it hard to believe something as explosive as this can be kept running for decades.'

'I have just explained how it was kept going for decades in Russia. I am an engineer too and not an economist. The fact is Andy common sense must tell us that with so many dollars outside America, used to buy and sell narcotics, the system is unstable. If for some reason the rich drug dealers in Asia, Russia and Latin America started to swap dollars for another currency, say the Euro perhaps, then the dollar could collapse.'

'Then we must agree to disagree,' Andy smiled. 'At least until I have more evidence.'

'Always a wise thing to do,' Asang laughed. 'Although, I can promise you I speak the truth.'

Andy cursed under his breath, after trying to send Maria a text message and discovering his mobile battery was flat. Still he thought he did not want to seem insecure making more phone calls; she could manage without him okay for just a few more hours.

With Asang's assistance the installation progressed smoothly, and they finished well ahead of schedule. It was high-fives all round when he told Asang, who immediately called his boss to let him know they would meet the deadline.

'Let's celebrate with a few vodkas,' Asang grinned. 'This talk about Russia is making me miss my adopted country.'

Piling back into Asang's SUV they rejoined the evening traffic and crossed town. Andy suggested the same bar he went to the previous evening with Maria, as it was a short walk from his hotel.

Finding a seat, they ordered two vodkas and made a toast to a successful first day. Over by the bar, Barris Vaughan was speaking loudly to no one in particular and was clearly very drunk. Andy tried to block him out of their conversation as he outlined his plan for the next day.

Common to tropical locations, the front of the restaurant was open and the sight of two police cars screaming to a halt outside halted their conversation abruptly. Four officers leaped out of the first car and quickly joined by two others from the second vehicle. A woman with a small girl trailed behind as they all trooped into the bar area. One officer was now crouching down beside the little girl aged ten or eleven, who whispered something and unmistakably pointed in the direction of Barris Vaughan. As if on cue, the other officers approached and grabbed hold of him, dragging Barris outside in his drunken state protesting loudly. The girl now quickly ushered outside with her mother watched from a safe distance, as he was subdued and bundled into the back of a car.

'What the hell was that all about?' Andy asked above the blaring sirens. 'That guy's staying at my hotel?'

Asang wore a pained expression. 'I heard one policeman say the girl accused him of beating her and forcing her to have sex.'

'The bastard, if that is true what will happen to him?'

'He will face a long prison sentence and possibly the death penalty.'

The atmosphere in the restaurant had become gloomy; Andy had still not contacted Maria and was growing concerned. He explained his dilemma to Asang, making the decision to leave. His friend understood, offering to take him, but he declined and set off on foot back to the hotel.

23

'You wait here, please.'

The officer blocking the entrance to the Laos Plaza nervously fingered an old SKS semi-automatic carbine, as he tried to explain to Andy why he could not let him inside. Growing angrier by the second, Andy was about to start remonstrating again with another senior officer when a woman's voice interrupted before he had a chance.

'Excuse me, Mr Davies. I may be able to help?'

Caroline whispered something to the officer and asked Andy to follow her inside the hotel. He felt tense as they marched through the lobby, made worse by the presence of more military talking to staff. With police ensconced in offices close to the reception desk, unsure what was taking place he meekly followed Caroline to a relatively quiet seating area at the back of the foyer.

'May I call you, Andy?'

'Yes, of course…look, what's happening?'

'I made friends with Maria earlier today. She told me all about you.'

Andy frowned, darting eyes around the foyer. 'You've spoken to Maria? Where is she?'

'There's been a serious incident. Maria is badly injured.'

'What?' Andy shook his head and tried to comprehend what Caroline was saying.

The Treaty

'Andy I want you to stay calm, the police are trying to find out what has happened.'

Andy leaped out of his chair. 'Maria!' he shouted. 'Where is she?'

Distraught and in a complete state of panic Andy started walking away, he had no idea where he was going, so he turned back and began pleading with Caroline.

'Please, tell me where she is, I must go to her now!'

It was only beginning to dawn this was the same woman they saw in the restaurant the night before. She was tall and carried an air of authority, especially when she raised her voice at him.

'Andy, *SIT DOWN* and I will explain!' Caroline shouted as other people dotted around the room began to take notice. Taken aback he complied returning to his seat. She began speaking softly. 'Maria is at the hospital and in good hands, there is nothing you can do. It's important we speak to the police before you leave the hotel.'

'The hospital,' Andy whispered, gazing down at the polished floor.

Caroline nodded. 'Yes, that's right. A man attacked her in your room and the police have arrested a suspect, a European. He was at the poolside at the same time as Maria; we believe he followed her as he was seen close to your room.'

Still in shock, Andy sat with his head in his hands remained staring down; he was on the edge of tears. When he did not respond, she placed her arm across his shoulder in an effort to try to comfort him.

'Andy, as soon as we have spoken to the police and explained you have been away from the hotel all day, we can leave straightaway for the hospital. It is not far from here, and one of the best in the country. She really is in good care.'

Helping him get to his feet, she took his arm and they

walked together across the foyer to a side office used by the investigating team. Introducing Andy, she seemed familiar with the people and remained during the interview. Asked about his movements and relationship with Maria, also did he know the man they had in custody, an Englishman called Barris Vaughan. Satisfied with his answers, supported by Caroline, they gave permission to leave for the hospital. According to the police, Maria was still in a coma after a violent assault. The journey to the Centre de Traumatologie et d'Orthopédie de Vientiane, passed in silence. On arrival, Andy waited in a small office for the doctor attending Maria, while Caroline stayed outside to make calls on her mobile.

Still in shock, he felt racked with guilt for leaving her all day in a strange country. Then at this low point, the door burst open snapping him back to reality, as Doctor Theillier wasted no time making this the worst day of his life.

'I'm sorry for the delay Mr Davies.' Pausing and scanning his notes to make sure he had addressed the correct person then continued. 'I have to tell you Maria's condition was very serious with a blood clot in a vessel in her brain. The rest of her injuries were not life threatening; broken ribs and some suspected internal injuries, with extensive bruising to her thighs, upper body and face.' He then paused for breath, avoiding eye contact with Andy while glancing back at his notes resumed speaking in a very soft and gentle tone. 'Mr Davies, I have to tell you we consulted first with Maria's parent in Argentina, and they gave their permission for the life support machine to be switched off. Her death was peaceful and without gaining consciousness she was not in any kind of pain.'

The doctor's word made little or no impact failing to penetrate Andy's unprepared conscious mind. Feeling hot, he continued to listen while breathing quickly to help sustain his concentration. His body had never experienced this level of grief or magnitude of personal loss, and with no reference points to gauge how to react. He could not know when this would happen, only later discovering new heights of emotion. Probably alone, in a poignant moment; driving a car, listening to a piece of music, hearing laughter that sounded like Maria. On the other hand, perhaps a clip of memory a flashing a smile, dancing - just being silly. That is when the true grief would strike at a time dictated by his sub-conscious mind. Speech impaired, muscular movements practically out of control, a gut wrenching shuddering would lead to him sobbing, into the depths of his sole yet unfathomed and only followed by feelings of utter and complete despair.

'It's difficult for you, I understand,' the doctor continued, placing a hand on Andy's shoulder. 'It has been made worse by being in a foreign country, but I can reassure you that even in Britain, she could not have been saved after sustaining such injuries. Placing his arm around Andy's shoulder, he guided him toward the door, expressing his regret once again.

'If you would like to see her to say goodbye, I will ask the nurse to take you to her room.'

Andy nodded his agreement saying he would like to see her, and was left standing alone in the corridor. A young nurse quickly appeared and escorted him to the intensive care section and a private room. Inside two nurses bustled around a bed removing tubes and connections to Maria's body. She lay as if sleeping - her pale face calm and serene. One nurse stopped what she was doing and speaking in a French/Laos patois asked kindly if he was the husband. Afterwards she wanted to talk with him about Maria's belongings and other necessary practical issues yet far from Andy's mind.

The nurses smiled sympathetically and exited the room.

Andy cautiously approached Maria's side. He did not really know what to do; she was so lifeless, so still. Touching her hand, he lifted it to his lips then gently laid it back down. She seemed almost childlike with her long black hair laying neatly each side of her face. The hospital gown she was wearing had come open at the neck showing a breast blackened by bruising from the blows she had received. Covering her chest with the garment he leaned across kissing her gently on the lips, and began to walk away without looking back, knowing this would be the last time he would ever see her.

Standing in the middle of a busy corridor, unsure what to do next, feeling almost hysterical, he suppressed mixed feelings of passion and anger. Nurses and patients ignored him as they negotiated their way passed. The sight of Caroline making her way toward him was a blessed relief. She already knew Maria was dead and guiding Andy they sat down on a hard plastic bench.

Initially saying nothing, she squeezed his hand, as she fought back her own tears. 'I'm so sorry, I've just been told. You must be devastated. She was a beautiful girl. I only wish there had been more I could have done for her.'

Moving her hand away, he got up and walked in circles, breathing deeply to control a sudden well of emotion trying to erupt to the surface.

Andy stopped in mid step and turned to Caroline. 'I'm just not sure what to do next. I mean, how, do you move on from here. What do I tell her parents - "sorry I got your daughter killed"?'

'That's a ridiculous thing to say. You could never in a million years have imagined this happening, nor prevented such a terrible tragedy.

The tiredness and strain of the past few hours began to kick-in and now he felt the need to be on his own.

'Thank you for all your help,' Andy smiled, 'but I think I

need to go back to my hotel now. I need to start sorting out whatever arrangements have to be made. I want to return to the UK as soon as possible.'

Standing she approached laying her arm in a motherly way across his shoulders.

'Yes, I understand just remember if there is anything further I can do - call me.'

She fished in her bag and produced a fake business card.

'I have good contacts here, and I can help sort things out through the Argentinean Embassy in Singapore. You do not have to worry, Andy; everything will be taken care of for you. Call me when you are back in London if you just need to talk, it may help knowing someone who was actually here with you.'

They formally shook hands and after studying her name, Caroline Lovelace-Jones, he placed the card in his pocket. She also offered to speak with the police again back at the hotel and oversee arrangement for transporting Maria's body back home to Buenos Aires. Under different circumstances, he would have asked why she was offering to do all this for him. She did not really know either of them and had no reason to be this helpful. However, these were not normal circumstances and since he was hardly listening, only later would this matter. Accepting her offers at face value and as acts of kindness, he thanked her again before leaving the hospital stepping outside into the bright sunshine.

24

'If everyone here is awake I would like to discuss something dear to your hearts; Bolivian Marching Powder, Charlie, Chinese Sky Candy, Sugar Doves, or whatever your favourite name is for certain illegal narcotics. Our plan this morning is to explore the impact of this highly lucrative illicit trade on the world economy.'

Professor Colin Trenched always struggled to interest his students during a Monday morning economics lecture, but talking about illegal narcotics appeared to do the trick.

'Most of this class is crack heads, Professor.'

'Thank you Douglas, I'm sure you're wrong, however, I will alert the Vice Chancellor as a simple precaution. Quick recap then on how we got to where we are today. Humans have been farming - we think - for around twelve thousand years, before then any increase in the human population depended solely on the availability of wild food. By three thousand years ago, we had reached a standard of living, based on discovering most of the necessities in life, the wheel, medicine, architecture, weights and measures, money etc. From then on, not a lot happened to improve the lifestyle of the average person, until much later. A day labourer living two thousand years before the birth of Christ was no worse off than a labourer living in the 1700's.'

The Treaty

'Excuse me Professor, what's a day labourer?'

'It's a fair description of what you will eventually be called Douglas, when the only job you can get is flipping burgers at MacDonald's.'

The lecture room erupted in roars of laughter, while Douglas sat cringing with embarrassment at his idiot questions.

'A day labourer, for the benefit of anyone else unfamiliar with this expression, is what most of us become in this modern age. Anyone who is not self-employed and receives a fixed salary or wage can be described as a day labourer. Returning to the mid-to-late seventeen hundreds the standard of living in most "civilized" parts of the world began to show a year on year improvement for all classes of the population, continuing to this day. Does anyone here know the reason why? OK, I will accept this deathly silence as a no. Well, yippee-doodad, join the club because the best economists in the world do not know either.'

'Could it be anything to do with compound interest?'

'Thank you Douglas, a gem of wisdom, there is life between those shoulders. Certainly if you had started investing in stocks and shares in the eighteen hundreds, continuously re-investing the profits; you would be very rich indeed. Despite numerous recessions, wars and major depressions, if you plot a graph you will see an almost continuous upward curve. Economists like Keynes tried to figure out the growing standard of living seventy years ago. D.N. McCloskey called it "the heart of the matter" and said the answer was twelve, and that real income per head exceeded what it was in 1780, in countries that have experienced modern economic growth - by this factor twelve. The question now is where this initial flow of investment capital came from. Can anyone tell me?'

The students looked at Professor Trenched with puzzled faces.

'Anyone at all OK, well obviously there were numerous sources. Slavery being one gave a boost to the western economies and by the eighteen thirties the British had become the leading drug-trafficking organization in the world. Building on their success the East India Company made a new industry out of controlling the manufacture and processing of opium in India and shipping it to China, swapping it for tea and other goods to export back to Europe and America. At the end of the East India Company monopoly entrepreneurs and buccaneers moved onto the scene. Scottish opium dealer William Jardine teamed with friend James Matheson to found the multi-million dollar Jardine Matheson Group or Jardine Group, check them out on Google they still exist as a very legitimate business. People like these pioneered the money laundering methods used by modern drug dealers today, investing the profits through legitimate insurance and banking businesses. It is by no co-incidence, that the HSBC Bank, formally known as the "Hong Kong Shanghai Bank" started life in the exact same place as this Mecca for drugs. Nothing these companies were doing was illegal in Britain. However, the Chinese Government had banned the import of Opium. Jardine and Matheson successfully built a property and banking empire and it is possible your own parents have funds invested in these very businesses via their pension funds. They were not alone and today dozens - maybe hundreds of rich Europeans and Americans owe the roots of their fortunes to narcotics. If you could calculate the value of their original investment in today's money, with the added interest, it's easy to understand how this huge snowball of cash will have played a vital part in building the conglomerates in America and Europe.'

'Excuse me, Professor. Are you saying we sell drugs to China now, today?'

The Treaty

Trudy Shupe was a feisty young American student and not afraid to voice her opinion, usually leading to a clash with Colin Trenched.

'Of course not Trudy, I will explain a little clearer. As we speak, there is an estimated four hundred billion dollars of US bills in circulation around the world; only one hundred billion of these remain in the USA. Just imagine the compound affect if cash earned through the sale of narcotics is being used to buy shares in the world's top performing companies over a long period; say two hundred years. Why would any sane government have wanted to stop this happening? Yes, Trudy.'

'Professor, three weeks ago at a lecture you told me to disregard conspiracy theories and this sounds just like one. What has happened in between to make you change your mind?'

'If the facts change Trudy, then I am entitled to change my opinions. I cannot tell you the exact detail, but let us just say a suspicion I once held that a drugs cartel or treaty existed between our two countries - is firmly back on the agenda. It remains as logical now for governments to control the sale and distribution of narcotics for the same reason they wish to control oil, gas or any such commodity. OK, I can see from your faces that this morning has been challenging so we will stop for the day. If anyone else has further questions about this lecture, then please call at my office. Thank you and see you all bright and early next Monday.'

25

Trudy ran to the café to meet with Brett and her friends. She had taken up Professor Trenched's offer of a discussion back at his room where she asked him more questions about the treaty. He had not been as forthcoming as she hoped only saying the reason he changed his mind could be due to new evidence he had recently come across making it possible that a narcotics treaty really did exist.

Trudy lived in London with her parents, where they occupied a three-storey house close to Governor Square. Her father Tom Shupe worked for the US Government and came to London through his job in Washington, holding the official title of 'US Trade Representative' that covered a multitude of sins. Inside the café, Brett was sitting close to a blonde girl from their group at the LSE. Changing her mind Trudy decided this was a good opportunity to leave, and collecting her books together, gave Brett a peck on the cheek then addressed the gathering with a cheery, 'Sorry people I have to go home for dinner with the parents, you know how it is when you're a sad person living at home. See you all tomorrow.'

'Lightweight,' Brett jeered as she sashayed toward the exit.

Spinning around, she extended her index finger. 'Swivel on this dick head!'

Hailing a black cab, she prepared for another stressful evening. Having promised her mother faithfully to be there for dinner and try to make peace with her father. They had not spoken for several days since she came home smashed out of her head, and spent most of the night in the bathroom throwing up. Trudy regarded Tom Shupe as an opinionated and obnoxious man, who expected her to get married and have kids in the same way as her mother and his own mother before him. He kept constantly banging on about why she did not get together with Brett, whose father worked with him at the Embassy. Trudy had known Brett from High School in Washington. His only ambition then, as now, was to get laid, and anyway they would have to wait and see what she did for herself.

'Hi Mom, I'm home, is Daddy back yet?'

'Hi honey, you're early, is everything okay? Daddy's downstairs.'

Trudy dropped her bag in the hall and made her way down the stairs to her father's office. She decided on the way home to make up with him as soon as she arrived ensuring the rest of the evening was spent reasonably civilized. The house, in a fashionable London square, had a large basement area with a separate entrance leading out onto a small cobbled mews. More than 100 years ago, this basement would have been the sole domain of staff, a cook, maid and probably a live-in butler. Her father had converted the pantry into an office where he kept his computer and work files. She cautiously poked her head through the half open door.

'Daddy, can I talk with you for a minute? I need to ask you about a lecture we had today.'

Tom Shupe stopped what he was doing at the keyboard and turned to face his daughter. He too was eager for normal relations; she rarely asked his advice and assumed this was by way of an apology. 'Hi honey, great to see you're home. Are you staying with us for dinner?'

She walked across the room and sat down on one of the chairs close to her father. 'Yes I said I would be home this evening. Daddy, our lecture today was with Professor Trenched, you know the guy, and I've spoken about him before.'

'Sure, you haven't been fighting with him again, have you?'

Trudy laughed. Usually she was ranting about his unreasonable manner toward her during lectures.

'No, we haven't been arguing this time, he was discussing narcotics and how they affect the global economy.'

'Trudy, that's not my area. It's been thirty years since I was at college.'

'Let me finish, please.'

Trudy was trying hard to be nice for once, so Tom decided to let her finish speaking. Her college work was new ground for them and he was keen to make it work.

'A few weeks ago I mentioned during a lecture about something I read on the net about a secret treaty that is supposed to have been signed between the Brits and the USA in the sixties...'

'Trudy, I think...'

She looked up at her father, and frowned.

'...No, I'm sorry, please carry on.'

'Anyway, as I was saying, this supposed treaty is unofficially to carve up all the main regions of the world where cocaine and opium are grown. He rubbished this, saying it was another conspiracy theory, and made me look like a complete idiot. Then today he spoke about something very similar, and may have evidence that it does actually exist, what is your view on this? Have you ever heard about the treaty?'

Tom tried to look calm, and thanks to his training managed to do this effectively. In one sentence, his daughter had described a secret he had spent most of his career trying to

The Treaty

keep quiet.

'Daddy have you been listening to me?'

'Yes, of course, honey. Trudy, my work takes me into different sectors of US Government; some of the stuff I come across is restricted information. I want to be honest with you and say that as far as I'm aware, nothing as comprehensive as that exists, but then I don't know everything. Did the Professor say he had any proof about this treaty, or was it coming from information he downloaded off the internet himself?'

'All he said was he had discovered something recently. He believes a significant proportion of the UK/US economy is underpinned by trading narcotics. Do you believe that's true, daddy?'

Tom Shupes primary task as senior CIA operative was his involvement in drugs. He spent a large part of his life coordinating deliveries and tracking unlicensed dealers. His job description was similar in many ways to the role played by an Administrator during the British colonial system in India. He worked with an elite group paid very well to perform their duties, and he did not intend to say anything that could rock the boat.

'Trudy, this man sounds like a bit of a clown to me, and I would take all this stuff with a-pinch-of-salt. Until someone comes up with real evidence it's just hearsay.'

'So Daddy, where does this leave me with Trenched? Do I blast him saying he's talking rubbish, or let it go?'

'If I were you, I would let it go. It's an issue so full of holes you could never plug all the gaps and make any sense of it to conclude, true or not.'

Trudy was disappointed, she had hoped for a killer fact, believing her father may have privileged information.

'I guess you're right, perhaps I should let it drop and move on. Thank you anyway, I've enjoyed our talk and hope you didn't mind my asking stupid questions.'

Tom smiled at his beautiful young daughter, and got up from his chair and embraced her as she stood up to leave the room.

'Sweetheart, of course I don't mind if you ask me a question, that's what I'm here for; you know you can always come to talk to me. Listen, I am sorry if I seem such a boring old dad usually, but I do love you and want to keep you safe.'

'I know that daddy, and sorry I behave so childishly sometimes, I promise there will be no more coming home drunk.'

Trudy headed for the door and Tom returned to his computer. She was halfway up the stairs when her mother called.

'If that's you, Trudy, tell your father dinner is going to be another ten minutes.'

Turning back to carryout her mother's instructions, she paused by the office door and could see he was on the phone.

'My daughter's college in London yes, Professor Trenched. He is that narcotic guru - has a lot of influence, especially with the UN. Okay Frank that's cool, good to speak with you too.'

Replacing the receiver Tom turned around and was surprised to see Trudy standing in the doorway.

'Trudy, honey, did you forget something?'

'Who were you talking to, daddy? I heard Trenched's name mentioned.'

'Oh just a colleague at work I was only gossiping. We didn't have much to talk about, so I told him the old treaty stories were still doing the rounds.'

'So you have heard about the treaty. I thought you said you knew nothing about it?'

'Not quite honey, I think I said there were many stories like this one doing the rounds. I was just saying to Frank they keep on re-surfacing, that is all.'

'Why did you specifically mention Professor Trenched and my University?'

'Trudy, honey, what's with the third degree, there was no particular reason - don't get all upset again. I was just gossiping about something with Frank.'

'Where is Frank, here in London? I haven't heard you mention his name before?'

'Sweetheart, why are you making such a big thing of this? I had to talk to Frank in New York, that's all, and I just finished off the conversation with your little story, nothing sinister at all.'

Trudy had the one important thing in common with all her other sisters on the planet, an innate sense that told her when any man was lying. She could not put her finger on why this would be, but she knew he was not telling the truth.

'Mom said to tell you dinner is in ten minutes.'

She turned to leave and ran up the stairs to the lounge.

'What have you and Daddy been discussing, Trudy?'

'Oh, some boring old stuff from Uni, not very interesting.'

'From where darling, where's Uni? That is not what they call your college now, is it?'

'No Mom, it is what the British guys call University. The name of my college is The London School of Economics.'

'Oh, so if it's a college, why do they call it the "school" of economics, then?'

'Mom, it's not important, OK, let me just wash my hands and then I will be back to help you with the dinner.

26

'Come on, Andy, you can't spend the rest of your life in that apartment. You have to socialize sometime. Trenched wants us to join him for dinner - the student party is optional, okay?'

Cousin James had been sending Andy texts and emails, and was now on the phone trying to persuade him to go to an LSE party.

'James, I have to give a presentation the following morning to a really important client, I can't afford to cock-it-up.'

'Listen, where's your presentation taking place?'

'Oh, it's at the Strand Palace Hotel.'

'For Christ's sake, that's only a minutes' walk. Stay the night in the hotel. You will be there in the morning and feeling as fresh as a daisy. Please come, it will be fun. It was you who wanted to meet Colin in the first place.'

Andy began to feel guilty; James had done him the favour of arranging a meeting with Colin Trenched.

'OK,' Andy sighed. 'Dinner and then I am back to the hotel. I have to prepare, this is a million dollars worth of equipment we're talking about here.'

'Perfect, I will let him know you are coming. I must go, I've got to get back to a meeting, ciao.'

It had been over four weeks now since Maria's death. Her funeral had taken place in Buenos Aires in private he did not even know the exact date. News of Barris Vaughan's conviction of her murder and the rape of the little girl in Vientiane appeared in the national press and he faced execution by firing squad. Since returning from Laos, Andy had thrown himself into work doing everything he possibly could to block out the events of the past few weeks. The dinner with Trenched will he thought, be cathartic, if only to hear finally the treaty saga was historic bullshit. Catching a train into London along with hundreds of tired looking commuters, he was ever thankful this was not part of his daily routine. With a meeting planned for 9.30am, in a hotel foyer close to Liverpool Street station, he did not have a lot of time. His clients were two Nigerian men planning a new telecoms business in Lagos. They had excellent credentials and were confident of placing a large order eventually. After they had finished, he decided to head straight over to the hotel and start getting things ready for tomorrow's presentation. He had all afternoon to prepare for the demonstration, and make other support calls. The Strand Palace was not that far from where he was in Liverpool Street, and they granted an early check-in. He passed the afternoon in the room, phoning colleagues in the US, who were arriving for work, and testing circuits he planned to show his customer the next day. At one particular stage, painful memories were disturbed when he logged onto the Laos switch, located only a few miles from where Maria died.

Andy had brought smart casual clothes with him as James instructed and, no longer able to concentrate on work, he decided to take a shower and get ready for dinner with Colin Trenched. He arranged to meet with James for a preliminary drink at a nearby pub called Ye Olde White Horse in Aldwych. According to James, students were not welcome making it an ideal venue, then afterwards they could walk around to the restaurant. Pacing the few hundred metres, James was already standing on the pavement in front of the pub.

His cousin gave a grin as he approached, and extended his arms ready to greet him. 'Hi Cous, my God you are looking good - lost some weight by the looks of you. This meal is just what you need.'

'You look pretty good yourself, for an old man,' Andy sneered.

The two-year age gap used to make a difference when they were children, and now Andy did not miss an opportunity to milk it. Moving inside the pub, James ordered a couple of pints from the bar and they sat at a free table.

'I was about to ask how you are, but I can only imagine you feel like shit.'

'No problem, James, I'm okay. As well, as can be expected as they say under the circumstances. I am trying to get on with my life. It's the only thing I can do, you know, move on.'

'So, this guy that attacked Maria, what is happening to him? Will he be brought back to the UK?'

'He's already been found guilty and will be executed anytime soon.'

'Too bloody right the bastard, sooner and the better.'

James went on to describe excruciating punishments Barris Vaughan deserved, before realizing how painful the subject still was for Andy.

'Sorry, mate, I'll shut up.'

'It's okay James. Hey, before I forget, I have been meaning to thank you for your introduction to Colin. He explained a few things about the documents saying he could understand why governments had a desire to control the global distribution of narcotics, and found it interesting what I was telling him, but he didn't think it could be proved one way or the other unless there was any credible evidence to support the theory.'

The Treaty

'What do you plan to do now? Why don't you just forget all about that nonsense and try to put it all behind you.'

'Maybe I should, it would make sense. There is nothing in it for me, anyway.'

He was almost completely in agreement with James, however, there was still a part of him that had a desire to find out more but he did not feel now was the right time to discuss his ideas in any detail. Leaving the pub, the two men walked toward the restaurant. James knew exactly where it was and entered first. Trenched sat facing the door, he chose a table for four by the window; and was talking to a woman sat with her back to them. As soon as Trenched spotted his guests he began waving manically, causing other diners to turn round. Trying hard to appear inconspicuous as possible, James led the way weaving among tables and quickly sitting down.

Marion Gubler was in her late forties, and was a visiting Professor at the LSE on a one-year exchange from Harvard. Calling the waiter Colin ordered wine and they chose from the menu. During the meal, Andy spoke to Marion asking about her work. A mathematician involved in pure research, sharing Colin Trenched's interest in narcotics. A recent research grant from the UN provided funding for her to produce a mathematical model estimating the global size of the illegal narcotics industry and to assess its impact on world economics. He was fascinated to learn they were analyzing data recorded by the East India Company, during their Opium trading days and projecting this model into modern times. Trenched explained to Marion, it was as a result of a discussion about the treaty with his Cousin James that he was first introduced to Andy. Marion began to give her view on the same topic.

'My father worked with Colonel Oliver North, who was implicated in a major enquiry during the eighties and early nineties. Daddy was not accused of handling drugs, although, he still had to defend himself against the rumours.'

She went on to tell them about claims against government agencies, and some US banks, that the same war machine used to defeat communism in Latin America, became fully integrated into the Colombia-based regional cocaine trade. Suspicions surrounded Oliver North's operations believed to be bringing tons of drugs into the United States.

'Did anyone produce the evidence?' asked Andy

'No, it all became so convoluted,' Marion replied. 'There were newspaper exposés and enquiries. George Bush Senior and Sir Henry Kissinger came out of it unscathed.'

James looked surprised. 'I didn't know Kissinger had been knighted? When did that happen - he is American?'

Colin jumped in, expressing his dislike of the honours system and royalty in general. 'James, you should read the newspapers; he has been a "Sir" since the mid nineties he was knighted by the Queen at Buckingham Palace. One of the few top honours we Brits hand out to Johnny Foreigner, I can't imagine what he had to do to get it.'

Laughing at his joke, Marion was not offended. 'I can assure you guys, you've had your monies worth from Dr Kissinger, he has been a close friend to the UK for a very long time.' She turned her attention back to Andy. 'Tell me what has made you so interested in this treaty saga do you know something the rest of us don't?'

Andy shook his head. 'No, not really, it is just within the space of a few weeks, several bad things have happened in my life and the subject of the treaty keeps cropping up. I would just like to get to the bottom of what has been going on, if anything at all.'

'I'm sorry Andy, I didn't mean to be insensitive, and Colin did tell me about your girlfriend.'

Trying to lighten the atmosphere Colin boomed out, possibly without thinking. 'Watch this space I am pretty certain

The Treaty

I know who has the authentic documents.' Marion looked surprised. 'Go on then, fill us in Colin, we need to know by the end of the evening.'

'If I told you, I would have to kill you,' he joked while making a sideways glance in Andy's direction.

Seeing Andy's discomfort, James jumped in with a cash offer.

'Listen, why don't I pay the bill and we can make our way around to the party. Come on, Andy, just for a couple of hours, it will be fun!'

27

'Who's that gorgeous guy with James?'
  'I don't see where you're looking.'
  'Over by the bar, doom brain.'
  'Trudy, he's at least forty and probably gay.'
  'Don't be so stupid, Brett, he's not a day over thirty. James is only thirty-six.'
  'I bet you twenty bucks that guy is over thirty-five, and the last woman he slept with was his mother.'
  'Now you're just being homophobic. Do you have a fear about your own sexuality or something?'
  'Jesus, Trudy, shut up! You talk a load of shit. I am just saying that man is probably gay - in my opinion, OK.'
  'Calm down! I'm going to find out, and then you can pay me the twenty dollars you owe me.'
  'Trudy, sit down! Don't forget your promise; you're staying with me tonight at my place.'
  'I'm going to say hello, not invite him to have sex. Let me passed, you dick-wad.'
  'I know what you're like, the minute you spot someone different they become a challenge and you have to have them. Trudy, promise that is not going to happen tonight?'
  'I can't promise anything, who knows what may happen when I'm drunk?'
  'You little bitch. You promised if I came here with you

The Treaty

we could spend the whole night together at my place.'

'Well, I'm sorry, I lied! A bit like you did at Christmas. The minute I was out the country, you were inside that tart Linda's knickers. Told me a few lies too, remember?'

Pushing her way passed Brett, to noisy cheers of support from their friends clustered together around the same beer soaked table. She went to greet James and his friend.

'Hey James, remember me?'

He turned to face Trudy. 'Oh, no!' he laughed. 'You're that very annoying American girl with the awkward questions when I gave a guest lecture last term on public sector economics.'

'Hey, that's not very nice.'

James laughed and greeted her with a peck on the cheek. 'How are you, still terrorising lecturers?'

'I'm doing my best,' she grinned mischievously.

'Andy, this is Trudy - she's a walking nightmare.'

'Hi Andy, listen, I know this is rude and very non-British, but I have a bet with a friend that you are not over thirty-five and not gay. It's worth about ten pounds if I win and then the drinks are on me. What do you say?'

Taken aback, he began laughing. 'Well, it looks like you've won. I'm thirty four and strictly a one Willy in the bed man.'

With a high-five, she shouted "YES", and rushed back to Brett demanding her winnings. They watched as he reluctantly paid-up, grumbling that he thought Andy was lying. Trudy returned with the promised beers, and after that, the alcohol began to take affect. Losing his inhibitions Andy started to enjoy the evening.

'Let's dance! Come on, Andy, and show me how it's done.'

Gripping the chair, adamant he did not dance, Trudy's noisy persuasion made him let go. A friend of Trudy appeared on cue to take care of James, who showed no resistance. Once on the floor it was back to the 1980's, catching up with reggae and the rude boy scene. She avoided glares from Brett, who seeing Andy's dance moves was even more convinced than ever that he was a gay.

'Quick!' Trudy cried, looking suddenly pale. 'I need air or I will pass-out. I have to go outside.'

Pushing through dancing students, she ran for the exit followed closely by Andy. A rich intake of oxygen temporarily brought relief from the nausea, causing her to stagger from the head-rush. Taking her arm for support, they leaned against a pavement safety barrier by the roadside.

'Oh my God, I'm so embarrassed; you must think I am a drunken idiot.'

'Don't worry, just stay still until the dizzy feeling passes and you should feel better? Where do you live?'

'Near Grosvenor Square,' she slurred, looking uncomfortably intoxicated, 'but I can't go home like this. Will you look after me?' Her eyes rolled and Andy grabbed hold of her arm.

'Look, no offence, is there a friend you can stay with instead? I can get you a taxi, it's no problem.'

'I can look after myself, thank you!' she shouted pulling away and staggering backwards. 'I'm perfectly capable; I don't need your pathetic taxi service!'

As she turned around it was too late to avoid rubbish bags left at the edge of the pavement, and tripping over the first plastic sack fell into the middle of the pile. Unable to stand upright, Andy helped her back to her feet. Fortunately, it was all dry waste; mainly paper and she emerged unscathed apart from a bruised ego.

'I'm just a homeless bag-lady!' she screamed dusting down her skirt.

Unsure what to do, Andy considered running inside and fetching one of her friends.

The Treaty

Trudy squatted down and held her head in her hands. 'My father is going to kill me,' she muttered, as she began to weep.

Worried about leaving her on her own he felt obliged to help. 'Okay, you can stay in my hotel room. However, you have to be quiet and leave early in the morning. I've got an important business meeting.'

Now looking brighter she nodded vigorously. 'I'll be as quiet as a little mouse, promise.' She used a slurred squeaky voice to imitate a mouse, and her hand to demonstrate how very small a mouse she would become. 'I'll be very, very quiet. You will forget I'm even there, and then I will be gone in the morning before you even wake up.'

From her drunken state, he doubted this would happen, and he presumed she could leave after breakfast. It did not make a lot of difference, he always had a double room and there were two separate beds. Making their way on foot to the hotel, with his arm around her waist for support, Andy called out goodnight to a bemused concierge. Taking the elevator up to his room, he let go of her to press the button and she immediately collapsed to the floor. Helping her to her feet, the elevator doors slid open and he dragged her down the corridor and swung open the door to room 305.

'My God, everything is spinning!' Trudy cried. 'I'm going to be sick!'

Now up on her feet she rushed for the toilet. Andy closed the door behind her and waited patiently for the inevitable hacking noises to begin, and then he unexpectedly heard a loud crash.

'Trudy, what is happening are you okay?'

Hearing no reply, he had visions of her lying on the floor choking in a pool of vomit.

'Trudy, are you all right? Listen, I'm coming in.'

Thankfully, she had not locked the door, and peering inside he immediately saw her sprawled on the floor, sending him into a panic.

'Trudy, wake-up, you'll choke!'

Showing no sign of life, he lightly slapped her face a few times and her eyes sprung open. She began wiping the vomit dribbling from around her lips.

'People die like this, how the hell did you get into this state?'

'Shut up, I want to die. Just leave me alone!'

'I'm not leaving you here. Come on, get up, where's your skirt gone?'

'It's in the bath. I was sick all over it. Take my T-shirt off, it stinks.'

Trying to avoid touching the vomit as he pulled the top over her head, Andy tossed the garment into the bathtub.

'Stop looking at me, pervert! Leave me here, I want to die.'

'Don't be so stupid and cover yourself up, use a towel or something.'

Helping her stand, Andy held the bath towel around her as they staggered over to the bed, and with a gentle push, she fell down onto the mattress and almost immediately went to sleep. Covering her over he went back into the chaos of the bathroom, and rinsing the vomit off her skirt and T-shirt hung them across the shower curtain rail to dry.

Shattered after the evening's excitement, he found water in the mini bar and relaxed at his desk. Hearing Trudy's shallow breathing he smiled at the disastrous end to his evening. With preparations to make for tomorrows meeting he idly checked his email, but his thoughts quickly turned to Maria, how he missed her so much. He blamed himself for Maria's death, for leaving her in the hotel - for taking her to Laos in the first place. The cocktail of alcohol and tiredness was taking its toll, making him feel melancholy. Heading back to the bathroom, he decided he needed sleep.

28

Colin Trenched's routine was always the same when he attended a college party; he would socialize for a while with staff and students before making a subtle exit. James and Andy had been preoccupied on the dance floor and Marion was engaged in deep conversation with a mature student, so this time he had been able to slip away unnoticed. Outside in the street he joined other late night Londoners making their way home. Waving his long gangly arm in the direction of a passing cab, he stood patiently as it made a swift u-turn and screeched to a halt beside him. Climbing in the back, he shouted his address to the cabbie as they sped away. Colin had lived alone in the same three-storey house in South London since his partner Michael passed away on March 11, 1989. Often lonely he had never met anyone else, concentrating on his research and teaching students. Property values had soared in the area of South London where he lived, and sometimes he even thought about retiring and moving nearer old friends in rural Oxfordshire, or perhaps to somewhere with a warmer climate. The problem was he loved his work at the University, and the authorities there seemed happy for him to continue.

As the taxi sped across Waterloo Bridge, he began to feel an old urge returning, possibly stimulated by the alcohol.

Already after midnight, he tapped the window separating himself from the driver as they reached the vicinity where he lived and asked him to pull over. He did not feel tired and planned to walk the last half a mile to his front door, taking a route across Clapham Common. Throughout the day, this green space provided 220 acres of land, where children could fly kites and joggers and cyclists compete to stay fit. At nighttime, it attracted a very different activity, and known to Colin as a notorious venue for casual sex.

Despite the obvious risk to his personal safety and, for reasons he could not understand, he made his way down the unlit pathway. The day had been warm, and the evening atmosphere made sticky from rising humidity. Clouds were hiding an almost full moon making it difficult to see well ahead. Despite this handicap, Colin picked up the sound of someone approaching then could see it was a lone male coming from the opposite direction. As the distance between them narrowed, he slowed his pace until they were close enough for eye contact. Without speaking a word, the stranger veered off the path and went toward a clump of bushes; both men understood this procedure and he immediately followed. Obscured by vegetation and near total darkness, Colin paused and looked around. Where had he gone? Just as he was about to look elsewhere, it was too late to prevent a savage blow from behind as the man plunged an eight-inch steel knife up to the hilt between his shoulder blades. After a short pause followed by a series of animal-like gasping noises, he sank to his knees. The assailant repeated the attack one more time making sure Professor Colin Trenched was dead. Calmly cleaning the blade on the Professors own jacket the assailant rejoined a fellow accomplice waiting at the edge of the park.

29

Sharp needles of light stabbed Andy awake. Looking across to the bed next to him, he checked for movement, and felt satisfied Trudy had not suffocated during the night. Aware he had to finish off his presentation; he crept out of bed and made his way quietly into the bathroom anxious not to wake her. Pleased with the penetratingly sharp action of the power shower massaging his neck, he imagined purging the alcohol out through his skin. Feeling refreshed, he towelled himself dry and finished off with a shave, all the while checking in the mirror for any signs of premature deterioration. After many more nights like the previous one, he thought he would age twenty years in no time.

Dressing casually, deciding he would change into his suit later after Trudy had left. He powered up his laptop and checked notes, modifying the presentation and making sure; he had not forgotten any important detail. Million dollar deals were scarce, and he was determined to make every effort to impress his potential customer. Later that same day in the afternoon, he planned to meet with the woman who helped him in Laos, Caroline Lovelace-Jones. He had received an email from her soon after arriving home in Britain, and had accepted her invitation to meet up. He wanted to thank her properly.

Stirring noises from Trudy preceded her becoming fully awake and sitting upright in bed. Andy turned away finishing off what he was doing only giving a short glance over his shoulder.

'Good morning young lady, welcome back to the land of the living.'

Flicking back the bed covers, she crawled on her hands and knees to the end of the bed and lay flat on her chest, with her head pointing toward him. At sometime during the night she had changed helping herself to a clean pair of his silk boxers taken from his over-night-bag.

'What are you doing? What time is it?'

Andy ignored the question. 'I've got an important meeting, remember,' he replied without looking away from the screen. 'You promised to leave early.'

With a groan, Trudy slid off the bed and with her arms folded tightly across her chest tiptoed over to where he was sitting and stood directly behind the chair resting on Andy's shoulders.

'What are those numbers for?' she asked, squinting at the glowing screen.

Struggling to concentrate, he tried to ignore the tingling sensation caused by her close proximity.

'How are you feeling? You were sick last night. Your skirt and top are in the bathroom, they should be dry.'

'I feel okay and thank you, Andy; you're very kind sorting out my clothes. Are you sure you're not gay?'

Reaching back, he lifted her elbows off his neck. 'I'll be deliriously gay when you leave. Get dressed and we can have breakfast.'

Thinking he was offended, she tried to backtrack. 'Sorry, I didn't mean that - I was thinking of the skirt, most of the men I meet wouldn't have bothered.'

'Trudy, my only concern is that you're out of here before my client arrives. I don't need extra hassle finding you something to wear.'

Ignoring these hints for her to get ready and leave, she danced from one foot to the other as if needing to pee. 'Is the air conditioning switched on in here, I'm freezing?'

'Trudy, please, I have a lot to do!'

'What did you say those numbers are for on the screen?'

Andy tapped the keypad with irritation, and turned to Trudy. 'They are calls being made using one of the telecom switches that I sell - go and get dressed.'

'Hey, a Montana code I might even know them.'

Andy was testing the switch and changing call rates.

'This is what I do for a living,' he sighed, 'and with your help, by leaving here soon, I'll probably sell another system.'

'Oops sorry, do you want me to leave? Am I holding you up? You did say I could stay for breakfast. I don't mind paying for myself.'

Andy blocked her out and continued with his work. Accepting defeat, Trudy skipped away into the bathroom. Relieved she had gone he tried to concentrate dismissing the imagery of her taking a shower. Then in what only seemed a few minutes she was back fully dressed. Despite the untidy hair and faint whiff of vomit, he could not help noticing how amazing she still looked. Smiling, scribbling her mobile number on a piece of paper, and helping herself to one his business cards scattered on the coffee table, she pecked him on the cheek and left.

30

Caroline suggested they meet at the original Tate Gallery along Millbank, not too far from Andy's hotel. His presentation had been a success, and he felt sure he had won the order. Finishing sooner than expected, he caught a taxi to the Tate and watched for her arrival from the top of the granite steps outside. Admiring the view of the River Thames, he spotted Caroline in the distance striding along the pavement with her perfectly groomed hair and full-length skirt almost brushing against the ground. She walked up the few steps and they met halfway.

'Sorry I'm late,' she called out to him. 'I was delayed by phone calls. I can't believe I live so close and I've kept you waiting.'

'There are worse places, its beautiful here.'

Caroline smiled and turned to face the Thames. 'Yes, I totally agree. When I'm staying in London I like to walk along the embankment and watch the boats pass by. Shall we go inside?'

They walked through the entrance and followed the signs downstairs to the restaurant. It was quiet at this time of day.

'So how's work?' Andy politely inquired. 'Have you had to travel anywhere else recently on your buying missions?'

For most of that day Caroline had been in meetings with

her boss, Sir Richard Parsons, to discuss their next move post Laos. Barris Vaughan had been a huge embarrassment, especially as he was British and a hired assassin. This revelation sent shockwaves through her people, who were convinced the killer was part of Fatima's organization; this discovery confirmed darker forces were at work. The police had still not found a motive for the husband and wife murder, which they now considered could have been to prevent publication of the treaty story. Sir Richard decided to take a risk, instructing Caroline to tell Andy the truth about her work and try to get him on side.

'I have not been totally honest with you about my work,' Caroline said, wiping her fingers on a napkin. 'I'm not really a buyer as I told you in Laos.'

He chuckled at this confession and started to tease. 'Let me guess, you're an international drug smuggler?'

She smiled, shaking her head, but then paused and looked suddenly serious. 'Andy, I work for a government agency in a special security division called MI-21.'

He laughed, presuming she was joking. Caroline looked more like Mary Poppins than a secret agent.'

'I'm telling you the truth. You have to believe me. I came out to Laos to keep watch on you and Maria, because of your friendship with Fatima. She is under British surveillance and is suspected of being connected with a major terrorist group in Spain.'

Andy dropped his smile he was having trouble taking this all in. 'How do you know about Fatima?'

'It's my job to know. We have been watching her now for some time.'

Confused, Andy blinked, completely thrown by the woman he had thought was sitting in front of him. 'Are you saying Fatima's people killed Maria?'

'No, that is precisely the reason I am telling you this. Maria was murdered by a psychotic killer who we think is working for another group and they could be based here in the UK. They may also want to harm you.'

This was shattering news. He dropped his shoulders and tried to take in the revelations, having not considered he was himself in any imminent danger.

'I have a second confession, which in some ways may be even harder for you to accept.' Caroline said cautiously. 'Andy, I am trying to be absolutely honest with you and get everything out into the open, then I will be asking for your help. It is possible I will be to blame for missing important clues that could have signaled Maria's killer was staying in the hotel. If I had been more vigilant and conducted, proper security checks on the other guests, he would have shown up as a suspect. The problem was I convinced myself we were looking for Fatima's people. I guess I got it wrong.'

Andy's temperament was explosive to say the least, and for several agonizing seconds he simmered like a volcano. Fearing they may have underestimated how he would react, Caroline started gathering her belongings in preparation for a quick exit.

'Shall we go somewhere less public?' she whispered, slipping off her chair.

Andy slammed down his fist and his eyes burned with rage. 'You've just told me Maria was murdered under your gaze, while you and your stupid colleagues knew we were both in danger. Then, casually let me go about my business as if nothing was happening - leaving that poor innocent girl to face a horrible agonizing death.'

Caroline darted eyes around the restaurant and made a feeble attempt to calm him down by reaching across and squeezing his hand, but Andy immediately yanked it away.

'For God's sake, why didn't you warn us in some way?' he screamed. 'I would never have left her! SHE WOULD BE ALIVE NOW?'

The Treaty

'Please, calm down, people are looking over.'

'I don't give a damn!'

'I'm sorry. Please, let's talk about this sensibly without shouting.'

Scraping his chair noisily across the floor, Andy jumped to his feet and stormed out of the restaurant. Tourists sitting at tables close by turned around and stared, as Caroline quickly paid the bill and chased after him. Exiting the gallery, she saw him disappear down the granite steps toward the main road. Wading through a party of schoolchildren, she removed her shoes and ran after him, displaying all the drama of a lover's tiff. Thankfully, he deliberately slowed before she completely ran out of breath.'

'Andy, wait, we have to keep calm! We need to talk! Please listen, my apartment is nearby. Let's go there and have a coffee and I can explain.'

Andy spun round on his heels. 'Calm is not an emotion I am feeling right now! Why the hell would I want to spend another second in your company?'

Caroline stopped running and slipped on her heels. 'It's more complicated than you think. Please! What happened may have been avoidable, although, with the benefit of hindsight we will never know. What we do know is if you were in any danger in Laos you must still be now and not just from Fatima, but also from someone else. Listen to me, these people are more dangerous as they believe you have the information they are trying to protect.'

Andy stopped walking backwards and stood in the middle of the pavement with his arms folded. Caroline reached out and attempted to take his hand again, but he sharply pulled it away.

'...Please,' she said softly, her blue watery eyes staring at him. 'You have to listen to me.'

Andy sighed. 'How far do you live from here, because I refuse to waste my day?'

'Close, only a few steps.'

'How close?'

'Just follow me.'

They turned down Page Street, a short distance from The Tate, and stopped outside a modern apartment block. Entering the building they passed a doorkeeper sat behind a desk, and walked through the lobby and up to her two-bed apartment. Decorated in whites and pastel shades it had a modern contemporary appearance. Shown into the bright sunny lounge, he sat on the same sofa shared by the Duchess of Cornwall and Sir Richard Parsons only a few weeks before.

'Would you like a coffee, or something stronger?'

'Coffee is fine.'

Andy seemed quiet, but she felt able to continue with their conversation - speaking as she boiled the kettle and prepared their drinks.

'I've listened and watched your interview with the police after Dominic and his wife was murdered,' she said stirring the drinks. 'You categorically denied copying any files from his computer. Andy, the police do not believe you. You have to tell me the truth.'

Anger flared again, and Andy stormed over to the kitchen. 'You must be out of your mind if you think I am going to tell you anything after what has happened. I don't even know who you really are! You could be working for Maria's killers for all I know.'

Winded by the force of his aggression, Caroline was a determined woman and was not about to give up over a few insults. 'Now you're talking like a real idiot. Funny as it might seem, I do actually care about what happens to you, Andy. You must understand you need protection - your life is in danger. If you work with my people, we will help you. All I need is for you to be honest and tell me anything you've found out from Fatima, Maria or Dominic,

The Treaty

and we can pool our knowledge and formulate a plan.'

'I don't understand what you think I have. What do you want me to do, make it up? It doesn't matter a damn if I know something or not, if these people are as clever as you say - they will find me eventually. How are you going to prevent anything happening?'

She knew he was right; she had to risk telling him more and convince him to work with her people.

'Andy, I am based mainly in Madrid,' she announced, handing him a cup of coffee, 'and we found out, ironically from Fatima, that she is searching for a secret document called the treaty. It may all be total rubbish, however, according to some people, including your friend Professor Trenched, this treaty is all part of a long running conspiracy theory saying that Britain and the USA is in cohorts, controlling world markets for heroin and cocaine. According to his literary agent, Dominic Marsh had a copy of a document and planned to publish a book, there are strong suspicions he was deliberately stopped, and anyone who gets even close to this story seems to end up dead.'

Andy frowned. 'How do you know Trenched?'

'He works for us. Trenched was turned several years ago after the Soviet block fell apart and when it was discovered he worked for the KGB.'

'You mean he was a spy?'

'Well, sort of, he was sharing information especially about narcotics. Trenched thought he was doing us all a favour involving the Russians, what he didn't know was this intelligence was being handed over to the Russian drug dealing Mafia.'

Andy privately recalled earlier conversations with Asang in Vientiane, who had lived in Russia and had told him the Mafia was well acquainted with the treaty.

'Why wasn't he prosecuted and sent to prison?'

'He decided to become an agent for us,' Caroline replied,

sitting down on the sofa. 'We needed to know exactly what the people at the UN were really up to.'

'When did you last meet with the Professor?' Andy asked, unsure if Trenched had told her about the meeting, where he had confessed to seeing a copy of the treaty.

'At a special security conference at the Palace of Westminster, both Fatima and you were mentioned in the discussions.'

'But you have not met with him since?'

Caroline shook her head. 'No, but I know you have. Why did you go to see him?'

'It was a private matter; I was introduced to Trenched by a friend of mine.'

'Andy, tell me the truth. Did you go there to find out more about the documents you discovered on Dominic Marsh's computer?'

Feeling isolated, he desperately wanted to share the information he had stumbled across in Laos about Princess Diana, and the documents Mardjono gave to her. He wanted to believe Caroline's sincerity, while common sense told him to stay silent.

'Listen, there's nothing more I can tell you that is of any use. You sound as if you know everything already.'

'Andy, we need your help. The only logical reason Fatima was so interested in you is that she believed you found something on Dominic's computer. I only want the truth.'

'Thanks, and I thought she just wanted me for my body.'

'Three lives have been lost, for Christ's sake. If you are keeping anything back, it may inadvertently protect the murderers. I believe we can work together and get to the bottom of exactly what happened to Maria, and why she died.'

Hearing the sincerity in her voice, Andy mellowed considerably from when he first arrived at the apartment. He stood up as if preparing to leave placing his empty cup on a small coffee table. I really don't think there is anything I can do to help you further. I am sorry if you feel I am not co-operating, I want to believe you mean well Caroline. It took courage to tell me about the situation in Laos. I just don't think I should get involved anymore than I already am.'

'Andy, if the treaty does exist, how would you feel about the families of innocent young soldiers and civilians being killed in wars, being perpetrated to defend our market share and control of narcotics industries around the world. How are the families and survivors going to feel when they know the truth?'

Andy sat down again next to Caroline on the sofa. 'Sorry, I don't understand, what has that got to do with all this?'

'Think it through, this could be the reason why the USA and Britain are so keen to be involved in places like Afghanistan, which is the source for over 80% of the heroin and other opiate based drugs sold in Europe and America. Who manufactured and supplied some of the best opium in the world for over one hundred and fifty years?'

Andy stared down at the wooden floor shaking his head. 'I don't know.'

'India!'

'India?'

'Yes, under the control of the British. The illegal narcotics industry is worth billions of dollars each year, it is almost as valuable as oil. The treaty may prove who is really behind this war - not this current generation of duped politicians, but sinister people who rule the west, and who have secretly been in charge for decades.'

'Now you're talking bullshit.' Andy laughed, jumping back to his feet. 'No politician, however stupid, could sanction that. We live in a democracy remember, with a free press, they would be exposed in seconds.'

'It is a lot more complicated than that - drug trafficking and revenue from opium in particular is embedded deep within our economy. They would find it almost impossible to unravel the evidence. It is not difficult to persuade even the most committed socialist they are doing the right thing, particularly when whole economies are at stake. You only have to look at the way our politician's rollover whenever there's a moral dispute with the Saudis that might endanger lucrative defense contracts.'

'I have to say Caroline, there is one thing I can now be sure of, and you've bought into this conspiracy big time. However, I am still not so convinced that working with you guys is worth placing myself in the firing line, when it may eventually turn out to be all to do with politicians trying to cover their arses.'

'What do you mean, do think we are just making this whole saga up for a bit of fun?'

'No, I'm certain you're convinced something is going on. However, from what you just said about wars and our troops in the Middle East, I suspect the same people who sent our soldiers to Afghanistan are now looking for a scapegoat and as if by magic, they have discovered this secret treaty. Suddenly it all becomes the fault of a bunch of dead guys for us fighting wars we should never have started in the first place.'

'Yes, Andy, but not all these men are dead and what if they still work behind the scenes making decisions and are responsible for killing innocent people?'

'And for that you need proof - and there isn't any. How convenient to blame people preferably the ones that can't fight back.'

Caroline was now on her feet and knew she was losing the argument. 'Who do you have in mind?' she asked.

'Well, I was waiting for you to mention names - one of the Royals, maybe? They're pretty defenseless when it comes to conspiracies.'

'For you to suggest that, Andy, you must know more about this than you admit.'

Believing he had said enough and was in danger of revealing too much information, he decided to leave.

'I have to go now. I am still very grateful to you for helping me in Laos, and appreciate this is a difficult situation for you, professionally speaking. You have a job to do and I must remember that.'

Moving to one side holding the door open, she knew she could not force him to work with them, or hand over any information he might have stumbled across. Saying goodbye, he held eye contact for a brief moment then walked out of the door. Marching toward Millbank Road, he deliberately avoided looking back and never expected to meet with her ever again.

Taking a taxi to Baker Street, he went over in his mind the discussion with Caroline and the shocking revelation she knew that both he and Maria were under some kind of threat. She had independently reached the same conclusion that maybe the treaty did exist. He was playing the devils advocate in trying to destroy her theory while secretly knowing it was probably correct. However, he could not discount his own explanation. Certain politicians fighting for survival would use dirty tricks and the treaty may be their invention to mask major international cock-ups. All conspiracies contain an element of the truth and perhaps in the past some treaty did exist to control markets for narcotics. Now unscrupulous individuals had seized on what is in reality history and used this as a cover-up.

Arriving at Baker Street station, Andy originally planned to take the Metropolitan line back to his apartment in Chalfont & Latimer. Changing his mind at the last minute he decided on the faster more modern Chiltern Line at mainline Marylebone Station. Leaving the cab, he made use of a side exit, crossed over to Melcombe Street where he bought an evening newspaper and idly scanned the front page as he paid at the counter.

LSE Professor found dead
Two men appeared in court today accused of murdering Professor Colin Trenched, a University Professor from the London School of Economics. Unemployed Gary Evans, 28, and builder Brian Westwood, 35, arrested on Monday night, appeared at South Western magistrates' court in Clapham East London, and spoke only to confirm their name, date of birth and say they were of no fixed abode. There was no application for bail and the two men were remanded in custody to appear at the Old Bailey at a date still to be confirmed........................

Stunned, Andy moved out of the way of pedestrians as he read the article and tried to absorb the shocking news.

...................Professor Trenched, 68, was killed on Clapham Common as he walked home. A colleague at the London School of Economics, Professor Marion Gubler, said they were all very shocked by what had happened, and academic colleagues and students would miss him. 'He made an important contribution to the understanding of economics and the affect of illegal narcotics on the global economy'. The professor worked internationally both here and in the USA, addressing private select committees in Washington and London...... Police are still appealing for witnesses.

At first Andy found himself doubting it could even be the same person, it seemed impossible. Hearing the ringtone of his cellphone, he snapped back to reality answering the call.

'It's Trudy, can you talk?'

'Yes'

'I was calling to find out if you've heard about Professor

The Treaty

Trenched. Brett just phoned and told me he is dead.'

'I know, I'm reading the paper now I'm stunned.'

'He must have gone to Clapham Common after the party. Andy, it's terrible, the poor man.'

'Trudy, where are you now? I desperately need to talk to someone.'

'I'm at my parent's house near Grosvenor Square. Where are you?'

'Marylebone Station. Can we meet as soon as possible?'

'Yes, yes, of course, no problem. Are you going to be OK?'

Andy rubbed his temple. 'I'm fine. Look, there's an All Bar One in Paddington Street. I'll wait for you outside.'

31

'Mom, just going to my room to make a call, then I am out to meet a friend. I may be back late.'

'All right honey, are you meeting Brett?'

'Yes, later.'

Trudy went to her room, closed the door and flicked open a laptop computer. Plugging in a special device, the same as used by the CIA for ultra secure conversations, she connected to a VoIP phone. Only one other person could accept her call. Hitting the button she began speaking, certain she was connected.

'Listen, they have killed another one - Professor Trenched. He was one of my lecturers at the LSE. Andy had been speaking to him hours before.'

'Baby this is bad news - you have to make sure you arrange to see his apartment soon - anything could happen to him. There is not much time left before they track him down. What was it like at the hotel?'

'I was a little too drunk, he wouldn't take the bait.'

'Trudy, you're losing your touch.'

'I managed to install the keystroke logger onto his laptop. Shall I send the IP address details?'

'Yes, baby, do not email use FTP direct to my server - only encrypted data, you understand?'

'Yes, of course. Still missing me?'

The Treaty

'All the time, we will be together again very soon.'
'OK, love you.'
'Love you too baby, good luck.'

Trudy unplugged the phone, placed it back in its hiding place behind the wardrobe and then secured her computer. She took a quick shower and thought about Fatima, and how pleased she sounded with her progress. The hot water prickled, sending a sensual shiver from her head to her toes and reminding her of the good times they had spent together. They met in Washington when Trudy was eighteen at a special political function she attended with her father. Guests, mainly diplomats from various embassies in Washington, had to be entertained, he asked her to look after a Moroccan official's daughter called Fatima. She remembered how beautiful she looked, and how the men had fallen over themselves to meet with them both. Even her father openly flirted. His boss, a leading US Senator, gave Fatima a card and asked for help with some translation work; saying it could benefit her later in life when she needed to live or work in the USA. They even arranged to meet up at her hotel before she left the US. Just two years later Fatima returned to Washington, this time as an official Arabic translator for a UN delegation. Her Daddy's boss, now Fatima's friend, had kept his promise. Despite a colourful security profile, she travelled freely on a diplomat passport. Fatima contacted her almost as soon as she arrived, and they arranged to meet. Trudy talked about her father's disastrous political career, with the possibility they would all have to leave the USA for a while and go to Europe. Tom Shupe and his boss were involved in an election scandal and narcotics deals going back to the 1980's. His boss, the Senator, Fatima's friend, was accused of trading crack cocaine in exchange for weapons.

Deciding they both needed a girl's night out she suggested a bar that did cheap cocktails. It mainly attracted gay and lesbian customers, Trudy felt safe in this environment and free from hassle by men. Fatima rarely drank alcohol, and as the cocktails flowed, their inhibitions went out of the window and they finished the night together at her hotel. Talking about their lives and Fatima's early days living in Paris and Marrakech, she told Trudy about the death of her husband Philippe and their baby daughter. This had come as a surprise to Trudy, but she soon understood when Fatima explained that life, as a single woman in her society was not an option. She loved her husband and baby and told how her life had been destroyed by something she called 'the treaty'. Hearing this tragic story, made her want to help her new friend to find the truth. She was also becoming very serious about the Muslim religion and listened intently when Fatima spoke about her faith, believing she shared so many of the same beliefs and values. In reality, she knew deep down the main attraction was that Fatima's life was exciting, and being involved in covert operations provided a way to get back at her father for all the hurt he caused.

32

Paddington Street was a short walk for Andy; he quickly found the bar and decided to sit outside. It had been another warm day as throngs of office workers arrived for a beer before setting off home to commuter land. With a cold pint in his hand, Andy managed to grab an empty table and with a clear view of the road he would see Trudy coming. While taking hold of the pint glass he drank a large gulp of beer, remembering to wipe the creamy foam from his top lip; it tasted amazing. His day had been a stressful one and the shock of hearing about Colin Trenched's death was almost too much. He wanted to believe this had been a terrible and tragic event, wrong place wrong time. The reality however had to be different. Andy could recall a similar incident several years before, again on Clapham Common, involving a prominent Cabinet Minister in the new Blair Government called Ron Davies - *no relation*. He also happened to be out for a late night stroll across Clapham Common, only in his case he luckily escaped with robbery at knifepoint. When asked why he was out so late in such a notorious area he claimed to have had a 'lapse of judgment'. Perhaps Colin may have had a 'lapse of judgment' and tried to resist a robbery, or it could have been a homophobic murder. He did know Colin was gay - James had told him. Then remembering his cousin was abroad on holiday and probably would not know anything about this, he made a mental note to send an email.

Despite Trudy being later than she said, time passed quickly as he slowly came to terms with Colin's death. He felt more vulnerable now than ever before. People around him were dropping like flies, and he had no one he could turn to. Putting robbery and homicide to one side, there was the real possibility considering the circumstances that this could have been a contract killing. Caroline admitted the Professor was working for the security services, he may have told someone important that he was on the trail of finding the treaty - he had after all spoken about it openly enough at dinner in front of James and Marion Gubler.

Seeing Trudy paying for a cab on the opposite side of the street, he signaled maniacally to attract her attention. She saw him and smiling, casually walked over to where he was sitting.

'Thanks for coming,' Andy announced, looking serious. 'I felt a bit shaken when I heard about the Professor.'

'Me too,' Trudy cried. 'I don't think it has sunk in properly yet. Does James know?'

'He's on holiday. I'll send him an email as soon as I get home. They've been friends for years. I think he'll be really upset.'

'What did they say happened in the newspaper?'

'That his body had been found on Clapham Common in the early hours of Monday morning, and two men are being held in police custody.'

Ordering a couple of drinks from the waiter, Andy gathered his thoughts while Trudy slipped off a light cotton jacket and made her self comfortable, she still looked a bit pale from her alcohol binge the previous night.

'What the hell was he doing in the park at that time at night, anyway?'

The Treaty

Andy shook his head. 'I dread to think. Poor Colin, he was a really pleasant man.'

'Yeah, I feel a bit guilty to be honest with you.'

'Why?'

'Well, to be truthful, we never really got along. I think our personalities clashed.'

'That's okay, you don't have to feel guilty just because you didn't see eye-to-eye.'

'I guess not.'

Andy reached across the table and stroked her hand. It felt therapeutic to care about someone else for a moment. He desperately needed to distract himself from feelings of grief.

'I'm sorry about last night. I acted like a stupid little girl.'

'No problem, you were drunk. It wasn't your fault.'

'I know, but you really didn't need a silly American girl hanging out in your room when you had an important meeting to plan. Was it successful?'

'Extremely, but forget about that, it is not important right now. Did you have problems at home?'

'It was cool. They thought I was with Brett the whole time. Daddy considers I am safe with him, if he only knew the true Brett.'

'Why safe, because he's American?'

'No, it's because he has threatened to blow Brett's head off if I come to any harm or get pregnant by him.'

Andy laughed. 'Are you and Brett an item, then?'

The waiter interrupted, placing their drinks on the table. Andy was having a beer, and Trudy strictly non-alcoholic cola.

'No, we went to the same school in Washington - there was a High School fling. His daddy works at the Embassy alongside mine. We are more like brother and sister, at each other's throats usually. Problem is, if he's not with a girl, he looks to me for a quick shag and doesn't like it every time I tell him to hit the highway.'

'What is your father's job at the Embassy is he a politician?'

'No, he is a trade official or something like that. I have asked once or twice, but it's so boring. I'm usually fast asleep before he gets the chance to finish talking.'

'What sort of stuff did Trenched lecture you on?'

'Oh, mainly international and European economic stuff, but his subject was the effect of illegal narcotics on the global economy.'

'Did you find that interesting - sounds heavy?'

Trudy sighed, recalling her many battles with the Professor over this subject. 'Sort of, it was confusing sometimes. I argued a lot with the Professor and I rather feel badly about it now he's gone. He always meant well.'

'What did you argue about?'

'The last time was over some conspiracy theory that a treaty exists controlling the world's major narcotics markets?'

Andy knew Colin had been banging on about the treaty conspiracy theory during his lectures.

'I do know a little about it. James discussed a treaty document with me and so did Colin Trenched. He talked through his theories during dinner.'

Trudy knew he was not telling her everything after briefings by Fatima, but biting her lip, she could hardly start quizzing him in detail at this early stage of their friendship.

'That doesn't surprise me,' Trudy replied. 'For the last few weeks the Professor talked about it all the time. Initially, he spoke of it in a lecture during our first term - he rubbished the treaty as another plot off the internet with no substance. Then a few weeks ago he announced during a lecture that positive proof for the treaty was on the way and it probably did exist.'

'What made him change his mind?'

'I really don't know, he just kept harping on that it would

The Treaty

be a huge scandal and could even bring down the governments in the UK and US, and also damage the Royal Family. God knows what they have to do with it.'

'He must have discovered something very significant to change his mind, or he would have kept quiet until he had got more proof.'

'That was the Professor all over,' Trudy smiled. 'He was quite animated when it came to any discussion involving the establishment, he truly hated royalty. We called him Trench the Red.'

Andy laughed. 'Did you and the other students believe these theories?'

'Yes, he was an international renowned expert on his subject and you had to listen. I was as vocal as anyone and asked daddy about the treaty.'

'Your father - what did he say?'

'Well, he told me there was no evidence either way, and to forget about it. It's just stuff from history, was about all I could get from him. One thing puzzled me though, after we finished talking, I left his room and when I returned with a message from Mom, he was on the phone and mentioned Trenched, then the treaty. He said he was talking to a work colleague, some person in New York I've never heard of.'

Trudy continued to chatter about the LSE and her friends, then what she planned to do on vacation. Andy mentally drifted away for a moment, just snatching enough to nod his head from time-to-time and appear interested. He could not stop thinking about what she had just told him about her father. It was almost as if two parallel worlds were in motion, and because of his insight into them both, he could see their paths merging. Events were happening all around him, yet the cause never seemed clear-cut. Dominic Marsh and his wife murdered, Maria beaten to death, Colin Trenched robbed and stabbed to death - could it be they were assassinated?

'Hey, are you still with me?' Trudy suddenly cried. 'I know I talk for America, but don't fall asleep.'

'I'm sorry Trudy, I am listening to you, I just had a few thoughts about Trenched; they keep popping into my head. Tell me again about your plans for the summer, are you working or going on a grand tour?'

'As I was saying during your little nap, my parents are back to the states for a few weeks and Brett suggested we InterRail around Europe. I want to go further and actually live somewhere different for a few months. Have you any travel plans coming up soon?'

'I'm often working outside the UK; my next trip is to Malaysia to look at installing a system in the capital, Kuala Lumpur.'

'Cool, I'll come and stay in your room again. I'll be as quiet as a little mouse. You won't even know I'm there.'

Recalling her saying this when she was drunk last night, they both laughed.

'Problem is Trudy my boss may not like it. They pick up all my bills, especially the airfare, it's not that cheap.'

'Not a problem. I can pay my own way, well, the airfare, anyway. Do you normally have a double room?' She was deliberately pushing her luck recalling Fatima's remark about timing, then pulled back a little. 'Only kidding, I'm sure you have a lot more interesting people to see when you are travelling. I know about Maria by the way, James filled me in. I'm really sorry.'

Taken by surprise, he had not expected this comment.

'Uh, yes, it's still very raw.'

Trudy watched his reaction carefully before asking, 'Had you known her for long?'

'No, that's the crazy thing it was only a matter of... I'm sorry, don't mean to be rude but I would rather not talk about it right now.'

The Treaty

Now it was Trudy's turn to stroke his hand and play the sympathetic role. 'Trust me to drop the bomb, but if you ever need someone to talk to you only have to ask, okay?'

'Thanks,' he smiled.

Taking a gulp of beer, they continued to talk. Andy found Trudy's stories about her young life in Montana soothing, and he was able to forget about the terrible events that had been happening around him over the past few weeks. In the past, her father had worked for a State Senator, his friend from Stanford University where they both studied in the late 1960's. Still working for the Senator, Andy learned he moved the family to Washington - then came to England in 2004.

'So Trudy, why was your father posted to London?'

She raised her eyebrows and giggled, as if preparing to tell him something shocking.

'Daddy was associated with another Senator earlier on in his career, who was accused of orchestrating several smear campaigns during the election run-up in 2002. He was advised it would be a good career move to work outside the US for a few years.'

One event in particular amused Trudy, a story about another candidate, the Senator for Proctor, who was badly behind in the polls. He claimed an advertisement placed by her father in the press made him look like a 'Gay hairdresser and a crook'. The advert said he was involved in a 1980's video wearing an open-front-shirt and gold chains while massaging a man's face. This still made her laugh and she giggled hysterically. Andy watched her animatedly describe the events, using funny facial expressions. She was very bubbly, he felt happy in her company and for a blissful moment he almost forgot the reason he had needed cheering up in the first place.

33

Trudy left the bar to meet her friends. She had invited Andy along but he had declined, unsure if he could stand another late night with a bunch of carefree students. It had been an emotional few days, and after hearing the tragic news about Professor Trenched he wanted to just go home and catch up on some sleep. The regular commuter trains out of Marylebone had finished, and he did not fancy waiting around for the next scheduled service, so he made his way back to Baker Street. Passing through the ticket barrier, he hurried down a flight of stairs to the platform where he joined a group of tired looking office workers, who like him, had stayed behind after work for a social drink before heading back to suburbia. Reading the electronic message board he could see his timing was spot on, with only minutes left to wait. Bang on time, a familiar rumble preceded the manic vision of a red blur appearing out of the pitch-black tunnel. As if heading toward them, the train screeched to a halt alongside the platform. A group of people stood close behind Andy as the doors slid open. Jumping aboard the carriage, he felt a minute prick at the top of his thigh. It felt like an insect bite, and moving to one side he allowed the other passengers to overtake as he massaged the area until the sensation disappeared. Comfort and Metropolitan Line are two words not often

The Treaty

used together and finding an empty seat, Andy rubbed his eyes trying to dispel the tiredness as the train began to vibrate and shake violently from side-to-side as it sped out of the station. After minutes of being aboard the train he felt suddenly drowsy and fell into a deep sleep.

Waking as they came to a thundering halt, he realized his vision was blurred. Craning to get his head closer to the window he tried to read the sign for Harrow-on-the-Hill, discovering he could not move his arms, legs or neck. Seemingly paralyzed and unable to speak, he began to fear he might have had some kind of stroke. Making gurgling noises as he attempted to talk, he tried to attract the attention of the people sat opposite by staring through panic-stricken eyes, but with his head lolling from side-to-side they assumed he was either on drugs or drunk and showed no inclination to get involved with him. Immediately after they began to exit the carriage he became aware of a man speaking close to him, but not in English or any language he understood. As the train pushed back into rural Hertfordshire, he guessed his carriage would be almost empty, this foreigner may be his only chance to get help - he had to communicate somehow. A woman with distinctive henna dyed hair moved to the seat opposite him, they seemed aware he was in trouble and as the train approached Chorleywood station, both worked together lifting Andy to his feet. With a strong arm around his waist, the man pulled him up, brushing an unshaven chin against his cheek and causing him to wince from the powerful smell of tobacco on the man's clothes and breath. Crushed between the pair as the carriage doors opened, they helped him off the train and onto the platform. At this time of night, the station was deserted, and they led him away from the lights toward the end of the empty station concourse - stumbling into near total darkness before being made to stop. The ground underneath his feet seemed rough and uneven, and he was unaware they were standing on the edge of the rail embankment. Senses dulled he barely reacted to the pain caused by the force of a Seberger silencer pressing into his temple. Possibly triggered by some kind of neurological reaction, he unexpectedly moved, shifting their centre of gravity and causing the couple holding him to lose their balance. As they stumbled and tried to regain control, Andy fell backward in the opposite direction, plunging headfirst down the grassy embankment and disappearing inside a thick gorse bush. Thorns tore through his clothes, and ripped into the soft tissue around his face and neck. Not content to leave him paralyzed, bleeding to death and hidden from view by rescuers, his captor aimed the silenced weapon at the gorse and indiscriminately fired sub-sonic bullets at him to ensure he was properly dead.

34

Cracks of light penetrated his dense prickly cage. Andy blinked back to consciousness and begun to assess his situation. Lying on his back with his head pointing downward, all movement caused him to gasp with pain from some yet unknown internal injury. Encountering a new problem, he found he was unable to move his arm, which was anchored to the clumps of earth and grass soaked with his dried blood. Through gaps in the foliage, he could see a rail track at the bottom of an embankment. Somehow, he had to leave the safety of his nest and attract attention, without rolling onto the electrified line below. It was still early morning and no trains were running yet. The fact it was getting light meant they would soon start coming.

Freeing his arm from nature's tentacles, he managed to move out into the open. On the opposite side of the grass embankment across the tracks, he could see a garden fence, and with any luck a house - perhaps, he thought, someone would see him from a window. Defying the excruciating pain caused by every movement, all he could think about was to survive, suppressing the urge to stop and sleep. For some reason a tune came into his head, the same stupid song churning repeatedly in his mind ... "how do you like your eggs in the morning...hmmm...I like mine with a kiss." Knowing he would die if the bleeding did not stop, each move he made increased the likelihood he was re-opening the wounds. Over-and-over in his mind he willed himself that he must not lose consciousness - "how do you like your eggs in the morning...hmmm...I like mine with a kiss" - six more inches, rest. Then more thoughts came, negative ones. Perhaps death wasn't so bad, in a few more hours he would be history; urban fox's, birds of prey and rats didn't really matter, when you're gone you're gone - just another of natures ready meals. "How do you like your eggs in the morning...hmmm...I like mine with a kiss" - six more inches. He could see a bedroom window. Problem was it was still very early, who would be staring out the back at this time. In addition, the house could be unoccupied; it was holiday season, family-touring Europe, no one would be out of bed for at least two or even three hours. "How do you like your eggs in the morning...hmm...I like mine with a kiss."

35

Anne Maguire checked her bedside clock every hour. It was still only 4:30am. Unable to sleep she decided to get out of bed and make tea in the hope this would help her to relax. Slipping on an old dressing gown hanging from her bedroom door and her favourite fluffy slippers, she tiptoed by her son Danny's room and headed slowly down the stairs. The view from her small lounge looked out extending all the way to the railway embankment at the bottom of their garden. She peeked through the curtains at the streaks of red and yellow light appearing through cracks in a fading night sky. Anne searched for a cigarette and found an unopened packet and a lighter on the table beside the sofa. Unlocking the rear door to the garden, she gave a shiver at the unexpected chill. Honey, her two-year-old cocker spaniel, brushed by her legs and raced out having seeing something move in the vegetable patch down by the fence. Beyond the fence was a deep gully, carved out almost a century before to transport a new breed of commuters from the sleepy towns and villages into the crowded metropolis. Hardly taking notice of the routine passing, these trains formed part of the daily sounds and environment they all lived in. At this hour it was eerily quiet and strange not to hear their whirring high-pitched electric motors and carriages thundering past at peak times.

Honey had seen a rabbit hiding amongst the lettuces, Anne watched the little intruder darting back through a hole under the fence, and narrowly avoiding Honey's ambitions to catch her. These little creatures may look sweet, Anne thought, but they were gradually destroying all the hard work she'd put in earlier that spring. Deciding to investigate, still clutching her cigarette, she tiptoed down the path of broken concrete slabs, holding her dressing gown closed tightly around her. She picked up a piece of wood and placed it in front of the hole in the fence hoping it would keep them out. Peering over the top of the fence, she could see a track leading through the overgrown grass and foliage to rabbit holes burrowed deep in the walls of the embankment. Then noticing movement near bushes on the other side of the tracks, she saw a dark shape larger than a fox or badger in the grass - it was human - a man!

'Are you injured?' she called out, 'stay where you are.'

Running back along the path into the house, she headed inside and quickly called the emergency services.

36

'Mr Davies, it looks as though you've had a very lucky escape.'

The Scottish hospital consultant paused as he continued reading more notes handed to him by a nurse, and then he began to recite a list of injuries.

'You lost a lot of blood. Had it not been unseasonably cold, restricting further loss, you may have died in the night. You also have a broken clavicle or collarbone and a broken talus.'

Andy frowned. 'What's a talus?'

'That's the bone in your foot joining the tibia and fibula to form the ankle joint,' the doctor replied, scratching his baldhead. 'The collarbone injury probably occurred when you fell down the embankment, you have a bullet wound in the ankle, lower leg and also two gun shot wounds in your abdomen and forearm, so no tennis for you this year. The x-ray shows a missile in the left lower thorax, moderate hemothorax and a wide mediastinum. Luckily, all these problems are curable with good medical care, and subject to any secondary infection you should be out of here fairly soon.' The doctor broke into a wry smile. 'One additional problem, if you plan to travel abroad soon, you will cause a few raised eyebrows when you pass through the airport scanner and the metal bullets are detected.'

While the doctor laughed at his own little joke, Andy merely looked on with concern.

'I'm sorry Doctor, but aren't you going to remove them? If you leave them in my body won't I get blood poisoning?'

'You've been watching too many movies, Andrew, probably ones where John Wayne sucks on a bottle of whiskey while a woman pokes about in his abdomen with a sharp knife digging out bullets. Most damage is at the point of entry, we really do not need to go to make the hole any larger trying to dig the bullets out. Seriously, your biggest risk is secondary infections from here in the hospital, also brought to you from the outside and therefore, I would advise against too many visitors. I understand your girlfriend is keen to see you but we should restrict it to her for the time being.'

Walking away, Andy almost called him back to ask the name of "his girlfriend", and then thought better of it. He was in an intensive care unit and could see several people hovering about outside talking with the staff. The door suddenly swung open and a bubbly ward sister stormed into the room.

'I've had the blood tests back and they show traces of a drug similar to flunitrazepam,' she said, looking at Andy as if he had done something wrong. 'Do you remember anytime when you may have been given it?'

Shocked unaware of drugs being involved his only memory was boarding the train at Baker Street and everything after that was blank. That is until he woke on the side of the rail track. A second nurse was standing in the open doorway waiting to speak.

'Andrew has a visitor, can she come in yet? It's his girlfriend.'

The ward sister sighed. 'Yes, okay, but only for a few minutes, doctors orders.'

Craning his neck, restricted by tubes inserted into almost

The Treaty

every orifice, it did not take long for Andy to recognize the trademark hair and long flowing skirt belonging to Caroline Lovelace-Jones. As the nurse moved to one side allowing her through she did an imitation knock-knock.

'Can I come in?' Caroline sang. She handed flowers to the nurse and walked over to his bedside, bent down and kissed him full on the lips. 'Andy darling whatever happened?'

Andy thought it rude to protest smiling at her audaciousness. 'This is a surprise, thank you for the flowers.'

Looking around she began explaining in a low voice, 'I'm sorry about the girlfriend bit, but not the kiss - it was nice. How are you?'

Andy glanced down at the tubes and at the bleeping machine. 'Oh, yeah, I'm feeling great.'

'Silly question, sorry. I was so shocked when I heard the news.'

Andy winced. 'It does seem like my life is taking a very strange detour at the moment.'

'Well I am not going to start saying I warned you however - you nearly died.'

'Yes, the doctor was kind enough to mention that.'

'Did this happen after you left my flat?'

'No later that evening. Caroline, I am not sure if you should, be here talking to me before I speak with the police. I would prefer not to end with a heart attack?'

'I know I shouldn't have barged in like this, but I just had to speak with you. Andy, what has happened ends any debate if these killings are connected with the treaty.'

'Is that the reason you have the security outside my room?'

'Yes, I've demanded full protection for you until we have the information that dictates otherwise.'

Still unsure of the situation, Andy showed he thought it was an over-reaction. 'I'm not persuaded. How do we know this was not just a robbery - my wallet went missing? Have they caught anyone do you know?'

'Andy, you are in denial. It had all the hallmarks of the hotel incident, even the police suspect it may have been the same couple who were seen on CCTV after the Dominic Marsh shooting.'

'But they could be part of an organized gang operating in London. What's so unusual about what has happened to me?'

'We need information from you, Andy. I am genuinely worried. Will you give this some thought? Did you see the people who did this? We want to work closely with you and offer proper protection, much better than you will receive from the police. If you need me for anything at all please call, I will be staying in London for a few more days.'

Leaning over the bed, she kissed him once more on the lips.

'Sorry,' she smiled, 'I have to milk these opportunities while you can't resist. See you again soon.'

With that, she spun around and bustled out into the corridor. The nurse walked over with the flowers in a vase and placed them by his bedside.

'She seems very nice Andrew, you are a lucky chap.'

Unable to roll over or hardly move, he forgot about his stomach wound and how much it hurt while trying not to laugh.

37

'Can you manage the steps, Andrew?'

'Yes, I am fine, Mrs Shupe, it is not a problem. I'm used to these things now.'

Andy was still convalescing and making a remarkable recovery according to his doctor. Walking with the aid of crutches, he expertly negotiated each stone riser leading to the front door of the Shupes house.

Trudy became a regular visitor and when he left hospital, she was quick to offer help, taking him home and acting as his nurse. He was still in denial over his attack, believing it was an over-complicated and brutal robbery. Trudy, however, had no doubts about the motive; Fatima had already predicted there would be an attempt on his life and knew it was a race against time to discover where he hid the treaty documents. While staying in his apartment she made every attempt to examine computer files and paper records. Frustrated by sophisticated anti-virus software, Andy had already removed the keystroke logger she installed on his laptop and blamed it on a downloaded virus.

Fatima's plan had been to track his computer IP address and movements across the internet, and discover passwords and user names. However, he had used a false IP masking his real one, which changed on a random basis.

Even if it were possible to reach his main storage server, they would have met an impenetrable firewall. Andy's friend, who hosted the server storing his secret files, was a spammer responsible for sending millions of junk email everyday, advertising medicines, Viagra, loans and the opportunity to update your bank account (sic). Experts around the world hunted for the location of where junk email came from, with instructions to try to block these computers. It turned into a game. Encrypted data could be anywhere, at any time - China, India, South America, Indonesia and then back to India hours later, making the task virtually impossible.

Tom Shupe, who was well aware his daughter had made friends with this Englishman, waited patiently inside the house ready to greet him. As Andy entered through the front door, he prepared to shake his hand, certain he was not the ideal man for his daughter. The list of reasons were plain enough, he was a weedy looking Brit, had an accent like a homosexual, was twelve years older than Trudy, drank alcohol and did not go to church. Throw in a lack of interest in football and no military service, he was as far from being the perfect match as you could possibly get.

'Good to meet you, Andrew. I am pleased to see you are back on your feet.'

'Thank you, sir, I appreciate your concern and thank you Mrs Shupe for the regular supply of cakes they were delicious.'

After taking, back the remains of his hand from Tom's iron grip, Andy air-kissed Mrs Shupe before shown into the lounge. The size of the property amazed him, sharing one of London's exclusive squares with multimillionaire neighbours. Tom was the equivalent rank to a senior British colonial employee back in another era, when Great Britain was the world's superpower, and he enjoyed similar rewards for helping rule the American empire.

The Treaty

They were joined by a girl in her late teens, Latvian born Natallia, who came in carrying a tray of alcohol-free fruit-drinks. Mrs Shupe called them through to the dining room, and Andy helped to his seat next to Mrs Shupe around a table decorated with flowers.

After saying grace Tom invited them to eat, Mrs Shupe began by asking questions about his brutal attack. 'So how long do you think you were lying by the train track, Andrew?'

Tom rested his elbow on the table and darted a look at his wife. 'Please, we did not invite Andrew to dinner so he could relive his attack.'

'No, it's okay, I don't mind,' Andy smiled, placing a napkin on his lap. 'I lay there most of the night. The whole time is a blur from when I stepped onto the train. I can only recall waking, and knowing I had to move out of the brambles so I could be seen and try to attract help.'

'It's amazing you regained consciousness,' replied Mrs Shupe.

'I lost over twenty percent of my blood and would have died within an hour, or so, if that woman had not spotted me. Fortunately, it was an unusually cold night, making my blood thicker and reducing the loss.'

'How fascinating, at what time did she find you?'

'Around five in the morning she was at the bottom of her garden and saw me over the fence.'

Trudy joined in the conversation. 'It was so lucky she was out of bed at that time. We went to her house and took flowers and chocolates to say thank you.'

'I think our Lord watched over you that night, Andrew. I hope you've been to church and given thanks to God.'

Muffling his response, he quickly changed the subject. 'That was a lovely meal Mrs Shupe, really delicious.'

'Call me Myra, please, Andrew. Mrs Shupe makes me feel so old, and thank Natallia, too. She is an excellent young cook. Right girls, let's clear these dishes away and let the men have some to time to talk politics, or whatever.'

'Mom, I am capable of talking politics as well,' Trudy replied, not wanting Andy to be alone with her father.

'I'm sure they can manage quite well without you; now please do as I ask.'

With the debate over, Trudy followed behind her mother into the kitchen still grumbling about unfairness and equality while the two men moved into the lounge. Andy was dreading this. Invited to sit down on a floral patterned settee, Tom positioned himself in his favourite armchair. Trudy continued to make cameo appearances, first asking how they wanted their coffee, and then pulling faces at Andy trying to make him laugh as she carried the drinks into the room.

'Well Andrew, you have certainly been tested, how did your employers respond to these events?'

'Very well, sir. I work for a US owned company and they have moved a sales engineer from New York to provide cover for me. I can also work at home using a computer system, and network into the telecoms equipment based in London or anywhere in the world.'

'Do the police have a suspect?'

'It looks as if it was a robbery that went very wrong, but I guess we may never really know, unless the culprits are caught.'

'This is not a common form of attack in England, is it?'

'The police told me it was rare, although, not unique and happens more often in Eastern Europe and Latin America where the drug is widely available.'

'Oh, so you were drugged?'

'Yes, they actually found the small needle entry point in my thigh. It's suspected they used one of those automatic controlled devices that diabetic use.'

'Trudy mentioned you knew Professor Trenched at her

The Treaty

college. That was a strange business how he died. What do you think to that?'

'It was very tragic, sir. I had not known Colin for long and he seemed a really pleasant person, a world expert on some topics.'

'How did you come to know him, you did not go to college there did you?'

'No, I was introduced by my cousin, an ex-student; they kept in touch on a regular basis professionally.'

'The guy was a homosexual according to the press, are there many of them teaching in schools over here?'

Andy stalled unsure what to say in response at his homophobia, accepting it reflected a generation.

Not waiting for his answer Tom continued, 'Trudy and Trenched were having a debate a few days before he died on economics and she asked my advice. It involved some treaty or other; did you know anything about this?'

Any mention of the treaty from this unexpected source triggered paranoia for Andy, and coming from an American it was particularly poignant.

'My cousin James and Professor Trenched talked about some treaty over dinner recently, but I did not really understand the subject.'

'Trudy asked my opinion, and I told her it was one of those old chestnuts that keep doing the conspiracy theory rounds. When I worked in Washington, I gave a view on this kind of story the whole time - particularly to the press trying to dig some dirt. If you do hear any more gossip, you should pass it on, it's always useful to have some other points of view.'

Andy wanted to scream back, "yeah, right", but managed to stay quiet. Trudy, listening outside, used the pause in conversation to make an entry.

'Daddy, I have to take Andy home soon he's not allowed to get too tired.'

Flashing a quick grin, she helped him up out of his chair and passed him his crutches.

'Well Andrew, it was good finally to meet you. I hope the recovery continues. Take good care of my daughter young man; she is my most precious asset.'

'Oh, daddy, don't be silly, I am taking care of Andy right now.'

The two men shook hands and Myra gave him a peck on the cheek.

'Now Andrew, I have packed a few little things for you to take back home. Trudy, please call and let me know you have arrived at the apartment, I am always so worried when you are driving over here on the wrong side of the road.'

The Treaty

38

Nuzzling his face close to her neckline placing a hand on top of her thigh, Andy gently moved until they were both comfortable.

Trudy was awake and aerobically spun around to face him. 'Did you sleep okay?'

'Yes, fine, how about you?'

'Like a dream as always when I'm with you. Are you happy with me, Andy?'

'Yes of course, what man wouldn't be?'

'You're so sweet. What did you think to daddy last night, he is a nightmare isn't he?'

'He loves you and is over protective. If I had a daughter I would be exactly the same, no other man could ever be good enough.'

'What did you talk about?'

'Just general stuff about my work and he mentioned Trenched; he is very homophobic.'

'Yes, he struggles with the concept. He is from a different generation, and he still believes a woman's place is in the kitchen - like the way he treats my mom. I have no idea what she thinks about the world; politics, economics, anything.'

Andy suddenly sat up, and smiled. 'Hey, I received an email last night asking me to go to Kuala Lumpur.'

'Why?'

'To finish off the work I should have carried out before going to hospital.'

Trudy frowned. 'But you are still unable to walk properly. You're not fit.'

'I can almost walk without the crutches now and it's a straightforward job testing. I'm keen to go and should be fine by the time I fly, provided the hospital shows me the green light.'

Trudy looks surprised and a little anxious. 'What about the long flight, surely that isn't good for you?'

'If I travel business class, it will be okay.'

Trudy lay with her legs entwined around Andy's and her face very close. 'You're so lucky. Take me with you. I will do anything you want - right now.'

Sliding beneath the thin summer duvet, she began fooling around making him hysterical, and seconds later reappeared pushing her face close and whispering. 'Please take me, Andy, I really want to go with you. I've never been there in my whole life?'

'Trudy, stop it, I can't take you it would cost a fortune.'

'I have my own money. I have hardly spent anything this summer. I will look on the internet, I'm sure there will be cheap flights. We can both travel together, you need a nurse, and I can be your nurse.'

He so desperately wanted to say yes to her, the only thing in his mind was the last time he travelled was with Maria.

'I would love you to come to stay with me in my hotel room. I am just so worried about what happened last time.'

'You mean Maria?'

'Yes, I did not take care of her.'

'Andy, you have to overcome this fear. If I stay here on my own, who will protect me from being run over, drugged and raped, or shot and murdered right outside my

The Treaty

front door. It would be so cool to go to Asia; I promise I will not get in your way. You can do whatever you like, I will not stop you.'

She was right; he had to overcome this irrational fear. Trudy started pulling more silly faces.

'Okay!' he cried. 'Before I say yes, there is just one more thing I want you to do for me.'

Giggling, she spun onto her front and slid downward kissing all around the bullet wound on his stomach. 'Yes, okay, anything. What do you want me to do to you?'

39

'Oh my God, just look at that view, it's so beautiful. What is the sea down below called?'

'It's the Bay of Bengal and further on is the Straits of Malacca. During the night we flew over India and the Himalayas.'

'You're so clever, how come you know all this stuff?'

'I just looked on the map...look; you've got one as well.'

Trudy felt silly when she realized there was a map on the screen embedded in the 747's headrest, but she remained excited. Once Andy decided they could travel together there was no stopping her, and that morning in his apartment, she had searched the internet and booked a flight to Kuala Lumpur with Malaysia Airlines. They got a great deal in their Golden Club Class. Andy paid for them both using his Amex card; he was pleased to get the problem solved. He was left with nagging doubts about taking her along, she was hopelessly incorrigible and he did not stand a chance of changing her mind.

'Do you normally stay in a Marriott?'

'Not always, depends on what is available in each city. I just like somewhere that's fairly central with good communications and broadband.'

'I'd like to visit some of the smaller places sometime, perhaps we can go on a backpacker trip next time and really

The Treaty

see local life?'

Tuning out of the conversation for a while, Andy sat with his eyes closed and began thinking how he could make sure Trudy would stay safe. Despite his public refusal to accept any plot against him he had this niggling doubt that it might be true and feared they could strike again - they, being whoever wanted his version of the treaty the most.

'Andy, are you asleep?'

'Yes.'

She playfully slapped him on the arm. 'No you're not.'

'I'm sorry. I was just planning the next few days in my head. I need to try to get work out of the way, so we can have some time off. You don't mind hanging out with me tomorrow, do you? You can watch me work and then we can explore the city in the evening together.'

She leaned over and kissed his cheek. 'Whatever, you want.'

40

Andy's mobile began vibrating in his trouser pocket signaling an incoming call. It was too early in the morning for Europe and he guessed it was the US again, for the fourth time.

'Duane, what do you want now? I'm really busy!'

'Andy, it's Caroline, where are you?'

'Oh, sorry, I thought it was my people again. I am in a telecoms switch room somewhere in Kuala Lumpur.'

'I thought we agreed you would tell me if you travelled?'

'I've been really busy. It's only for a few days.'

Caroline responded with a deep sigh. 'I'm going to call you later. Shall I phone your mobile or your hotel? I will give you the name of our contact in the city, just if you have any emergencies. Are you travelling alone this time?'

'No, I am with a friend and thanks, but we are going to be fine. No one even knows I have left the UK, apart from you. I will call later; it's a crucial stage of the install.'

He placed the phone back down on the desk and then grabbed Trudy around the waist.

She jumped and slammed her glossy magazine shut. 'Andy, stop it! What if that engineer comes back?'

'Oh, he will be gone for hours, its lunchtime. I only want a kiss.'

She pecked him on the tip of his nose. 'Well, you are certainly showing signs of a full recovery. Come on, get finished

The Treaty

here and then we can hit the town for beers and shopping.'

'You're a hard taskmaster. Pass that circuit board and don't touch any of the components, the static electricity from your body could damage them.'

She stooped down, carefully picking up the delicate circuitry and passed it over.

'Andy, what crossed your mind the other day when I mentioned my father's interest in Professor Trenched? Did you think it was odd as well, or am I being paranoid?'

'Just give me a minute; I have to make sure this is all plugged in correctly. Okay, that looks fine.' Andy turned to her, surprised by this change in conversation. 'What's brought this on? Your father could not have had anything to do with Trenched, could he?'

'Well, I'm not sure, there are things I haven't told you about daddy that really bother me - in fact, I've never discussed this with anyone. When you live at home as a child most things that happen in your household you regard as normal, and it was only as I got older I realized daddy had some odd relationships.'

'Surely that's the same for everyone. We all have our own peculiarities and ways of doing things.'

'But he seemed to deal with weird people, holding meetings late at night. Mom and Dad argued about some of the things that went on. He was even having an affair with a family friend I called Auntie Sarah.'

'Wow, did your mother, know that?'

'I'm not sure, maybe. As long as he did not leave her, I don't think she cared. Auntie Sarah came to the house regularly with Uncle John. She was very attractive, always wore makeup and stylish clothes. She made mom look drab. I caught them together when I was about ten years old. Mom was at my grandfather's place while I stayed home with daddy. He thought I was at the next doors house playing with my friend, but I came back and saw

Aunty Sarah's handbag in the lounge and her coat on the chair.'

'Maybe your mom asked her to visit to make sure you were okay, assuming a man on his own could not cope looking after a little girl.'

'That's a generous thought Andy, but I heard something going on upstairs and being inquisitive crept up to find out what was happening. Without giving all the gory detail, they were going at it like rabbits. I watched for a while, then went back downstairs and returned to my friend's house, he never knew I had been home.'

'Did you tell anyone, your friend?'

'No. You see, that is the odd thing, it did not really shock me that much. I thought it was funny. What I am saying is I just accepted events taking place in our home as normal.'

Andy looked puzzled. 'So, how's this connected with Trenched?'

'The point I'm making is these unusual events and little snippets of conversation that I've overheard always seem to lead to actions some place else.'

Andy moved away from the switch and knelt down beside Trudy. 'Do you believe your father could have influenced a course of actions leading to Trenched's death?'

'Maybe, what do you think?'

'I'm not sure what to say. When I spoke with your father, he mentioned Trenched. I told you before that he's clearly homophobic, but as far as we are aware he doesn't have any other connection with the LSE.'

'Sorry Andy, that's not true. My father knows Marion Gubler pretty well. She worked closely with Trenched and was the person who recommended I went to the LSE. When Marion first arrived in England, she came to our home and clearly knew daddy, if you know what I mean. You do know her reputation at the LSE. I'm sure James told you - anything in trousers.'

The Treaty

Andy began to piece together earlier events that may have been relevant. 'James and I had dinner with Marion and the Professor the night Colin died. He told everyone he might have the information that proved the treaty was genuine. If Marion and your father work together, is it possible they are both with the same organization - the CIA, or something like that?'

'I don't know, but I think we would be in denial if we refused to accept there is something going on here. Is there a way we can convince everyone that Professor Trenched was perhaps wrong or that this treaty does or does not exist?'

Andy was growing concerned by the thread of Trudy's line of conversation. 'I'm not too sure why you think I may be able to provide an answer?'

Andy placed his hands on Trudy's hips and drew her closer. He really believed he could trust her now; she had too much to lose. It was highly possible her father knew about the treaty and was connected with Professor Trenched's death.

'There was something I found out in Laos that I haven't told anyone yet.'

Trudy concentrated and looked into his eyes without expression; filled with anticipation about what he was going to say and believing this was going to be a significant breakthrough.

'I was introduced to a man called Asang, a company lawyer. He had remained friends with another man called Mardjano Deradjat, and according to Asang, Mardjano orchestrated and wrote the official treaty more than thirty years ago.'

'Has this Asang seen the documents?'

'Yes, and so have I, they were stored on a computer at Maria's house.'

'Why didn't you tell me when we discussed this before?

Remember my debate with Trenched, he first said it did not exist, and then suddenly changed his mind - was that after meeting with you? Did you tell him what you had seen?'

Andy nodded. 'Yes, and this may have got him killed. It also explains the attempt on my life and that is why I have avoided telling anyone else - including you. Let's face it Trudy, it could be a pile of shit and not worth being killed for. The document I have could be a forgery, we will never know until the originals are found.'

Trudy leaned in closer. 'Did you just say you've got an actual copy of the treaty?'

'It's really crucial you keep this a secret,' he whispered, realizing his mistake. Both our lives could be in danger if it's suspected I have a copy in my possession.'

'Do you know where the original treaty documents are?'

'Yes, I mean, possibly.'

Her eyes lit up and sparkled. 'You actually know where to find the originals?'

'Mardjano may have them, if he is alive. We don't know anything for certain. We would have to find him first.'

'So where does this Mardjono guy live?'

'He is somewhere in Indonesia on an island in the middle of Sumatra.'

'Isn't that close to here?'

'Yes, it's a neighbouring country with Malaysia.'

'Cool. Well, if we are so close to the place, why don't we take time out and see if we can find him at least we can discover if he or the treaty, actually exists - or doesn't, whatever the case may be.'

Reluctant to commit Andy resumed work, and Trudy jumped down off the edge of the desk and stood over him as he brought the cabinet to life.

'Think about it Andy, at worst it will be a great adventure and at best we get to speak to Mardjono, he tells us the real story. You will be able to talk to the police or whoever, tell them you do not have any information. Bring closure to the whole affair.'

He began tidying his equipment ready to leave. 'I'm just not sure I want to get that involved, it's not my problem. Surely the story will die a natural death when everyone tires hearing about it - then we can forget about it.'

'Darling, you know that is not an option, what about Maria and Colin Trenched? I know you want to believe the attack on you was just a coincidence, but your life could still be in danger. We have to find out the truth once and for all!'

41

Trudy danced naked out of the bathroom and over to the bed chanting "old man, old man!" flicking wet hair into his face. Andy grabbed her around the waist and they began to play fight, which inevitably led to sex. Taking a shower afterwards, standing under a blanket of hot water he gave more thought to what Trudy had said about going to visit Mardjono. Maybe it was a good idea to see if they could find the old man and discover if he did still have the original documents, who knows he may even agree to sell them.

Trudy dried her hair, satisfied she was gradually winning and getting her own way. Confident Andy would eventually change his mind she began idly searching the internet for information about Indonesia and pestering him for key locations close to where Mardjono lived. He eventually caved in and gave her Asang's printout showing the full address.

'I've no idea how far it is from Medan, but he did say it was on an island in the middle of this enormous lake.'

Trudy keyed the place names into Google Earth, and within seconds, she was hovering over a lake in the north of Sumatra.

'Found it!' she squealed. 'It's called Lake Toba.'

Andy looked at the screen. 'That sounds familiar.

The Treaty

Mardjono lives in a small village called Tuk-Tuk. Can you see it?'

'I've found a town called Prapat right on the edge of the lake. Perhaps that is where we would get a boat.'

'Yes, that rings a bell.'

'Can we go?' she asked in her little girl's voice. 'Can we, Andy?'

'Trudy, I've been thinking, maybe I should go alone. It is too dangerous. I agree we need to find Mardjono and try to put an end to all this treaty nonsense, but I'm scared what might happen to you.'

'Baby, it's like I said before, I am already involved. Besides, if my father was involved with Trenched's death it might be safer for you if I stick around.'

Andy sighed and rolled his eyes.

Beaming quickly she asked, 'Is that a yes, then?'

'I suppose.'

'Cool! I will look for flights while you are at your breakfast meeting.'

Andy had to attend a breakfast meeting with his client at an office in the city. Checking his appearance, she gave him a wifely kiss on his way out of the door, straightened his tie then mischievously bared her breasts as he went to leave the room.

'Keep the door locked,' Andy grinned. 'I'll see you in a couple of hours. If you need me call my mobile.'

Blowing her a kiss, he closed the hotel door behind him. Bursting with excitement Trudy stood very still and listened to him walk down the corridor. Jumping back on the internet, she studied satellite images of Lake Toba the landscape looked amazing. From Medan, there was a single road leading to Lake Toba, passing through huge areas of rubber plantations and forests dotted with small towns and villages along the route. The only way to get there was by making this six or seven hour's journey and eventually crossing on some kind of ferryboat.

Excited by this new adventure, she had not forgotten the true nature of her mission - to find the treaty for Fatima. Amongst the many difficulties she faced was now a growing affection and loyalty toward Andy. He was a lot of fun, very loving and kind; in addition, she knew his life was under threat. Yet, she could not afford to fail Fatima, who needed those documents to gain the advantage by publishing them in the Arab media uncensored and ultimately avenge her husband's killers. The only practical option to save Andy that she could think of was to speak with Fatima and try to persuade her to spare his life by sharing the data when they found it. This way he could approach the authorities in Britain and she could do her own thing with the Arab media. Jumping up off the bed, she connected the secure VoIP phone to her computer.

Seconds later, Fatima's sleepy voice was on the end of the phone. 'Where are you? I've been waiting for you to make contact?'

'Sorry, I'm with Andy in Kuala Lumpur. Listen, he has told me where he thinks the original treaty documents might be - we are going to look for them tomorrow.'

Now fully awake, she barked back in full voice. 'Baby, that's wonderful news! I love you so much. You must bring me the papers. I have my people in Malaysia and Indonesia. Do you want me to come to help you? I can be there late tomorrow.'

'No, it's too soon. First, we have to search for this man called Mardjono, a lawyer who was involved in drafting the original treaty - he lives on a small island in the middle of a lake. It is not certain we will find him and it could all be a waste of time. Fatima, if we do find the treaty, what will happen to Andy? He is a good man; I would not want him to come to any harm.'

Seconds passed in silence, and Trudy began to wonder if

The Treaty

the connection had dropped.

'Fatima, are you still there? What do you think?'

'You have forgotten,' Fatima replied in a slow clear tone. 'He is not part of our plan and he will be killed eventually. There is very little we can do to prevent this happening. It was only through luck and incompetence that he survived the last time. Baby, I need those papers first. There is no other option, do you understand?'

Frightened and unsure what to, Trudy regained her composure. 'But why does he have to die? Once this information is in the public domain and the guilty people are named, they won't dare harm him.'

Fatima raised her voice. 'Trudy! You are being naïve. These are your people - American and British. They will find a way to silence him and prevent any publication in Europe or the USA. We need to release the treaty to the Arab world first - with the original papers if you can find them but even copies will be enough I am convinced of that. There will be no censorship. This will help to destroy our enemies and restore the faithful. The lands of the Prophets in Afghanistan returned and the wealth from the poppy given back to our people. God is with you, stay true to your faith you cannot let me down. We gave Jesus, son of Mary, clear evidence, and aided him with the Holy Spirit. Is whenever a messenger comes to you with that which you did not desire, you swell with pride? Some messengers you call impostors, and some you slew.'

Her recital from the holy book, echoed across the ether and then the phone went dead. Trudy knew her verdict was final and what may happen to them both. Sitting on the edge of the bed, taking deep breaths, she tried to stay calm and jumped to her feet as she began hearing noises outside the hotel room. Andy came breezing in.

'Just getting out of bed?' he smiled, placing his shoulder bag on the table.

'Yes,' Trudy nodded, fussing with her hair. 'How come you're back so soon?'

'I was in the taxi heading to the place when the guy phoned and cancelled the meeting. I'm actually glad, as now we can have breakfast together and book the flights to Medan.'

'Yes, sounds like a good idea.'

'Is everything OK? You look pale.'

'No, I'm fine, it must be the jetlag. My stomach feels a little upset from all that food we ate last night.'

'Do you want a few more minutes in bed? I can work quietly if you need to sleep.'

'No, I'll be fine after I've had a shower.'

'Are you sure, I don't mind?'

'Stop making such a fuss, I'm fine!' she snapped, revealing a yet unseen side to her personality.

Gathering up her clean clothes, she stormed off into the bathroom leaving Andy confused. Shrugging his shoulders, he dialled the number for the airline, letting her strange behaviour pass as just a girl thing.

The Treaty

42

Medan airport was crowded with dozens of people milling around the arrivals gate. Tripping over a suitcase Andy was frustrated as he battled to remain calm and held Trudy's arm, as if expecting her to disappear into the mass of bodies.

'Excuse me, sir, you need a taxi?' a thin man in a grey suit asked. 'We have very good taxi, nearly new, just around the corner, please come with me.'

Andy stopped walking and caught his breath. 'We're going to Lake Toba. Do you know where that is?'

'Yes I can get you to Lake Toba, no problem sir, please come.'

'How far is this taxi?' Andy asked abruptly, still holding Trudy's arm. 'I'm not leaving the airport on foot?'

'Just over here, sir, please come.'

Around the next corner, they saw a clean white mini-bus parked at the roadside with the words 'taxi' painted in enormous letters. When Andy saw this, he almost exploded with anger.

'Hang on, I wanted a saloon car! I'm not travelling hundreds of miles in a van.'

Trudy tried to calm him. 'It's okay, at least we will have room, and it is better than being squeezed into the back of some old car. It looks new.'

The man organizing their taxi went to speak with the driver, who stood at the side of the vehicle smoking a cigarette.

'You have to watch these guys they will suck the money out of your wallet in no time.'

'Andy, he seems OK, he wants the business. Relax.'

The man in the suit walked briskly over to them. 'The journey to Lake Toba is four or fives hours, and will cost fifty thousand rupiah. We wait now for other passengers, then go.'

'What other passengers?' Andy cried.

'We wait for more people.'

He turned sharply to Trudy. 'There's no way I'm waiting here for hours. Let's find a taxi that'll take us to the lake. Thank you, but no thank you.'

As they walked away, the man chased after them and threw his hands in the air. 'Okay! Okay!' he shouted. 'We leave now but you must pay three hundred and fifty thousand rupiah.'

'How much - you've got to be joking?'

Trudy quickly did the mental arithmetic. 'It's less than fifty US dollars, if I've got my math right.'

Andy turned back to the man. 'Okay, fifty US dollars for all the seats if we can go now - in the next ten minutes?'

'Yes, no problem.'

Climbing on board, they sat together in the back behind the driver. It was comfortable and they had plenty of room to spread out. Powering up the vehicle it began moving away from the airport along modern roads with signs pointing toward Medan City centre. Surprised at seeing so many Mosques, Trudy pointed out practically all the women wore a hijab and some with full veils.

'I didn't know this was a Muslim country,' she whispered. 'We're in Asia; this is like the Middle East.'

'I didn't know, either,' Andy replied. 'It seems full-on

The Treaty

Muslim just shows you how ignorant we are in the West. I read it on the net before we left the hotel that Indonesia has the largest population of Muslims in any one country.'

As they reached the edge of the city, the scenery gradually began to change from the run-down dwellings at the outskirts to a more lush tropical landscape. Passing neat fields filled with Cassava, the plant that produces Tapioca, reminded Andy of one of his pet childhood horrors.

'I used to hate Tapioca pudding when I was a kid,' he smiled looking out of the window. 'It tasted like warm phlegm.'

Trudy screwed up her face and slapped him on the arm. 'You're disgusting! That sounds awful. How did your mother cook it?'

'She made it into a milk pudding and we all swallowed the stuff down without complaining.'

'Sounds like torture.'

'You can say that again. Do you like cooking?'

'I hate it. My mum thinks all women should be good in the kitchen it really frustrates her. Hey look!' Trudy suddenly cried pointing out a small Christian church with a steeple and roof all made from corrugated tin. 'What's a church doing here? I thought you said this was all Muslim?'

'No, there are Protestants and Catholics in small numbers. The Dutch introduced Christianity when they ruled here for a few centuries. This used to be the place in the 1600's for spices. Ships came over from Europe taking months to arrive, and in the early days less than twenty-five percent of the crew made it back home again.'

'Why did they do it if it was so dangerous?'

'Money, I guess. The ones that survived made fortunes from the sale of the spices - it was a hugely profitable venture.'

Trudy sat with her head resting on Andy's shoulder. 'I

wonder what it was like spending months on a ship, not knowing if you would ever see your family and friends again. I could not have done it.'

Motoring through the undulating countryside the scenery changed to thick-forested rubber plantations, regimental rows of trees each with a cup attached collecting the latex sap. Every few miles the driver would overtake huge trucks laden with complete tree trunks, on their way for crushing and the valuable palm oil extracted.

'Where are we, honey?' Trudy yawned. 'The scenery looks different, there are more trees?'

'This would have been a hardwood rain forest a few years ago, but now, thanks to us, they've chopped it down and planted palm trees.'

'Why?'

'To extract the oil, and use it to produce bio-diesel and shampoo.'

'Shampoo - we need some, remind me later.'

The shrill noise of a mobile roused them. Lurching across the cab the driver answered overtaking a truck. After an animated conversation, he threw the phone down on the front passenger seat and wrenched at the steering wheel, swerving in front of the monster vehicle and narrowly avoiding a head-on collision with a car hurtling toward them in the opposite direction. Andy cursed and looked over his shoulder; amazed the truck did not jack-knife and spill its load over the highway. Leaning forward he stuck his head into the front cabin. The driver nodded and dabbed the brake pedal. As they entered, a small cluster of houses with shops on either side of the road, the driver indicated and pulled the taxi over. Parking opposite a restaurant, they piled out of the van and, feeling the ground beneath their feet once again, followed the driver inside. Sitting at a table in the restaurant covered with a corrugated iron roof, the waiter immediately brought over

The Treaty

dishes of spicy looking food. Nervous of stomach upsets Andy suggested they drank only the bottled Cola, leaving the bemused driver to eat alone. Sitting in silence Trudy dared to risk finding a toilet, and made signs at a woman peering through a curtain dividing the eating area. She understood and ushered her inside their private quarters. Seconds later Andy watched as a police car drew alongside their vehicle and two casually dressed officers came into the restaurant. The more senior looking of the officers spoke with the driver, who responded by producing his identity card and waving it in Andy's face, indicating he needed to show his ID. Finding his passport, Andy handed it over and the officer thumbed through the pages and paused at his photograph before passing it back. He then scanned the room, speaking again and pointing toward the backroom. Trudy reappeared, and seeing the police officers looked concerned as she made her way toward them. Showing her passport to the officer, he gave it the same cursory examination and seeming satisfied chatted informally to the waiter accepting complimentary cans of coke before leaving.

'What was all that about?' Trudy whispered.

'Probably just a routine check, it's strange, even though you were in the toilet they seemed to know there were two of us here.'

'What do you mean?'

'Never mind, forget it. Maybe my tiredness is playing tricks on me.'

For the remainder of their journey the well-fed driver floored the mini-bus toward a towering Barisan Mountain Range, and rallying round a tight bend the sparkling blue waters of Lake Toba came suddenly into view. Surrounded by peaks over a thousand metres tall the giant basin covered more than a thousand square kilometers and the lake was over four hundred metres deep.

Arriving in Parapat, the driver parked over by the ferry terminal and waited for Andy to pay the fare. Handing over the equivalent of a hundred US dollars, double the fare, brought a huge smile to his tired looking face. Walking down to the quay, they boarded an ancient wooden ferryboat and mesmerized by exotic sights and smells, Trudy watched a group of small boys dive into the water and happily retrieve coins thrown by waiting passengers. A short distance away, wooden houses backed onto the lakeside and a woman waist deep in the shallow warm water bathed a child.

'Look Andy, it's just like a National Geographic documentary. Imagine waking up each morning and bathing in the lake with your family?'

Overwhelmed by the magnificence of the surroundings, Andy tried to imagine what it looked like after the event. A massive eruption spread volcanic ash high into the atmosphere for thousands of square miles covering large parts of the Indian sub-continent and Malaysia, causing the earth to suffer years of winters. A large percentage of all vegetation destroyed leaving perhaps only a few thousand ancestors on our planet who survived.

Parked at the rear of the boat was a Japanese SUV with blacked out windows. Looking out of place Andy wondered who could afford such a luxury. In less than forty minutes, they have reached the main island terminal, and watched the SUV disembark and speed off along narrow roads. Staying onboard, the boat maneuvered in the black waters and continued hugging the edge of the island stopping by another small wooden jetty, which turned out to be the rear to their lodgings. Trudy, helped down onto the short boardwalk by eager crewmembers struggled with her bag. Andy jumped down beside her and together they climbed a flight of steps leading directly into the guesthouse. Samosir Cottages looked surprisingly modern; it

The Treaty

had a restaurant and lounge area linked to neat rows of wooden chalets dotted around the periphery - all with breathtaking views of the lake.

'This is great Andy, we have a shower, and the room is big enough - what do you think?'

'Not quite the Marriott, but it will do for a couple of nights. Come on, let's leave our things here, I need a drink and something to eat before I pass out with hunger.'

43

The giant lizard lay rigid across Mardjono's useless legs. From his bed, positioned beneath the open window, he looked across sparkling water reflecting shards of silver and peppered with blue. Few people in the village of Tuk-Tuk knew of his true origin or background, only that he had arrived a few years before unable to walk and moved into this house by the shore. The front room of the cottage was a bookshop, lined from floor to ceiling with neat rows of new and worn paperbacks and hardbacks. New customers soon learned the ritual; first choose a novel, then pay by removing your shoes and entering the old man's private room.

Mardjono was content with his lifestyle, despite his disability, and rarely thought about the time before when he was a young lawyer who trained in Jakarta, and moved to live in Holland. He worked for the infamous Bilderberg Group and in those days, rubbed shoulders with the world's most influential people. He was a close confidant of Prince Bernhard the husband and consort of Queen Juliana of Holland, Bilderberg's first Chairman in 1954. During his time working abroad, the project he was most proud of was drafting the original legal framework for the treaty. This involved endless meetings with committee members and the originator of the idea Prince Philip, husband of the Queen of England. He became close to Philip, and got to know him well, becoming a trusted advisor and making the inevitable rejection harder when it finally happened. Mardjono would tell himself they were great times and had few lingering regrets. He had a good lifestyle living on Lake Toba with all the respect and friends any man required.

Leaving Holland he moved to Bangkok, where during a chance meeting with a military commander from his Bilderberg days, who served in the Laos military government, he was offered the important job as a lawyer working for the new state telephone organization in Vientiane. Afterwards there was the shooting and he almost died, leaving him paralyzed and forced to flee in secret to Indonesia, to the house by the shore. Princess Diana had personally called him in Laos to warn him his life was in danger, and told him she would need to hold onto the original copy of the treaty he had given her to rectify any wrong in the future. He trusted her, and travelled north to stay with friends until he could be sure all was safe. He had never expected anyone would wish to harm him and, after fleeing the country barely alive, left in isolation with many questions unanswered. At least he thought he could rely on Princess Diana to do the right thing.

The man and woman browsing the bookshelves outside Mardjono's room whispered as they sifted through racks of popular paperbacks. Andy selected a well-read Stephen King novel, while Trudy remained undecided. Staff at the hotel told them Mardjono owned the bookshop in the village. It was all too easy. Andy looked around for someone to pay, and spotted a man in the back room lying on a bed with a lizard on his belly. Reading the note in English pinned to the wall, they removed their shoes and entered.

'Please come in, don't stand there. What did you chose?'

'Stephen King,' Andy smiled, edging his way inside the

bright wooden room.

'Ah, yes, Stephen King, very popular. Where are you from?'

Approaching his bedside, wary of the huge colourful lizard sat frozen on top of the old man, Andy looked on in awe at the spectacular view of Lake Toba outside his window.

'England and America,' he smiled shaking Mardjono by the hand. 'I'm Andrew, and this is my partner, Trudy.'

'Hi,' Trudy smiled shyly.

'I met a friend of yours in Laos, Nhia Tou Yang. He asked me to send you his regards.'

'Nhia Tou Yang, my old friend Nhia Tou Yang! Its months since I heard from him, possibly longer, it could be a year. How is he keeping? He must have told you I'm living here.'

Taking in the surreal background to their conversation, unsure of the etiquette when addressing a man lying prostrate in his bed, Andy replied. 'Yes, I met him several months ago when I was working in Vientiane; he told me that you previously had his job before the accident.'

Sitting up, he moved the lizard off his leg. 'It was no accident - terrorists in the north near Lunag Prabang shot me. They almost killed me, but I was lucky to only lose the use of my legs.'

Mardjono called out to a young girl loitering in the shop, who acted as fulltime nurse, companion and shop assistant. She returned dragging two chairs and closed the door behind her.

'Would you like tea? I have asked for tea; please tell me more about Nhia Tou Yang. Did he say if he would come to visit me? I will call him again and tell him you have been to see me.'

'Nhia told me you met with Princess Diana when she visited Vientiane. How did you manage to see her?'

Mardjono smiled. 'You certainly ask a lot of questions.'

The Treaty

'I'm sorry.'

'No, no, it's fine. Well, I spoke with someone at the hotel saying I knew Prince Philip. The Princess came to her phone and we talked about my time in Europe. I told her I had important papers and wanted to discuss these with her.'

'Was she interested?'

'Yes, I think she was curious. She told me her interest was the charity for clearing land mines. I explained I wanted to show her some original and historic documents and we arranged to meet at the Laos Plaza that same afternoon. My purpose was to negotiate more of the narcotics money for my charity in Laos, and for the farmers who grow the poppy.'

Trudy continued listening in silence as Andy pumped the old man with questions.

'Did Diana offer help?'

'Yes, and then asked me for a favour in return - to borrow my papers and make copies for her to keep. She promised to return all the documents the following day. I was a little uncertain but not too worried as I also had another set.'

Reaching down at the bedside, he opened a tin box and extracted faded carbon printed documents originally produced on a manual typewriter, passing them over to Andy.

'I still have these.'

Taking hold of the flimsy sheets he lay them in his lap and carefully turned each page scanning the words and recalling what he had seen on Dominic's computer; they looked to be the same. For the first time he was finally convinced the treaty was for real.

'Did Diana return the documents the next day as promised?' Andy asked, remaining in control of his excitement.

Heaving a sigh, while stroking the lizard, Mardjono's answer revealed his true feeling and lingering disappointment.

'I never saw her or the documents again. I thought she would let me know how my copy of the treaty may have helped, but soon after was killed in that tragic car accident in Paris.'

'So she definitely had an original signed copy of the treaty?'

Mardjono nodded. 'Yes.'

Andy could see the old man was getting tired and probably a little depressed regurgitating all these non-too-happy memories.

'It's probably time for us to leave, thank you Mardjono for such an interesting afternoon and I hope it continues to go well for you. If we find out anymore about the treaty in Europe I will let you know.'

'Good to meet you both and thank you for coming here to see me. I'm so pleased to hear about Asang. I am an old man now.

They both stood up to leave. Reaching out and taking hold of Mardjono's frail hand, he wished him well once again promising they would visit before leaving the island.

The Treaty

44

Walking back toward the centre of Tuk-Tuk village along a route bordered by a row of small windowless wooden houses, Andy paused at a fork in the road and watched a large humpbacked cow grazing peacefully on a tuft of grass.

Breaking the silence, he turned to Trudy. 'What do you think we should do now?'

'Well, we can either go left or right,' she smiled, hands on hips.

'I mean in regards to what we have just heard, as in Diana and the treaty. It seems certain the treaty is for real.'

'Let's forget about that for now,' Trudy sighed, affectionately tugging on his arm. 'I fancy having something nice to eat, and then we can consider what to do next. There's no point worrying about it anymore this evening.'

'You're absolutely right,' he replied, wrapping his arms around her waist. 'I'm pleased you came with me on this trip, I've become very fond of you. Thanks for being such a great friend.'

After kissing affectionately, they continued walking toward a cluster of buildings in the centre of the village. Racked with guilt at her continuing deceit, Trudy found it hard to hold back the truth. They stopped by a chalkboard outside a restaurant and read from the menu.

'Look, Magic Mushroom Omelet!' Andy laughed.

'Can they really be hallucinogenic mushrooms?'

'It wouldn't surprise me. I was offered cannabis several times when we arrived today.'

Gingerly climbing a flight of rickety wooden steps leading onto an open balcony, they came into a room with yet more breathtaking views across the lake. Wearing a beautiful red and gold traditional Tapis Sarong, the waitress came to the table. Ordering a couple of dishes to share, a chicken sate and grilled fish with rice, they sat back and enjoyed a beer. Reflecting on the bizarre meeting with Mardjono, Andy felt unsure what to do next. He could ask Mardjono for his copy of the treaty and take it to the police, but then there was no guarantee they would do anything with it. He now knew the treaty was for real. It frightened him to think that a large percentage of the global economy remained reliant on the US and Britain controlling markets for narcotics - and here was the proof. It seemed clear that as soon as this all became public knowledge, the repercussions would be enormous. Considering destroying the evidence, believing ignorance might be a better alternative to the treaty falling into the wrong hands, he reminded himself that at present with or without the treaty he was a dead man.

Tucking into the delicious food, Trudy's thoughts had gone back to earlier worries about how to escape her terrible dilemma. Finally, unable to bottle it up anymore, she came out with a plan, which may save his life.

'Andy, now we know the truth about the treaty, doesn't this mean you are still in danger? There may be another attempt on your life.'

'Yes, it's been on my mind since Mardjono confirmed my worst fears, and to be absolutely honest I don't really know what to do next.'

'Listen why don't we go off somewhere for a while we could travel Asia or perhaps South America. Maybe they

The Treaty

will forget about you.'

Andy stopped laughing. 'What are you talking about? I have a job and a life in England. I can't just give it all up and disappear anyway, what about your family and University? We cannot run away. It's a great idea, but it's just not possible.'

'Of course it's possible!' she snapped. 'There is something I haven't told you that could make this really easy to do. A few years ago I was left a large sum of money by my Grandparents in a trust, I have access to it now, we can go anywhere in the world and no one will ever find us.'

Andy picked over his food, shaping the rice into hillocks around the edge of his plate and then watched with confusion as they surreally melted like butter. Feeling incredibly strange all a sudden, he stopped eating and took a sip of beer. Trudy dropped her fork and knocked Andy's beer glass over, spilling the foamy liquid all over the table.

'Andy, I feel funny.'

'Yeah, me too,' he replied, glazing over.

Trudy giggled at the changing appearance of Andy's face. She suddenly felt sick and disorientated. The room changed colour and she began hearing strange noises.

'Andy I do not feel well,' she mumbled her face cold and pale. 'Stop the room moving, switch off the bright lights.'

'We need to get back to the hotel,' Andy laughed uncontrollably. 'Before the room sucks us in.'

'Stop laughing at me!' Trudy cried. 'Stop laughing. Why are you laughing?'

Andy tried to stand up, but his legs gave way and he flopped back down onto his chair.

'What is happening Andy, what's going on?'

From across the room a man who came into the restaurant after them was sitting alone at a table watching them.

'I want my bed.' Trudy cried, watching the light fixtures emulsify and drip in swirling patterns of vivid colour.

Andy successfully stood up and staggered to the toilet.

'Be back in a minute,' he slurred over his shoulder.

'Where are you going? Andy, please! Where are you going?'

He locked the door behind him and battled with his mind. Trudy panicked and slipped down off her chair and onto the floor. She was weak and her head was spinning. The walls were caving in and the table legs had turned into thin human legs covered in hair.

'Andy!'

The waitress ran out of the back room and helped Trudy to her feet. She had seen her earlier walking out of the hotel down by the lake with a man, but Trudy did not understand a word she was saying. There was shouting and people flashing around helping her from the restaurant back toward their hotel. Andy's eyes sprung open some moments later. He sat on the toilet, his feet had melted into the floor and unable to move. His vision was clear he could feel his heart pounding inside his chest. A feverish nightmare ensued as he battled with insanity. Covering his eyes, he breathed slowly and managed to regain some composure. Holding onto the wall, he dragged himself to his feet. Unlocking the door, stepped out into the bright lights of the restaurant and walked over to the table. Trudy was gone. Breathing heavily he was starting to panic; she was nowhere to be seen. In the dark shadows of the restaurant, glowing eyes watched him, and terrified he stumbled down the steep stairs out into the street heading toward the hotel. Arriving at the wooden steps taking him down toward the jetty by the lake, he cautiously negotiated each riser while clutching the handrail. Passing at the turning to his room, he continued drawn by the shimmering water Sitting down with his legs dangling over the edge of the pier he stared mournfully into the black. Surrounded by plants, bushes and seeing them morph into different shapes and sizes producing a soft kaleidoscope of colours on the surface of the water. Suddenly feeling incredibly hot he began tearing at his T-shirt. He wrestled to pull it over his head, screaming and cursing into the still night; with one final tug, as he pulled it over his head losing his balance slipped off the side and disappeared. Causing hardly ripple the still innocence belied the treacherous currents swirling beneath the mass of water. Quickly descending, trapped in a spiraling current, he fought to get back up to the surface. With lungs ready to explode, he soon realized he could no longer hold his breath and stopped the futile struggle. The bright lights dimmed and the noises stopped. Immediately feeling calmer, he heard his name being called, a solitary voice, which sounded like someone he knew - his mother or was it Maria. Giant globules of colour floated passed, peaceful, warm and safe - to the sounds of the sirens call.

'Andy, Andy...'

Then in a mass of unexpected turbulence, the liquid tentacles lost their grip and a human shape, now clearly visible, disrupted the flow of the current and releasing him as he shot to the surface like a cork from a bottle. Strong hands grasped his lifeless body, dragging him to the surface and hauling him onto the lakeside. Unconscious and unaware of the drama, seen by a man, the owner of the hotel, who rushed to his aid bringing more help with him. Once the lungs recovered and were empty of fluid, the island doctor arrived and attended to him in a small bedroom.

Sleeping for almost twelve hours, Andy woke up in unfamiliar surroundings; the sun streamed through the window and the birds sang loudly outside the door. He looked to his left expecting to see Maria asleep beside him; but she was not there.

'Where is Maria?' Andy whispered.

A member of staff was standing by the door looking out across the lake when Andy woke. The young girl named Rusty, a local Batak girl, walked over to the bed.

'Where is Maria?' he asked.

The girl looked confused and ran out of the room. Moment's later Hendrik the manager appeared.

'There is no Maria,' he told Andy. 'You mean Trudy.'

Andy closed his eyes, and nodded.

Resting for a while longer, he decided he was well enough to return to his own room, he borrowed a dressing gown and shuffled back to find the drapes closed and no sign of Trudy anywhere. When he looked closer even more alarmingly, there was no sign of her clothes, shoes or even the bag she brought with her - it was all gone. His headache immediately disappeared, and quickly dressing he hurried to reception and asked if they had seen her. Rusty, who seemed almost permanently to be at work, described how earlier that morning his woman friend had left the hotel carrying a bag and driven away in a black SUV. Speechless Andy appeared confused, and then began a noisy protest saying his girlfriend was the victim of an outrageous kidnap and asked someone to call the police. Hendrik, the manger reappeared and on hearing the story, reluctantly agreed to phone the only police officer stationed on the island, while suspecting Trudy would probably reappear before he even arrived. Andy however was completely convinced she went with those people against her will, for reasons he could not reveal to them. At the forefront of his mind, he knew this all had something to do with their discovery of Mardjono and the treaty and he knew he had to act fast.

The Treaty

45

'Good morning Caroline, how is sunny Madrid?'

'*Buenos Dias*, Richard. Madrid is not so sunny; in fact, it is raining! I may as well be back in London.'

'Did you know Andrew Davies has left the country again?'

'Yes, he is working for a few days in Kuala Lumpur. I've spoken to him and alerted our local people to keep a close eye on them both.'

'Them? So he's not travelling on his own, who's he with?'

'An LSE student called Trudy Shupe, American; they met before he was hospitalized. At one stage we were both visiting him in the hospital it was embarrassing.'

Sir Richard Parsons rarely telephoned Caroline directly, and she anticipated this conversation was leading to something more important.

'It's beginning to make sense,' he explained. 'Our chaps at MI-6 have intercepted conversations between some American, who they have under surveillance with Fatima. They are sure she is still in Marrakech, but this other fellow is calling from a remote region of Northern Sumatra, and has apparently met with a girl called Trudy. Can this be the same Trudy Shupe?'

Taken aback by what Richard was saying she agreed it more than possible.

'Listen Caroline, I want you to go to find them.'

'Excuse me?'

'I want you to go to Sumatra, wherever that is, and find them.'

'But…'

'Look, I appreciate you already have a lot of work to do.'

'More than I can handle,' she sighed.

'Like I said all your efforts are very much appreciated. It is just I cannot allow this whole situation to mushroom into another Laos fiasco, especially involving an American citizen. Downing Street has reacted badly to all the continuing rumours circulating about Prince Philip; they want them quashed finally. If anything happens to the girl and it is linked to the treaty, all hell will be let loose on this side.'

'I understand I will make arrangements immediately. Can you authorize our people in Kuala Lumpur and Medan to provide any back office services I may need?'

'I will take care of that and Caroline - be careful.'

Richard Parsons ended the call and sank back into his black leather executive chair. He was confident Caroline would sort out whatever was going on and pleased she had been available to leave at short notice. Leaving his desk, he paced over to the window looking across London's Millbank and the River Thames. Richard was an experienced professional in the security service and very familiar with the risks involved with their work. The treaty was starting to escalate and could get out of hand, especially if Fatima's people found what they appeared to be after. He was depending on Caroline to stop her.

He himself was no stranger to stories about illegal accords between the US and Britain, and from his discussions with Camilla knew exactly what was going on. He first made his own discovery during his military days on a six-month secondment to the US army. This was during the 1980's,

The Treaty

and it quickly became clear there was a chain of command trading arms and dealing drugs in Latin America, with most of the dealing and management organized by a private company called Healthy Verve. He knew this company was still in existence and assumed they were by now a legitimate and respectable business, with the passage of time. This whole episode of his life seemed surreal and despite the scandal he discovered long ago, it was all well above his pay scale and he did not choose to become involved. In the past weeks, new stories kept emerging in the press, and most recently one in the Daily Express making a direct link between Prince Philip and Healthy Verve claiming he was a secret investor using a blind trust fund - something Camilla had confirmed was true. None of this unduly bothered the old chap, who at 84 had more important health issues to concentrate on, and anyway Philip and scandal had persisted for years, he usually ignored it never making any comment and waited for the press to get fed up before moving on with something else. Richard's main problem was his own boss - the Prime Minister, whose ignorance of the treaty was embarrassing. Despite 'the special relationship' with America, the poor man was not aware this agreement between the two countries was still in operation and leading toward a huge international scandal.

46

'Baby, are you feeling okay, are my people looking after you?'

'Yes I'm fine, everything's fine,' Trudy replied, speaking softly into the mobile.

'Do you have my treaty safe?'

'Yes, I have it right here.'

'Keep it safe for me, baby, we cannot afford to lose it. Now I can start my campaign. I knew you would help me and not let me down.'

Staying silent, she let Fatima continue talking on the mobile her captors handed to her. After being assisted out of the restaurant the previous night she had been bundled into a black SUV, and taken to a private house a few miles away. Waking early the next morning Trudy realized mushrooms caused the hallucinations they suffered and after a briefing by her captors, she told them about Mardjono when it became clear Andy's life was in danger.

Returning to their hotel, she saw Andy sleeping in another room. Unable to communicate with him she had to leave in silence, collecting her bag and passport with no chance to explain about Fatima, or say goodbye. There was no other choice - his life was at stake.

'Listen baby, we can talk on this phone but please, you must not contact me anymore until you arrive here - is that okay?'

'Where will they take me, Fatima?'

'Home, here with me baby, in Morocco - you will love this place, it is beautiful. When you arrive we can let your people know you are safe - is that okay baby, you do still love me?'

'Yes, of course.'

'Good, now put Allam back on the line, I need to speak with him.'

Her minder took hold of the phone and began talking in Arabic. Trudy looked out through the tinted windows of the SUV and across the deck of the ferry loaded with goods, mainly hardwood taken from the small forests on the island. A teenage girl waist deep in the lake, dampened her hair with soft rainwater warmed by endless days of tropical sun, and began rhythmically flicking the long tresses from side to side. The boat began to move as Trudy began to cry. Gentle silent tears, there was no turning back; she had so desperately wanted to tell Andy the truth and now it was too late.

47

'If anything bad has happened to my girl I'll tear your frik'n head apart with my bare hands.'

Andy tried to explain again to Tom Shupe how his daughter had left him at the hotel voluntarily, and then realized the line was dead. Trudy's father was clearly not a happy man.

Passing the receiver back to Rusty, he wandered restlessly down to the jetty. Squatting by the exact spot where he had fallen in the night before he aimlessly scanned the surface to see if he could locate his mobile phone lying hundreds of metres on the bottom of the lake. There was no sign Trudy had been at all unhappy. Only the day before she had been all over him like a rash, kissing and touching showing genuine affection. It simply did not add up, something must have happened to her. Hearing his name being called, this time for real, he turned to see Rusty standing in the hotel entrance waving a piece of paper.

'Mr Andy, I have message for you. A woman called just now, you must go to her at Ambarita. She wants talk with you, it very important.'

'Was it Trudy - did she say her name?'

Rusty shook her head. 'I not sure Mr Andy, she spoke too quickly for me. I no understand. Ambarita close from here, about five kilometres.'

The Treaty

'You're sure she didn't say her name or why she wanted to meet?'

'I very sorry, but nothing else, she stopped the phone.'

'OK, Rusty. Thanks.'

It had to be Trudy, who else could it be?

Andy walked back inside the hotel and spotted Hendrik sitting in the lounge room watching a DVD.

'Hendrik, I need to get to Ambarita urgently! Can you get me a taxi?'

'That is not a problem,' he smiled, pressing the pause button on the remote control. 'One will be here in twenty minutes.'

'I need faster, Hendrik. Will the boss take me in his car?'

'He is not here Mr Andy; he has gone to the mainland. May I ask if everything is okay, has your friend returned?'

'No, I really need to get to Ambarita. It's an emergency!'

'You can take my bike, I don't need it today.'

'Thanks, Hendrik.'

The last time Andy had ridden a motorbike was when he was 16, and it was not a pleasant experience. Despite this, he followed him to the small car park beneath the hotel. The bike was a Honda Super Cub, the Asian equivalent to the Ford's Model T or the Volkswagen. Honda produced millions of these bikes, seen all over Asia transporting whole families around. Hendrik demonstrated the simple controls while Andy sat astride the bike and opened the throttle.

'Try please, Mr. Andy,' Hendrik smiled.

Andy placed a hand on Hendrik's shoulder. 'Thank you for your help.'

Roaring away in a cloud of exhaust fumes, he headed north hugging the shoreline. Rallying passed neat rows of wooden houses with no fixed doors or windows; he managed to avoid huge potholes in the middle of the road. Hendrik had told him to look out for a traditional Batak house. He would recognize this, as sadly there were only a few remaining. Rounding a sharp bend the wooden house loomed ahead, there was no place name to mark Ambarita, and he only guessed this was it. Standing the bike in the centre of a courtyard and close to some ancient stone seats arranged in a bizarre circle it seemed to be deserted and just a little eerie. Striding around the outside of the building, he couldn't find an entrance and was startled when a man suddenly appeared. Dressed in a Manchester United football shirt, the man claimed he was a guide for this historic village and offered to give him the full tour. Andy explained he was meeting a friend. The guide instantly turned back looking toward the house saying a woman was already inside the Batak House, and perhaps waiting for him. Handing over the few coins, Andy made for the stairs and squeezing through a trapdoor size hole blinked into the darkness and waited for his eyes to adjust. The only light came from a row of small windows along one wall of this empty room. In one corner was a raised plinth and gradually he focused on someone - a woman seated on the plinth with her legs dangling down over the side.

48

'Caroline! What the hell are you doing?'

Grinning broadly, she came out of the shadows and planted a kiss on Andy's cheek. Having undergone a dramatic makeover, she looked amazing with short blonde hair and wearing a sexy cropped top and a pair of Miss Sixty jeans.

'I was missing you,' she smiled.

'You must've really missed me to travel seven thousand miles. What's happened to you, you look different? How did you find this place? I never gave you the location.'

'My job description darling is Intelligence Officer. It wasn't rocket science, particularly with the amount of communications signals you've both been spraying into the ether over the past few days.'

'Well, as it happens, I'm really pleased to see you, but why here - in this weird house?'

'My boss sent me to find you and on the way over I heard Trudy had gone missing.'

'You heard right.'

'She finally saw sense and did a runner, then?'

Andy turned to Caroline and narrowed his eyes. 'Do you think this is some kind of joke, some stupid game?'

'I'm sorry, Andy, I should not have said that. You must be extremely worried.'

'Yes, believe it or not, I am!'

'Look, we have been monitoring calls linked to you and Trudy via GCHQ, and there has been a lot of chatter mentioning both Fatima and Trudy coming from this part of the world. We did not want another situation to develop like Maria. Our communications people at MI-6 intercepted a short burst from Trudy's mobile at this precise location; I suspected you would be close. My back-office staff found your hotel and left you the message. What happened to your mobile, I've been trying to call you for hours?'

Andy looked furtive. 'It's at the bottom of Lake Toba. Come on, let's go outside, it's so dark in here it gives me the creeps.'

Caroline struggled through the narrow doorway with her Gucci rucksack. They walked over to the moped and sat on the stone seats used in the old days by village elders.

'Andy, listen, I have to tell you something and before I do promise me you won't kick-off again. You may not like this?'

Nodding, he steeled himself for what was to come; realizing there had to be a strong motive for Caroline's presence here on the island.

'As you know we have picked up *chatter* from this region mentioning Fatima. Well, we also had the same coming through linking her to Trudy. This is why my boss sent me here. We are almost one hundred percent certain Trudy and Fatima know each other. In fact, we can prove they met in the USA on several occasions and, before you say anything, this was confirmed by MI-6 and wasn't passed on to me so please don't start shouting.'

As the blood drained from his face, he looked both stunned and horrified by her revelations and felt deeply, deeply embarrassed by his own staggering naiveté for a second time.

Andy stood up and kicked a stone across the ground. 'I

don't believe this!'

'Andy, calm down.'

'She was here helping me! It was her suggestion to help clear my name of any suspicion related to the treaty.'

'It's not your fault!'

'She wanted the treaty documents for Fatima. I wondered why she was so interested in the stupid thing. I can't believe it, how could I be such a sucker - again?'

Andy walked away trying to stem the erupting anger, then rushed back toward Caroline and pointed a finger at his forehead.

'It's written here, isn't it, tattooed across my forehead - *STUPID DUMB ASS SUCKER*!'

'Andy, please! She is a young girl, a young student and there is the possibility she had no choice. Fatima is a very powerful woman who could easily have threatened to kill her if she didn't co-operate.'

'Oh, please, spare me the bullshit! Look, we have to find her. She was last seen driving away in a black SUV.'

'How long ago was that?'

'I'm not sure probably three hours ago.'

'Well, I've heard nothing from the mainland. I've got my driver positioned at the main port.'

'When does the next ferry leave?'

Caroline glanced at the slender gold Rolex around her wrist. 'In about fifteen minutes!'

Andy leaped onto the moped and struck the tiny Honda into action. 'We have to stop that ferry!'

Swinging her Gucci rucksack over her shoulder Caroline straddled the bike. The bag contained a simple full length silk dress for evening wear, clean underwear, makeup, plastic bin liner if it rained, and a Heckler & Koch Mark 23 Caliber .45 automatic pistol; the same gun used by special forces and US Navy Seals.

'Okay, I'm on!' she shouted over the noise of the engine.

'Let's go!'

Releasing the clutch, Andy revved the 50cc, four-stroke engine and began to maneuver out onto the road. With the throttle wide open, needing more power for the return trip with two on board, Caroline gripped so tight he could hardly breathe. She soon learned which way to lean on cornering and shrieked with delight as they sped down a steep incline. With her cropped top trucked-up around the midriff, idle men and young boys sitting around whistled and shouted as they zoomed passed. It was not long before Andy saw the lake up ahead and a ferry next to the pier with vehicles on it all ready to leave. Straight away, he saw the black SUV and quickly applied the brakes skidding to a halt.

'That's the SUV that took Trudy!'

Caroline frowned. 'How do you know?'

'I just know. It has to be! I can't imagine there's many on the island.'

'What shall we do?'

'Make sure it doesn't leave without us.'

Andy moved closer to the boat, trying hard not to be noticed by the driver of the SUV or by Trudy. Caroline prepared to jump aboard, and Andy looked in surprise as she extracted the gun and released the safety placing it back inside the bag.

'Are you sure you are going to be okay?' he whispered.

'Why, are you worried about me?' she winked.

'Maybe I am.'

'Listen, I will get Trudy. Find us a fast boat so we can get the hell out of here.'

She leaped aboard and raced across the deck toward the SUV. Guessing Trudy was inside she tapped the driver's side window. As it slid open, she immediately saw her sat in the back beside a large looking man, the only other person being the male driver. He seemed surprised and even more

The Treaty

so when she began speaking in a classic softly spoken English accent.

'Excuse me I wonder if you can help me?'

Then without waiting for a response, she whipped out the gun already in her hand and pointed directly at the driver's head.

'*SIT STILL! TRUDY I WANT YOU TO LEAVE THE VEHICLE - MOVE! OPEN THE DOOR OR I'LL BLOW YOUR FRIGGIN HEAD OFF - NOW!*'

The electronic lock snapped open and Trudy grabbed her bag with the treaty inside and climbed out. She pushed her along the deck walking backwards; keeping the gun trained on the two men both wide-eyed with shock and bemusement.

'*RUN - GO!*' she shouted at Trudy. '*JUMP OFF THE BOAT!*'

The rope securing the ferry to the shore was released and the crewmember clambered back onboard.

Still shouting as Trudy hesitated, Caroline yelled again. '*I SAID JUMP!*'

The men had left the SUV, and both were holding a gun. Trudy leaped from the moving boat, closely followed by Caroline who landed softly amid sacks and boxes stacked at the quayside. The ferry had already started powering away as Andy called them over to a waiting speedboat. Running toward him Trudy wrapped her arms around his neck.

'No time for that, let's get out of here!' Caroline yelled.

They all leaped aboard and the boatman immediately whacked the boat into full-throttle, pushing back the still water in a huge wave. Veering left away from the ferry once ahead they began to turn right back on course toward Parapat where they hoped to arrive before the ferry. Trudy and Andy sat together nearer the bow, while Caroline was last onboard at the back. She had managed to retrieve her bin liner and stow the gun back inside the Gucci bag, wrapping the whole pack to keep it dry from the inevitable spray.

'*TRUDY*!' Caroline shouted over the noise of the engine. '*GIVE ME THE TREATY?*'

Andy looked in surprise as Trudy withdrew Mardjono's carbon copies of the treaty out of her bag as they bounced at high speed across the choppy water advancing toward the crimson mountains. Glancing over his shoulder at the SUV on the boat he watched it slowly growing smaller, and suddenly saw the rear window open and something poke out through the back.

'*OH GOD*!' he shouted.

Seconds later, the water all around began to boil from continuous bursts of AK-47 gunfire, and the boatman raked with automatic gunshot. Blood splattered across Andy's face, as the boat swerved out of control and suddenly flipped into the air throwing them all into the water. Hitting her head on, the side as she went in Trudy disappeared beneath the depths with the copies of the treaty still in her hand. For the second time in less than 24 hours, Andy was floundering, this time in the middle of Lake Toba. Caroline looked around desperately for Trudy and signaling to Andy dived athletically beneath the surface disappearing for what felt like minutes, and then suddenly burst to the surface with Trudy in her arms. Onshore another fisherman watched the drama unfold, and realizing they needed help he powered up his boat and burned to their rescue. Clinging onto Andy, Trudy was still dazed with bruises to her neck and face. Persuading the driver to drop them out of site of the ferry port, they waded the last few metres onto dry land. Their boatman remained somewhere in the water presumed dead and they could do nothing apart from explain to the authorities what happened. Trying to remain inconspicuous, the bedraggled

The Treaty

trio, led by Caroline, ducked and dived along rows of market stalls toward a prearranged venue at a café where her driver originally dropped her off. Years of experience had taught her; never enter the box until all your exits are clear.

49

Caroline walked with Andy through the busy concourse and stood outside Kuala Lumpur's Subang Airport terminal building.

'Sorry, to keep you waiting,' she smiled, lighting a cigarette. 'It took ages to sort everything out with the Indonesian authorities. I am sitting in on a meeting tomorrow at their Embassy in Kuala Lumpur to explain what happened. There shouldn't be any problems, so feel free to leave for the UK whenever you are ready. Where's Trudy disappeared to?'

'Oh, you missed that little drama,' Andy sighed. 'Her father's in town and they've taken her to the US Embassy to meet with him. He's taking her back to the UK tonight.'

'Andy, you did your best. Her father is lucky to have Trudy back at all, but more to the point how about you?'

'I'm fine, I can't believe what you did back there Caroline, you could've been killed. Why did you risk your life for Trudy?'

'Maybe I did it for you,' she smiled, taking his hand and giving it a squeeze. 'At the end of the day we prevented Fatima getting hold of Mardjono's copy of the treaty, I call that a result. It's a shame all those lovely papers are still floating in Lake Toba as I would really liked to have seen them. Oh well, nothing we can do about that now.'

Andy knew Caroline was teasing him, but he was deter-

The Treaty

mined to stay his hand and refused to acknowledge he also had a copy of the documents. Pulling up alongside them, Abu, a British Embassy driver, waited in the car with the engine running. Andy surprised Caroline with a spontaneous kiss on the cheek.

'I know I've been very rude to you, but I'm grateful for what you did back there. Thank you, Caroline.'

'You don't have to thank me, it's my job. Maybe we can meet for dinner next time we are both in London.'

'Yes, I would like that.'

'And please Andy, stay in your room tonight. Do not go wandering off around the city. This is still very much Fatima territory and she must be really pissed-off with you right now, so take care.'

Andy walked over to the waiting Limousine and gave a wave as it pulled away. Relaxing back in the comfortable leather seat it felt good; this was the first time he had been alone since leaving the island. Throughout their journey from Lake Toba to Medan, Caroline had spent most of her time negotiating with the Indonesian authorities. Trudy slept, saying little about what happened after she left him in the restaurant; her only explanation was that Fatima tricked her. She did try to persuade Fatima not to pursue the treaty for his sake, and admitted she should not have lied and that her feelings toward him were genuine. For Andy, there was no going back after her betrayal; it was impossible to trust her again. There was no anger only a feeling of great sadness.

50

'How does the Laurent Perrier Bar at the Savoy Hotel sound?' Caroline asked. 'Will that be okay for you?'

'Yes, it's not far from where I'm working. I should be able to find it.'

'Well, I am pleased you arrived back safely. I must hurry if I am going to be there on time. Don't you be late, twelve-thirty, ciao?'

Andy had not spoken with Caroline since returning from Malaysia, and he looked forward to catching-up with any news about Trudy and Fatima. He had spent the morning working in a client's office a short taxi ride from the Savoy. The journey took less than ten minutes. Paying off the cab, he stepped back to admire the Savoy's imposing facade and nineteenth century architecture then hesitated, a little unnerved by the grandeur, before walking toward the door. The uniformed flunky opened it wide allowing him inside; Andy straightened his posture and nodded a thank you, a little conscious he was not wearing a smart business suit. Making his way through the plush foyer, he soon discovered the bar where they arranged to meet, and with a sigh of relief spotted Caroline sitting at the bar. Turning in her seat dressed smartly in autumn colours she saw him and began waving. Andy walked over as she stood to greet him.

The Treaty

'You look well,' Caroline beamed, standing back and admiring his good looks.

'Thanks, you're looking pretty hot yourself.'

They moved over to a table with more comfortable lounge chairs, directed by a waiter who materialized from nowhere. He topped up Caroline's champagne producing a glass for Andy.

'I try my best,' she grinned. Eager to make the best use of their time and capitalize on any goodwill existing between them, she plunged in with a question. 'I hate to drag this up again so soon, but when I mentioned to my boss we were meeting today he began pushing for information. I will be straight with you, Andy; his target is to get his hands on the original signed...'

'Wait a minute,' Andy interrupted, raising his hand, 'did you come here to see me or get gold stars from your boss?'

'What do you mean?' Caroline frowned.

'I've just walked through the door and you are asking me bloody questions again about the treaty.'

'This will not take long and then after we can relax and enjoy ourselves. I need to find out more, this is important.'

'Two minutes, otherwise I am out of here.'

Caroline smiled and sipped her champagne. 'I love it when you get angry.'

Andy was not laughing. 'Just get on with it.'

'Okay, did you learn anything from Maria when she lived with Dominic Marsh, which may still be of interest to us?'

'Not that I can recall,' he sighed, glancing around to make sure no one was listening. 'You read my witness statement. I'm not sure how much you already know regarding the association between Prince Philip and the treaty. I'm mentioning this because when we met Mardjono he discussed both Philip and Princess Diana.'

'What you've told me is all I know, and the stupid rumours that have been circulating in the press, however, none of it supported by a shred of evidence. Why, do you have proof?'

Andy shook his head. 'No, of course not, Mardjono gave his original signed treaty to Diana, and she never returned it to him, it must still be out there somewhere and the question is where?'

Pushing back in her seat, deep in thought, it began to make sense to Caroline why Richard was increasingly paranoid about this whole saga. At first she thought maybe, it was fear of the political fallout in pure historic terms, but the possibility of an agreement between the US and Britain - with some part played in the negotiations by Prince Philip, would give a new dimension to any crisis.

'Okay, your two minutes are up,' Andy smiled, tapping his watch.

'Come on, surely you can't be serious. I would have thought you would be itching to find out any news regarding Trudy and Fatima.'

'I must admit, I hoped you'd tell me something.'

Taking another gulp of Champagne, Caroline wiggled her nose as she swallowed, reacting to the sharp fizzy sensation caused by the bubbles. 'I've been discovering more about Trudy. Do you want to hear, or is she history now?'

'No, go on, please.'

'Well, according to CIA files, Fatima and Trudy had known each other for several years and were friends in Washington. They used a device supplied to CIA operatives, probably stolen from her own father, which enabled encrypted calls from a Laptop computer direct to Fatima and...are you okay hearing this in public?'

Andy had gone quiet and looked serious, she was ever mindful of his unpredictable nature.

'Yes I'm fine, carry on,' he nodded.

'Fatima really does get about and we are no closer to finding out what it is she's up to, apart from making stren-

The Treaty

uous efforts to find a copy of the treaty. Trudy on the other hand has left the LSE and has gone back to the US. Have you heard anything more from her?'

'No, not a word, apart from an email saying she was sorry and that was it.'

'Trudy is a very lucky girl. My brief was not to let her deliver the documents she stole from Mardjono - under any circumstances.'

'You would've shot her if she had refused to go with you?'

'Work it out.'

Ending the conversation on that note, Andy switched back to discussing the missing documents.

'I want closure on all this Caroline, to put it behind me. I am taking a trip up to Althorp where it started to see if there is anything I've overlooked. It will also be a good opportunity to visit Janet and her husband Jack - she was Dominic Marsh's housekeeper and a good friend to Maria.'

'That sounds like a really good idea. It seems ridiculous, but it's a part of the country I've never been to. I would like to see it myself.'

'Well, you are more than welcome to come with me. It's only two hours drive from Central London, and I can pick you up and take you along.'

'When did you have mind?'

'I thought maybe soon. Next Saturday?'

'I'm in London on the Friday for a meeting. Why don't we make a weekend of it and stay somewhere Saturday night, then have a really good look around?'

Not having considered anything this elaborate, Andy did not immediately respond.

'Of course, if you prefer not to, we can travel back the same day. I just thought we could explore the area a little more.'

'Yes, why not, it sounds like a plan. I will arrange for somewhere to stay, there are a few decent places in the area. I particularly want to explore the church and visit Althorp house; having more time makes sense.'

'Are you sure about this? It all sounds expensive. I am happy to pay my way, no favour you understand?'

He laughed at her joke. 'Of course, it's the least I can do to say thank you and, besides, I will really enjoy your company.'

She reached out and touched his hand. 'I told you before, there's no need to thank me.'

51

'Excuse me sir, the Prime Minister has requested a short meeting after his appointment today with the Queen.'

'Is it Tuesday again already? That should be fine hardly going anywhere. Let me know if I need to prepare anything.'

'Yes thank you, sir.'

The Queen's private secretary ended the call to Prince Philip's apartment at Windsor Castle, and immediately phoned the Prime Minister's office to confirm the arrangements. Philip did not have to guess why the PM wanted to see him so urgently. Throughout the week tabloid newspapers, in particular the Daily Express had been running stories implicating Philip with the American company Healthy Verve. Most of the articles contained a semblance of truth, but none contained a scrap of evidence. Surprised by some revelations claiming the Indonesian lawyer, Mardjono, had been discovered on a remote island and was willing to tell all. Philip felt relieved to learn he didn't have any documents to support his story, claiming he was forced to hand them over to people he believed worked for Philip and the Americans. Only wishing Mardjono was right and they did have all the documents back Philip considered how on reflection, he had been careless letting him have a signed copy of the treaty in the first place. If it was true that Mardjono didn't have any evidence, then this was welcome news. The most recent independent report he received coming from Camilla, was that all of Mardjono's documents were lost during some altercation between British spooks and some mysterious foreign group, and were last seen floating in one of the deepest lakes in the world. This would he hoped be an end to the matter and one more problem out of the way.

'Excuse me sir, the Prime Minister is here. Shall I bring him in?'

'Yes, yes bring him in and, Michael, get some coffee and a small brandy and soda for me.'

The PM came into the room as Philip reached for his stick and began to struggle to his feet.

'Prime Minister what a surprise, good to see you old chap. Are you feeling guilty that you visit my wife once a week, but never call on me?'

Laughing falsely the PM cleared his throat, 'Please, don't get up sir, I'm so sorry to disturb you at such short notice.'

Collapsing back in his chair, they waited for Michael to set out the coffee and place Philip's brandy next to him on a small table.

'Don't stand on ceremony Prime Minister take the weight of your feet.'

'Close the door Michael, no interruptions for half-an-hour there's a good chap. So, what's this all about?'

'There is a matter receiving a lot of attention in the media at the moment. I felt we should discuss it before tomorrow's question time in Parliament. Do you still see the papers?'

'Yes, I'm not completely blind. The Telegraph most days, but it's not what it was you know, going downhill fast I reckon - full of rubbish.'

'Well, you may have noticed one item that has been mentioned on television in a documentary and was covered on the wireless by the BBC Today program, regarding some

The Treaty

historic documents originating from the 1960's. Apparently, some of my predecessors are accused of making an agreement with America and this agreement was said to have been signed in your presence.'

Philip enjoyed listening to the Prime Minister tiptoeing around this delicate subject and he intended to give him a hard time.

'It's a good thing you trained as a lawyer Prime Minister,' he chuckled mischievously. 'You will be more aware than most that spreading scandalous rumours without a shred of evidence is a very serious matter. However, in my capacity as the senior member of the royal family, this is not the first time such stories have appeared. There is actually very little I can do to stop them without making matters far worse.'

'I do understand sir, my family and I suffer this exposure in much the same way. My difficulty with this particular event is there are other issues that I have been warned may enter the public domain in the very near future - fore-warned is forearmed as they say.'

'Now you're speaking in riddles,' Philip frowned.

'As you are probably aware, the Chancellor of the Exchequer's office has to work closely with the US Treasury department these days, especially since the Americans introduced their USA Patriot ACT to control terrorists laundering huge sums of money.'

Philip remained poker-faced whist clearly uneasy with the direction the Prime Minister's conversation was leading.

'Yes, go on.'

'I understand that many years ago your own finances were moved, and investments were made in a range of overseas trust funds managed abroad. The question that has been posed is where the initial and subsequent reported rise in income came from, we are not aware you had such wealth when you entered the royal family.'

'My first answer for you Prime Minister is that I stopped dealing with these affairs more than fifty ago. I have a financial manager who looks after my investments and you had better go and ask him your impertinent questions.

'Sir, I realize how disrespectful this may seem, but I can promise you we have acted on the information supplied by the US Treasury as discreetly as we can, which included speaking with your advisors. We have found no one able to explain where the initial private funds came from and subsequent rise in income, hence my coming to you for some kind of explanation. I am sorry to be longwinded, but according to a report that was apparently being leaked in Washington and the UK, you currently have invested wealth in excess of ten billion dollars.'

Philip looked stunned, then ready to explode, before relaxing back in his chair and laughing loudly. 'My word, congratulations Prime Minister, you have just won top prize for the biggest heap of blithering old rubbish I have ever heard.' Fuming with indignation Philip went onto to say, 'I could not put together ten million pounds without taking a mortgage on this pile of stone, and that's if I owned it in the first place.'

The Prime Minister laughed falsely and shuffled uncomfortably in his chair.

'Didn't you know Prime Minster; I'm a man of straw. I came into this family penniless apart from my naval officer's salary. I have no money of my own, apart from what I've scrimped and saved over the years from gifts and official handouts.'

The PM had clearly touched a raw nerve and just as he was about to find a way of escaping his embarrassment, a gentle tap on the door saved the day. Michael made a well-timed entrance.

'Can I get you more coffee and another glass of brandy sir - also your tablets and a glass of water?'

The Treaty

'Thank you Michael, good feller, I have to watch myself getting too excited, it's my blood pressure you know. That will be all for now Michael, the Prime Minister is leaving soon.'

After waiting in silence for Michael to finish pouring more coffee and handing over the tablet, the Prime Minister watched as Philip swallowed the pill and took a sip of water.

'My intention was not to cause offence,' the Prime Minister awkwardly smiled. 'I'm simply the messenger tasked with making you aware of what is officially being stated. Apparently, most of the money credited in your name arises from a complex network of trust funds all linked to a significant holding in a relatively unknown organization called Healthy Verve International. It has even been reported you made a private visit to their annual conference this year during your holiday in America, but again no one has been able to confirm if this is true or not. All I am trying to do is seek a rationale explanation, so that when the Chancellor or I stand up in Parliament we can end the speculation.'

Philip had calmed down after taking a sip of brandy, and paused to consider how to respond. He always knew if would become more difficult to keep his affairs secret in the face of ever increasing scrutiny by governments and the media, but he had hoped he could get through in his own lifetime. His finance man had repeatedly assured him there would never be any way of directly linking him to the money and he had to believe this was still the same situation today.

'Yes, yes, I am sorry too, one gets tired, especially when you reach my age and still have to defend ones self against this utter blithering drivel. Surely there must come a time in my life when this stops, preferably before I kick the bucket.'

'Well, as you said earlier sir, without proof there is little anyone can do. Your financial advisors both home and abroad have already confirmed you do not have any investments in this company and rightly refuse to provide further information about your private affairs. I have asked the questions and I will relay your answers back to the cabinet. It is my belief this is probably all part of some long running conspiracy designed to discredit my government and you and your family. Since you have just assured me that none of these accusations are true, I willingly accept your word and will make my own views on this matter known.'

Sitting straight in his chair and clearly happy to hear the Prime Minister's change of tune, Philip brightened, becoming friendlier. 'Obviously I would appreciate your help Prime Minister. I am quite defenseless against these rumours, being the innocent party.'

'Of course, I will do my level best to make sure you are not embarrassed any further by such intrusive enquiries. There is just one other matter. I am about to announce the date for my retirement as Prime Minister having decided it's time to stand down. I have informed Her Majesty the Queen and will be looking to pursue an active career in some other suitable role. The Queen has mentioned she is considering a proposal for the creation of a roving ambassador working for the Commonwealth. I am still some way off reaching sixty, and if her majesty should consider my background and experience worthy of such a title then I will be more than interested.'

'Yes, that would perhaps be an excellent idea,' Philip smiled. 'I will definitely recommend to the Queen she takes your vast experience and negotiating skills into account in the coming months. There is another opportunity you may want to consider for a similar kind of ambassadorial role. I require someone of your stature to help me

The Treaty

with my work at The World Wildlife Fund. It is a very prestigious part-time position and will come with two grace and favour residences in London and the Bahamas, plus six-figure remuneration for expenses. I will be more than happy to recommend you.'

'Thank you very much indeed, sir. I am most definitely interested, and again, my apology if this meeting was stressful for you. Please consider the whole matter closed. I will ensure it's sorted out completely to everyone's satisfaction.'

Standing ready to leave, the Prime Minister walked briskly over to Prince Philip, bowing to shake his hand. The two great men no longer needed to speak their thoughts; a simple glance and eye contact sealed the agreement. The Prime Minister left the room.

52

Caroline sank back into the kiwi leather seats of Andy's carbon black BMW M3 Coupe, like an excited schoolchild, badgering him for more information.

'Come on, Andy tell me more! Where are we staying?'

'OK, first we are going to check-in at Fawsley Hall, a five-hundred year old manor house in the middle of gardens designed by Capability Brown.'

'That all sounds fabulous.'

'It looked pretty good on the net. There's a beauty salon, fitness studio and steam room sauna and spa bath. Apparently, it's a splendid place for an intimate romantic getaway or a grand memorable gathering.'

Laughing, Caroline gave a dig to his ribs causing him to wrestle with the steering wheel for a split second.

'Careful, you will make me crash.'

'You memorized all that from the brochure, you fraud.'

The hotel was a two-hour drive from Caroline's apartment in London, ending down narrow winding country lanes surrounded by the sights and smells of autumn.

'A season of mist and mellow fruitfulness,' Caroline smiled.

'Sorry?'

'It's Keats *Ode to autumn.*'

'I never liked poetry that much. I went to a state comprehensive school. It was dangerous taking too much interest in the arts or literature; you were risked being branded a homosexual.'

'That's outrageous I've always loved poetry and literature.'

Approaching Fawsley Hall, Andy told Caroline a little bit more about the house. 'Apparently the building is a mix of Tudor and Georgian architecture. Queen Victoria, Charles I and Queen Elizabeth I all stayed here.'

'My goodness, you are a mind of information, Mr Davies. I wasn't expecting a guided tour.'

'Am I boring you?'

'Of course not silly, I'm only joking.'

Andy's plan was to check-in, have some lunch and then go out sightseeing and return later that evening for dinner. Parking his car, they retrieved their overnight bags and walked together the few yards into the reception. After a quick tour of the Great Hall with its huge ornate ceiling they headed upstairs to their separate adjoining rooms.

After depositing his bag Andy went back out into the corridor to check Caroline, and seeing her door was open ajar he popped his head inside. 'Everything OK for you in here?'

'Oh Andy, this is gorgeous. I can't believe the view across the park; it must have cost you a small fortune. Champagne too, how lovely, I vote we open it now!'

'Hey, hold on, I thought we could save it for later when we get back.'

'You're not thinking of getting me tipsy are you Mr Davies, and then having your wicked way with me - and if not ... why not?'

Moving closer she teasingly slipped her arm around his waist. Without resisting, he was in her grip and responded by kissing her passionately. They had only been in the hotel less than thirty minutes and, while this was not part of Andy's original plan, Caroline was working to a different agenda...

Reaching out for his champagne glass on the bedside cabinet, Andy drained the last drops into his mouth and collapsed back down onto the pillow. Caroline did a flip, and propped on one elbow pressed her lips to his, sharing the champagne.

'You taste yummy,' she smiled, glancing down at his bare chest.

'Would you like me to pass your glass?'

'No, stay still I am really comfortable, I never intend to let you move.'

'Oh God,' Andy smirked, 'you're not going to turn into a crazed woman and start stalking me, are you?'

Caroline frowned and lifted her head; she was smiling despite his cruel remark. 'Excuse me, how dare you say that. Didn't you realize, I only want you for sex and now I've had you I'm off back to Madrid and my great life.'

'So, you've simply used me for my body and this is just an empty meaningless relationship. I knew it, women - they're all the same.'

Jumping out of bed, she rummaged through her handbag and found a cigarette. Andy watched her move across the room while admiring her beautiful slim figure. She crouched by the half-open window and lit the cigarette.

'Someone will see you and call the police. How will you explain that to your boss?' Andy teased.

She laughed saying he would probably ask for photographic evidence.

'Andy, what's the plan? Are you going to show me Althorp?'

'Yes, I thought perhaps after lunch we could drive to the village and see where Maria lived and this whole treaty thing began. Then perhaps call on Janet Briggs, pay homage to Althorp House and visit the little church where all the

The Treaty

Spencer's are buried, except for Diana.'

Closing the window, Caroline disappeared into the bathroom and returned seconds later shivering as she leapt back into bed.

'I can't believe how beautiful this place is,' she giggled excitedly, snuggling up to Andy. 'It's so pleasant to get out of London once in a while.'

'You can say that again.'

'So we look around Althorp House then the Church? What do you hope to find - a box with a secret code that contains the original copy of the treaty?'

'Don't take the piss,' Andy replied, kissing her lips and finding the smell of cigarette smoke on her breath strangely erotic.

Laughing hysterically Caroline began to choke. 'Pass my Champagne darling, I need a drink.'

She sipped the flat wine and recovered her composure, still very much amused.

'How did you become involved with MI-21?'

'Oh, it's a long story. I was originally a schoolteacher.'

'A schoolteacher, that's a bit of a career leap. What made you do it?'

'Okay, but you realize if I tell you about my life I will have to kill you or marry you, which is it going to be?'

'There's not really a lot to choose between the two, so just tell me, what made you give up being a teacher and become a spook?'

'My father was a Barrister and sent me to Benenden, an all girls' public school in Kent. I went on to Oxford to read English and that is when one of the other ex-Benenden girls first tried to recruit me. I did not tell anyone apart from my dad who thought it was a lot of nonsense, so I decided to ignore her. The year I graduated unemployment was at record levels and when I was offered a teaching job in London I decided to take it to get some pennies in the bank.'

'So your Oxford degree didn't count for very much, then?'

'I didn't know what to do after graduating.'

'When did you join-up?'

'I'm getting there - be patient. By coincidence, the girl from Benenden turned out to be working in the same school as me. We started socializing together, and that's when I discovered she had been recruited by MI-5. It sounded exciting compared to being a boring teacher so the next time the subject was raised I decided to join.

'This sounds like something in a movie. You must be pretty good at spying to have reached such a senior position.'

'Andy, you watch too much TV. My work is not considered spying; a lot of it is intelligence gathering, strategy and surveillance.'

'Yeah, spying!' he laughed.

Ignoring his sarcasm, she continued. 'I've worked for MI-5 and now MI-21 for nearly twenty years, the transfer to Madrid was an important career move.'

'You've been pretty successful. It must have been something else that propelled you to the top?' She began fooling around again making him laugh. 'Come on, don't try to distract me, you must have done something very special to have climbed so far up the career ladder.'

She stopped playing, and balancing on her elbow looked down with a stare. 'Excuse me who is it interrogating who in this bed, I've already said enough and it's certain you will have to marry me to carry on living.'

Andy was so intrigued by Caroline's secret he was tempted to accept her proposal.

'Okay, if you really have to know, I helped manage a very important Russian agent, and I was only one of five people who knew that the deputy head of the KGB in London was actually a double agent.'

The Treaty

'Oh my god, I've got instant images of Michael Caine as Harry Palmer in *The Ipcress File*. What would have happened if you had leaked information to the Russians?'

'He would've been killed immediately.'

'That's really scary. When did you learn to fire guns and start carrying a weapon? I was shocked when you did that SAS thing on the boat - in fact; it frightened the shit out of me!'

Caroline smiled. 'You're like a little boy, aren't you? I will take you out on a shooting range and teach you how to fire a Kalashnikov, its great fun. I have a question for you now?'

'Fire away.'

'How did you manage to spend the night with Fatima when you were in Madrid? We always thought she was a lesbian.'

Andy blushed. 'It felt perfectly natural. If she is a lesbian then she's one hell of an actress.'

'What is she really like, Andy? I only ever see the intelligence stuff about her, not the real person. Do you think you got very close to her?'

'It's hard to know. I suspect she was working the whole time I was with her, but there were moments when I think the attraction was genuine enough. We talked, like we are doing now. She asked me if I had slept with a black woman before, which I thought was a bit strange.'

'And had you?'

'What difference does it make? The fact is she is an incredibly beautiful woman, and I can understand why both men and women are attracted to her.'

'Were you really, really attracted? What was she like in bed?'

Andy playfully protested at this last question. 'That's outrageous, you can't ask me that.'

'I just did. Come on stud rate me and Fatima out of ten.'

At that moment Andy decided to begin his own attack by leaping on top of her and pinning her by the shoulders, then in a mock Humphrey Bogart accent said, 'So, baby, it's time to show you who the real man is around here.'

Caroline began giggling and screaming too loudly. '*HELP ME, I'M BEING ATTACKED, MAKE HIM STOP*!'

'Go ahead scream away, baby, this guy's got no fear of dames. I'm just going to take what I want, anyway.'

Laughing at his stupid voice, she thought about using one of her judo moves then gave in without a struggle.

53

'Oh well, that was a waste of time.'

'It doesn't matter Andy, we have an excuse to come back here again sometime.'

'Yes, but I should have checked beforehand, I just expected Althorp House to be open at least until the end of September.'

They had stopped off at the Althorp Coaching Inn, in the middle of Great Brington and a few yards from St Mary's church.

'What shall we do instead, then?' Caroline asked.

'Maybe we could drive passed Maria's old house and call to say hello to Janet Briggs. What do you think?'

'I'm just enjoying being out here with you, it's so good to escape the city.'

Driving to the village of Upper Harlestone, three miles away, they left a wooded area and passed by clinically clean ploughed fields stripped bare of the summer harvest. Silenced by its natural beauty, Andy recalled memories of Maria and the day they met. Even though it was only a few months ago after all that had happened it seemed like an eternity.

Caroline turned and touched his arm. 'You're quiet, how are you feeling about being back here?'

'I'm okay. This was the way we came when I first met

with Maria. There had been a torrential storm, like a mini-tornado, trees and debris littered the road. I hurt my foot and couldn't drive; Maria asked me if I wanted to come here to Dominic's house.

'Perhaps she was after your body as well?'

'How did you guess?'

'And I thought you were such a shy boy.'

'I am.'

'Yeah right,' Caroline laughed. So, Andy, this story about Princess Diana, do you really believe she may have kept Mardjono's version of the original treaty, and why would she have left it here?'

'He did sound genuine, and was upset she hadn't returned the documents to him. Diana used to visit here regularly, so there is every chance this was a safe haven out of London.'

'That's funny, because I interviewed his literary agent and he told me Dominic had confessed he believed a copy of the treaty had originated from Northamptonshire. There was a courier label or something showing where the package came from; it does seem a coincidence that Dominic lived so close.

'Listen Caroline, there is something more Maria told me which I think will confirm this. She said the treaty documents in the safe deposit box at the bank in Buenos Aires, were held in the name of Susan Barrantes, the mother of Sarah Ferguson and a close friend of Diana.'

Caroline looked surprised. 'She was killed in a car accident - why didn't you say about this before, it wasn't exactly a secret?'

Andy muttered an apology. 'Yes that's right and it was because she died and the items were never claimed. Maria's father felt he could just take them without permission.'

'It's beginning to all make sense I can remember Princess

The Treaty

Diana making a visit to Argentina and seeing pictures of her with Fergie's mother.'

Andy relaxed; happy he got away so easily withholding this vital information. 'Well, there you have it! We must be on the right track. Now all we need to know is where she's hidden the real treaty documents and not just photocopies - we need the ones with the signatures to be believed.'

'If only it were that easy,' Caroline sighed. 'I suspect she squirreled those papers away somewhere very safe as insurance - a lasting hold over Philip and Charles.'

A row of terraced thatched cottages emerged as they reached the village, and rounding a bend he slowed outside a large redbrick house.

Andy pointed out of the window. 'That's where Dominic lived and down the side is the driveway leading to the back door.'

'It looks as if someone new has moved in,' Caroline observed.

'I would've liked to visit Toby, their son, but he is with his grandparents and it seems pointless he would never remember who I was. Janet Briggs lives farther back, we passed her cottage coming through the village, but I am not sure which one.'

'I can knock on a door and ask if you like?'

Turning around, the road was eerily quiet as they approached the stone houses. Caroline jumped out of the car and began walking toward the first gate of a terraced row. Pushing it open, she confidently strode down the path and knocked enthusiastically. An elderly woman peered through the gap and listened to Caroline's enquiry. Releasing the chain on the door, she swung it wide open and pointed toward her neighbours' house. Seeing this as his cue, Andy switched off the car engine and met Caroline at the gate. Weaving down the path together, they knocked on the door as if couple of Jehovah Witnesses on a recruitment drive. As it opened, he immediately recognized Janet's husband.

'Hello, Jack, remember me, it's Andy! I came here to visit with Maria a few months ago.'

'Andy, of course I do what a nice surprise.'

'Is Mrs Briggs home? I'm sorry not to have let you know I would be coming.'

'No problem, Janet's up at the church. She does the flowers on a Saturday afternoon ready for the service in the morning. Would you like a cup of tea?'

'Thank you Jack, a cup of tea sounds wonderful. This is my friend Caroline. I brought her along to show her there is life outside London.'

He laughed sharing the view city folk were ignorant about the countryside. Caroline towered above him as he showed them into the lounge, and leaving Caroline sat on the cottage style settee he followed Jack into the kitchen.

'How have you been? Has Mrs Briggs found another job yet or is she a lady of leisure?'

Jack carried on filling the kettle, looking in unfamiliar cupboards for the best cups and saucers that Janet normally used for visitors.

'Oh she is used to being at home all day, we are both pensioners and do not really need to work. She enjoyed looking after the house and spending time with Emma and little Toby, he became like a Grandson. How are you, Andy? We have been worried about you. I know you had not known Maria long.'

Andy sat down at the wooden kitchen table, and nodded. 'It still hurts. It must be awful for you too, Jack. I mean, with Dominic, Emma and Maria. How have you coped?'

'Everything happens for a reason, I suppose. Life can be cruel. Life can be beautiful. There is not really an answer. You just have to carry on and return to normal.'

The Treaty

'That can't be easy.'

'No, but time will ease the pain.'

'Yes it will,' Andy smiled, looking around the kitchen. 'I like this place Jack you've done a fine job on the decorating.'

'Oh Andy please, it's awful. Who in their right mind decides to paint a kitchen brown?'

Both men laugh and feel better for it.

'Now, who is this woman you've brought here?' Jack winked, pouring the drinks. 'She's quite a looker.'

'Caroline is a friend of mine. She is helping me with something. She is also interested in Althorp House and especially Princess Diana. You and Janet both worked there didn't you?'

Returning to the lounge Andy carried the tea tray, placing it on a side table sitting next to Caroline. Jack made himself comfortable in his armchair before answering Andy's question.

'We both worked at Althorp House for years. It is where we first met. Janet was cleaning inside and I was out in the grounds. There were a lot of us in those days. It was hard work, but we had fun all right, especially in the summer and around harvest. The Mrs certainly made us graft hard for a living.'

Jack seemed set to launch into what could possibly be a long anthology on the life and times of Althorp, so Caroline quickly jumped in and asked a question. 'Was that Princess Diana's stepmother Raine Spencer?'

'No, I'm talking years before her time; this was when we only ever saw the housekeeper, Mrs Pendrey, a very strict lady.'

'Did you ever see much of Diana when she was younger?' Andy asked.

'Yes, after Lord Albert died, they all moved into Althorp. She was a lovely girl and became very fond of Janet - treated her like an Aunt. Whenever she and Charlie, the present

Lord Spencer, had a bust-up, Janet was the first person Diana came to for help.'

'How often, did she visit Althorp after getting married?'

'Oh, I couldn't be sure.' Jack moved closer while lowering his voice, emphasizing the need for their full attention. 'Listen, there's a story I got to tell you. The problem is, it makes me a little upset, so you will have to bear with me.'

'Please, take your time,' Caroline smiled before sipping her tea.

'Well, I was out working, doing a bit of gardening for neighbours. Janet was alone while our Gary was still at...'

'Sorry, who's Gary?' Andy frowned.

'He was our son, but he isn't with us anymore. I'll tell you about him in a minute. Janet was here on her own when this car or jeep pulled up outside, one of them four-wheel drive things, and who should get out of the driver's seat, Diana herself. Janet said she rushed to open the front door; they hadn't spoken for years, not since she went off to London. Diana had sent regular cards at Christmas, and when her boys William and Harry were born, she sent a thank you letter for clothes Janet knitted, but that were all. We knew she came to Althorp occasionally but never managed to see her.'

'What did Janet do?' Caroline asked

'Well, once she had overcome her surprise, she invited her in and sat her down where you're sitting now.'

'Oh really, that is quite surreal. Andy she was here on this same seat.' Caroline was gushing as Andy touched her arm signaling for her to shut up.

'Sorry Jack, please continue.'

'Thing was, she was clutching these two big brown envelopes, about half the size of a newspaper. She chatted for a bit and asked how everyone was, then asked Janet if she could do her a favour.' Jack gave a chuckle. 'Well, I ask you, what would be your response if Princess Diana asked

The Treaty

for a favour - she said "yes, anything, just name it", or something along those lines. Diana showed her one packet, which had a long name and address wrote on the front. It was going abroad, somewhere called Bonos Ares. I saw it, here on the sideboard.'

'I think that's in Argentina, probably Buenos Aires.'

'Yes, that's it Andy, Argie land. Anyway, she asked if she could leave this package in our house and one of them courier vans you see darting about everywhere would collect it the next morning. Janet said yes of course, it didn't cause her any bother.'

'What happened to the other package?'

'Well, Janet put the one for collection on this sideboard here then Diana handed her the second package that didn't have writing on it.'

'Was it the same size, Jack?' asked Caroline

'Yes, both the same size, I saw them myself. She asked Janet to put this second one in a very safe place and she would collect it later on. This is the strange part; she said she was having problems keeping some of her things safe. Well, Janet never gave it a second's thought. Diana didn't need to explain anything to her - she knew what that young brother was like when they were kids, whatever it was she had Charlie wanted it as well.'

'What happened then, Jack?'

'She told Janet she was going abroad somewhere and would call round for the other package later on.'

'When did she come back?'

'Well, here's the thing, she never did, and not that long afterwards she was killed in that terrible car accident. It was a real shock for everybody. I could spend hours telling all about the funeral here in the village.'

'How much of it did you see from here, Jack?'

'Quite a lot I had to take Janet up the Church the evening before she was buried.'

Andy looked puzzled. 'Why was that, I thought the funeral took place on the Althorp Estate?'

'I don't quite know what was going on Andy, there were a few rum things happening if you ask me and I couldn't get an answer from our Janet.'

Caroline joined in with the conversation. 'Jack, you've completely lost me, did Janet say why she went to the Church the evening before?'

'It was an odd business,' he replied, sipping his tea. 'She had this phone call asking if she could take the keys up to the church. The Vicar had gone off somewhere and they needed to get access. I was down the pub and when I got home about ten o'clock, there was a note asking me to go up there and bring her home. I had a few pints so I probably should not have driven. When I got up there I saw this big Army lorry parked outside the Church with some lads in uniform standing around having a smoke and chatting to a couple of police chaps. I told them I was Janet's husband and they let me go inside the church.'

Andy reached out placing his cup and saucer on the little table, clearly intrigued. 'Did you find out why the Army was there?'

'Yes, they came to build one of them Bailey bridge things across the lake in the grounds up at the house to reach Dog Island.'

'Dog Island?' echoed a bemused Caroline.

'That's what we call it round here. The Spencer's always used the island to bury their pet dogs.' Jack did not appear to think anything of this while Andy and Caroline gave one another old-fashioned looks. 'I went into the Church, very spooky going in through that big old door. The light was on and I could see across into the Spencer Chapel.'

'Do they have their own room inside the church?'

'More than a room, Andy, I should think a good quarter of the building is for them Spencer's and all their ancestors.

The Treaty

Well, here is the funny bit. I couldn't see our Janet anywhere and the iron gates to the Spencer chapel were wide open, which was unusual. I walked over to have a look and called her name, when she suddenly appeared almost from nowhere and gave me a fright she did. What's more, the blinking great concrete flagstone that covers the steps down to the crypt, where they keep the coffins, was wide open. Janet just walked out as bold as brass. When I asked what she had been up to, she told me to mind my own business. I tell you Andy, we have been married forty something years and I never seen her look so queer, as if she had seen a ghost or something.'

Caroline sat on the edge of the sofa poised with another question.

'So, what next Jack, did you both go home?'

'Yes, eventually, she went outside and spoke with somebody, could have been either a police officer or the Parson. I kept out of the way in case they smelt my breath; they told her to leave her church key with them for the whole night and it would be there for her next morning. Anyway, next day when I took her back to the church early to finish sorting out the flowers it was still unlocked and everything was all back to normal.'

'What do you mean, as in no sign of people?'

'Andy, you would not ever have known the night before had happened. The big iron gates of the chapel was closed and everything was tidy, the only clue I could see was fresh cement sealing that blinking great concrete slab covering the entrance to the crypt.'

'Jack that's fascinating,' Andy beamed. 'It must have really made you wonder what was going on. I presume the courier collected the packet for Argentina. What happened to the other envelope when Diana didn't return to collect it herself?'

He remained silent and appeared to be composing himself.

'Well...' Jack replied, with watery red eyes, 'the chap called next morning in one of them vans and collected the packet for abroad. Janet put the other one at the back of her wardrobe - same place she hid the Christmas presents every year from young Gary. A day or two later we got this funny call from some bloke in London, said he was from the blinking Sun Newspaper. He asked for Gary first, and then when Janet told him he was out at work he left a message, I can remember every damn word. "Tell Gary we need to see the documents before we can agree anything, but we are interested." When Janet heard this, she slammed the phone down and raced upstairs to our room and the wardrobe to check Diana's packet. Sure enough, the little blighter had opened it and tried to seal it up again. She went barmy, and when he came home that evening his feet hardly touched the floor - "how dare he touch her things," she screamed. He had broken the trust Diana had shown in her, she would never forgive him.'

'How did he know about the package in the first place?' asked Caroline.

'It wasn't that surprising, Janet was so excited, she told us both as soon as we got home that Diana had called to see her, and he saw the envelope waiting for collection, then heard her mention to me there was another one. It didn't take the little devil five minutes to work out where she'd hidden it - he'd known about the Christmas present hiding place for years.'

'So he opened the packet to see what was inside?'

'Yes, but Gary wasn't very good at reading, neither am I for that matter. He said it was all about America and Britain, then a lot of legal stuff he couldn't understand.'

'Did Gary tell the man at The Sun about this?' Andy asked.

'Yes, that's why they wanted to see it, I suppose, but Janet was certain it wasn't going anywhere and moved it

The Treaty

away to a new hiding place. Gary reckoned some bloke in the pub told him the paper would pay a thousand pounds for stories like that.'

Did Gary contact the man at The Sun again?'

Jack paused. 'No, the poor little blighter never got a chance. The next day on his way home from work he came off his motorbike and was killed.'

Shocked, Caroline instinctively reached out to Jack, patting his arm. 'Jack, I'm so sorry. It must be very difficult for you to talk about this now.'

'I'm all right,' he replied, blowing into an off-white handkerchief that he had fished out of his trouser pocket. 'It's supposed to do some good to talk about it - not like Janet, bottling everything up all the time. The Ambulance chap reckoned Gary had said just before he went unconsciousness, that he was dazzled by bright lights, but folk in a car following didn't see any other vehicles pass them and said he suddenly swerved and ploughed into a tree at the roadside.'

'That must have been a dreadful time for you both. I just can't begin to imagine how you've managed to deal with everything that's happened. You both must be very strong people.'

'Thank you, Caroline, it's not been easy. Dominic, Emma and now Maria being killed haven't made things any easier. It's hard to hide the pain.'

Andy shifted uncomfortably in his seat he managed to push his emotions about Maria's death deep down.

'Time's a good healer they say,' he smiles sympathetically, glancing over at Andy. 'Isn't that right, my boy?'

He slowly nodded.

Were the police involved?' asked Caroline.

'Yes they came about a week after Gary died. Two men and a young woman, we thought they had more news about how it happened.'

'Were they in uniform?'

'No, they had the ordinary clothes on. Detectives I suspect.'

'Did they come to give you more information about the accident?'

'Here's the thing, they said it was possible Gary may have killed himself, committed suicide, of course, we knew Gary would've never done that. The woman with them had this notebook and asked loads of questions about his health, did he have a girlfriend, had there been any rows. When it got to that bit, poor Janet broke down, remembering the flaming argument they had the day before.'

'What were the other two officers doing while this was going on?'

'They asked if they could look at his bedroom, then disappeared for ages rooting around in all the rooms.'

'Did they show you any identification or any official papers?'

'I don't remember seeing any, but then we were too upset at the time to bother asking.' Caroline gave Andy a very piercing look indicating to him that the visitors Jack described were not police.

Jack had stopped talking and sat looking mournful. Andy decided they were outstaying their welcome and it was time to leave.

'Jack, I can't tell you how grateful we are to hear your story, and how very sorry we are to hear about Gary.'

Jack straightened his posture and forced a smile. 'That's okay, Andy, it's been hard for all of us. Our only blessing is that we get to see little Toby every now and again. He's a little ray of hope.'

Andy smiled. 'We should leave and find Janet to say hello. Jack, one more thing, that package Diana left here, did Janet ever show it to you again?'

He stood up and walked toward the cottage door to see them both out. 'She never spoke to me about it again,' he paused. 'And the only time I did ask she went into such a blinking mood, I never mentioned it again. For all I know she could have ripped it up and burnt it, good riddance to the damn thing.'

Standing by the open door Andy took his hand shaking it warmly.

'Take care Jack, we will go to find your Janet.'

Caroline took his hand and bent down to give him a kiss on the cheek.

54

Jack watched them drive off in the direction of Great Brington, toward the Church of St Mary the Virgin.

Andy slapped the steering wheel and turned to Caroline. 'That's unbelievable, I've been halfway around the world looking for this damn treaty, almost getting killed in the process, and it's been here in this village all the time.'

'We don't know that for certain. Janet may well have burnt it, as Jack suggested. After all the trouble it caused them who could blame her?'

'Would Janet destroy something Diana asked her to look after, I don't think so. She would see it as her duty to keep her promise beyond the grave.'

'We have to be careful this is delicate, she lost her son.'

'I know but I lost someone too, remember. I need to find the underlying cause of all this - I need to know the truth.'

Caroline did not respond having forgotten the price Andy had already paid for his involvement with the treaty - she now hoped they would be in time to avoid any new even more devastating developments.

Pulling up outside the church, Andy maneuvered the car and parked alongside a wall opposite an ancient monument. The car park now deserted apart from one other stationary vehicle with foreign registration plates. Inside, the occupant, a lone woman with henna died hair, chatted animatedly on

The Treaty

a mobile phone. With less than thirty minutes to go before the official closing time, they remained seated in the car absorbing the pure sanctity of the location. Surrounded by beautiful countryside, from the top of the eight-hundred year old rectangular tower there was a spectacular, unbroken view to the horizon crossing the Chiltern Hundreds to the South West of England, opposite the flat lands of, East Anglia. Through the ornate wrought iron gate, a neat gravel pathway led to the church door and resting-place for nineteen generations of Spencer's with the noticeable exception of the late Princess Diana.

'Are you religious, Caroline?' Andy asked, breaking the silence.

'No, not now, I was from about age fourteen. My mother died of cancer. I went to church regularly until my late twenties then my father died.'

'What did he die from?'

'Cancer, the same, seems to run in my family.'

'Why did you stop believing in God when he died?'

'Oh, I don't know, really. It just did not add up anymore. The work I did was violent and unforgiving, and not in the true spirit of Christianity, you could say. The last time I was with my father was at the hospital. Even though he was asleep, I knew in his mind he was thinking of me. He always phoned at least twice a week and was there when I needed him - regardless of the crisis; never judging, just holding me until whatever pain I was feeling had left. As I sat by his bed knowing he would soon be gone, I turned away for a few seconds; it could not have been more than ten seconds fifteen max, distracted by a trivial event outside. When I looked back, the clear plastic oxygen mask was dry and he had stopped breathing - he was dead. That was it, gone. No more talking, no familiar goodbye - no speak to you later - just gone without a word. Death is final; and there are so many things that you remember later you needed to talk about. It was then I decided life and death are simple matters and we must not get serious about any of it.'

Andy had not seen Caroline look this emotional before, she was a woman made from steel, but not entirely. Seeing her discomfort, he changed the subject.

'Here's a puzzle for you - Princess Diana, arguably the most famous member of the Spencer family in its five-hundred year history, is the only one to have died and not be laid to rest in this church. Instead, she is on an island in the middle of a lake that was previously used to bury the family's pets.'

'Yes, I agree, it does seem like an odd decision - especially when you see what a wonderful resting place this church would have been.

'I can remember reading an interview with a retired housekeeper who worked at Althorp. The only people to witness the burial were Prince Charles, his sons, Diana's mother and one of her closest friends. As for that story about removing the graves of the family pets to make room for her - you would have expected a public outcry.'

'Look, there's a bicycle - do you think it could belong to Janet Briggs?'

'Yes probably, let's go inside and find out.'

The Treaty

55

'Are you alone, Camilla?'

'Yes Richard, what's happening?'

'They are definitely in the village outside the Church, it's clear they're onto something.'

'Are you sure she never mentioned visiting Althorp, it seems so odd.'

'I'm certain. We spent most of Friday in meetings together and not a word about Davies or going to Althorp. As far as I was concerned her plan was to go home to Madrid on Friday night.'

'Maybe that was an excuse - you know, she didn't want to tell you she saw another man.'

'I hardly think that would be appropriate, especially if it was Davies - a key suspect linked to Fatima.'

'Then what do you think she is up to? You must have some idea.'

'Camilla, if I knew that I wouldn't be on the phone to you. Davies must have told her something relevant about the treaty, and for her own reasons she chose not to tell me or anyone else, as far as I know, and we have to consider this - she could be working on her own.'

'What do you propose?'

'I recommend the contract goes ahead on Davies, he does pose a real threat.'

'Is there no alternative, Richard? What harm can he do?'

'As I said to you before, Philip's policy of containment and damage limitation is right, just poorly executed.'

'What about Caroline, surely not her as well, you have no proof she has turned.'

'What can we do, she is not talking to me about this new situation? Normally I would have received a full report of her planned movements and who she was meeting, especially someone as important as Davies. There would have been a request for back-office services.'

'Richard, I have to leave it to you. Please do the best you can and make sure things are done by the book, let me know the outcome.'

Switching off the secure Brent phone, he continued to stare at a computer screen on his desk. The images were clear enough; Davies's car was parked near the local church in Great Brington. If their investigation were allowed to continue it could perhaps be only a matter of days before the once historic document, completed at the height of the cold war, was revealed - destroying everything in its path. Richard had known Caroline for nearly twenty years and briefly they were lovers. This was the most difficult decision he had ever taken.

The Treaty

56

Andy pushed against the heavy oak door and held it open for Caroline, the inside was deceivingly larger than he had expected. A woman crouched down by a vase of flowers glanced over her shoulder. Andy smiled, recognizing Janet straight away and walked toward her.

'Mrs Briggs it's Andrew I hope you remember me.'

Standing upright, she peered over her glasses before breaking into a grin. 'Yes, I can see it's you now. What a lovely surprise.'

'Jack told us you were here, so we thought we would drop by. This is my friend, Caroline.'

Caroline came forward and shook hands with Janet. 'I've heard such a lot about you, what a beautiful church.'

'Yes, it is. I really enjoy helping to keep it pleasant.' Mrs. Briggs looked suddenly sad, and reached out and touched Andy's arm. How have you been, Andrew?'

Andy smiled back. 'It's been a tough few months.'

'Yes, it has. So much hurt.'

He then gently squeezed her hand. 'I'm sorry I haven't been to visit since Maria left us. It was just too painful for me to come here. I was abroad with her when she was attacked.'

'We read about it in the newspaper and I knew you would make contact in your own good time.' Janet's eyes were brimming with tears. 'Oh dear, so many terrible things have happened lately. It was just her time. Are you staying nearby Andrew or just visiting for the day?'

Andy looked to Caroline, and back again at Janet. 'We are spending the weekend at Fawsley Hall. I needed to visit the area and say goodbye to Maria.'

'She was such a sweet girl. Little Toby loved her very much.'

'How is he?'

'He's young, so he will be fine. Sometimes he asks where his mummy and daddy have gone, but I doubt he understands. His grandparents are very good people.'

'We stopped by your house first and saw Jack.'

'He would have been very pleased to see you. We have few visitors around the house these days. I hope he looked after you?'

'Yes, he made us tea and even found your secret stash of chocolate biscuits - he seems to be coping well.'

'Jack's been my rock these past few months. I don't think I could have coped without him.'

'He told a fascinating story about how Princess Diana dropped by your house not that long before she died, and how you had tea together. That must have been amazing!'

'Oh, it was just one of those things, Andrew. I try not to think about it too often, it was a period of great sadness for us.'

'Jack mentioned Gary, I am very sorry. I didn't know anything about him when I came to visit.'

'I'm not even sure I told Maria about Gary, she may have learned how he died from someone else, I don't know.'

Andy then went for the close, it was now or never. 'Driving here from your house, we couldn't help discussing what became of that second package Diana gave you. Was it destroyed or did you keep it safe as she asked?'

Janet had never spoken about this to anyone and at first

The Treaty

felt angry with Jack for discussing private business. Oddly, coming from Andy his innocent question made it seem less important.

'I've never said what happened to it, Andrew, because Diana asked me to look after it. The contents were special to her and before she left my house, she said she would be back to collect it. I believed it was my duty to make sure it was there for her when she needed it.'

As Janet spoke those last few words, she looked toward the north side of the chancel, the Spencer family chapel.

'I've simply complied with her wish to make sure her private possessions remain just that - private.'

Undefeated, Andy made one further attempt to decode this cryptic answer. 'Were you here when Diana's body was brought back to Althorp?'

Once again, she took her time choosing her words with deliberate care. 'Yes, I was privileged to be here Andrew, when she was returned to God.'

'What did you think of the island in the lake being her last resting place?'

'My goodness you've got a lot of questions, worse than some of those journalists we had around here after she died.'

'I'm sorry if I'm being intrusive Mrs Briggs, we are just curious to hear your first hand experience of such a historic event.'

Janet turned her attention back toward her floral display. 'My Diana would have hated the thought of being alone on that island, and she will never be lonely while I am here to keep her company.' Janet turned and looked over at the Spencer chapel again before peering down at her watch. 'Oh my goodness look at the time Andrew, I must finish off in here as I have to lockup at five o'clock. Please forgive my rudeness; it is wonderful to see you and Caroline. You are more than welcome to come back to my house, I will cook us all a nice meal if you have the time.'

'Thank you that is very kind, but we have made plans back at Fawsley Hall this evening. I will drive over tomorrow morning before we head back to London if that's okay with you?'

'Yes, it will be good to see you both again. You can stay for Sunday lunch if you like. You get off and have a lovely evening and I will see you again tomorrow.'

Waving them off she returned to her flowers, neither Andy nor Caroline spoke until they reached the car. Andy could barely contain his excitement.

'I don't believe it, this is all starting to make sense. Janet has probably hidden the bloody treaty in the church somewhere, you know, to be close to Diana's spirit.'

Caroline nodded and lit a cigarette. 'Yes, maybe she is not buried on the island as everyone thinks and is really in the church along with all the rest of the Spencer's. The treaty could even be in Princess Diana's own coffin. Have you thought of that?'

Andy excitedly grabbed Caroline's shoulder. 'Oh my God, Caroline you are a genius!'

'Yes, that's true...'

'I still can't believe what we have just heard,' Andy beamed. 'It's been almost ten years since Diana died and all this time Janet has held the destruct key for Prince Charles and the rest of the Royals. It is so unbelievable you simply could not make it up - little Janet, guardian of the treaty.'

'This really does change everything. I suppose it is possible they could have gone through the motions of the burial. After the service, her spirit is committed to the ground, but maybe she is not physically on Dog Island. In all probability, she is at rest in the church alongside her ancestors. Lord Spencer has publicly admitted he never said exactly where on the island she is buried and he wouldn't even

The Treaty

reveal the name of the Clergy who conducted the service.'

'Caroline you are probably right and you can kind of understand why they would have done this under the circumstances. The church would've been a nightmare to secure and it is a public place. Shortly after Diana's death this area would've been crawling with all kinds of lunatics and the drain on the local police resources untenable.'

Turning in her seat to face him as if to make a statement Caroline reached out and touched his arm. 'I've something I need to share with you, Andy. Maybe I should have mentioned this before, but there you go I did not. On Friday afternoon I had a meeting with my boss Sir Richard Parsons and he told me we are no longer interested in finding the treaty.'

Shocked, Andy pushed back in his seat increasing the distance between them; instinctively feeling a double-cross was coming.

'Caroline, I hope you are not here under false pretenses, why didn't you say something earlier?'

'Calm down and let me finish. I was amazed to hear this myself, especially when my boss said The Prime Minister was planning to make an announcement to Parliament to quash publicity surrounding Prince Philip. Apparently, he will say that it was all part of a conspiracy against the Prince, and that he is satisfied no such narcotics treaty ever existed.'

'But we know that is flagrantly not true, he has done some kind of deal - it's obvious.'

She looked sheepish, guilty having kept him in the dark. 'I think you could be right. I was equally shocked when I heard this, it all seems very wrong. It seems certain Philip has managed to convince the Prime Minister or someone in government somehow, that there was a conspiracy against him.'

'So, bearing in mind what you've just learned this afternoon about the possible whereabouts of the treaty, do you intend to make an official report?'

'Well actually I am not here in an official capacity; I'm here with you on what has turned into a very romantic weekend. My boss thinks I am in Madrid, and I've said nothing about our plan to visit this place.'

Andy became thoughtful as he digested this new situation. Feeling defeated and betrayed by what he had just heard, this seemed very much like the final blow. With the tacit involvement by the Prime Minister, who he previously believed was not party to any of the workings of the treaty. The whole government system was gradually being sucked-in and corrupted and there was nothing he - or probably anyone else could do to stop it from happening.

'Caroline, I do wonder if we should stop searching for the treaty. I mean what is the point? Sitting here outside this church perhaps we have reached the end of the road and its time to give up the search and leave things as they are. We should consider this out of respect for Princess Diana's memory and for the sake of sons, William and Harry. I mean, what is to be gained just carrying on? Prince Philip is already very old and his involvement will have a natural ending before very long - what do you think?'

'You really are a great guy and this will be a very unselfish act on your part if you stop now. However, what about the others - Mrs Briggs, James, Trudy even me. We have all become linked in someway. The dark forces operating behind the treaty have been consistent. Anyone, anyone at all - who has seen the documents or knows something about them - has been eliminated.'

Andy snapped back, feeling she was accusing him of acting weak. 'Well, who in authority can I trust? The nearest I got was to confide in Colin Trenched, a respected senior university lecturer who quickly ended up dead. The courts

The Treaty

are not going to sanction examining her coffin on the island and to search the Spencer crypt, based solely on unsubstantiated evidence. I think we have to accept that without the signed documents, Prince Philip and the Royals have gotten away with it and together with any Americans that have been involved. You can bet your life that corporate USA with help from establishment Britain, will remain hard at work keeping this whole thing under wraps for as long as possible.'

'There is a way,' Caroline smiled, posting the stub end of her cigarette out the open car window. 'We can use the copy documents that we know exist. Andy, you have a copy of the treaty - please, admit this to me - I am on your side now. Maybe it is time we used it. It might be our only way out.'

He stared blankly across the open fields, trying to evaluate his situation. He knew he needed professional help. Caroline was genuine, she had told him all about her early life and work in the security services. Surely now he thought he could trust her and perhaps together they will make the correct decisions.

'Andy darling, I know how tough this must be for you in view of what you have suffered to date. But I promise I do have a solution that will end the killing, and more to the point - remove you from danger. Trust me please?'

'Okay,' Andy sighed, 'I admit it I do still have a complete copy including the correspondence between Mardjono and the committee in Holland - so what. How can this make a difference now? They allege Prince Philip orchestrated and has managed the treaty for over thirty years. Caroline, I will agree to give these to you; however, I need your word no one else will be harmed as a result of our actions.'

Smiling, taking his hand she gave a gentle squeeze between her palms whilst suppressing her burgeoning excitement, and reassured him this was the right decision.

'Baby, have the faith, I hold your interests at heart.' Laughing she then quipped, 'Besides, you will be no use to me in bed if you're dead.'

'I will arrange for you to have a copy in the next 24 hours, it will be encrypted and I will give you the relevant passwords. Now look me in the eye Caroline and swear to me once again - this is not a double cross - considering you still work for MI-21!'

She looked at Andy, fluttering her eyelids in a moment of distraction.

'I promise you my people will not get to see a single page and you will be safe.'

'So what do you intend to do with it, then - how are you going to make a difference, use blackmail?'

'That is quite close to the truth. Andy, I shouldn't really be telling you this - but I will. Sir Richard Parsons, my ultimate boss, is an ex-lover of mine - we go back almost twenty years. He once told me he knew Camilla, The Duchess of Cornwall, when they were only teenagers, they had brief love affair before he left to join the army. It is almost certain he is still in contact with her. In fact for reasons I can't say - I know he is. My plan is to ask him to negotiate through Camilla. Our proposition will be that providing all of the killing stops, and then the only known copy of the treaty they are aware of - will be kept hidden. This way we have them by the balls. They achieve their objective of damage limitation, no one writing about the treaty. You are out of danger along with any other people, such as Mrs Briggs, Trudy and your Cousin James - including myself I should add.'

'If the treaty is to remain hidden, why do you need to see a copy?'

'I have to show them part of it to prove it exists, maybe even the whole document - remember they have their own

The Treaty

version anyway.'

'Why would you be at risk, you are part of their system?'

'Andy, I'm already very involved and it's highly likely I know too much for comfort. What do you think about this as a plan?'

'Well, if you can make it happen and they agree, it does seem to be the only alternative - unless the real signed documents turn up, which seems pretty unlikely in the next century if they are in Princess Diana's crypt.'

'Exactly!'

'The other problem is it will mean the UK and USA involvement controlling the market for narcotics is going to carry on.'

'Yes, but Andy, that problem is too huge and complex for us to solve. We have to accept that greater minds than ours have attempted to resolve the issues of drugs in society for the best part of two hundred years.'

Feeling a lot happier Andy was now smiling; relieved she had come up with what seemed to be an excellent new plan of action.

Although harbouring niggling doubts, he felt it necessary to accept her word and turned his attention back to more immediate needs.

'I feel we've reached a new crossroads Caroline and perhaps should celebrate your plan with a toast - let's see if the pub has any decent champagne?'

Leaning over and taking hold of his knee, she giggled. 'I've a much better idea; let's have the champagne back at the hotel.'

'Sounds good to me - I still need to go inside the pub to use their toilet, are you staying or coming in with me?'

Still giggling, Caroline leaned across and gave him a peck on the cheek. 'No, I will stay. Be as fast as you can.'

Watching him jog around the corner, she reached inside her Gucci bag and took out her government issue Brent mobile. Hitting a key, she waited for a husky woman's voice to finish her greeting.

'Salam ali cum.'

'Peace be with you - I will have the treaty soon, it's been a success.'

'That's wonderful. Bring it to me as soon as possible?'

'I must go, he is returning. Speak to you soon.'

The call ended as Andy caught sight of her stowing the phone back in her bag.

'You were fast; did you remember to wash your hands?'

'Of course cheeky, and who was that on the phone?'

'I was checking for messages.'

'Thought perhaps you were calling someone to tell them you finally had access to the treaty.'

'Don't be silly, Andy, I have already said you can trust me.'

Pulling out of the car park Andy caused the wheels of the BMW to spin scattering loose gravel chippings that narrowly missed the vehicle parked up a short distance from them. The woman sitting behind the wheel appeared not to notice and continued to clutch a phone to her ear. Turning right he headed back down a narrow lane through the neighboring village of Little Brington. Here they joined a country road leading toward the main highway. Rounding a sharp bend Caroline was the first to see a temporary traffic sign warning of road works, then a man in a hardhat and orange high visibility vest holding up a stop sign.

'Careful, Andy, looks like a burst water main!'

Slamming on the brakes he came to a sudden halt. 'Shit, must have just happened. It looks closed ahead, can I reverse?'

'Yes, but there is a car coming up fast from behind, you could've taken a left earlier.'

Feathery bulbous rain clouds hung overhead casting a

shadow across the man in the yellow hardhat. In just a few more seconds it would all be over; he had rehearsed this scene many times. The car pulls to a halt and he will approach the driver's window, wait for it to open and then fire. This would be his last chance; he had to succeed. The assassin had a 9mm Parabellum semi-automatic silenced pistol, with a range of fifty metres. He would aim for the head and heart at close range. The get-away-vehicle parked behind the van blocked off the road. The woman they had seen earlier parked by the church, approached in her car preventing reverse access and their escape. After it was all over, a short drive to the airport and by plane to the Czech Republic. Their mission finally accomplished.

Just as predicted Andy moved the vehicle to pull alongside then began to slide the car window open. The workman stepped out clutching the gun securely beneath his reflective jacket. Holding the stop sign in his left hand he bent over to speak with Andy, his face now close to the open window. In a split second Andy caught the strong scent of tobacco, wakening a powerful suppressed memory, this flashback triggered a hard-wired reaction taking over control. With a massive flood of adrenalin he slammed the car into reverse, flooring the accelerator and speeding back toward the approaching vehicle. The image in his rear view mirror was the face of the driver now desperately trying to stop her car, a face that matched perfectly with the one stored in his memory. These were the same two people who left him for dead by the railway embankment. Without a pause ignoring frantic pleas from Caroline, he ripped into the front of the car with his rear bumper, the impact catapulting the woman headfirst through her front window screen.

Yelling at Caroline to take cover while thrashing to maneuver the BMW out from the wreckage, Andy booted the accelerator, targeting the workman taking aim with his gun.

'He's going to shoot, get down!'

Panic-stricken, Caroline attempted in a final desperate and futile effort to evade the missiles, bullets tore through the glass striking her in the head and chest. With 1.5 tons of metal charged by a 350bhp engine bearing down it was the assassin's turn to flee. Struck by a glancing blow he was dispatched hurtling across the road and onto the grass verge. Jumping out of the car consumed by an inconsolable rage, Andy snatched up the gun and pointing directly at his crumpled body, ignored his weak plea for mercy. Squeezing the automatic trigger he continued firing until the magazine was completely empty.

The Treaty

57

'You're extremely lucky to get bail, these are really serious charges.'

'I appreciate that Brian, but I am totally innocent. That killer was out to get me for a second time and Caroline may still die. What was I supposed to do - wait for him to recover and try to shoot me again?'

Andy was sitting in his solicitor's office together with cousin James, who had been at his side since Andy was released from police custody. Brian Johnson had not dealt with a high profile case like this one before and wanted to do the best for his client.

'You've been charged with manslaughter, two people died and it could so easily have been murder. The law states you can use reasonable force to defend your self. You blasted a man to pieces who lay helpless at the roadside with two broken legs - shooting him to death.'

Immediately after the incident, a man out walking his dog discovered the carnage, seeing Andy collapsed on his knees by the side of his car cradling Caroline's unconscious body in his arms. The dog walker called the emergency services. Caroline was taken by helicopter to hospital; the dead man and woman remained where they were during a detailed forensic examination. The assassin's female accomplice had died the instant she went through the front windscreen of her car. Andy gave a full explanation before being arrested and taken into custody. The police while sympathetic had little choice based on the lack of any other motive and independent witnesses, charging him with manslaughter later releasing him on bail.

'Will I go to prison?' Andy mumbled, as he sat slumped in a chair showing dark rings under his eyes caused through lack of sleep.

The young solicitor was sympathetic since it was obvious he acted spontaneously, however; he was forced to explain the real dilemma the court would face.

'The problem is this man was defenseless despite what you say he tried to do. He was innocent until proven guilty and you denied both of those people natural justice by taking the law into your own hands. The fact you went on to deliberately kill him may lead to a custodial sentence. However, we will plead mitigating circumstances, as you were in shock after you say he tried to shoot you first.'

Angrily responding Andy yelled back, 'It's not me just saying he tried to kill me - he nearly did.'

James jumped out of his chair and calmed him down. 'Andy, please mate, take it steady, Brian is only trying to help by playing the devils advocate. It is a fact from the prosecution point of view there were no other witnesses apart from Caroline, and we have to face facts she may not survive. If Caroline dies it will be your word they have to go on and you will have to prove there was a motive - since you killed the only other living witness.'

Andy accepted his situation was dire. He could hardly tell the police the real reason behind the shooting and why he was innocent. That he was being assassinated on the orders of Prince Philip and other senior British establishment figures, all because he knew about the treaty. They would he thought, immediately have him sectioned as a raving loony.

The Treaty

Once having agreed to meet the bail conditions he asked Brian for permission to go back home for a fresh change of clothes. Part of the terms was he lived with Cousin James, and surrendered his passport. Tony Celentano, Andy's UK boss, supported his bail application on the grounds he be released to complete essential work. The US owned company was initially reluctant, and he knew this was the last straw; his career was in the balance. In some ways he could understand their attitude toward him. For the past six months, he had been in and out of hospital suffering one crisis after another, and had now been charged with manslaughter or worse.

James travelled back with him to his apartment, and together they searched on the Internet for press reports of similar cases and the length of prison sentence. After just five minutes research he realized there were few options for the court, and knew he faced at least five years in jail. He could perhaps try confessing everything to the police - telling them all he knew, but this would seriously compromise a whole raft of other innocent people including James, Janet Briggs, Trudy and Caroline. It was unlikely he would be believed since even the Prime Minister labeled the whole affair a conspiracy with no real evidence. Sinking deeper into depression he went to the kitchen to look for a beer. With James following together they shared the single can of larger he found in the fridge.

Disturbed by a bleeping noise coming from his desktop computer Andy realized it was his phone connected through the PC. Sprinting back to the lounge he cautiously tapped a key accepting the caller.

'Hello, who's this?'

'Baby, how are you? I heard about what happened?'

Immediately recognizing the heavy accented voice of Fatima coming through the speaker, conscious of James listening he snatched up a handset next to the system.

'I'm so sorry what happened to you and that lady, your friend Caroline - how is she? Will she make a full recovery? I was so upset when I heard the news.'

'Fatima, forgive me for asking, but how do you know Caroline, and why have you contacted me?'

'Andy baby, Caroline and her people have been watching me for years - I have met her during several interviews. She is a good woman I don't hate her for doing her job and I think she liked me too.'

'Well she never mentioned to me that you two were friends and we talked about a lot of things only last week - never about you. This is not your reason for making contact.' Andy was not being strictly honest since they had discussed Fatima; in fact, it began to make some sense why Caroline had asked so many questions.

'Are you still there?' Fatima asked.

'Yes. I don't understand why Caroline would like you - she thinks you are a terrorist and more importantly why would you tell me about this?'

'Andy, I was helping Caroline and I can help you now. In return you may still want to help me bring the people who are trying so hard to kill you to justice. You know what it is I want.'

'And do you know I have been charged and will probably go to prison?'

'Yes, there is a good chance if you go to prison you will never come out, one way or another you will either be kept inside, commit suicide or have a fatal accident - trust me, I know how your people work.'

Andy believed this to be true; it would be the ideal opportunity to get rid of him one way or another. Every year well over one hundred inmates die in British prisons by committing suicide - one more death would go relatively unnoticed.

'So what do you have in mind, turn me into a terrorist

and mass murder like your brother?'

He knew this would hurt her, Caroline had told him they suspected Fatima's brother was associated with the Madrid train bombing the year before, however, there was no proof Fatima had any involvement.

'Baby, my love for God is too great to harm those who are innocent. I love you in the name of God and want you to experience peace and freedom. You defended yourself and the life of my friend Caroline, I owe you a debt and yes, I do need your help and I can pay for this. You need to leave England, please pay attention to what I have to say.'

Listening without making any further comment James looked on in silence filled with curiosity, then watched as Andy hit a key casually disconnecting her call.

58

Boarding a train at Chalfont and Latimer station, Andy moved down the carriage and sat in the first empty seat next to the exit. Surrounded by London bound commuters he observed people crushed up beside him. Waiting, poised for the sliding doors to begin closing, he jumped to his feet and stepped down onto the platform a split second before they slammed shut. Seeing no one else leave the train, he watched the swaying coaches gather speed and rapidly disappear out of sight. Confident he was not being followed Andy dodged through a passage leading into the station car park, and walked quickly along rows of vehicles searching for a particular dark blue Mondeo. Spotting the anonymous Ford, checking the registration number and flipping the lock, he stowed his one small bag in the boot. Climbing into the driver's seat, powering up the engine he slowly moved off toward the exit. Time was of the essence; with a long drive to Plymouth then boarding the overnight ferry to Santander in Northern Spain.

So far, Fatima's plan was working, she had given precise details telling him to return to his apartment three days after their phone conversation and check his mail. Recalling his excitement seeing the hand delivered packages on the floor of the hallway just as she promised, he had torn open the first envelope and withdrawn a Visa debit card with no name printed on it - just the usual long number and issue date. The note inside explained he could use this anonymous card at any ATM around the world.

The second slightly bulkier envelope contained a red covered Irish passport, International Driving License and a Spanish SIM card for his mobile. Turning the pages of the passport, he immediately saw his face - the same image he had sent to Fatima by email. Then reading out his new name for the first time, it sounded strange "Patrick De-Morgan." She had not forgotten to include keys for the Mondeo and instructions to reach the bank account.

Completing the road trip in five hours, arriving at Plymouth docks, he caught sight of the enormous 40,000 ton Pont-Aven, capable of carrying over 2,000 passengers and 600 cars. During boarding he was concerned about the slim chance someone might recognize him, an old acquaintance perhaps from his past. After a drink in the bar he bought snacks to take to his cabin and settled down in the windowless room. Lying back on the bed feeling tired after the drive he soon drifted off to sleep. Within seconds he was dreaming of travelling again, this time with Maria, and they were going home to meet her parents in Buenos Aires. Excited she told him about her father and that he should not be nervous meeting him. Then in a bizarre twist the way it happens in dreams, Caroline began speaking animatedly from the back seat of the car, while Maria had disappeared. Waking with a start from the hazy nightmare, he tried to forget the incident flicking on the TV. His cousin James had been opposed to him leaving, saying there was still a chance he would not go to prison, perhaps receiving a suspended sentence. Andy argued he was not prepared to take the chance, knowing once he was in custody anything could happen to him. He was not particularly close to his own family and apart from James, with Maria gone; this was an opportunity for a fresh start in life. Poignantly the tiny windowless cabin resembled a cell, reinforcing the gloom and a reminder of what incarceration in a prison would really be like. Eventually, with the help of another beer and the steady rocking of the ship pushing back through the autumn swell, he went to sleep, on thoughts that maybe he would never return to his home country again...

Waking refreshed and approaching the port at Santander after the 24 hour sea crossing, Andy was feeling positive about his future - even excited by the prospect of a new beginning. A crewmember began barking instructions through the ships intercom, asking drivers to re-join their vehicles below deck. Remembering his bag, he trooped down metal steps leading into the ships cavernous hold. Passengers slammed car doors in the confined spaces struggled to stow away luggage, strapping small children into their safety harness. Waiting in the Mondeo, his fingers nervously tapped on the steering wheel, trying to second-guess where Fatima would be taking him. Logically he expected it to be Madrid, but she also had another home in Paris.

Loud mechanical noises signaled the opening of the gaping ships hold. As daylight burst in through the widening gaps, unseen actions at the front of the queue triggered an ensemble of throbbing motors. Then as the line of vehicles began to move, Andy powered his engine and followed behind negotiating the Ford down a steep metal gantry. Crossing over the gangway he pulled out the line of traffic to avoid the customs and immigration control, and parked the Mondeo by the quayside. Next, searching for his mobile phone expertly fitted the Spanish SIM card and waited for Fatima to make contact with new instructions. Constantly checking the small mobile he began to feel

The Treaty

conspicuous fearful of attracting the attention of some jobsworth or port official. Deciding to make a move he was about to drive away and risk passing through customs and immigration when the unfamiliar ring tone made him jump.

'Fatima, is that you?'

'Yes, are you okay - are you in Santander?'

'Where do you think - of course Santander, I arrived an hour ago and have to move from here soon.'

'You have not been reported missing by the media yet, so it should be safe to go through immigration. Drive to the hotel Bahia, it is close. Go there and check-in and don't forget your new name is Patrick,' she laughed; only half-joking.

'At what time will I be contacted again, I need to know?'

'Don't worry, just stay in your room, my people are on their way and will make contact very soon. I have arranged for them to take you to a safe house. Afterwards we will decide when to leave and bring you here to Marrakech.'

'Marrakech, I thought Paris or Madrid? What the hell am I going to do in Morocco?'

'I am looking forward to seeing you again, you will like it here it's very beautiful.' There was a pause. 'You brought me everything - the copy of the treaty. I know you told Caroline you have this?'

Taken aback, Andy knew there was only one other person who could know this for definite and that was Caroline, and he only told her less than one hour before the shooting. It was then he pictured her replacing a mobile inside a shoulder bag when they sat outside the church - after he returned from the pub. Could she have been calling Fatima?

'Are you still there Andy, you do have the papers and letters for me don't you? I am so excited at last we can reveal the truth.'

Thinking fast, unable to comprehend a betrayal by Caroline, there had to be some other explanation. Maybe she was bluffing and had guessed this was true, making the story up as she went along. Or, once again, could it be he was astonishingly naïve. Was it possible that Caroline had changed her loyalty and now worked for - or even alongside Fatima? It was simply too much to contemplate and off his scale of comprehension. All he could think of at that very moment was he needed a delaying tactic and it had to be good.

'Yes Fatima, but they're only duplicates - you need the original signed version otherwise they will be dismissed as forgeries by the British and Americans.'

'No, you are wrong, baby. Anyway, I am not interested in what your media says, the people I care about will believe when they recognize the truth. They will rise up causing a revolution, uniting the Middle East, Africa and Asia, against the Zionists and infidels. A new fatwa on your Royals will destroy their lives - anger and revenge for ravaging our countries and stealing its wealth for centuries.'

Shocked by her true purpose, Andy raced to temper his emotions and then decided to deal another card - his ace. 'There is another way Fatima, if you can wait a little longer. Caroline and I may have discovered where the authentic signed copy of the treaty is hidden. We came very close to finding it, and once you have this you really will be believed throughout the world, including the UK and America.'

Hearing her laughter made him feel angry.

'Fatima, I am trying to help you - it is true what I am saying! I'm sure I know where the original files are. Why waste more time with duplicates?'

'Baby, I love you, even when your life is in so much danger you tease me. You cannot possibly know where the

The Treaty

real treaty is hidden. Maria will have told you. All the original documents are still somewhere in Buenos Aires, protected by the sisters of Peron. Please, no more games, we must move quickly, go now to the hotel and wait for my call.'

'Maria didn't tell me anything. Caroline and I are certain they are in England, you must be wrong.'

Sounding angry as if her patience was almost exhausted, Fatima barked back at him. 'I'm not wrong, even Maria knew this; she was herself a member of the Peron Organization. I am sure your girlfriend did share this with you. Please Andy no more games I have to go; this line may not be safe - to the hotel quickly, ciao.'

Listening to the abrupt silence and with the mobile phone still pressed firmly to his ear, Andy looked out of the car window across the murky black water toward distance ships on the horizon. His own fate was sealed; he was cut adrift from those he could trust and with his life in jeopardy. In the way that it sometimes happens when everything seems lost, he suddenly found inspiration and made a split second decision. He would switch to another hotel in an effort to regain control. Cautiously powering the car engine and starting to move away toward the immigration booth, the Mondeo was waved through without inspection. He continued following signs out of the harbour, and away from Santander's busy centre.

Shadowed by the Picos de Europa's, avoiding the main highway, he rallied through tight mountain passes travelling along narrow country roads. After driving for two hours north from Santander, he noticed an unusual building displaying a modern sign for a hotel. It was a converted monastery outside a town called Cangas Onis, dating back to the days of the crusades. Checking-in under his new name, Patrick De Morgan, Andy settled into a clean, well-furnished room with luxuries no monk could ever dream of. Unsure if he would be staying, he began to sort through his belongings before stretching out on the bed to consider his next move. Closing his eyes in contemplation, he thought about Maria. Even when their relationship hit a low point and he discovered she was involved with Fatima, he had never stopped loving her for one minute. In one recurring dream they were together, but he couldn't see her face; it was always hidden behind her delicate small hands. Another time he was convinced he heard her crying - deep sobs that chilled his spine, reminiscent of that sad day in his apartment when she made her confessions to him.

Sitting upright, reaching for his bag, he recalled her small silver locket always worn around her neck. It was in a plain envelope he brought with him, all he could carry that would remind him of the past. A passport-sized photograph of his mother, mixed in with pieces of jewelry handed to him for safekeeping by the nurse after Maria died. Thinking they were only of sentimental value, he kept these believing that perhaps one day he would return them in person to her family. Emptying the contents onto the bed, he immediately noticed the silver locket. Never having closely examined it before, Andy fiddled with the delicate catch and opened the small case. Inside were two pictures. One was an unmistakable miniature of Princess Diana, opposite the iconic Eva Peron. Gently easing them out of their tiny frame, he saw scratched on the surface behind Diana in swirling writing, "Dios en mujer" (God in woman) and underneath Peron, "Madre de Cristo" (Mother of Christ). Replacing the pictures, he lay back down and struggled to understand the meaning represented by these two women. His first thought was that perhaps Maria was just a fan. However, from the inscriptions beneath the images they appeared to have a religious significance.

Fatima, who earlier mentioned the Peron movement,

seemed to think Maria should have told him more about this organization, which was obviously connected in some-way to Eva Peron. Both he and Caroline were convinced they found where the original treaty was - in the crypt with Diana, as he suspected, or the other remote possibility, was Janet had somehow placed it inside Diana's coffin - before the burial on the island at Althorp. One thing was certain; he could not dismiss Fatima, who seemed definite she was right and that the authentic treaty was still in Argentina. Just maybe he thought Diana or Mrs Briggs sent the original documents to Buenos Aires, leaving Janet with the copies and knowing if they were discovered they would be rubbished as forgeries. The more he considered this new theory the more he thought about the story Jack told them about Diana's visit to his home. Had both he and Caroline been unbelievably stupid? Jack will have told that same tale to dozens of other visitors; he even said it was therapeutic to talk about it. A regular in the village pub that was visited by hoards of tourists, perhaps he even earned a few free beers on the strength of his tale, embellishing it just a little over the years. It all sounded so genuine, they could not dispute the death of his son and Caroline was not a complete fool and she believed it was true. He had to consider the possibility that all the later events at the church did take place and Diana left a package or something with Janet Briggs for safekeeping. Moreover, with Janet's co-operation they were encouraged to believe the treaty was in the UK - diverting everyone's attention from the true hiding place six thousand miles away. Could it be Diana set out to take precautions in the event of her absence - predicting her own early demise? Protecting those closest to her, particularly Susan Barrantes? Eventually, Andy became more and more frustrated by not knowing enough and decided to leave his room in search of the hotel's internet terminal. Anxious not to use his own laptop and give clues to his whereabouts, the hotel had a computer for customers to use. Googling anything he could find on Eva Peron and her links with women's movements, he quickly discovered she had in fact launched her own party in 1947, attracting support from women in Argentina. The last recorded militant activity by the group was in 1990, confirming it remained in operation years after Eva Peron had died. With the arrival of Princess Diana on the scene, and with encouragement from Susan Barrantes, Andy considered the possibility perhaps Diana joined the Peron movement and was contemplating an involvement in international politics, fighting for the rights of women. The foundations erected by Eva, would have been perfect for Diana, and with the treaty in her reserve arsenal; she could have made quite an impact on the world. Suddenly, with all this new information to consider Andy felt an overpowering urge to leave immediately for Argentina and find out more? There were so many unresolved issues and personal demons to face. Who really was Maria, and what was she trying to achieve?

The Treaty

59

The 400 kilometer virtually non-stop drive through the night to Madrid's Barajas airport lasted 6 hours. Andy abandoned the car leaving the keys in the glove box. After checking-in and passing through security, he made his way to the departure terminal and by early evening had exchanged Europe's autumn skies for summertime.
Watching out the aircraft window the Boeing 747 Aerolineas Argentinas flight touched down at Buenos Aires Pistarini Airport. Passing through immigration and collecting his luggage, he went in search of the tourist information booth. After choosing a hotel in his price range, he booked a room in the comically named, Hotel Rodney. Andy knew nothing about this city and was surprised by its size and modern European style architecture. He arrived at the hotel and settled into a room, badly in need of decoration. Deciding to press straight ahead with his plan, he began to search through his bag for Maria's notebook and her parent's phone number. Starting to make the call after only a few rings, a woman's voice answered and in short Spanish phrases he asked to speak with either of Maria's parent. There was a pause and a new female voice came on the line. Listening patiently while Andy explained who he was, she could only understand parts of their conversation interrupting asking him to speak

English.

'Thank you, I am sorry about my Spanish.'

'No problem, how can I help you?'

'My name is Andrew Davies I was a close friend of Maria's when she was living in England.'

'Yes!' the woman gasped, sounding surprised. 'She spoke about you. I am Mercedes - Maria's sister.'

'She mentioned you too; it's great to finally speak with you. Is it possible to meet? I have some of Maria's personal belongings that you may want to keep.'

'Yes, thank you Andy, that is very kind, my mother will be pleased when I tell her. Where are you staying?'

'On Junín at the Hotel Rodney, do you know it?'

'Yes, I work in the city. Are you free tomorrow at around midday?'

'Sure.'

'We could meet at the Café Tortoni and make arrangements for you to visit our house.'

'Okay, that sounds great.'

'It is in the centre just take a taxi.'

'Perfect. See you tomorrow I will look forward to meeting you.'

'Ciao.'

Replacing the receiver, Andy felt pleased having made contact with the family so soon after arriving in Buenos Aires, although he did wonder why she wanted to meet him alone. Disregarding this as a problem, he was grateful for the opportunity to explain what had happened, even though he was nervous they might blame him for Maria's death.

The next morning with little to do but wait until he met with Mercedes, Andy used the time to investigate the city. Buying a guide book, he headed for the Casa Rosada, the celebrated Pink Palace where Eva Peron spoke from her

The Treaty

balcony to a reputed two million people filling the plaza below. Years later after Evita had gone the collapse of their currency the Peso followed. Andy learned this was in part due to the rising strength of the US dollar. Bank deposits were frozen in 2002 and remained locked in accounts for nearly 12 months. Many middleclass people like Maria's parents were made practically destitute overnight, and when they did finally access their accounts; the money on deposit had devalued by half against the dollar. This resulted in the now famous riots and demonstrations from the balconies of the apartment blocks, starting with men and women banging pots and pans in unison, loud enough for their leaders to hear in measured tones the growing anger and frustration of the people.

In the early 1990's, around the same time Princess Diana visited Buenos Aires, the country had experienced something of a boom in their economy. With the feeling of wealth, it was a time for new ideas and opportunities - enough reason perhaps for Diana herself to like this country and want to play a role in shaping a new party for women. The Eva Peron Organization believed to be dormant was a shadowy association, with the aim to bring increased power to disenfranchised women. Andy thought that in Diana, they perhaps found a new leader, who bequeathed to them another weapon. This time it wasn't anything so crude as a home made bomb, but a real weapon of mass destruction in the form of *the treaty*.

Argentinean women had every reason to be angry with the West and in particular the British. Andy observed a number of limbless war veterans hanging around the plaza as he toured the city, begging for money. These were almost certainly casualties of the ill-fated Falklands War.

It was not hard to find the Café Tortoni along the Avenue de Mayo, located in a major tourist area. This was the most famous coffee shop in the country visited by crowned heads of Europe, full of rich nostalgia, the walls lined with celebrity pictures. Andy arrived ahead of schedule and found a seat in full view of the door. He had not until that moment considered how he would recognize Mercedes. Few women came alone and those that did were clearly of the wrong age group. Arriving late, she hurried through the door, anxiously scanning the room before seeing Andy. Making her way over to his table, looking taller and slightly older she was her sister's double. With the same shaped face sharing Maria's trademark jet black hair, Andy stood to greet her having recognized her immediately. Kissing her on both cheeks he felt a surge of emotion as if Maria had simply returned from a long absence.

'Hi Mercedes, how did you recognize me, I was worried I would miss you?'

'Hola, it was easy, Maria sent me your picture soon after you met, taken when you were in London visiting the Queen's Palace.'

'Yes, I remember, the first time we went out together. We finished the day sitting in a park eating fish and chips, it's an English tradition.'

'Did you have any problem finding this place? Have you been waiting long?'

'No, not at all, I have a tourist map. Thank you for meeting me at such short notice; you must be surprised at my sudden appearance in Buenos Aires?'

'I have been expecting you at anytime. I asked my parents to invite you to the funeral, but they were in shock, it was too soon for them. Maria did tell me about you, I was certain it wasn't your fault.'

Interrupted by the brusque manner of the middle-aged male waiter, Mercedes asked what he wanted to drink and ordered more coffee for him and cola for herself.

'Laos is a safe place for Westerners to visit and the man was English, we had no reason to be worried about our safety.' Mercedes didn't want to talk about her sister's death and quickly changed the subject. 'So what can I show you, have you seen any other sights? I don't have to work this afternoon, shall we go somewhere and we can talk about a plan to visit my family soon?'

'Do you think it will be a problem meeting them? I don't want to upset your mother or father.'

'No, not at all, we should talk first. It will make it easier for them and for you.'

'Yes, I agree. Let's go sightseeing, I would like to see the English Tower, sorry, you renamed it after the war The Monumental Tower.'

Mercedes laughter was eerily identical to Maria's. She explained most people still called it the English Tower; it was donated by the English community on the centennial of the May Revolution and renamed after the Falklands War.

The tour lasted through the afternoon finishing at an Italian restaurant in Junín close to his hotel. Happier than he had been in months, Buenos Aires seemed a wonderful place to be right now. Mercedes was bright, cheerful, giggling at Andy and his attempts at speaking Spanish.

'Why do you British drink so much?' she asked.

He was drinking his third glass of beer and suddenly felt oafish.

'I don't consider this a lot,' Andy smiled speaking defensively. 'In England three or four glasses are not unusual spread over an afternoon.'

'Maria told me even your girls get very drunk when they go out. Why is that?'

He could not give a rational explanation, only that it was probably due to the English reserve and needing alcohol to feel more liberated. Mercedes continued chatting. 'I enjoyed today, do like our city?'

'It's a wonderful place. Mercedes, I hope you don't mind, but tell me more about Maria. What was she like? I have an image of her, was she a happy child.'

'Yes, but we had many fights. I'm the older sister and became very jealous when everyone said how pretty she was.'

'You look very attractive to me.'

Dropping her eye contact, she looked away feeling embarrassed, and leaving Andy to curse under his breath.

'Sorry, I didn't mean to embarrass you. I meant you are attractive, so I couldn't understand why people would say your sister was more attractive - I will stop talking if you like?'

She grinned at his bumbling English behaviour. 'You do not have to explain why you paid me a compliment, it's just I'm not used to receiving them. If you were an Argentinean man, I would be listening to how great and wonderful you are.'

Feeling happier, he ordered wine leaving the remains of his beer and filled their glasses with the delicious Argentinean Rutini. As the minutes passed the illusion of being safe and free grew stronger - an illusion destroyed in 20 seconds.

'I called you at the hotel this morning, but you had already left.'

'Yes, I went to the Casa Rosada, it was very interesting.'

'I asked for you by name, but they did not recognize it at the hotel, there was only one Englishman staying there called Patrick. Why do you have a different name?'

This was a calculated question, and she had chosen her timing taking him completely by surprise. His furtive behavior, glancing around to see if anyone was listening only compounded his guilt.

'It is a bit complicated. I am travelling under a different name. How much did Maria tell you about her life in

England? Did you know she was in hospital and what happened to her employers?'

'Of course, she told me everything. I was shocked when they were killed and we called the hospital everyday while Maria was there, she was very happy to be staying with you.'

'We were both happy. I did hope we would be together for a long time.'

'When they told me at the hotel you had a different name I decided to read the English news and searched for Andrew Davies. A report on a website described a shooting, a man and woman died at the scene close to where Maria lived. Was that you?'

Reeling from this second broadside, and the ease with which she had unpicked his masquerade, he took a sip of iced water and bought more time before answering, knowing full well he had to tell her everything.

'Before I explain, can I ask you a personal question?'

Sitting perfectly calm, Mercedes never flinched. She held full eye contact and smiled. 'Yes, anything you like.'

'Do you know a woman called Fatima Labaua?'

'Yes, I expect Maria told you about her. She is one of our sisters. We are members of the same organization.'

'Which is?'

Now it was Mercedes turn to break her stare making furtive glances around before saying quietly, 'The Eva Peron Organization - but please, I cannot talk about that in here.'

'Perhaps we should go somewhere more private, my hotel?'

Nodding her agreement, they prepared to leave, asking for the bill. Andy paid in cash and began walking in silence to The Hotel Rodney five minutes away. Passing a respectable looking young woman with two small children pushing an old baby's pram, Andy observed how she used the carriage to hold bundles of waste cardboard scavenged from amongst the piles of rubbish at the roadside.

'That woman looks so young, is there no other work for her to do, they must be very poor.'

Mercedes gave a cursory glance in her direction. 'She probably lost everything when the banks closed. This country went from being one of the richest per head of population in the world - to having more than 50% of the people living in poverty. Imagine if that happened in Britain?'

'I think there would be riots equally as large as the ones that happened here - if not worse.' Andy commented.

Reaching the hotel, ignoring the disapproving glances from the woman behind the reception desk, Andy directed Mercedes up to his room. Once inside he immediately sat down in the one armchair, tired from the affects of alcohol and jet lag, while Mercedes perched primly on the edge of his bed with her feet firmly on the floor.

'Andy, Patrick, which name, do you prefer me to use. Why are you really here in Buenos Aires?'

'I'm sorry for all the subterfuge, please call me Andy. It would have been difficult explaining everything in the first few minutes of our meeting and I am not sure how much you already know what has been happening to me?'

'After Maria died all the information stopped, I did have some contact with Fatima before Maria came to England, but not since then. We stopped speaking, she has her own agenda.'

'Maria seemed very close to Fatima at one time, are you saying this did not involve you - The Peron Organization.'

'We had a disagreement with Fatima, and Maria sided with her against the wishes of our family, it's a long story but first, why have you really come all this way, explain about that shooting. If you are dangerous I may want to leave the room now!'

Hearing this, Andy decided he would be honest and tell her briefly what happened after Maria died. Mentioning Caroline Lovelace-Jones and their mission to find a set of documents called the treaty, and how this was the same information being pursued by Fatima.

'Andy, I already know a lot about this. It was my father who sold the copy of the treaty to Dominic Marsh in the first place. You still haven't told me why you left England to come here, why were you arrested for shooting that man?'

'It was a setup; he tried to assassinate both Caroline and myself. I managed to knock him over with the car after he shot at us and wounded Caroline. When I saw what he had done to her I got out of the car, picked up his gun and pulled the trigger. I killed him before he killed me - it was as simple as that. His wife died in the car. I reversed into her when we were trying to escape. The police accused me of manslaughter killing both people, which in England means at least five years in prison, more than long enough for my enemies to have another go at killing me.'

'But what do you plan to do now? Will you try to stay here in South America? Andy, why shouldn't I tell the police? You sound like a dangerous man.'

'I'm honestly not a threat to you or anyone else, quite the opposite. I do need your help in explaining some of the things that have happened, particularly between Maria and Fatima. I still don't get the connection. What does the Eva Peron organizations have to do with the treaty?'

60

The roar from a passing truck shook the building, rattling the windows and startling Andy awake. Massaging his neck, he climbed out of the armchair and stumbled toward the bathroom, passing by Mercedes curled up lying across the double bed. They had talked for hours, long into the night. It became too late for her to return home, so she decided to sleep in his room. Pleased he had not frightened her off considering he had confessed to killing two people, a surreal event that he still had not properly come to terms with. Despite their obvious differences the fact they both new Maria gave them a bond, and for the first time Andy felt he was able to talk about what happened to someone who new her as well as he did.

Studying his face in the bathroom mirror, he went over in his mind what had been discussed the night before, the Eva Peron Organization and the involvement of Princess Diana. She came to Buenos Aires in 1995 on an official visit, after her divorce from Prince Charles. Having been introduced to Argentina by her sister-in-law Sarah, whose mother Susan Barrantes had made her home on a ranch some distance from the capital. According to Mercedes, Diana seriously considered relocating in the belief her life in Great Britain was under threat. She likely knew she was a target for aggression, and her knowledge of the treaty had

The Treaty

marked her out; also given the fact she now had the authentically signed copy and the original letters and documents. Mercedes claimed that following her blessing by the Pope and praying together with Mother Teresa, Diana moved closer to God through the Catholic Church. Her growing popularity in Argentina brought fresh hope to women - some called her their new Evita.

At first Mercedes claimed to know nothing about the origin or whereabouts of the treaty, and avoided Andy's question on this subject. Then she gradually revealed Princess Diana's plan to use these documents to wreak revenge on her ex-husband, knowing she held the key to Prince Philip's power. Fatima became involved with the Peron Organization via another associated Muslim group, sharing a common goal to empower women. It rapidly became clear to Fatima and members of Peron that fundamental differences existed between them.

Princess Diana believed she could prevent her ex-husband becoming the King of England and forcing both him and his family into exile. After the Queens abdication and in Charles's absence, her own son Prince William, unsullied by corruption, would be invited to take the crown. Once he was established, it could only be a matter of time before she then persuaded him to convert to Catholicism, returning England to the true faith. Her plan was not to allow any of this to happen until the timing was right. She was desperate to wait until William reached maturity; they would have a normal upbringing and not be plunged into the limelight too soon. However a date had been set for the documents release, July 1, 2011, marking Diana's 50th birthday. When Andy asked how it could still work now Diana was dead, Mercedes remained adamant the project was on track. The treaty she said will be unveiled, causing the downfall of the monarchy. She believed the British and American economies would be seriously damaged by the documents release, proving deep corruption and failure to sustain their ailing democracies. This change in the political landscape will allow other countries to expand especially those in Latin America, with the help of China.

Andy was puzzled how a copy of the secret files first came to be in Britain. Mercedes explained this had been part of a scheme to disrupt Fatima's campaign. To release information into the public domain via Great Britain, before Fatima had a chance, knowing these copy documents would be dismissed as forgeries in Europe and the US. Later, on the date agreed with Princess Diana's last wishes, the Peron Organization will release the signed authentic documents proving the conspiracy is true.

In answer to how Maria became so involved with Fatima, her explanation came as a painful reminder to Andy. Maria had fallen under Fatima's spell during a brief love affair. Mercedes could see his pride was wounded and tried to reassure him that Maria was confused and had been desperately in love with him too. Maria convinced her father to let her work in England for Dominic Marsh, her motive being to steal a copy of the treaty for Fatima before he had a chance to get anything into print. The Peron Organization disowned her and so too the family with the exception of Mercedes. After Dominic and Emma's death, Maria realized her own stupidity and begged for their forgiveness.

Exiting the bathroom fully dressed he invited Mercedes to stay for breakfast. There was still so much more they needed to discuss. Mercedes offered to take him to the place where Maria is laid to rest. She told him the cemetery was at Recoleta, and the coffin placed inside their family mausoleum. Still somewhat in denial about Maria's death he considered this would be the most difficult part of his journey.

Eating breakfast and confirming he was staying on at the

The Treaty

hotel for another night, afterwards they left together in a taxi. Mercedes continued to play tour guide, pointing out the sights as they passed by the famous Plaza de Mayo and a group of women protestors.

'They are called the Madres de la Plaza,' Mercedes explained. 'They walk around the square demanding more information and justice for the deaths of their loved ones who were killed during the "dirty war". Thousands of civilians disappeared in Argentina during the military rule and were presumed murdered by our police and army. Look over there is the Cathedral Metropolitan,' Mercedes smiles. 'It holds the tomb of General Jose de San Martin - Argentina's greatest independence hero. It is very beautiful you have to agree?'

Coming from Europe Andy had seen many beautiful churches, but he decided it was a particularly handsome building asking, 'Do you worship there yourself?'

'Sometimes, with my father, he is close friends with people from the church.'

'Is your father more religious than most Argentineans of his generation?'

'Maybe, a little more - our family has good pedigree in the Catholic Church. As you know my family name is Farnese - we are distant relatives of Pope Clement VIII from the sixteenth century.'

'Wow, that's amazing - have you studied your family's history?'

'No, not really,' she giggled. 'I have learned most of this from my father who is very proud of his Italian ancestry.'

'Maria said you were all Argentineans now - is that how you see yourself?'

'Yes, I've no links with Italy or Spain for that matter, which is where our mother's family is from, but I believe in God, the link with the Church is important - it's worth fighting for.' Puzzled by this last comment he let it pass.

Arriving at the cemetery Andy was not prepared for what he was about to see in Recoleta. The area was the size of a busy suburb or small town, displaying a mass of ornately decorated structures. Winged angels looked out across domes and spires separated by mature trees. Strolling among the crowded architecture, he struggled to take in the diversity and acreage devoted to housing the dead.

'This place is amazing, how many people are buried in here?'

'According to Padre, since the cemetery was founded, there have been over three hundred thousand burials in five thousand tombs. He brought us here when we were children to visit our family mausoleum.'

Stopping alongside one particularly imposing tomb, decorated with fresh flowers attached to the doors, she pointed to a brass plaque midway among a line of other tributes and the embossed image of a woman fixed to the black marble column.

'This belongs to the Duarte, and is the final resting place for our beloved Eva Duarte-Peron, or Evita.'

Running his fingers over the raised image, Andy felt a tingle of reverence at the sight of her name. This was no ordinary girl. She became a woman feared by politicians for her power and influence, was a symbol of hope for millions of Argentineans, and won votes for women with a potential to inspire people across the world.

Mercedes went ahead, leaving Andy standing alone by the monument. In a sudden flash of inspiration the idea came, what a fantastic hiding place this would be for the treaty. Who would venture inside a tomb, comprising of a deep chamber full of dusty coffins? The temperature below ground was constant and Buenos Aires climate perfect; preserving the documents for decades. Hurrying away, he found Mercedes sitting on a wooden bench shel-

The Treaty

tering from the sun underneath the spread of a mature cypress tree.

'Listen, I've just had a brilliant idea! What a great place to hide the treaty - right here in Recoleta cemetery.'

Sitting on her hands and staring down at her shoes, she lifted her head back with a huge grin. 'Where in particular would you hide it - 5,000 tombs, several hundred thousand hiding places - which would you choose?'

Watching her, it was then the penny dropped.

'You do know where it is - it's here somewhere! I'm not asking you to say exactly where, but agree I'm right, did Maria know the real location - did she always know it was right here in Argentina all along?'

'No, she did not, there are only a very small number of people who have that knowledge, and it's sacred to us.'

'But she never told me anything about the Eva Peron Organization, or much about you for that matter - she was very good at keeping secrets.'

'After Susan Barrantes died, the Peron Organization gave instructions that only a select number of people should know the whereabouts of the original treaty. Maybe if Maria had been trusted with this knowledge she would not have made such a tragic mistake.'

'I see.'

'Please, Andy, forget this for now - come, I want you to meet my sister.'

Meekly he followed, dreading finding out if he had the emotional strength to cope with this awkward confrontation.

Walking passed manicured lawns; she stopped alongside a clean white marble structure smaller than many of the others. It looked old by comparison but well maintained. A solid wrought iron gate blocked the entrance, and there - fixed to a marble column, was a startling photograph of Maria, taken when she was still a girl. Unprepared, despite this being the purpose of his visit he could not halt the flow of tears. Since she died, he had not grieved properly, only shutting out the dreadful reality in all the chaos that had followed. Not being at her funeral, and the attempt on his life resulting in weeks of hospital treatment, had meant he had managed to suppress a volcano of emotion building up below the surface - a real shuddering gut wrenching sorrow.

Mercedes put her arm tenderly around his shoulder, and then she too began to cry. It was at this moment something strange happened and they heard a voice coming from another place saying. "Shush...I love you, it's all right. I am okay." There was no mistaking it was the voice of Maria and turning to stare at Mercedes, he imagined seeing Maria, and then watched as she melted into the image of her sister.

Squeezing his arm, stroking her fingers across his cheek, Mercedes looked crazed - her eyes drilling into him as she repeated over-and-over in Spanish; 'Conoces al Dios, Conoces al Dios, do you know God - I mean really know and understand the meaning of God.' Breathless, speaking without a pause - she ranted on; 'Andy, sometimes when I wake the thought of my love for dear sweet Jesus fills me with excitement, empowering me to carry on with our mission. You must help me now - Maria has gone from us, she spoke to you, she is a messenger from God, you did see her, she was here - admit you saw her? God is our protector and will help us, we will use the weapons of the Princess to remove the heretics and win the battle for the return of the blessed Mother of Christ.'

Stunned into silence he listened, dumbfounded, and heard voices screaming inside his head - telling him to run from what he didn't understand. Breaking her grip, he wrenched away - confused, distraught and desperately unhappy.

Walking off in shock, he tried to make sense of what he

The Treaty

had just heard - convinced that he was either losing his mind if he believed Maria spoke or was he just overpowered by the emotion of her being so close.

Mercedes caught up and began shouting. 'What's the matter, Andy? Did I frighten you - why are you so unhappy hearing her? It was Maria, not some ghost?'

'I'm not sure what I heard. It could've been my imagination.'

'Then did I imagine it too. Andy, we did hear the same thing together - answer please, do not be afraid, you did hear her. Listen, I speak often when I visit here, she is close to us because we love her so much, it's quite normal.'

'It maybe normal for you, but hearing voices from the dead is not something I've previously experienced or ever believed was possible - maybe I will have to do some re-thinking, just give me more time.'

'Jesus came back from the dead and he speaks to those people who love him all the time - only Maria's body has died, her spirit is alive and with us now.'

Sitting down on one of the numerous wooden benches dotted about the gardens, in front of them was a beautiful display of deep red Poinsettias, *Flor de Pascua*, symbolizing the blood of Christ; and sanctifying their semi-religious debate.

'I want to believe what you're saying and for the sake of no more argument let's agree you're right and I heard Maria's voice. Please tell me how God can approve of you keeping this narcotics agreement a secret from the world for so long. When for several decades the increased production and distribution of these killer drugs has ruined millions of people's lives?'

'Andrew, we have been given the opportunity to use the treaty for the good. The church blessed our plan when The Pope issued a Toro Papal or Papal Bull you say in English. He decreed the lands taken by the British, and the other heretics were really the territory of my ancestors from

Spain and Portugal, they are Papal States. When Prince William is King, he will return to the church along with all his people. It has taken over four hundred years, soon the treaty will be used to make this happen - we can wait a little longer.'

'I just don't know what to make of this Mercedes, its all way over my head. What can I do about it? I know nothing about this I'm not even religious - what is it you want me to do?'

'Unfortunately for you, Andy, you are right at the centre of what's happening and we do need your help. Please, tomorrow I want you to meet with my father and our friends. I will show you inside the Cathedral Metropolitan where we come together.'

'But what can I do, I've nothing to offer you and your friends? Have you forgotten - I'm a fugitive.'

'Then for now we can help you, and you can stay here safe in Buenos Aires - be part of our family. This can be your new home.'

'Thank you, that's a kind offer, especially in view of what happened to Maria - but if I meet with your father, what is he expecting me to do? Are you asking me to betray my own country, I'm not ready to do that whatever the cost to me?'

'Andy, first we don't blame you for Maria's death and second you are not betraying anyone by helping our cause. You will help to bring your people home - to the house of God. They have already suffered - for hundreds of years, heretics with no faith, told lies that mere mortals could be in charge of the house of God - you will return to the one true faith.'

'Mercedes, I've already told you, I'm not religious full stop, so this is all lost on me. I worry more about the treaty on the moral issues, and that is why I became so involved. If you want me to continue helping your cause, with the eventual exposure of the guilty people then yes, I will meet with your father, but I will not condone you to wage war against my country.'

Taking hold of his hand and giving a gentle squeeze, they caught the afternoon sun, standing between the columns outside the imposing entrance to the cemetery.

'*Bien*, that's a starting point. I will arrange a time, would you like me to come back to the hotel with you now or do you want to be alone?'

'I don't want to seem rude, but yes, I would prefer to go back alone. I need some time to think.'

'Okay, but cheer up, Andy, you look unhappy. We will celebrate your arrival, my mother will love you like a son, and I like your devoted sister. Please don't change your mind; I really want this to work for all of us.'

Leaving the cemetery precincts and walking out to the main road watched by Mercedes, Andy caught a taxi back to the hotel. Cruising through the busy streets, he tried to understand what he really heard outside Maria's tomb. Believing only rational genetic, physiological or biochemical explanations for hearing voices, he thought perhaps Mercedes must have experienced similar sensations on a previous visit, and from his reaction assumed he heard something as well. When he came to Buenos Aires on impulse, Andy never imagined this new scenario and was not sure he had made the right choice leaving Fatima. At least she was only interested in using the treaty to help existing Muslims and Muslim nations, also to expose the evil people behind the treaty. This was a common objective they both shared. He could see logic in why Mercedes was keen to involve him; he had the local knowledge and was fully up to speed on what the treaty was all about, with contacts in the UK and the Far East.

Arriving back at his hotel, after a quick shower he went out to eat. Seeing an Internet café he decided to catch up on the news and found a press report mentioning Caroline, she was conscious and expected to make a full recovery. Checking Mercedes story about her distant relation the Pope, using Wikipedia, he discovered her family name Farnese linked to Pope Clement VIII. In 1600, he was in the chair when Queen Elizabeth granted permission for a bunch of adventures to go off and discover a route to the East, in defiance of the Papal Bull Mercedes mentioned. The Catholic Church had already excommunicated Elizabeth so there was not a lot more the Pope could do to her. Nevertheless, he did not forgive Queen Elizabeth for defying him, or any of her subjects, meaning the judgment was still very much in place 400 years down the line - condemning the British Royal Family together with all their non-Catholic subjects as heretics.

This gave Mercedes father reason enough to take umbrage and offer his support to any project helping them win back what Catholics regarded as belonging to them by divine right. It was not just the Falkland Islands they wanted to be returned - it was all lands to the West of Spain and Portugal. On yet another flank, he knew Fatima was pioneering her own similar operation, hell-bent on causing disruption to make way for her Muslim revolt. Meanwhile back home in Great Britain, no one had a clue what was happening, citizens ignorant of this two-pronged attack by a group of religious fundamentalists - planning to fill the vacuum created by the demise of the Church of England. Britain had become a morally bankrupt country managed by a corrupt establishment and whose people had lost their faith. Obsessed with property values and who thought nothing of buying an empty church and living inside the house of God with their animals. To counter this demise in religious standards a new generation of migrants was settling in the UK, many of them Catholic and Muslim. By the time Prince William ascended to the

The Treaty

throne this new religious army will be firmly in place.

In the USA, revelations of the treaty could trigger a religious civil war between millions of Catholics and Christian fundamentalists. A tipping point reached when it is realized how much of their nation's wealth depends on the production and sale of illegal narcotics. With the Narco dollar underpinning corporate America, bolstering share values, the collapse in the currency would cause economic meltdown.

For Andy and the people back home only two clear choices remained - Muslim or Catholic - who would win?

THE END

POSTSCRIPT

In a poor state of health confined to his bed suffering from Gout, Pope Clement VIII, will have listened to the message read aloud, and received from one of his many spies living in the English Court of Queen Elizabeth 1.

After a delay of exactly one year, the Queen had finally granted a charter to a group of adventurers for trade in the *East "Where Spaniards and Portuguese have not any castle, fort, blockhouse, or commandment."* This was the start of the East India Company and the beginning of the British Empire.

Pope Clement was coming to the end of an otherwise very successful decade for his church. The remarkable reconciliation of Henry IV of France in 1593 when Henry embraced Catholicism, the Synod of Brest held in Lithuania reuniting this country with Rome and finally, during the jubilee of 1600, three million pilgrims visited the holy places. Seeing the return of England to Catholicism was no longer a possibility in his lifetime after this outrageous decision. Her illegal act ignored past Papal Bulls issued by his predecessors since 1481. The Church had divided the world between Spain and Portugal instructing them to colonize and setup Catholic Missions in the new lands. England's decision to explore the East and together with the Dutch ended their monopoly. In 1588, the earlier orders of excommunication against Elizabeth for other offences against Rome and her treatment of Queen Mary was renewed, there was little more he could do to punish her. The Pope, a pious man, trained in the law was unable to forgive and forget wrongdoers easily and vowed Elizabeth and her successors punished for breaking the law occupying and stealing lands rightfully owned by his Church.

By ignoring The Pope, Elizabeth could not know at the time, she was laying the foundation for the remarkable rise of British imperialism and the colonization of large parts of the globe. On the last day of December 1600, with the full support of their Sovereign Queen behind them, a group of 217 investors formed a new company called the Governor and Company of Merchants of London trading into the East Indies - *The East India Company*. Having met together earlier in the year they managed to raise £63,373 enough money to build several ships. Only one more hurdle prevented them sailing - persuading Elizabeth to grant her permission for them to leave.

Few travellers had made the journey from England to India and those that did make it returned with tales of wealth and new opportunities. The land route was difficult fraught with danger, ships could ferry the goods and provisions which is why pioneers chose to go by sea. Sailing around the Cape Horn, hugging the African coast they crossed over the Indian Ocean, meeting regular opposition from the Portuguese and Spanish.

The odds of returning home was less than twenty-five percent, these lucky adventurers became rich beyond their wildest dreams. Carrying mixed cargoes of spices silks and objects unseen in seventeenth centaury England, they went on to sell these for huge fortunes.

For the next hundred years or so the British, French,

Spanish, Dutch and Portuguese carved out territories and by the late eighteenth century the British was winning, dominating large sections of India. Employees sent out to work in the colonies were well paid compared to their fellow citizens back home where the top post of Governor received around £4,800 compared to an average wage in England of only £250 per year. Besides the salary, they also had opportunities for making even more cash; receiving "presents" and some arrived back home super-rich.

One example is possibly the best known for his success in India uniting this vast country. Robert Clive left his family home in Shropshire when just eighteen and was sent to work in Madras as a clerk. Arriving in 1744, he was said to be miserable and homesick during the first two years and on one occasion attempted suicide with a pistol but fortunately changed his mind. Later during a conflict with a French settlement, Clive received a commendation for bravery and clearly enjoyed the excitement and drama of both war and politics. Gradually, due to numerous and more serious altercations with the French and other warring factions, he emerged a very successful leader. Historians describe Major General Robert Clive 1st Baron Clive of Plassey, as the hero of his day, a soldier-of-fortune and commander who established the military supremacy of the East India Company.

Not so frequently discussed, is the darker side and the investigations that followed his tour of duty after being accused of taking bribes and becoming involved in corruption. In one single private arrangement made between Clive and an Indian Prince, the Mir Jafar, he accepted payment of £234,000, which was only the first of many such presents he was to receive.

The new territories won by Clive and others, added to the net wealth of the East India Company, allowing them to become key players in an industry new to the British -

The Treaty

dealing drugs. The Southern Indian Mughal Empire was in steep decline and Clive was able to direct the consolidation of a drug empire based around opium in India. The poppies were grown throughout the region and harvested, after processing the opium was sold in China or exchanged for tea and shipped back to Europe. Huge fortunes were made during this period of European and American history with much of the wealth used to kick-start the industrial revolution in Britain. It can perhaps be argued, by calculating the affects of investment and resulting increased wealth through compound interest this caused the rise in living standards throughout the *civilized* world - which many enjoy to this day.

For Clive it certainly paid off, returning to England when he was still only 28 years old a very wealthy man, paying off all his fathers' debts and winning a seat in Parliament. After his marriage to Margaret Maskellyne, he was persuaded by The East India Company to return to India and, ironically, help solve the enormous problems they were having with corruption - which arguably he was instrumental in starting. By now, the regular taking of opium was endemic amongst the Europeans and by the time he reached his forties, Clive was himself addicted to the drug. With his health wrecked, he returned to the UK and is thought to have committed suicide aged 48. Later his biographer wrote, *"There was a spirit of plunder and a passion for the rapid accumulation of wealth among all ranks at that time."* Who was perhaps trying to excuse this great man for his actions! The whole atmosphere was said to be corrupt from a modern point of view and only later did it seem to improve with the arrival of Lord Wellesley. Offered a gift by the company of £100,000 resulting from the spoils of Seringapatnam, he was said to have refused. By the 1800's the East India Company controlled poppy-growing areas on the Ganges plain between Patna and

Benares, dominating the Asian market for the drug.

With a virtual monopoly, controlling supply and setting prices, imports into the UK and Europe grew steadily as the use of the opium became widespread. Sold for its medicinal purpose and taken recreationally by celebrities of the day, poet and philosopher Samuel Taylor Coleridge was said to consume opium in copious quantities. China was by far the biggest market where they mixed opium with tobacco - a practice introduced by the Dutch - and smoked using special opium pipes. During Robert Clive's time in India, they were shipping two thousand chests of opium a year and one hundred years later; this had grown to 70,000 chests per year. Despite the disastrous affects this was having on the Chinese population, whose government tried to stem the trade by banning the sale of opium, the foreigners were determined to keep it coming. With the first Opium War between China and Great Britain in 1839, the Chinese tried to ban the sale of the narcotics, demanding all foreign traders surrender their opium. Then in 1841, the British defeated the Chinese and took possession of Hong Kong, making the sale of the drug legal after their second victory in 1856 - against the wishes of the Chinese government. It was not until 1910, after 150 years, they finally managed to persuade the British to stop selling opium into China from their India colony.

Meanwhile the American Government imposed a tax on opium and morphine then later restricting its use and passed the Pure Food and Drug Act, requiring pharmaceutical companies to label their patent medicines with their complete contents. In the USA, the availability of opiates declined further and by 1923, the U.S. Treasury Department's Narcotics Division banned all legal narcotics sales, introducing the start of a thriving black market. At this time, most illegal heroin smuggled into Europe and the USA came from China, until after the communist revolution when the source moved to Southeast Asia, and particularly Laos, Thailand and Burma. The French who occupied these areas in Southeast Asia actively encouraged Hmong farmers to expand their opium production so that the French could retain their opium monopoly. After 1946, Burma gained its independence from Britain, and opium cultivation flourished.

In the U.S., the heroin trade flourished dominated by Corsican gangsters and U.S. Mafia drug distributors when it is reported President Nixon seriously looked into ways of working with the gangs to control the market. Raw Turkish opium refined in Marseilles laboratories (the "French Connection,") was sold to junkies on New York City streets. In the 1950s, the U.S. preoccupation with stopping the spread of Communism led to alliances with drug producing warlords in the Golden Triangle. The U.S. and France supplied the drug warlords and their armies with ammunition, arms, and air transport for the production and sale of opium. The result was an explosion in the availability and illegal flow of heroin into the United States and into the hands of drug dealers and addicts. During the U.S. war in Vietnam, the Central Intelligence Agency (CIA) set up a charter airline, Air America, to transport raw opium from Burma and Laos. During this period, the amount of heroin addicts in the U.S. reached an estimated 750,000.

Richard Nixon's arrival at the White House in America, signals the first clear sign of a foreign policy to control drug supply together with increased border controls and treatment. Attorney General Daniel Patrick Moynihan wrote in a cover memo to William Rogers Secretary of State in 1969. *'Heroin brought into the East Coast is grown in Turkey and Syria, and processed in France…it seems to me possible to make clear to the governments involved that in our view to acquiesce in the traffic is to be an accomplice to it, and henceforth we will regard this as a hostile act.'*

Readers of this book may recall the name William Rogers, Secretary of State, appearing in this story, perhaps confirming he would have had a legitimate cause for signing "The Treaty." Moreover, clearly other American politicians, Attorney General Daniel Patrick Moynihan, expressed concern and possibly their willingness - to influence foreign governments becoming involved in controlling the production and therefore the value and sales of narcotics - which may well, have required an international agreement. *The Treaty!*

The Treaty

Acknowledgements

Writing real people fiction is not without controversy since by definition names of real people have been included. How can I say this - it is what it is - FICTION a blend of historic facts casting real people in a fictionalized role. The characterization of Prince Philip for example, was necessary since in his case he is unique. The same qualities apply to Ex-President George Bush Senior, Camilla, The Duchess of Cornwall and Diana Princess of Wales. During my research for this story, I was shocked to discover the tragic death and circumstances surrounding the accident of Susan Barrantes, mother of Sarah Ferguson. This happened only 12 months after Princess Diana's death and I wish to express our sincere condolences to that family. Anyone else who believes they have been characterized in this book without their permission is mistaken. All other names and characters are based on life experience and figments of my imagination.

Published works used for reference
I have dipped in and out of some published works using extracts included in the Prologue. Quotations respectfully used in the story came from the English translation of The

Koran by S.V. Mir Ahmed Ali and Edited by Yasin T. al-Jibouri, published by Tahrike Tarsile Quran, Inc, New York. I included these to illustrate Fatima's deep faith. My very sincere thanks to these authors and also the current copyright owners and publishers of the 'History of British India' by P.E. Roberts last reprinted in 1941 and also 'The Quest for Drug Control by David F. Musto, M.D and Pamela Korsmeyer, published by Yale University Press in 2002. Numerous other sources of inspiration came from the Treaty of Nanjing 1842; articles and references on the Internet to Britain's opium trade in the Far East and the use of opiates over the centuries. My sincere and grateful thanks to the authors for any sentences or paragraphs I may have included in the summary pages.

And Finally:
Thank you ____ Gracias Danke Merci Mauliate Barak llahu fik Shukriya

To my partner Susan Crozier for her untiring support, Paul Raven, Melissa Crozier and Imogene Harper who read the very first drafts of the book and encouraged me to carry on writing. To the many friends around the world who have contributed in some way, the Batak people of TukTuk who live in paradise on Lake Toba. Finally, the critical appraisal conducted by my Copy Editors Chris and Simon who saw it through with me to the end.

The Treaty

David J Grant